I0729014

CAPITAL'S PUNISHMENT

CAPITAL'S PUNISHMENT

BY

JOHN DANIELSKI

www.penmorepress.com

Capital's Punishment by John M. Danielski
Copyright © 2017 John M. Danielski

All rights reserved. No part of this book may be used or reproduced by any means without the written permission of the publisher except in the case of brief quotation embodied in critical articles and reviews.

ISBN-13: 978-1-946409-24-9 (Paperback)
ISBN :-978-1-946409-25-6 (e-book)

BISAC Subject Headings:
FIC014000FICTION / Historical
FIC032000FICTION / War & Military

Editing: Terri Carter

Cover Illustration by Christine Horner

Address all correspondence to:

Penmore Press LLC
920 N Javelina Pl
Tucson AZ 85748

Previously, in "Blue Water Scarlet Tide"

It is August, 1814. The misbegotten War of 1812 drags on into its third year. Royal Marine Captain Thomas Pennywhistle, a veteran exploring officer, scouts behind enemy lines. He seeks a suitable site for a major British amphibious landing in the Chesapeake. Rear Admiral George Cockburn, RN, has commanded successful raids up and down the Chesapeake and is resolved to strike a decisive blow against the Americans by seizing their capital city. Major General Robert Ross, the British Army Commander, is of a milder disposition but a skilled soldier who learned his trade under the Duke of Wellington. The two chieftains have formed an excellent operational partnership.

Pennywhistle's scouting has discovered that the American forces are scattered, unprofessional, and inexperienced. Brigadier General William Winder, the American commander, is an inept officer. Politicians from Washington make matters worse by interfering with Army operations.

Two exceptions to American amateurism promise hope for the Republic. Captain John Tracy leads a tough cadre of United States Marines but he must battle an insidious secessionist conspiracy as well as the British. He fights as ingeniously as Pennywhistle and bears a striking resemblance to him as well. Commodore Joshua Barney bedevils the British with a flotilla of gunboats. His battery of heavy cannon may prove the salvation of the United States.

Pennywhistle is assisted by the redoubtable Sergeant Andrew Dale, Lieutenant Peter Spottswood a capable officer with whom he served in the Adriatic, and Lieutenant John Manton, a former servant who, thanks to battlefield gallantry, is now a subaltern in the 4th Regiment of Foot. Two escaped slaves, Gabriel and Isaac, provide crucial information and enlist in a new British fighting force, The Colonial Marines.

Along the way, Pennywhistle uses his knowledge of science to modify the design of Congreve Rockets to make them much more deadly in battle. Armed with these, he wipes out a militia regiment led by Colonel Daniel Parke, who bears a ruinous secret.

A beautiful and deadly forest huntress named Sammie Jo tries to kill Pennywhistle. Whether she is patriotic or homicidal is unclear. Although she merits execution as an illegal combatant, a bushwhacker, he spares her life, motivated by both chivalry and strong physical attraction. The ripple effect of that decision will have far-reaching consequences for him, personally and professionally.

Both sides are poised for the battle that will decide the fate of Washington. The 7,000 men of the American Army are posted at Bladensburg, six miles northeast of the Capitol Building. The men are game but most have never seen battle. They are in a triangular formation of three lines, with the apex of the triangle pointed at the Bladensburg Bridge. That bridge over the Anacostia River represents the last physical barrier to the British advance. If the Americans hold it, it is a shield. If the British take it, it is a dagger pointed at the heart of the Republic.

The first elements of a British force of 4,500 soldiers and marines are reaching the outskirts of Bladensburg. They are all veterans who have beaten the best Napoleon can throw at them. The Redcoats will begin their final deployments in ten minutes. The next few hours will shape American History forever.

DEDICATION

This book is dedicated to Dave S. He was a patient ear as I read him each new installment. His kind suggestions kept me intellectually honest.

Acknowledgments

I would like to thank James Danielski and Chris Wozny for their many helpful recommendations and insights during the writing and editing process.

Map derived from Old Tybee Ranger and James Danielski with thanks

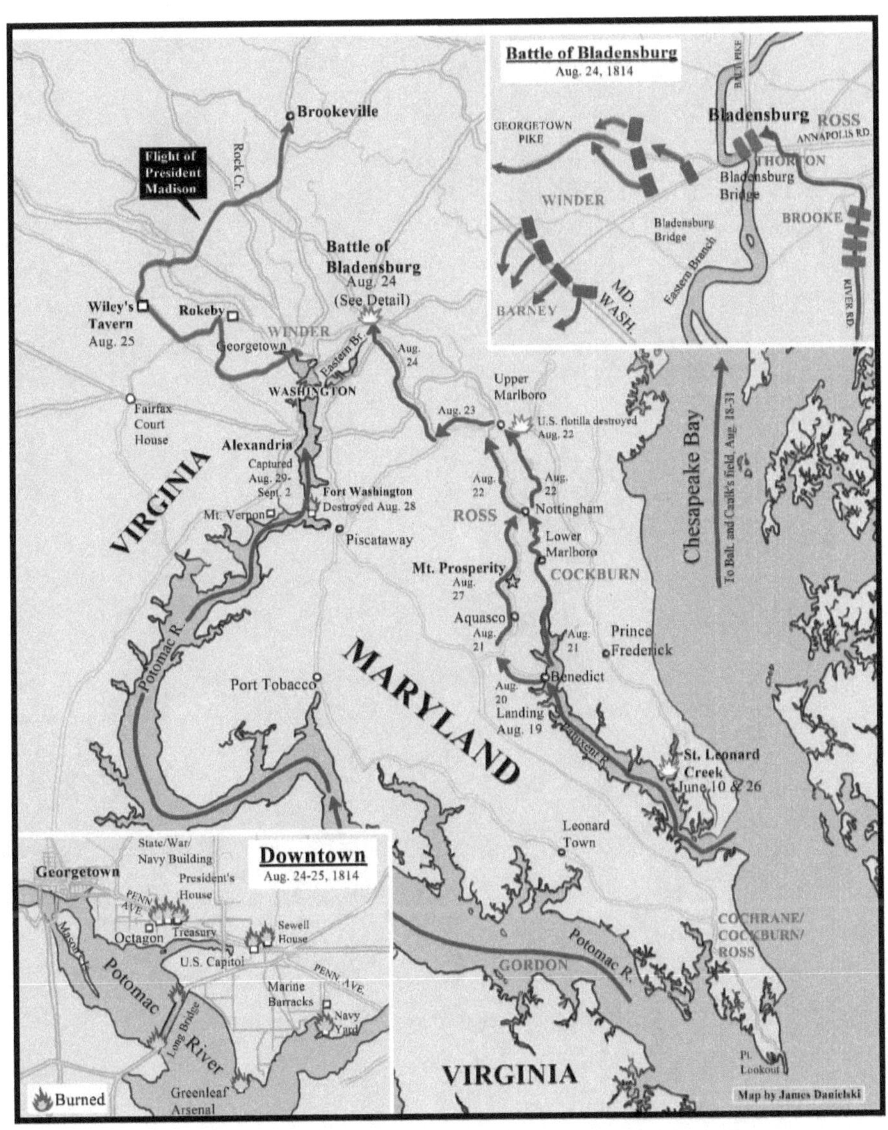

War of 1812. Map of British attack on Washington

Chapter One

Bladensburg, Maryland 24 August, 1814

"Don't touch them animals, you two-legged jackasses! Lay a finger on them and I'll put a load of buckshot so far up your arse you'll be waddling around like a duck in a tar pit."

"That ain't the way you're supposed talk to guardian angels, Grannie. We just need a little food to do our jobs."

"If you're guardian angels then I'm The First Lady."

Thomas Pennywhistle listened carefully to the conversation proceeding twenty yards away. The barn's corner concealed him but he heard every syllable perfectly. The words were harsh, the tones shrill, and the mood discordant. He found the exchange compelling even though he was neglecting his duty by eavesdropping. His job was to scout ahead for the Royal Marine Rocket Troop, not act as a protector of oppressed souls.

He reached into his haversack and wrapped his fingers around the butt of the ducksfoot. He was probably being hasty but his intuition argued it was imperative he prepare for action. He preferred to believe his intellect sovereign, yet his willingness to heed instinctive presentiments of danger had saved his life on countless occasions. Those flashes of warning sometimes defied reason but professional soldiers did not survive long if they relied on logic alone.

The ugly pistol was heavy and imperfectly balanced but stout enough to use as a bludgeon in a last ditch fight. It was useless at distances beyond ten feet, but at point blank range against a densely packed body of men, it packed a deadly wallop. The seven short, 50 caliber barrels flared in a sixty degree arc and resembled a duck's foot. One pull of the trigger ignited all of the charges simultaneously. The pocket volley gun had been designed to give a ship's captain the power to quell a mutiny, although it was also exceedingly useful in repelling boarders. It worked just as well on land but was not a weapon for those squeamish about spilling blood.

The tall, spare woman of perhaps seventy years who was haranguing three men was an American; citizen of a country whose nearby army was bracing itself for a British attack. She was highly agitated and the men looked annoyed at her words. The discomfiture of an old woman in an enemy country was certainly not his concern and he should just walk away and await the arrival of his marines. But the old woman had grit, gravitas, and a damn-your-eyes courage that reminded him of his grandmother. He felt an instinctive empathy for her plight as misplaced sentimentality reared its annoying head. She had chosen to stay behind to defend her property after the other 1500 inhabitants had sensibly fled Bladensburg because of the impending battle.

"I ain't agoin' nowhere," rasped the woman to three scruffy men. "I aim to stay fixed to this spot until Judgment Day if I have to." She wore a blue gingham dress that had been fashionable twenty years before. A matching bonnet framed a lined, determined face that had likely once been considered pretty. She swayed slowly back and forth in an old maple rocking chair set in the middle of a muddy barnyard. She was surrounded by half-a-hundred chickens, pigs, cows, and goats contentedly clucking, oinking, mooing, and bleating as they unburdened themselves of the contents of their bowels and bladders.

"These here animals is all I got. I know if I leave I'll never see 'em again. I don't care if bullets start flying, I ain't agonna lose them to the British, and certainly not to you. Now why don't you gents clear off and forage elsewhere. You're supposed to be on my side." She full-cocked the ancient, rusty double-barreled shotgun she held in her lap and leveled it at the three men; her expression that of a wary banker guarding a vault. "I don't want to hurt no one, but don't y'all come any closer."

The three men surrounding her looked ragged, dirty, unshaven, and very hungry yet their portly physiques clothed in the uniforms of Maryland Militia proclaimed they were strangers to real privation. They cast covetous eyes on the animals as they brandished long knives. They looked to be trying to decide whether to gorge themselves on chicken, steak, or ham.

"You ain't very patriotic, denying food to Uncle Sam's best," said a man with a large Roman nose who appeared to be the group's leader. His tone turned mocking. "You better be polite to us old lady or we will burn down your farm too."

The old woman snapped back. "You don't look like no soldiers to me. Powerful likely you're deserters I'm thinkin'. My late husband was a regular in the Maryland Line in the last war so I can spot a real fightin' man a mile off. You'uns ain't it."

"We done more than our share you stupid old biddy," sneered Roman nose. "Now why don't you put that shootin' iron away and let us fill our bellies?" The trio moved slowly and menacingly toward her.

She did not hesitate and pulled the twin triggers. Instead of the *clack woosh bang* of a flintlock ignition there was only the sound of flints snapping fruitlessly at frizzens with no sparks forthcoming. "Damnation" she sputtered in sheer frustration.

"You bloody old witch," snarled the second of the trio, a horse-faced man with cheeks full of scars.

The three came at her in a rush. They grabbed the base of her rocker and hoisted it to waist level. "One, two, three, heave," yelled Roman-nose. They threw her and her chair into the air and a second later both crashed into the deep mud like a pile of old firewood and rags.

"Ha Ha Ha." The nasty trio laughed derisively. They appeared to find the sight of a mud-cloaked old woman the funniest thing they had ever seen. They slapped their knees and doubled over as their twittering laughter deepened into long, vulgar guffaws straight from their base of their bloated bellies.

Pennywhistle's hatred for bullies boiled up. He whipped out the ducksfoot and broke into a run. These disgusting specimens of humanity were vermin in need of pest control. They were worthless as prisoners since they likely possessed no current information on an army they had deserted. The men were all clustered together: perfect.

His long muscled legs covered the distance in seconds, catching them completely unaware. Two had their backs to him but Roman-nose sensed movement and pivoted to face the angry Englishman. He blinked in surprise and terror. "What the he..."

Boom! The seven barrels flared to life and blood splattered in all directions. The animals squawked and bellowed.

Roman-nose's red grey intestines popped out as two rounds ripped a long trench into his belly. The second man absorbed three bullets that shredded his kidneys and never even saw his assailant. The third man had started to turn as two balls penetrated between his middle left ribs and plunged into his heart.

Pennywhistle immediately reversed the pistol to club but the men showed no signs of life. He noted with satisfaction the blood had missed his uniform completely. He looked down in contempt as the three distorted faces slowly faded into the deep mud. He had long ago abandoned any gentlemanly qualms about shooting an enemy in the back. Professional soldiers never shirked a fight but never took unnecessary risks either. The most successful predators employed surprise and attacked only from advantage. A stern attack was far safer than one made bows on.

The old lady watched in astonishment. Pennywhistle walked over, extended his hand, and gently helped her to her feet. He brushed some of the mud off her dress in an effort to help her regain lost dignity. She stared at his face and scarlet coat in complete puzzlement. "Why?" She asked. "I'm your enemy, ain't I?"

Pennywhistle looked at her thoughtfully. "The American army is my objective, madam. I may be the enemy of Mr. Madison and his misbegotten administration but I count myself a firm friend of women who display courage, regardless of the flag they favor. You were willing to hazard your life for what you had built and I consider that most worthy."

"Thanks, mister. 'Tis just a small spread but I'm right proud of it."

"I respect real soldiers," Pennywhistle continued, "but had no wish to see worthless louts impersonating them devour the fruits of a life's labor. I know American commanders have punished desertion with death of late, so I have merely acted as their surrogate. We Britons abhor looting and pay for what we take, although I will admit sometimes our men occasionally get out of hand and steal. Those soldiers are flogged."

"I shall inform our people to respect your farm during our advance and I give my most solemn word that neither you nor your property will be disturbed. The war will end eventually and I believe the historic ties of language and kinship between our two peoples will be swiftly resumed. If I can, by some small action, speed the return of that former amity, then I am gratified."

"That's a right handsome gesture you made, mister. You really did save my bacon. The word of an honest gentleman means a lot and I can see that you are one and are telling me the Gospel truth. Never expected rescue from a lobsterbac... uh...uh... Englishman. Guess you folk in red coats ain't all devils. Wouldn't normally do this with a limey," she extended her hand, "but you're a real neighborly young fella with a lot of pluck. I am right pleased to know ya. I'm Henrietta Harper and you are?"

Pennywhistle shook the offered hand gently, pleased by her willingness to see an actual man instead of an evil archetype. "Thomas Pennywhistle, your servant ma'am. Enjoy the remainder of the day and be in no fear of life, limb, or property. I wish I could stay to help with the bodies but I cannot tarry as my duty commands me away."

"Don't you worry none, young sir. My hired hand Lem will be by directly and he will take care of those varmints before they get too ripe. They might even be useful if he plows 'em in between the corn rows. Bandits like that will probably make better fertilizer than soldiers." She let out a scornful laugh straight from a core evidently made from hickory. "They came to steal from me but now they can earn me some money."

"Capital thinking! I wish you well, Mrs. Harper." He bowed quickly then pivoted on his heel and marched smartly away, leaving her with a smile of surprised pleasure that God had answered her prayers in a most unexpected way.

She watched him for a full minute and thought of the son who had died in infancy. If he had lived, she was sure he would have grown into as fine a man as Pennywhistle.

Pennywhistle briefly reproached himself as he walked. He had swerved from the straight-line path of duty yet he could not deny the brief diversion had brought him great satisfaction. If he had done nothing it would have passed unnoticed save by God, but such situations furnished the truest evidence of your real character. The welfare of an enemy civilian need not have concerned him, yet one could hardly claim to be a man of honor if one allowed aggression against the old and weak when one possessed the power to arrest it. The matter had nothing to do with the allegiances demanded by war but everything to do with a higher allegiance demanded by basic humanity.

The elderly farmwife was an unimportant consideration in the grand scheme of things yet her very triviality made her important to his integrity. Compromise on the little things and it would not be long before you compromised on the big ones. Like a seductive whore with the pox, war constantly whispered alluring invitations to barbarism and sought to unshackle dangerous emotions by circumventing reason. Only by keeping your honor burnished bright could you resist her siren song of temptation.

The scorching sun brilliantly illuminated his scarlet uniform which stood in stark contrast to the dun color of the deserted street. The humid air rippled with the electricity of impending battle and added urgency to his brisk steps. He moved with the confident, disciplined strides of the professional soldier, a jungle cat with training; his alert eyes incessantly sweeping the street ahead for any sign of an American presence. His mind shifted into an altered state of deep focus; his physical sword remained sheathed but he raised the one in his mind to the *en garde* position. His hearing and sense of smell increased in range and acuity.

No scars wronged the spare cheekbones, blunt nose, and full lips of a memorable face that was shaped like an inverted triangle. Numerous black and blue marks cursed his back and chest, souvenirs of a very rough week. While he was no model for Praxiteles, he was supremely fit. A dozen years of combat on three continents had schooled the thirty-year-old in the predatory wariness essential for staying alive. Its price was a cynical heart and a disfigured soul.

Tension showed in his pursed lips, the coiled crows-feet on either side of his emerald eyes, and on the taut skin of his cheekbones. His deeply tanned skin concealed the paleness of vasoconstriction, his body was automatically shunting blood away from the surface to reduce bleeding from potential wounds. His breathing remained deep and steady as his sphincter muscles tightened and his genitals retracted slightly.

He batted away annoying clouds of mosquitoes every few seconds. They were attracted by the rivulets of sweat coursing down his forehead that were natural concomitants of the obscene heat. The heavy air was suffused with the scents of magnolias, pines, and boxwood as well as the mating proclamations of cicadas, blue jays, and bullfrogs. His hyper-observant mind calmly noted them as well as dozens of other considerations and then filtered them out. They were merely background irrelevancies that could not be allowed to divert attention from the hard duty ahead. He canted his head determinedly forward; the stern resolve on his face proclaiming that he was a man ready for any trouble.

His right index finger trembled briefly and it worried him. Usually that tremor manifested after a fight not before. It had happened four times over the past week and had become more pronounced each time. Every soldier who had seen extensive service moved toward a personal threshold of combat exhaustion beyond which he simply ceased to function. He wondered if he was approaching his own limit.

He stopped briefly, bent down, and examined a host of tracks. The numerous shoe and boot impressions were all civilian and in random patterns. No enemy militia had marched this way, indicating the Americans would make no attempt to defend the Lowndes Hill side of the Bladensburg Bridge. He stood up and resumed his brisk walk, pleased that the Americans had ceded the high ground to the British.

The superb cut of his scarlet coat and the perfect hang of his pebble-grey trousers combined to emphasize the athleticism of his six-foot-two inch frame. The double-breasted coat had clearly seen use yet glowed with a lustrous sheen only possible with the most expensive broadcloth. Sunlight glinted off the gold in its epaulettes and buttons. The collar was high and stiff, the back terminated in short swallow tails, and the waist was noticeably cinched. The heavily starched cuffs were navy blue, as was the collar. The crimson silk sash of command circled his waist. Gieves of Savile Row was expensive but good tailoring always put an extra spring of confidence in a man's step and sent a message to the other ranks that a true gentleman commanded them.

The searing sun caused the gold in his gorget to sparkle as well, making it an attractive target for enemy rifleman. The small, crescent shaped object emblazoned with the arms of King George hung suspended from a blue ribbon round his neck. It was a scaled-down and spruced-up reminder of the days of chivalry; its steel ancestor had functioned as a knight's neck plate.

His gold-tasseled black hessian boots were confections of James Hoby, Wellington's preferred bootmaker, and dazzled with a polish so high that a man could see his own reflection in them. The only flaw in the entire ensemble was a small patch near the left epaulette covering a bullet's intrusion; proof its wearer was no bandbox soldier.

Sunlight glinted off a small object in the street and he stopped to pick it up. It was a silver locket adorned with intricate gold filigree work. It contained a striking portrait of a lovely young lady along with small lock of her auburn hair; the sort of thing a woman gave to a fiancée or husband. His eyes moistened slightly. The woman resembled his beloved Carlotta; like the locket, a casualty of war.

He angrily chased away the bittersweet memory and focused coldly on deduction. That such a thing of high personal value would end up in his hand told him that its owner must have been fleeing in haste and fear. Fear was infectious. If the Yankee civilians were rattled, they might well spread it to their militia.

He removed the plumed black coachman's hat that was a trademark of the Royal Marines and splashed his head with water from his canteen. He could almost visualize a puff of steam rising. As a reluctant concession to the heat, he undid the black silk stock girdling his neck and left his throat bare. He had already told his marines to throw away their hated leather stocks, most felt them akin to dog collars, and discipline had not collapsed.

The real problem was that his wool coat was ill-suited to weather that was proving torrid even for an area that was infamous for summer heat. The coat was not made for the comfort of its wearer but for the effect it would have on the men. Indeed, its brilliant color made him a prominent target for American sharpshooters. Greater rank carried greater risk because an officer had to be an eye-catching beacon of indomitability so that the serried ranks of red marching behind might draw courage from his example.

Nelson had reluctantly followed his subordinate's advice and had worn a plain, undress uniform at Trafalgar. Yet his sense of theatre could not resist adorning it with four glittering, outsize orders of chivalry and that vanity had cost him his life. Fame definitely had its drawbacks, but Pennywhistle, as an anonymous Briton in scarlet, faced no greater hazard than any other officer doing his duty.

The muggy air of the heavily-wooded tidewater was a good friend to rust, so a quick weapons check was in order. He unsheathed his thirty-inch cutlass and flourished it about several times. The black leather grip beneath the clam shell guard fit his hand perfectly and the gold and red sword knot was more than strong enough to ensure the cutlass would stay attached to his wrist should his grip be temporarily lost. The blade glistened with the oil he had applied just after dawn. He dropped a square of thin leather wadding on the upturned blade from a foot above and smiled in satisfaction as it was sliced neatly in two. Wilkinson's of London had done a fine job fashioning a compact weapon that was ideal for close-quarter fighting on pitching decks at sea.

He returned the cutlass to its scabbard and unslung the Ferguson he had been carrying over his left shoulder. The four-foot rifle was a rarity that needed no ramrod; a breech-loading weapon years ahead of its time. He checked the action of the trigger guard which raised and lowered the rotating breech screw. The liberal coating of tallow and beeswax on the screw made the movement easy and smooth.

He pulled the trigger to test the flint and was rewarded with a large shower of sparks. The flint's edge was sharp and even, and he guessed it was good for fifteen more shots. He loaded the .65 caliber weapon with his usual precision and attached a 30-inch bayonet.

Satisfied that he was well-fixed for a fight, he slung the weapon, extracted his pocket spyglass from his coat, and extended it to its full foot length. He had paid a small fortune for the glass crafted by Jesse Ramsden, London's finest maker of precision instruments, but it had been a sound investment. A good glass was as important to an officer in the field as a good horse was to a jockey at Epsom. With a magnification factor of seven, the Ramsden was far superior to those of other manufacturers and always gave sharp, clear images.

He scanned the street for the approach of the Royal Marine Rocket Troop bearing Congreve Rockets. He furled and stowed his glass when they marched into view five minutes later.

*****

Sammie Jo Matthews carefully observed Pennywhistle's progress from her perch on the second floor of an elegant

Federalist home. The tall twenty-two-year-old had come looking to contribute to the American cause and knew action followed the marine as surely as thunder followed lightning. She reminded herself that the home was really just a brick version of the tree platforms she employed hunting deer in the deep forest.

Her alert eyes became those of Artemis and stalked Pennywhistle and the 26 men of The Royal Marine Rocket Troop as they traversed the main street of what was now a ghost town. The Troop wore royal blue trousers and navy blue tunics with white facings and brick red collars and cuffs. Added to Pennywhistle's scarlet and grey, the group was as conspicuous as a rainbow over a beach of volcanic sand.

Sammie Jo loaded the *Widowmaker* with meticulous care. The five-foot-long, .44 caliber Pennsylvania Rifle had been given its name by General Daniel Morgan in the Revolution. Her father had been a sharpshooter in Morgan's Rifles and the weapon bore 25 X-marks with crosses atop each. Located below the brass patchbox, each representation of the Union Jack signified the extinction of a British officer.

He had bequeathed the weapon to his daughter who had added to its legendary reputation for precision by winning five turkey shoots. Her skill had caused intense embarrassment to the county bucks that lusted after her beauty but missed the essential toughness of her core. In her skilled hands, her rifle could place a ball square in the middle of a man's forehead at two hundred and twenty five yards. The only reason that Pennywhistle had survived an early morning encounter was that he had bent his head forward at the last second.

Muzzle flashes winked at Pennywhistle from across the Anacostia River. He walked half a block toward the river bank and stopped when he had a clear view of the enemy. He unshipped his spyglass and pointed it at the first of the three lines of the American Army. He focused in on the Baltimore Artillery and swept the glass slowly along its front. Satisfied it was just the desultory pot shots of nervous militia in support of the artillery and that the battery was unlikely to open fire, he snapped his glass shut. The troop resumed its progress. A quarter-mile later he found a shallow ravine which would provide cover for his rocketeers.

He ordered the men to set up the launching stands for their Congreve Rockets. The Congreves resembled fireworks on six-foot poles and were fired off in the same way. Congreve warheads featured 6, 12, or 24 lb. spherical case shot, commonly known as shrapnel. The warheads contained a timed fuse that burst the container and rained a shower of hot lead on anyone unlucky enough to be underneath.

The Americans had 28 field pieces, mostly 6-pounders. The British had only Congreve's for artillery. A lot was riding on their effectiveness.

Sammie Jo had never seen rockets in action before, but had heard even veteran troops were fearful of them. A conventional solid shot traveled slowly enough that sometimes you could follow its flight and guess its impact point, but a Congreve traveled blindingly fast along a trajectory that defied predictability. A Congreve also shot unearthly gouts of flame from its exhaust port and made terrible hissing sounds akin to an angry dragon.

It crossed her mind stopping Pennywhistle might stop the rockets, but the Marine had gallantly spared her life when she had tried to bushwhack him seven hours earlier. Most officers would have summarily hanged her as an illegitimate combatant outside the laws of war. She had promised the

Englishman she would never target him again and was determined to honor her pledge. It was far better to seek higher-ranking game.

She had passed through the British lines disguised as a pregnant Amish woman driving an old buggy pulled by an ancient horse. Upon gaining her present post, she had quickly changed back into her usual attire of hickory-colored wool shirt, cedar brown bib-and-brace overalls, black brogans, and a cream slouch hat

Something caught her eye, a flash of sun on metal. It came from a house directly across the street. It was there for a second, then gone. Someone had a gun! A minute passed. She saw it again, followed immediately by oval face that resembled a plate of mashed potatoes splashed with curdled milk. The head was topped with a straw panama hat. Straw-hat did not duck back down, likely thinking he remained unseen in a ghost town. He looked to be about fifty and had a long rifle similar to hers.

The head of the long red-coated column entered the town and British advance scouts passed directly beneath her window. The 1100 men of Thornton's Brigade formed the British army vanguard and marched proudly with flags flapping, drums pounding and fifes trilling.

Straw-hat scanned the street carefully. He had the same idea as she. Well, almost the same idea. As she watched him line up his sights on Pennywhistle, a stab of fear made her heart flutter and mad instinct overpowered patriotism. She grabbed her rifle, aimed quickly, and fired. Straw-hat's head disintegrated like an old tomato pulped by an anvil and he disappeared from view.

What had she just done? Even with British fifes and drums playing loudly, the crack of a rifle was unmistakable. Several red-coated light infantrymen looked up from the flanks of the column and raced toward her hide. She was an idiot! She had just betrayed her country and destroyed her own carefully laid plan. The men would be inside the house in under a minute. She needed to run, but kept her head and loaded her rifle before doing so.

She grabbed her accoutrements, dashed down the rear stairs to the servant's hall, and bolted out the back door. She unhitched the buggy reins from the post, jumped aboard, and applied the whip liberally.

"There he goes!" shouted a light infantry sergeant. He naturally assumed the fleeing figure in men's clothing was a man. He and four privates darted from the house and saw a black buggy disappearing into the distance. They all fired, although a hit at this distance was problematic. Their marksmanship proved better than expected.

One bullet clipped Sammie Jo's hat and another hit the horse in the neck. It was a bad wound. The animal coughed and wheezed; had not much life left in him. She whipped him harder and he staggered forward perhaps a quarter mile then dropped to the ground stone dead. She heard shots behind her and knew it was time to trust her athletic legs.

She clutched her rifle, leaped down, and broke into a fast run. She could hear clipped foot falls and they sounded closer with each passing second. She needed a place to hide, somewhere she could get off at least one round. She shot a glance over her shoulder, saw there were four of them. She thrust her head determinedly forward and her long legs put on a burst of speed. The distance from her pursuers lengthened.

She had always been a fast runner. Pa said she was half jack rabbit, half deer. She had heard that small, active men typically found their way into light infantry service and the men behind her looked at least five inches shorter than she. She would turn on them quick as wildcat if they got too close. She could out-wrestle most men and also carried a long, wide-bladed hunting knife that with a bit more maturity might have been called a sword. If she went down, she would not die alone.

The footfalls behind gradually grew fainter, and after a minute, stopped altogether. She turned and saw that the lobster-backs had begun trotting back toward the advancing column. Exposed enemy backsides; a beautiful sight for a huntress. She calculated the distance at two hundred and fifty yards. There was almost no wind and she had a clear line of sight. She lined up the last man in her 'V' sights and took a deep breath. She let it out slowly as she gently squeezed the double set trigger. The rifle slammed against her shoulder and smoke blocked her view. A second later, she saw the man lying prone on his face. Her pa would have been proud of that shot. Funny, she still wanted his admiration even though she knew she had never had his approval.

The other redcoats turned in surprise and anger. She could not hear the words but they were clearly arguing. The sergeant shook his head, gesticulated for few seconds, and motioned his men away from Sammie Jo. She guessed his thoughts exactly. A nest of snipers was worth further action, but not a single operator when an entire enemy army lay just ahead.

Good, it would give her a chance to kill more redcoats. A wave of heat swept across her forehead and every nerve-ending in her body tingled and danced. She had assisted her country in a small way and smiled in satisfaction. The stern voice of conscience scolded that she had also dispatched an American to save an Englishman, but she angrily vowed she would never again fall prey to a foolish impulse spawned by the memory of a handsome face. She told herself she had given her word to spare the Englishman's life and shooting a man that meant to take that life was merely an extension of her promise. It was a thin rationalization but it held because the excitement of the chase was upon her.

Her eyes widened, her nostrils flared, and her breath came in short, excited bursts. She dashed for a hedgerow that would give concealment. She needed to think. She inserted a new flint and carefully reloaded her weapon. Tonight, she would carve two flags on the *Widowmaker*. Well, perhaps only one since the American had been a personal enemy rather than a patriotic one.

The savage joy of the hunter was an extraordinary feeling but not one a woman was supposed to understand. Her Calvinist father had warned her she was an unwomanly reprobate, a bad lot, a dark seed. He never beat her, but the constant lashing of a tongue far sharper than a rapier's tip was much worse as it damaged the spirit rather than the body. Bodily wounds at least healed. She had often fled to the woods after his outbursts and had gradually discovered that the forest not only supplied balm to psychic wounds, but great wisdom to those who would heed its informed whispers.

Her dour pa, Jacob Matthews, had felt that any act which brought simple joy must be a sin. He had been a good soldier and a free-wheeling terror to women and respectability in his early days but when he had had his "Great Awakening" everything changed. He became as devout and narrow-minded as he had been devil-may-care and tolerant. He came to believe all mankind were sinners in the hands of an angry God that dangled man precariously above a pit of fire.

He had no patience with her belief that God was best discovered alone in the profound silence of his greatest cathedral, the deep forest. No words were needed, she had told him. The soaring choirs of majestic pines preached silent sermons that rendered dogma and ritual unnecessary. Truths of nature were direct and clear, just like the central message of Jesus. You had but to look around you to feel the power and glory of God.

She held her breath for a minute as two redcoats passed by her hide. She said a quick prayer in her mind, and it apparently worked as the two soldiers did not bother to look over the hedge.

Jacob Matthews held that sin hid best when people were solitary and talk of religion in the woods reeked of outright paganism. The 'saved' prayed together communally that each person might police another's soul for signs of ungodliness. He once claimed he caught a whiff of the Devil's brimstone perfume when she had innocently asked him what the point was of trying to do good if God had already determined who was saved and who was not.

She had worked hard to come to Jesus because she liked his central message of love, but quite a number of His male representatives had displayed more interest in stealing her virtue than saving her soul. Matters finally reached a breaking point when she ran away from a lascivious preacher who had tried to give her a very private, particularly intimate baptizing. Her father ignored her protests and instead placed the blame squarely on her, saying she was a temptress, not an obedient woman. He demanded she pray for deliverance from her lustful nature and focus on the domestic arts so that her gifts would serve the Lord's goals rather than her own selfish ones.

She came to regard the local Baptist Meeting House as a hotel for hypocrites, rather than a hospital for souls. Jesus had loved even criminals and prostitutes, but had no kind words for men whose base actions belied their pious tongues. Just as Jesus had cast out demons, she finally cast from her heart the minions of conventional religion. She vowed to captain her own soul and never allow another to chart her course through the sea of spirituality.

She peered cautiously above the hedgerow and saw no scouts in her immediate vicinity.

The Good Book told her she should feel remorse for the two men she had killed, but she instead felt exhilaration and triumph that she had brought down the most difficult quarry of all. She wondered if she should strike out toward the main American army, but decided her former post in the brick home was not a bad one after all.

The sound of a rifle would be drowned in the tumult of noise, once the engagement became general. No one would take notice of a single shot, even if it came from behind. If she moved from time to time, there was no reason she could not continue to account for British soldiers. She wanted a chance against that ogre Cockburn. The British Admiral was the most hated man in America and his death would be greeted with loud cheers and huzzahs.

*****

Sergeant Andrew Dale had spotted a tall pregnant woman fifteen minutes earlier and recognized her as Sammie Jo. Her height and the distinctive motions of her whip hand had enabled him to see through her Amish disguise. He needed to warn Captain Pennywhistle that she was about and likely up to no good, but he could not leave his post just now.

Disguised in a ghillie suit, he had been detailed by Pennywhistle to watch the Bladensburg Bridge and not report in until the main British column was close. Pennywhistle wanted them to have the most up-to-date information possible on the disposition of the American forces.

While he could not leave his post, his canine companion could. Blarney was a bloodhound that was as smart as he was ugly. His amazing nose could scent a fox in a chicken coop at a mile.

Dale hastily scribbled a note and attached it to the dog's collar. "Find Pennywhistle," he whispered. Blarney gave a happy "woof" and dashed off. In the confusion of battle, a four-legged beast stood a better chance of getting through than a man.

*****

Daniel Parke loaded his Springfield and shouldered it carefully. He stood in line with the 500 men of the 5th Maryland Regiment, not as a colonel who had lost a regiment but as a humble volunteer, no different from any other private soldier. Rank mattered little to him now, redemption mattered a great deal.

He was in the second of the three lines of American Army, well back from the first, but he was certain the regiment would see action today. It calmed him not to have to worry about giving the correct commands to others. He need only be responsible for his own conduct today and he would make certain it was exemplary.

He felt less fatalistic than he had earlier. He might well survive the battle.

Capital's Punishment

There would have to be a lot of changes back home. They would be painful, but nothing could equal the pain of seeing his command destroyed because of his mistakes. They had been his neighbors, his friends, indeed in a few cases, his relatives. If he lived, he would have a lifetime to atone for his errors of judgment. He held onto that; it gave him a reason to want to survive.

And of course, he wanted to see Archie again. He could not grasp why God had fixed his canon against something that seemed so natural to him, but perhaps that was the nature of temptation. He hated himself after each encounter, yet at the time it always felt powerfully right. He had told himself a thousand times that it had to stop, but had not been strong enough to overcome his peculiar lusts. Maybe what happened to his command was not divine retribution for his crimes against nature, but it was certainly a warning that if any word leaked, there would undoubtedly be legal retribution.

Sodomy not only violated God's Law, it emphatically contravened man's. A public trial would be ruinous to his reputation as well as his family. Many men faced with that possibility resorted to the gentleman's solution--a locked library door, a decanter of whiskey, and a loaded pistol. He had to make sure things never got anywhere close to that.

He was an eligible widower. A wife would steady him and hold the dark part of his nature in check. There were certainly eligible women who had little interest in conjugal relations but great interest in position and prestige. He already had children; at least he had done his manly duties in that regard. There was no need for further heirs; perhaps an older woman past childbearing. His children were just entering their teens. They needed a father more than ever.

*****

Pennywhistle heard a rifle shot, but it was not the report of a British Baker. The noise was the distinctive crack of an American weapon like the one Sammie Jo...no, that simply was not possible. He scanned the street quickly and saw no trace of an American presence.

He returned to his work of positioning the triangular launching stands. There was no reason the Congreves had to be exposed to enemy fire, since their flight paths arched severely. As long as he spotted for the shooters, things should go well at minimal risk to themselves.

He had added three fins for guidance at the base of each Congreve Rocket under his command. The rest of the Army's Congreves lacked fins and it was anyone's guess where their salvos would land. The rockets sometimes even turned back upon their shooters. He prevailed upon the other rocket commanders to allow him to open the barrage. First impressions were important. He wanted the enemy to believe all of them would be as accurate as the finned rockets.

He unfurled his glass and again panned it carefully over the Baltimore Artillery on the opposite bank of the Anacostia. He estimated the six-gun battery of 6-pounders was one-third of a mile from his position. Beyond musket range, but well within that of the Congreves. The battery was posted fifty yards back from the western terminus of the one hundred and twenty-one foot long Bladensburg Bridge. It puzzled him that the Americans had neglected to do the obvious and destroy the bridge.

He could not see every cannon because of the earthworks that partly concealed them. 150 artillerymen manned the battery and there looked to be the same number of infantryman acting in support. Between them they would strongly dispute any attempt to cross the bridge.

A quarter-mile away on his side of the river, he saw Lieutenant William Colonel Thornton waving his sword in encouragement at British light infantry advancing toward the bridge. His men wore swallow-tailed brick-red coatees and ash-grey trousers like line infantry but their tall black shakos sported green plumes instead of red and white. Their uniforms were frayed at the edges and displayed plenty of patches; to be expected of soldiers who had seen hard service.

The American infantry on the opposite bank opened up a spotty fire on the scattered skirmishers. The British light infantry advanced in groups of four, rather than as an unbroken line. They moved in spurts and dashes, taking full advantage of natural gullies.

They fired their .75 caliber Brown Bess muskets in chain order, each group separated by ten paces from the next in line. The right-hand soldier of each chain took three paces forward, fired, then retired to the rear. He was followed in sequence by the second, third, and fourth man. By the time the fourth man had fired, the first man had reloaded and was ready to begin the sequence again. Chain-firing kept the Americans under constant pressure, giving them no respite from flying lead.

Scattered houses also provided plenty of cover and the chains used them cleverly as they leapfrogged forward. They would fire quickly, then drop and vanish from sight. The Americans fired a few desultory volleys but could not get a clear shot at them. It was the reverse of the Revolutionary War. American troops firing generalized volleys in the open, the British firing aimed shots from cover.

"Forward 85th," bellowed Thornton, "Take the bridge! Column by companies at the quarter distance and advance at the quick step! Form line on the far side!" Bugles echoed Thornton's words and the 100 scattered skirmishers expertly formed themselves into a column with a four man front to accommodate the width of the bridge. They advanced determinedly at 105 paces a minute, their weapons carried at support arms.

Their faces were determined and expectant, their shoulders squared with expert precision, and their strides bold and sure. All were products of a confidence that sprang from having beaten seven Marshals of France in the Peninsula. Their heads were inclined slightly forward as if meeting a hailstorm, this one of lead. The planks vibrated slightly from their perfectly cadenced steps.

Thornton waved his sword vigorously above him and then back and to the sides, beckoning new troops forward. The sunlight flashed brightly off the superb Birmingham steel making him a natural target for riflemen schooled to kill officers. "Forward my hearties! The day will soon be ours!" His strong and steady voice radiated disdain for American marksmanship but complete confidence that his redcoats would always prevail against men he regarded as little better than armed rabble.

One company of light infantry had discovered the Anacostia was fordable just to the right of the bridge. Guns and cartridge boxes held above their heads, they waded into the shallow, muddy stream. The water came to the waists of most men and to the pectorals of the shortest. All focused their attention on the opposite shore and ignored the angry buzz of lead whizzing just above their heads. As was usual with green troops, the Americans fired just a little too high.

*****

A mile to the rear of Thornton, Lieutenant John Manton's light company of the 4th Foot pounded hard to close the distance. General Ross had decided to engage the Americans with the forces immediately available rather than wait for all of his men to assemble. It had caught the Americans off guard but the rest of his men were doing their damnedest to reach the field in time.

Manton heard the distant rattling of musket fire and smelled the familiar scent of acrid smoke that signaled battle had commenced. His mouth grew dry as a desert sepulcher even as cascades of sweat poured down his forehead from the extreme heat. He was tired from the last burst of marching at the Moore Quickstep, three steps at the walk followed by three at the trot, but the expected reserve of nervous energy kicked in as he felt the 'God of Battles' casting his spell of madness. He had been through Salamanca and Vitoria: both large, bloody battles and knew exactly what to expect. Today would be a much smaller engagement, but he hoped the results would be just as conclusive.

The Americans had fought better than expected in recent skirmishes, but were not up to French standards. Excitement and fear challenged each other for dominance, but excitement won. He silently mouthed the comforting words of the Bard as he marched, "Of all of the wonders that I have yet heard, it seems to me most strange that men should fear, seeing that death, a necessary end, will come when it will come."

When your time was up that was it; no precaution, good luck talisman, or protection could stop the inevitable. Until then you were perfectly safe so worrying was pointless. The muscles in his anus puckered as his stomach gurgled in disagreement. He tasted bile in his mouth but told himself it was merely some bad salt pork he had eaten a few hours earlier. No, he would survive the day!

Chapter Two

Parke's eagerness turned to anxiety when he saw the vexed look on the face of the normally sanguine Lieutenant Colonel Joseph Sterrett, commander of the 5th. The colonel stormed toward Parke looking like a man with an insoluble problem. He gathered he was about to be favored with an audience. Military etiquette was applied lightly to him because of his former position as a regimental commander. Perhaps his advice was sought.

"Well, Daniel. They've done it. We are ordered to move from the orchard. Take a position a quarter-mile to the rear on top of that small hill."

"Why on earth would we want to do that, Joe? We are sheltered here and in a good position to support Pinkney's men to our front."

"Orders, apparently from Secretary Monroe. He feels it would be wiser to occupy higher ground."

"What authority does he have to issue orders and countermand Winder's instructions, Joe? He's the Secretary of State, for God's sake! He's not in anyone's chain of command. The new position puts us out of real supporting distance from our front line with no cover whatsoever."

"None that I can think of, but no one appears to have the courage to tell him to go to the blazes. So I will issue the orders and hope for the best."

"It seems like no one is really in charge. General Winder is like a ghost, much talked about but never seen. I heard a rumor earlier that a troop of cavalry was ordered to demolish the bridge with axes, but I have not seen a solitary horseman near it. Leaving the bridge in one piece is criminally foolish and almost an invitation to attack."

"Sadly, I believe you're right. Too many command whisperings instead of one clear-voice one. I just got word the President arrived fifteen minutes ago. Perhaps Secretary Monroe is issuing orders with his backing. Well, we will do what we can and hope for the best."

"That does not sound like much of a plan."

"It's not. We have been dealt a bad hand and all we can do is play it out. Good luck to you today, Daniel."

"Godspeed to you, Joe." Sterrett departed and Parke felt a huge surge of fatalism overpower his earlier optimism. Higher command had no thought of assuming the offensive. The Marylanders were merely to become fat, fixed targets and see how much hard pounding they could absorb. The question seemed not if they would be beaten, merely how badly.

*****

While a company of British light infantry waded steadily toward the opposite shore, a platoon under Ensign Jonathan Browne had reached the midpoint of the Bladensburg Bridge. "C'mon my brave lads! Forward to glory!" He shouted shrilly with the unaffected enthusiasm and pride available only to the young and inexperienced. The irony of a youth referring to men considerably older than he as lads escaped him. He boldly pointed a Pattern '96 Heavy Cavalry Saber toward the enemy. The 35-inch blade made the weapon entirely too large for his small frame and he held it clumsily.

He was just seventeen, hardly ever had to shave, and his voice still squeaked. He had been a King's Officer for just six months. This was his first battle and he wanted to honor his father, the general, by being mentioned in dispatches. He waved his sword energetically and the column followed.

Boom! Two of the 6-pounders across the river spoke their deadly words; the sound of balls in flight, that of barrels of beer slowly rolling over an oak floor. The gunners aimed their shot to graze the ground fifty yards in front of the bridge because ricocheting solid shot was generally more accurate and did more damage than shot flying directly through the air. Like stones skipped upon a lake, the balls bounced twice then bounded up to strike the redcoats at armpit level. The chests of Browne and four of his men disintegrated into gobbets of flesh and heart muscle. The British advance stopped in shock. Greasy blood slicked the bridge planks as the smell of old iron permeated the air.

Discipline held and five men quickly marched up to replace the fallen. Captain Robert Litton dashed ahead of his advancing company, sword held high and lungs blaring, to assume command. He was a one-eyed veteran of several battles, but was only four years older than Browne. The damage would have been far worse with canister. He wondered why the Americans were not using it.

"Hip hip huzzah, hip hip huzzah, hip hip huzzah!" The Americans cheered lustily. The cannoneers started to reload. Captain Karl Kramer, the battery commander, frowned. The damage could have been so much greater if they had been given canister--the supreme anti-personnel weapon that transformed a cannon into a giant shotgun. Someone had made a mistake. They had been sent only solid shot while some other battery, likely well to the rear, had their consignment of canister. He cursed the stupidity of those in charge; careless mistakes seemed the order of the day and might cost them the battle. Nevertheless, he vowed to make do.

The 150 riflemen of Major William Pinkney's command fired a volley at the redcoats remaining on the bridge. A few more British collapsed, but they were replaced as quickly as they fell. Pinkney's men reloaded, but slowly. Rifles always took more time than muskets.

Thornton saw the bloody mess on the bridge, put the spurs to his horse and galloped forward. He slowed the horse to a canter as he neared the bridge, then to an unhurried walk as the animal moved onto the planks. A gallop across would have suggested haste pushed by fear. A measured, deliberate advance was appropriate.

The men needed inspiration, a display of steadfastness. Leading from the front in a crisis was a critical part of command, even more so with senior officers than subalterns. The men needed to see and hear their commander out in front. If necessary, show the men how to die. The best officers always shouted *"follow me"* never *"go get 'em."* Thornton would be first across the bridge.

Pennywhistle carefully panned his glass over the American Army searching for targets for his Congreves. He guessed they numbered close to 7,000 men. His own army numbered a little more than 4,000. He snapped his glass shut and commanded the rocketeers to zero their rockets a hundred yards in front of Thornton. He checked his Blancpain and noted the time as just a quarter past noon.

His sword flashed down. *Woosh! Woosh*! The first five Congreve's shot skyward from their stands. They trailed red-orange flames and arced into the sky at two hundred miles an hour. Three of them landed square on one 6-pounder, smashing it and its crew into a confused mixture of metal and tangles of flesh. The other two crashed into the supporting infantry killing several and scattering the rest.

Thornton crossed the bridge slowly and deliberately, waving his sword as he did. A spent bullet ricocheted off its hilt, shaking his grip slightly. A second bullet removed the plume from his hat as he reached the far bank and a third took the fringe off his right epaulette a second later. He halted his horse and turned in his saddle, a contemptuous smile on his face. "See boys, they couldn't hit an elephant at this distance! C'mon! Double quick time!" His men raced across and began to form a line for a general advance.

Thornton and his men were on the same side of the river as the Americans. There was no natural barrier to stop them. Now it was up to the American militia; success depended on training, discipline, and experience. The British greatly overmatched the Americans in all three respects.

Thornton's men were at the top of a slight rise of ground and the Baltimore Artillery's cannon barrels had been elevated to score hits. A quick downhill advance might deny the Americans a chance to depress the barrels sufficiently to inflict further casualties.

The Congreves had exploded directly on the guns and one was destroyed. The others appeared intact but with far fewer men alive to serve them. It was the perfect opportunity. Buglers sounded the advance for the light infantry and drummers beat it out for the line infantry who were moving up in support. The light infantry advanced in loose order, with two feet between each man, making them more problematic targets for artillery.

Some of Pinkney's riflemen fired a ragged volley at Thornton's men. Several redcoats dropped wounded to the ground, but most of the shots flew high.

Woosh! *Woosh*! Pennywhistle let fly the second salvo of Congreves. All burst to the immediate rear of Pinkney's command.

The salvo felled a score of Americans and planted a seed of panic. Congreves were not supposed to be accurate! They had been told not to worry! A few started to run, although the rest seemed mostly uncertain. "Fall back and regroup!" shouted Pinkney. It took the men a full minute to recover their wits. The retreat could not be called orderly, but it fell short of a rout. A quarter of the men fled the field, but what remained formed up just to the rear of the 6-pounders.

At the same moment, the first redcoats wading the Anacostia splashed ashore in the marsh reeds. The company formed in front of a long white fence between two willow trees. A short advance would enable them to impose themselves astride Pinkney's line of retreat. Captain Robin Martyn, their commander, a Peninsular War veteran of ten year's service, heard the bugles, and saw Thornton's men moving down the hill. If his advance were timed right, it would catch the Americans between two fires.

The Baltimore Artillery fired off another round toward Thornton's men. Their barrels were wedged over the top of the four-foot-high earthworks and there was no time to disengage them, remove the quoins, and bring the barrels to a more level position. Their imagined protection proved a severe disadvantage. Most of the battery's solid shot flew high.

Canister would have been much better against men advancing in loose order.

Pennywhistle dashed over to the other Congreve operators and ordered them to fire. Most rockets would probably miss, but if even a few told, there would be chaos.

Woosh Woosh! Flaming parabolas of orange light shot through the air. Most of the rockets zigzagged wildly and did no damage other than upsetting already jangled nerves.

But just as you cannot randomly broadcast seeds without a few germinating, two rockets landed true and deadly. One burst at the ideal height of twenty feet over cannons number three and four and showered them with lethal shards of metal. The large, heavy fragments acted as bullets, knives, cleavers, and cudgels. They punched, ripped, hacked, and crushed flesh and bone. The guns were minimally damaged, but all of the crews were either dead or wounded.

The second rocket felled only two men, but one of them was Major Pinkney. Without his leadership, his men simply milled about, appalled, like cattle on the edge of a stampede. It would take precious little to push them over the edge.

Thornton and Martyn saw the situation at the same moment and ordered the same response. *Charge!* The men dashed forward, bayonets leveled, an evil glint in every British eye. The Americans were the nut, the converging British forces the nutcracker. All semblance of order in the American forces vanished when the British forces finally broke into a run, sunlight sparkling on the tips of their hungry bayonets. A stray shot killed Thornton's horse, but he threw himself clear and continued the charge on foot.

At thirty yards distance, the Americans simply turned tail and headed toward the rear, heedless of any thought save basic self-preservation. The guns were swiftly overrun and the militia scattered. The American front line was gone. Despite the mad excitement of victory, British soldiers obeyed orders and paused to regroup and reorder their lines. The battle was only thirty minutes old.

*****

Parke saw madly running fugitives burst out of the apple orchard behind the Baltimore Artillery and knew these men had lost all conception of duty. "Save yourselves," shouted men who rushed past their own line. "See you on the other side of the Potomac!" yelled others. Sterrett's stern voice echoed down the line. "Ignore them. Steady, men, steady. Hold with your teeth, with your nails, but hold; for the honor of the Old Line State! We'll give 'em the devil's own hiding!"

The 5th Maryland Regiment stood firm, posted on a small rise three hundred yards to the rear of the apple orchard. True to Sterrett's bold words, they refused to be infected by panic. The tide surged past them, like waves parting before a breakwater. The two ranks kept their alignment and waited.

Parke was proud to stand with them. This was a smart, disciplined regiment composed of men of substance and quality. All of the men had decent training. They also had real uniforms, most well-tailored, swallow-tailed royal blue coatees with crimson collars and cuffs with bone white trousers. Their black shakos were tall like the British but more rounded and sported a wide red band midway up the crown.

Men of the 1st Maryland, Colonel John Ragan commanding, and 2nd Maryland, commanded by Colonel Jonathan Schutz, stood in echelon to the right and slightly in front of the 5th. Each contained 675 men of all ranks. Unlike the 5th, the commanders of these two regiments were not using the officially prescribed drill manual of Colonel

Alexander Smyth and had formed their men into an older, three-rank arrangement; one that usually resulted in a less efficient delivery of firepower. The front rank kneeled, the second rank fired over their heads, and the third rank fired through gaps in the second rank.

Both the 1st and 2nd had been hastily organized and possessed little training. Most wore black top hats but their coats and trousers were only vaguely military and came in various shades of brown, buff, butternut, and blue. The majority of both were products of repeated sweepings of the Baltimore waterfront. The rest were mostly unemployed young men and itinerant farm workers. They were all in their late teens and early twenties, men from the margins of society whose deaths would go unnoticed save by their own families. As with most conflicts, the current struggle was a rich man's war but a poor man's fight.

Parke reckoned that while the rank-and-file were not men of quality, they were well-intentioned and patriotic. Their officers were chiefly merchants whose portly physiques represented comfortable, well-tended prosperity; the sort of folk who meant well but knew battle only from Moroccan leather-bound books. He had heard that a few very old noncommissioned officers who had seen action in the Revolution were spread thinly among their ranks. Would that the rumor were true!

The weapons of all three regiments were at least new. Rather than the antique fowling pieces and duck guns with which some units had to make do, all of the Maryland regiments were armed with .69 caliber Springfield's, pattern 1795. The Springfield was a close copy of the Charleville that had won fame for Napoleon's armies.

The Springfield, like the British Brown Bess, weighed in at ten pounds and was an inaccurate, single-shot, smoothbore; a good marksman with either was lucky to hit a man-sized target six times out of ten at one hundred yards. It took sixteen separate motions to load and discharge a piece so three shots a minute was considered an excellent rate of fire.

Muskets were best employed in volley fire with one solid block of soldiers blazing away at another tight mass at close range; generally under one hundred yards and sometimes as close as thirty. The militia occasionally practiced target shooting at musters, but in battle many just pointed their weapons in the general direction of the enemy and fired on command. Muskets gave off tremendous amounts of smoke so after a few volleys it was hard to see much of anything.

Accuracy counted for little, speed counted for much. Victory went to the side that could put the greatest amount of lead in the air in the shortest time. A bayonet charge, launched after lead had cut the enemy to ribbons and unmanned their resolve, usually finished a fight.

Brightly colored uniforms were preferred in battle since they could be spotted much more readily in the choking smog, rather than civilian dress of dowdy earth tones. Commands to retreat, advance, fire, surrender, or dozens of other actions were pounded out on drums, blared on bugles, or trilled on whistles because all were much easier to hear in the din of battle than the human voice.

Parke felt there was still hope. The men of the 1st and 2nd might be amateurs, but their faces looked determined and 1350 muskets at close range would powerfully enunciate the American viewpoint. Added to the 500 muskets of the 5th, the combined firepower stood a real chance of stopping the British if it were intelligently employed.

A big if, considering the ineptitude he had seen displayed by the higher echelons of command. The disgrace of the fleeing militia made Parke determined to give a good account of himself. He fervently hoped that the men of the other regiments would see things the same way.

*****

Pennywhistle's rockets were gone. He told his unarmed rocket troop to report to the rear as stretcher bearers. He shouldered his Ferguson rifle and realized he was a free agent in the battle unfolding. Spottswood had his company along with the redoubtable Sergeant Dale and would make good use of it. Anyway, it was a mile-and-a-half to the rear, not yet engaged, and he was in the thick of a fight.

He debated alternatives, then noticed a young officer fall, not twenty yards from him. The way the man fell made no sense. He had to have been hit from behind.

He ran over to the body. It was a young ensign, probably not more than eighteen; a boy in a man's uniform. He was still alive but consciousness was already fading from his eyes. Blood dribbled from his mouth like soap bubbles as he struggled to focus on Pennywhistle. He tried to speak but all that came out was incoherent whisper.

Pennywhistle shushed him, told him to converse his strength. His words were gentle but his mind became coldly clinical as he performed a quick examination. He cast his mind back to the Edinburgh University anatomy theatre watching surgeons perform a dissection. A foolish duel had terminated his fledging medical career but the knowledge gained there had proven useful on many occasions.

The bullet had entered the right epaulette from above and behind, and had struck downward from there, penetrating the

37

lungs and lodging at the base of the spine. It was very similar to the wound that killed Nelson. The wheezing told him the ensign was drowning in his own blood. There was nothing to be done.

The teenager looked at him with pleading eyes seeking reassurance this was not the end. He gripped the boy's hand, at least able to let him know he would not die alone. The hand spasmed a few seconds later then relaxed permanently.

Pennywhistle's mind registered it as an expert shot and it stoked his rising anger from a suspicion that would not be banished. He looked up and his mind shifted into a sharply clear, focused state. He calculated the angle of the shot and plotted its trajectory back to its point of origin, a red brick home, second floor, a hundred yards distant with excellent concealment, clear field of fire.

Blarney raced up at that moment. He patted the dog several times and Blarney responded with his characteristic doggy grin. He pulled the note from the collar and a second later his face flushed with anger as his suspicions were confirmed.

No! No one could be that reckless. It was madness! Spurning her reprieve in the interest of some silly, misguided patriotism struck him as unbridled foolhardiness. "God damn it!" he said in sheer exasperation. He rarely swore and when he did it was usually at arrogance, recklessness, or stupidity. This time, it was all three. What was it about these ill-mannered Yankees? Did they understand neither honor nor mercy?

His mind stayed coldly clear and he observed Rear Admiral George Cockburn and his aide, Lieutenant James Scott, approach on horseback, not more than three hundred yards distant. Cockburn looked his usual boldly confident self, contemptuous of any danger. His brilliantly planned and executed raids up and down the Chesapeake over the last year had caused great consternation among the Yankees as well as millions of dollars in damages. He had become a bogeyman fixture in stories told to American children. *Behave or Cockburn will get you!*

That bloody twit! The subaltern was only practice. She was stalking much bigger game. Cockburn would be at the outside range of her rifle, but there was absolutely no wind and she had the advantage of elevation and a fixed firing position. She could definitely do it.

His anger seized control and he ran toward the home, hoping against hope he would not find what he expected. He slammed the half-open front door aside and darted up the stairs. He stopped at the top landing, calmed his racing heart, and looked for an open door. His right hand squeezed the hilt of his cutlass. He took a deep breath and walked through with dread purpose.

Their expressions reflected mutual shock, yet no great surprise to either. Sammie Jo had never looked more beautiful or more lethal. A wisp of smoke curled up from the muzzle of her firelock. It was clear what business she had been about.

She did not try to run or hide, but stood rock still and regarded him with both resignation and defiance. He had warned her he would kill her if he ever saw her near a battlefield. She clearly expected him to be as good as his word.

Pennywhistle knew what he had to do, what he must do, but he simply could not. He compulsively clenched and unclenched the hilt of his cutlass several times in deep frustration, then relaxed his grip. He was losing his edge and it appalled him. Two years ago in Spain, he would not have given it a moment's consideration.

God, she looked delicious and ripe for plucking. Why did the richest fruit always entice at the end of a long, dangerous climb? Her five-foot-eleven-inch frame was powerfully athletic, but curved in all of the right womanly places. She was the living incarnation of Diana, Goddess of the Hunt. Her lips parted, her bosom heaved, and her breathing came in gasps. Did the act of killing excite her or was it something very different?

It was madness, it was folly, it was a total dereliction of his duty. A battle raged outside, he was desperately needed, but he did not care. For once, king and country could wait. Killing was becoming all too easy; understanding the passion of love, all too hard.

He advanced toward her then stopped, still as a statue.

The day outside was torrid, but nothing compared to the rising heat in the gaming room. Their eyes met, locked, and blazed with fire. A wealth of meaning danced between them. They rushed madly at each other and collided in a grand conflagration of long wet kisses and frantically roving hands. Tongues were delightfully active, but the only conversation proceeded with fingertips. Complexities of life departed, everything became exceedingly simple. She wanted him: he wanted her.

It troubled him for a fraction of a second. Was it merely one skilled killer embracing his distaff counterpart, two dark entities merging? They swiftly tore the clothing from each other like starving people who had just discovered a hidden cache of food. It was utterly without elegance or ceremony; unadulterated, searing desire smashing anything resembling rationality. They needed each other for reasons neither could explain.

He lifted her forcefully by the hips and laid her out on the green baize of the billiard table. She quickly extended her long arms and pulled his sweating body down atop hers. He took her hard and vigorously, without words. It was pure, raw, animal passion heightened by the danger of imminent extinction. Their wild bucking motions moved at precisely the same frenzied tempo and complimented each other perfectly. Her long legs and athletic body furled him splendidly, better than the most tightly tailored gloves. They emitted a steady stream of low, beast-like yelps, cries, and grunts, but the most telling sound was that of their superheated breathing. It ended in two simultaneous explosions five minutes later, both parties bathed in sweat, panting hard, and grinning broadly in sheer joy.

They did not speak for some minutes after, merely caressed each other gently as their breathing returned to normal and the sexual flush departed their beaming faces. He felt real affection in her touch. It surprised him; perhaps the coupling presaged something more than the triumph of lust.

"Well jubilation and praise the Lo-ad! Yoah a sly boots, Sugah Plu-um. I ain't nevuh daynced the goat's jig lahk th-at! Dayum if yuh didn't put just the rat balls into just the rat pocket. Done blew all muh loose coahns clean off!" She turned to kiss him.

He punched her. Not too hard, just enough to be sure she was lights-out until the end of the day. She lapsed into blissful unconsciousness. She would sleep through the remainder of the horror ahead. He hated doing it, but knew she would be back at her deadly business in short order if he did not. Cruel to be kind, Shakespeare said. He did not think the bruise would show after a few days.

He knew he was a fool to spare her, but someone had to look out for her welfare and protect her in spite of herself. She had called him 'sugar plum' just now as she had upon their first meeting. It had annoyed him at first but as the hours of her captivity advanced, he came to find it oddly charming. He had responded by sarcastically referring to her as "Hawkeye," and she had smiled at the nickname.

He looked at her exquisite oblong face framed by shoulder-length honey-blonde hair she usually kept wrapped in a bun; high cheekbones, bee-stung lips, deep-set eyes, and determined jaw line. He liked her, might even fall for her, but he was a gentleman and she an ignorant rustic. It made no sense. He was glad they would never meet again.

He dressed quickly and glanced down at her lovely form, surprisingly innocent in quiet repose. He found a blanket, carefully covered her nakedness, and gently placed a pillow under her head. He mentally wished her well, and dashed back down the stairs, trading post-coital heaven for a hell of violent madness. The vanguard of Brooke's Brigade had just entered the town.

Despite the reek of brimstone, the clouds of dust stirred by thousands of marching feet, the spit-spat of muskets and booms of cannon fire, he sauntered onto the street smiling stupidly and feeling relaxed and renewed. He and Sammie Jo were oddly suited for long-term relationship based on sexual needs. Rather a pity that it was hardly a sufficient foundation for a permanent connection.

He breathed slowly and deeply for a full minute, drove all carnal thoughts from his brain, and focused on his duty ahead. A vision of her ample breasts returned a second later and danced merrily on the edge of his consciousness. No, blast it! He chased the image away with the fervor of an Inquisition priest performing an exorcism. He unfurled his spyglass and moved it in a slow, wide arc as he assessed the situation across the river. He could not shake the feeling that some part of Sammie Jo's loveliness had insinuated itself permanently into his brain.

Was her essence some kind of infestation similar to the fungal blight he had sometimes seen on oak trees? Green blight was pretty to look at, but eventually fatal to the tree. *Damn it concentrate! Remember your duty!* screamed his conscience. *You can hear the whine of bullets, what the blazes is wrong with you?*

Why did the prospect of her in creamy, diaphanous, *décolletage à la française* gowns, jeweled earrings, and long silk gloves bewitch him so? It was madness. She would be as out of place in England as a giraffe in the Arctic.

His relatives would be barely able to understand her heavy Southern dialect and he had felt like Gulliver, washed ashore in a strange land when he first heard her speak.

"Ah may be just a pore cuntruh gull with no fuhmul edgycation, but ahm a lot moe than the apple dumplin yuh think ah em. Doan deny it, ah kin see thay-at in yoah ahs playhun as day-uh. Ah re-ad the Gawd Bo-ak just fahn and ah cipha rat well too. I lo- ak in the newspapuhs regulah to discovuh the naysties yo bow- ass Cockburn has done brow- ht down on our he-ads. That bayustard doan se- am to git th- at we murikans er fahtun fuh sayluh's rats."

Why on earth would sailors fight for creatures that were the bane of ships? It took him a full minute to understand she actually meant sailor's rights. In the hours she had spent in his company as a prisoner, he had used his ear for languages to decipher her talk. She languidly drawled every word and he typically could utter two sentences in the time it took her to speak one. She often turned one vowel into two, so bill became *bee-hill,* bed *be-od,* talk *ta-wk* and clam became *clay- yum.*

Her R's were particularly confusing to speakers of the King's English. Sometimes she pronounced them with an "ah" sound so sugar became *suguh,* order *awduh,* and sir *suh.* Other times she transformed them into Y's and hair emerged as *heya* and thirsty came out as *thy-st-y.* Sometimes R's disappeared entirely so you spoke a *wuhd* and *huhd* a sound.

G's frequently went missing as well and common functions came out as *larnin, eatin,* and *wukin.*

You *bawled* water for *suppah* when it got *doc,* added *sawt* to *me- ats,* and used *yarbs* to give food extra taste. You bought things at a *stowe, toted* goods *a fur piece* rather than carried them a long distance, and gave a *yale* when you wanted to get folks attention. *Y'all* wormed its way into almost every sentence and the words done and thing had a curious utility. "*I already done tole yuh about thaht thar thang*" was a phrase she favored.

She could curse a blue streak but hell came out as *hale* and shit as *she- at.*

She peppered her speech with legions of country expressions. Chief among them were "hold your potato" and "cut your own weeds." The first meant "be patient" and the second "mind your own business." Business sprang from her lips as "bidness."

Polite salon habitués in England would laugh at her bumpkin manners and ridicule her lack of ladylike deportment. One woman had died for his love, while another calmly moved on and found a better man. His combat judgment was excellent. The opposite obtained for his assessments about women. It was far more sensible to focus on what he did best and shun the mawkish observation of La Rochefoucauld "that a life without women is like a spring time without roses."

Damn! He had been daydreaming while bullets were flying. Unconscionable! He shook his head twice and snapped himself back to reality.

*****

Brooke's Brigade began its deployment. The 44th Foot would advance in column across the bridge followed by the 4th, sans its light company. They would move north and west and edge round the American left flank while Thornton occupied the attention of their center and right. Pennywhistle slung his Ferguson over his shoulder and decided to march with the men headed to the bridge. He would target enemy officers as usual. There would also be casualties among the officers on his side and he could serve as a replacement where needed.

He could see Thornton's men forming on the opposite bank at the edge of the orchard. They stood calmly in place, awaiting the advance of Brooke's Brigade. Their line was two ranks deep and six hundred feet long. The musket fire had stopped temporarily, although there was a steady booming from Barney's heavy artillery on the Washington Turnpike. Without a clear line of sight for their solid shot, most of the rounds buried themselves harmlessly in the ground. The only casualties of the cannonade were a few squirrels, rabbits, and willow trees.

Manton's light company of the 4th marched past and Manton waved to him. Manton had been his servant a lifetime ago in Spain. It was rare for someone with Manton's background to obtain a commission but conspicuous gallantry as a volunteer at Salamanca had provided a way to breech the barricades of class. Pennywhistle was delighted that the career begun in the Peninsular Campaign had progressed well. He quick stepped over and moved alongside. "Good day, John! Your people march exceptionally well. You have come a long way in a short time. I don't think there is a more proficient subaltern in the British Army."

"I shall be forever in your debt, Captain. You changed my life and Juanita's." He smiled broadly. "She is expecting you know!" It was still hard for him to call Pennywhistle by his first name. "You certainly look cheerful this morning. The heat actually seems to agree with you," said Manton with surprise. His men marched handsomely but the effects of the unforgiving sun showed on their beet-red faces.

A smile blossomed on Pennywhistle's face. One kind of heat certainly agreed with him, although he had no idea it was so obvious. "I made a few changes on some Congreves. They worked well and I am simply flushed with success. The rockets are exhausted, Spottswood has my company, and I am become a mere supernumerary. Wondered if I might tag along and make myself useful?"

"I'd be honored to have you....Tom. We are going into action directly. We are short an officer as it happens. Mr. Drake died in a pointless little skirmish yesterday; ran into trouble with some militia led by a damned US Marine. Have to admit the militia fought well and their leader was something extraordinary. I don't know how to say this without sounding a bit mad, but he was the spitting image of you! It quite unsettled me. I thought I was seeing things, thought perhaps my fevered brain was reacting to the heat and combat. It must sound ridiculous, but the more I think on it, the more I am sure of what I saw."

Pennywhistle's face turned grave. "You are not mistaken. I have met the man. His name is Captain John Tracy. He is a formidable and resourceful antagonist. I believe I know exactly who he is. There is only one explanation that makes sense, but I do not like it. His age would be exactly right."

Manton's time as Pennywhistle's batman had taught him to read the marine's moods and conflicts with clarity and accuracy. He had always been discretion itself with regard to secrets and Pennywhistle clearly had one. The captain wore a faraway look. He was weighing something, sorting variables, searching for an alternate answer to the equation. The way he arched his eyebrows suggested he could no longer reject something which caused him deep distress.

Manton spoke with patience. "I have a feeling we will both be seeing him today. Is he..." He hesitated for a second, "Is he some very distant relation, perhaps from some long-forgotten cadet branch of your family?"

Pennywhistle walked a little faster, staring straight ahead. It was a full minute before he spoke. "He is not from a cadet branch, John. He is my father's son. My father was apparently less than chaste during his service in Virginia in the last war." He let his breath out in a long sigh. "I confess I am disappointed. I idolized my father, he was a fine man. It is always difficult for an admiring son to accept a parent had warts and to acknowledge that he was human, that he had needs. He was young, unmarried, and often in great danger. He fought in most of the battles of the Southern Campaign. I suppose he did what most do, sought comfort where he could find it. I am hardly qualified to lecture on chastity.

"I have to confess, I am quite curious about who she was. Knowing my father, she must have been someone quite remarkable." His voice grew angry. "But that is pointless, idle speculation. I will probably never find out and it is the height of folly to waste my energies chasing answers that would never bring me peace anyway." He muttered several imprecations under his breath.

Manton knew he should drop the subject but he could not. Information on an opponent's cast of mind crossed the line from gossip to military necessity. "I think he is a great deal like you, Tom. That makes him dangerous. He pulled a maneuver on me that was exactly what you would have done. Do you suppose he knows?"

Pennywhistle stopped dead in his tracks and faced Manton. "I have fought him twice and even spoken briefly to him. I even looked him deep in the eye for a split second and it told me all I needed to know about the hardness of his resolve. If he is in charge of the US Marines today, and I suspect this is so, he will assume the offensive if at all possible."

"Other than the Virginia drawl, even his voice sounds like mine. He will have reasoned out the truth, rejected it angrily, and then finally accepted it. A part of me finds it painful to acknowledge him, but another is most curious and would enjoy a long talk with him. It is a very strange feeling to suddenly acquire a brother, particularly one fighting for the other side. I confess I am pleased that he is a fine officer. He might just as well have been a shiftless ne'er-do-well. Still, were that so, I should never have encountered him upon the battlefield.

"I think it comes down to what he merits not just as a brother, but as a man. He may be a vexatious adversary, but he is a staunch warrior and deserves the full details of his heritage. Legitimate or not, he is a Pennywhistle by blood and should know our successes and our failures."

He laughed ruefully. "But I am letting imagination run away with me. None of us may survive the battle ahead. If I meet Tracy in the next hour it will be my duty to kill him. He will think it his duty to do the same to me. He would not respect me if I hesitated, nor I him. I have heard people on both sides speak of this stupid little war as an extended family quarrel. In my case it is literally true."

Chapter Three

A horseman galloped up to Manton with the expected orders. "Well, Tom, time to play our part. Let's get the men formed and ford the river."

Pennywhistle nodded. "Thanks for listening to my ruminations. You are most patient. You were always a good servant. You have become an even better officer and friend. I'll post myself at the left end of the line as we advance."

Manton nodded. "Honored, as always. My company is ordered to detach itself from Brooke's Brigade and directed to take up position in echelon to the left rear of Thornton's men to protect his flank as he advances." He shook Pennywhistle's hand, wished him luck, and took his leave. He walked over to the bugler, gave him instructions, and drew his sword. The bugler blew the appropriate flourishes and the company formed into a loose skirmish line.

The company advanced methodically, Manton and Pennywhistle walking slowly in advance of the men. The two officers held their swords aloft with their elbows straight and locked, the blades at 45-degree angles with the surface of the river.

The sluggish Anacostia stank badly in the high summer heat. Offal and excrement from a local slaughterhouse were regularly dumped into it, as was the effluvia from several tanners and dyers. It was also choked with slowly revolving pinwheels of fast-rotting vegetables. The produce had been hastily cast into it by panicked farmers determined to deny sustenance to the invaders.

Pennywhistle wrinkled his nose in distaste at the chocolate-colored murk he was wading through as it had a consistency closer to tar than water. Some of the men actually pinched their noses to ward off the noxious vapors. A few desultory shots from stray militia men punctuated the British advance, serving notice the Americans had not vanished entirely, but mostly their progress was uncontested. The company formed up on the opposite bank, linking up with Thornton's extreme left.

The objective was clear: drive off the militia directly in their front, preferably in abject panic so that their fear might be quickly spread to their brethren. The rest of Brooke's Brigade poured across the bridge, formed up, and performed a smart right wheel. They marched away from Manton's men, intending to attack north of the Washington Turnpike. They would move around the American left and slice into their rear, aiming for the ammunition trains. The maneuver would relieve pressure on Thornton's men who would lead the main assault.

*****

Across the river, Cockburn and Lieutenant Scott dismounted and watched with great interest as rocketeers set up a battery of Congreves. Scott suggested Cockburn make himself less conspicuous. The gold on his *chapeau de bras* was a tempting target for American sharpshooters. "Oh pooh!" said Cockburn dismissively. "We are in no danger here!"

A second later, a bullet whined past, missing Cockburn's hands by a quarter inch but severing the left stirrup of his horse's saddle. A marine who instinctively reached up to grab the falling stirrup took a bullet through the head.

Cockburn frowned briefly but continued to act as if he were merely taking a pleasant stroll in St. James Park. Cockburn spoke to Corporal Haynes, a hard-bitten marine of ten years' service who greatly respected Cockburn's toughness. Haynes smiled broadly, greatly honored an admiral would gift him with a few minutes of his valuable time. "Make sure you aim your rockets high," said Cockburn. "We want to target the second line of militia men. They will be immediately to the rear of that large apple orchard. Don't open fire until you see our men advance with the bayonet."

*****

Daniel Parke waited but not patiently. His heart hammered and he sweated freely both from the ridiculous heat and the excitement. He heard bugles blow and drums thunder. He saw a line of red and steel advance out of the orchard. The British marched slowly, majestically, menacingly, their weapons held horizontal and waist high. The light companies of the 21st and 44th, as well as several line companies borrowed from the 85th, advanced behind Manton's men. Their weathered, craggy faces looked stern and confident. His moment of truth was at hand. He was ready, and so was the 5th Maryland.

At one hundred yards range, 1st Maryland fired a volley at the advancing British. As often happened with a three rank firing arrangement, a few men in the front line were hit by bullets fired by jittery soldiers in the third. Most rounds flew slightly high since the inexperienced men aimed at enemy chests rather than their legs.

When the smoke cleared, there were gaps in the British line, but very small ones. They vanished quickly as file closers stepped into each breach. The volley did nothing to arrest British momentum and the red line advanced inexorably up the low hill. The 1st Maryland reloaded as the 2nd Maryland advanced on their right and prepared to deliver their own volley.

The British line abruptly halted fifty yards out. Pennywhistle locked his sights onto what he took to be a colonel. "Make ready, front rank kneel!" echoed down the line. Hundreds of soldiers brought muskets vertical to their chests. Their thumbs full cocked them with a loud, collective *click*. "Present!" The redcoats leveled them toward the enemy. Pennywhistle's finger moved lightly to the Ferguson's trigger.

The men of the 1st wavered and their expressions showed naked fear. At this distance, war suddenly became *very* personal. The faces of their opponents were clear and their expressions unmistakable: hardy veterans, unacquainted with qualities like mercy and/or restraint. The torrent of lead would be very bad.

Woosh! Woosh! Woosh! Ten Congreves tore into the sky. *Wham! Wham! Wham!* They burst directly over the heads of the 1st, showered them with a storm of jagged metal shards.

British swords flashed down and a dozen officers yelled, "Fire!" Scarlet flame darted forth from hundreds of muskets. The British did not fire high. They aimed for the kneecaps and allowed for the rise of their balls. The volley was like a whip of hot lava and the Americans fell in neat rows, exactly as they had stood seconds before. Pennywhistle's shot caught the 1st's colonel just below his left pectoral.

Panic hit the Marylanders like a plague of locusts, moving fast and swarming over their reserves of courage. First one American ran, and then his neighbor, and then his neighbor. Panic spread quickly if not cauterized by strong leadership, but with their commander dead, there was no heroic father figure to rally them. Hence, it took thirty seconds for the regiment to change from a disciplined block of men to a horde of fleeing fugitives out of all control. They scampered up the hill like rabbits.

The British line did not bother to reload but resumed their methodical advance, bayonets leveled. Cold steel would decide the business.

The 2nd Maryland advanced slightly, tried to fill the gap left by the 1st. Their weapons were loaded. They waited for the command to fire. The British were thirty yards out now. Their faces looked grim and unforgiving.

Later, survivors from the 2nd would never know quite what happened, what triggered the panic. One man simply ran. Others saw him, following his lead. Panic spread like wildfire stoked by a strong wind. The 2nd Maryland dissolved in an instant. Officers stormed and shouted but no one listened. A rabble fled up the hill.

"Steady men, steady. We will stand firm and give them what for!" Colonel Sterrett shouted confidently at the 5th. A fierce smile blossomed on his face. If panic was a disease, then self-assured leadership was the vaccine. Battlefield leadership was about getting men to perform commonplace parade ground actions in a distinctly un-commonplace setting.

Sterrett's men stood tall, silent and implacable. *Good,* thought Sterrett. *We will make our volley a stiff one.*

As if to complement his resolve, the Washington Artillery fired a blast of canister at the advancing British. Two hundred pieces of lead tore into the British line. Gaps opened, but the red menace barreled on.

The horde of fugitives streaming past his regiment dismayed Parke, but if anything, it stiffened his resolve to stand and fight. The men on either side of him looked just as determined as he. One man retched and shook briefly, but recovered and did not leave his place in line. Another man wet himself but stayed put. The two long ranks were as solid as granite and would be just as steady meeting the British advance.

A dappled grey thoroughbred bearing a high-ranking officer blazed across the confused landscape, the rider apparently seeking to bring order out of chaos. Parke had only seen him once, but thought he recognized General William Winder, the army's commander. Winder galloped up to Colonel Sterrett appearing haggard and harried; his face that of a man confronted with a dozen tasks but only granted the time to perform six.

"Colonel, withdraw your men. You will be overrun." He pointed to the west. "I want you to reform your men further back up the hill-- say four hundred yards yonder."

Sterrett looked at Winder as if the general had taken leave of his senses. "General, my men are poised to deliver a volley. We can stop the redcoats! I know it. We can't abandon our position!"

Winder looked at him with disdain. "I have already given orders to the Washington Artillery to withdraw. You will be without support if you stay here and I don't have time to argue. We will make our stand at the top of the hill."

Sterrett stared blankly at Winder, appalled. It was insanity but he would do his duty and obey orders. "Fall back by companies. Reform at the top of the hill. Smartly now!" The men looked bewildered and angry. The order made no sense to them, he could tell. They had not signed on to flee like a herd of frightened ponies. Nevertheless, they obeyed and began an orderly withdrawal. Winder galloped off to remonstrate with the Washington Artillery.

*****

Manton and Pennywhistle saw the 5th retreat and were puzzled why it had not delivered a volley. Thornton and Brooke halted the British advance. Pennywhistle dashed over to Manton when he saw Colonel Thornton gallop over. The three conferred for two quick minutes. They all noticed the 5th's right dangled in the air, completely unprotected.

The British line methodically extended itself to the left, and then the redcoats reloaded their weapons. The orderly evolution took only a minute. The red line overlapped the now retreating Americans and was in a perfect position to pour in enfilade fire on the 5th. The British resumed their methodical advance up the hill.

*****

The Washington Artillery slammed two further blasts of canister into the British and cheered after each salvo. They were doing real damage. Winder galloped up. He reined his horse in and shouted at Captain Benjamin Burch, the battery commander. "Damn it, I told you to withdraw! Why have you not obeyed? Get the battery out of here!"

Burch kept his voice polite but shot him a fiery glance, a mixture of contempt and anger. "Yes sir, very good sir." He had already disobeyed the order once. He issued the orders and the men limbered up the half-dozen 6-pounders and prepared to withdraw.

*****

Parke was halfway up the hill. He marched in good cadence, but hated what he was doing. His mind screamed that this was all wrong, but Sterrett was a good man and probably could limit the worst effects of Winder's foolish order. The mercury must have topped one hundred and everyone perspired heavily. The heavy wool uniforms became as wet as if just pulled from washtubs and the moldy smell of incipient mildew filled the air.

Winder galloped insanely across the field, having seen the British extending their line. He reined in his heavily-lathered horse in front of an exasperated Colonel Sterrett. "Colonel, halt your regiment and face your men about. Extend your line fifty yards to the right. We must make our stand here and now!" His rasping voice betrayed a hint of hysteria.

"General, I must protest!" said Sterrett, half remonstrating, half pleading. "You can't swap horses in midstream. Let me complete my withdrawal and reform at the top of the hill!" The men were already bewildered and this might well send things spiraling into chaos. Confusion and irresolution at the highest levels of command unmanned troops far faster than enemy action.

"Do as I say, damn it, or I shall relieve you here and now!"

"Yes sir." Sterrett saluted. He had no choice. Winder was fool enough to carry out his threat and there was no one else who enjoyed the men's confidence. Better to stay in command and try to make the best of a bad order. He reluctantly issued the requisite instructions and Winder sped away, apparently satisfied and undoubtedly off to cause trouble somewhere else.

The several companies turned and faced the British. They started to change from column into line. With bullets whining past and nerves ragged, the maneuver proceeded much more slowly than it had on the parade ground. In actual battle, everything was simple, but even the simplest thing was difficult.

Woosh! Woosh! Woosh! More Congreves flew into the sky. All but one was a clean miss, but a single rocket landed square in the heart of the 5th who were frantically struggling to form two coherent lines. Ten men fell. Pennywhistle had been tracking Colonel Sterrett and gently squeezed the trigger of the Ferguson. Sterrett dropped, shot through the heart.

The British line continued its steady advance, marching at nearly right angles to the 5th. The red line halted at sixty yards distance. The men full-cocked their weapons and waited stoically for one simple word. "Fire!" yelled a dozen officers. A torrent of lead slammed into the Marylanders at a perfectly oblique angle, ripping their line into tattered fragments as easily as a child shredded tissue paper.

The combination of events was simply too much for the 5th. They broke and ran up the hill. Parke was the last to leave. He might have made some bad mistakes with his regiment, but he had done nothing that approached what Winder had just done. He reluctantly shouldered his musket and quick marched up the hill. He showed the enemy his backside and silently dared them to shoot.

In sheer frustration, he stopped, turned, and angrily discharged his weapon at the oncoming line of red. He was not sure if he hit anyone but it felt good to at least take action. He thought there must be a few troops left who would fight and he determined to seek them out.

*****

Captain John Tracy, USMC, could not credit his eyes. The front two lines of the American Army were gone. There was only one left and he was in it. Blast that fool Winder; mostly never around, then everywhere at exactly the wrong moments. Winder was a lawyer by trade, a political general out of his depth on a real battlefield. He only got his job because his cousin, Levin, was the Federalist governor of Maryland. The Republican administration hoped his appointment would dampen Federalist opposition to the War. If he made an appearance near Tracy's men, he would shoot the man himself and consequences be damned.

His own US Marines stood firm and resolute. They were small in number but well trained, motivated, and battle-hardened veterans. The marines on the field today represented one-fourth of the entire US Marine Corps. They looked with disdain at the legions of fugitives dashing past. He knew nothing short of an earthquake could budge his marines.

The marines and the veteran sailors alongside them totaled only 480. They had all been part of Commodore Joshua Barney's gunboat flotilla and reposed complete trust in their veteran leader. The flotilla had been destroyed so they were making themselves useful as infantrymen and artillerists. With few exceptions, they were the only Americans on the field experienced in battle.

Five big guns stood behind them that Barney had salvaged from the flotilla; three 12-pounders and two 18-pounders. The sailors and marines manning them were all skilled artillerists and itching to smash the red-coated invaders. The guns commanded the Washington Turnpike, the main thoroughfare leading to Washington. The British were not going anywhere near the Capital unless they were overcome.

Tracy felt sorry for the fugitives. Winder had not even designated a rally point in case the day went against them. They fled along the Georgetown Road rather than the

Washington turnpike, i.e., away from the battle, rather than to its rear. They were too distant to play a further part in the battle if they were rallied. But Tracy had seen the whipped cur look in their eyes and knew they were broken reeds beyond rational appeals. He could hardly blame them for looking after themselves when the high command had failed to do so.

Tracy spotted a small, unimpressive figure in black on horseback who was being swept along by the tide of fugitives. It was President James Madison himself. A powerful group of treasonous New Englanders called the Knights of the Golden Horseshoe had wanted Tracy to turn assassin. He now had the perfect opportunity to kill the President. Tracy was a loyal Marine and had no intention of doing so, but had felt it was his duty to play along with them. He wanted to discover the full extent of their malice and intended to expose them as traitors when the time was right.

The range was right and the confusion was perfect cover for the shot. As he was congratulating himself on frustrating the Knight's plan by simply doing nothing, he saw another Marine Captain that he did not recognize taking careful aim at the President. What the blazes? He, Samuel Miller, and Quartermaster Samuel Bacon, were the only Marine Captains on the field today.

It hit him in a flash. The imposter belonged to the Knights. They did have a fallback plan to use another killer to act if Tracy did not. Those devious bastards! The man was almost exactly his height and build. That was no accident. In any inquiry after the fight, men might say they saw a Marine officer firing and he would likely be blamed.

Tracy hesitated not a second. He brought his rifle swiftly to the point, aimed, and fired. The imposter dropped like a man whose skeleton was reduced to sawdust. Tracy raced through the crowd of disorganized militia and reached the corpse moments later. He quickly searched the body and found a packet of documents that looked important. He had no time to inventory them and stuffed them into his coat pocket.

He waded into the swirling mob of disheartened militia, much thicker now than a minute before, and after considerable pushing, shoving, and elbowing, finally reached Barney's guns. At least the enemies he faced now were honorable ones who fought in the open.

Barney's flotilla men stood by their cannons unfazed by the initial British success; portfires burning, ammunition chests fully stocked, and gun crews ready. Tracy's men, Barney's, and a company of just-arrived US Army regulars formed a solid bulwark that was not going anywhere soon. The iron in their postures and faces screamed a silent challenge at the advancing British. Tracy hoped the newly-arriving militia from Washington would rally behind them.

The British would have to advance directly up the hill into the jaws of Barney's guns. The militiamen on either side of the guns were raw troops but Tracy hoped the conduct of the Navy and Marines would put some spirit into them. Tracy posted his Marines in a small ravine that concealed the bulk of them from the British. He had enough men for a surprise counter-attack once the cannons had smashed the British with waves of canister.

He was tired of the Americans just defending. He would act like a Marine--attack, seize the imitative, and carry the fight to the enemy. Trust in the power of maneuver and use fast movement to slide around enemy strong points. He wondered if militia on either side of his position could perform even a simple maneuver without degenerating into rabble beyond military control. Beall's Annapolis Regiment looked spry enough, but he could only expect reliable action from his professionals.

*****

Thornton halted the British line after the rout of the 5th. He saw one more line a few hundred yards ahead. Big guns anchored it. Big guns meant Barney's men. Cockburn had warned the Army Barney was exceedingly tough and dangerous. Thornton conferred with Brooke. In the chaos, their commands had become jumbled. It took a quarter-hour to straighten things out. Thornton would go straight up the hill and Brooke would move around the enemy left at the same time. Thornton had the worse and bloodier task but the guns had to be taken.

Pennywhistle extended his Ramsden and methodically surveyed Barney's position. He observed men shifting position with a smart step and perfectly spaced files, clearly Regulars. The men wore blue tunics with scarlet collars and cuffs and bone-white trousers covered to the knee by buttoned-up black gaiters. Their coat fronts displayed v-shaped facings of butter yellow. Each sleeve above the cuff and the top of each coattail displayed three gold buttons framed by wide, chevron shaped buttonholes of the same yellow.

Most distinctively, their hair was worn powdered and clubbed. Only US Marines wore their hair in that old-fashioned way.

The officer commanding them sported an enormous black *chapeau de bras*—literally a hat of arms—that was meant to attract the notice of friend and foe alike. Napoleon's famous bicorn was considered a big hat but this behemoth was fully a third larger. It made the tall officer appear a giant.

The hat was shaped like a half-circle and worn in a fore-and-aft rig. It was two and-a-half feet long and its crown added a foot to the officer's height. Its twin brims extended ten inches from the front and back of his head respectively. The brims curved downward and the white fringe dangling from the front brim extended nearly as far as his chin, while its opposite number reached well below the top of his high scarlet collar. A black cockade with a small silver eagle at its center marked the apex of the crown and an eight-inch crimson plume surged upwards from the cockade's top edge to further enhance the illusion of height.

The uniform coat beneath the hat was of the finest blue broadcloth and displayed the single gold epaulette of a captain on the right shoulder. Only one captain in the 500-man US Marine Corps stood over six feet. It was the man with his face, John Tracy, a half-brother whose existence he had discovered less than a week ago over the wrong side of a pistol.

He briskly walked over to Thornton and Brooke. "Those are Marines supporting Barney," he warned. "They will defend their position as vigorously as Leonidas defended the Pass of Thermopylae. We will have to drive them very hard." A bold, head-on charge would be dangerous, yet it seemed the only available option. "I know the man in charge. I believe he will attempt some sort of counter-stroke. Please allow me the honor of spearheading the attack." He was eager to smite Tracy in battle, but a part of him strangely hoped Tracy would survive the encounter. He mentally cursed himself for his continued decline into weak sentimentality.

Pennywhistle assumed Barney's men would double-shot the big 18-pounders, ship killers, with canister. These naval monsters had barrels nine feet long weighing 4600 pounds and each was served by ten-man crews. The discharge from each piece would send 400 lead balls flying through the air.

The three 12-pounders, crewed exclusively by US Marines, would likely be charged the same way, although it was just possible they might use solid shot to mow down close-ordered ranks: bouncing bowling balls striking pins. Barney would probably reserve his fire until he could not miss. Canister was most effective at ranges under four hundred yards.

Commodore Joshua Barney, USN, was observing the redcoats with his pocket spyglass at the same moment Pennywhistle was watching him. The ruddy-faced, fifty five year old radiated an overwhelming confidence that transmitted itself to the men under his command. His lively blue eyes glowed with eagerness, yet he was a man who never acted precipitately. His *sang-froid* sprang from numerous combats at sea in a remarkable career that had begun during the Revolutionary War. He had once served as a captain in the French Navy; had commanded a string of successful privateers, and his flotilla of gunboats had vexed the British mightily for the past two months.

Barney saw Thornton's redcoats assembling in the gully at the foot of the hill, preparing for a general advance. He noted Brooke's men moving round to the north but Thornton's men were the immediate threat.

"Should I bring more cases of shot forward, Commodore?" asked a very earnest thirteen year-old named Bill Adams. A little Rat Terrier dashed up behind the boy and assumed a sitting position as if he too awaited orders. Adams had wounded a British soldier with a lucky shot the day before. He was very eager to show the world that yesterday was no fluke and that while he was short of stature, his heart was the size of a lion's.

"We're fixed fine for solid shot, but we could do with more canister for the long eighteens. Glad you are on top of things, Adams. We'll make an artilleryman of you yet! Perhaps your little dog too!"

"Aye aye, sir. I'll see to it right away, sir. Jake's my helper and my good luck charm, Commodore, smartest dog in the Republic!" Adams smiled, snapped a salute, and raced off toward the ammunition trains as eagerly as if he had been a pirate told a chest of doubloons lay near. Jake raced after him barking joyfully.

As he watched Adams go, he hoped the boy lived to see fourteen. A lot of hard pounding lay ahead and powder monkeys were always in the thick of a fight. They were sometimes targeted by enemy marksmen and needed three things for survival: pluck, fast legs, and a guardian angel willing to pull extra duty.

Barney was glad most powder monkeys possessed the youthful certainty that they were immortal. The twelve teenaged boys Tracy had furnished him had learned their duties quickly and had performed splendidly today. Tracy had rescued them from their own stupidity when they had drunkenly bushwhacked a British column as a test of manhood. They might have lacked judgment, but they possessed a fighting spirit that was marvelous to behold.

Tracy had beaten a British infantry company in a small, sharp engagement the day before. He had commandeered their services and shown them British invincibility was a myth. The boys believed with absolute confidence that the Americans would prevail today and Barney could see their youthful zeal was infectious. Would that General Winder possessed the same certainty!

Half-a-mile to Barney's rear, Captain John Maxwell's troop of Dragoons cantered up to the main body of 140 commanded by a frustrated Lieutenant Colonel Jacint Laval. He saluted Laval. "Have you received any orders yet, Colonel? We ought to do something to stem the tide of fugitives." One of the important duties of the cavalry was to round up broken troops and herd them back toward the main battle.

"No, I haven't Captain, and it's damn irregular. I received orders from Winder to advance then Secretary Monroe galloped up and countermanded them. Told me to hold myself in reserve here for, how did he put it, *the decisive moment*. It has been an hour and I have received no orders. I grow tired of watching a battle rage and our boys run, and not being able to do a thing."

Maxwell nodded in agreement. "Winder is a real piece of work, but is he even in charge? The battle seems to be fighting itself. I hate waiting."

*****

Lieutenant Colonel William Scott reached the rear edge of the third line as Maxwell and Laval conversed. He had 300 well-disciplined US Regulars with him, an amalgam of bits of the 12th, 36th, and 38th Regiments, worth their weight in gold among militia.

He sent a runner on ahead to find Winder or whomever was in charge. He had received so many contradictory orders over the last five hours his head still spun. Stand fast, defend the Capitol itself, act as a last-ditch reserve force. Advance and join the main body of troops outside Bladensburg. Wait, reverse course and join up with some spare marines to defend the Navy Yard. Make for Bladensburg again with extreme haste. His men had answered the final summons with every reserve of strength. They had jogged most of the last four miles to the battlefield. They were tired and thirsty but they would fight. The runner returned, could not find Winder. He was somewhere on horseback.

Scott could see redcoats approaching from two directions. One line advanced from directly ahead and a second chased fugitives on their left. He looked behind and saw more red-faced militia arriving from Washington. He needed orders, they needed orders. His side had enough men, someone just needed to tell them the right place to attack.

He saw Secretary of State James Monroe galloping toward him and his face fell. *Please God, not another order from that man*, he thought in disgust. There must be a real soldier somewhere in the American lines.

Chapter Four

Pennywhistle made the company's final dispositions. Manton was still in command, but deferred to his senior's more experienced judgment. The men did not give trust easily, so Manton explained things succinctly. "Captain Pennywhistle was seconded to the light company of the 88th at Salamanca at the Duke of Wellington's request because all of their officers had been killed. He led them brilliantly and His Grace mentioned him prominently in dispatches. I am sure you know Wellington is as stingy with praise as a miser is tight-fisted with coin. You will never find a braver man or a more cunning leader."

The men's faces reflected approval. The 88th, The Connaught Rangers, were a very tough bunch of hard-drinking, hard-fighting Irishmen. If the Rangers and Wellington believed in this man, they could certainly do so as well.

The American line lay five hundred yards uphill. The big guns looked menacing and Pennywhistle knew how a chipmunk must feel spying a hawk diving at him. He saw smoke rising from gunner's glowing portfires and several artillerists adjusting the positions of their pieces with handspikes.

No matter what his men did, the assault ahead was going to be a very bloody business. Manton's company would be the tip of the sword. He had been through enough battles to know gallantry and heart were sometimes just not enough. The tip of the sword would probably be blunted. The soldiers of the 4th were good men, but the chances of carrying the heights on the first try were fair at best. The trick was to have the determination to never give up, to keep coming back until the object had been accomplished.

Pennywhistle hated frontal attacks, simple brute force opposing simple brute force. With big guns on their side, the Americans had considerably more brute force. If only he had been a little smarter, he might have devised a clever feint to divert attention, but his creativity crashed into a wall of bloody inevitability. There was simply no possibility of a flanking move.

Pennywhistle knew a good portion of the redcoats would die in the next few minutes. Experience enabled him to suppress the overwhelming instinct for self-preservation, the animal urge to burrow deep in the earth and hide from a predator. He must show the men they were predators--not prey. He would stand tall, advance against the storms of lead, and taunt death with aplomb and dash.

He would send a message as old as the Spartans and one that they would have understood perfectly--there was no point to living if it was done in dishonor. The whole "return with your shield or upon it" message was overused and pure showmanship, yet it had power because it spoke to an unchanging, noble ideal. His own studied theatricality was as dangerous as it was bombastic, yet the essence of leadership was to use clever histrionics to inspire even the faintest of hearts.

It was not that he did not feel fear, quite the contrary. Battlefield rookies actually had things easier since they had no real idea of the horror that lay ahead and could still be comforted by illusions. Rather than getting easier to play the hero, it grew more difficult each time he did it. Courage was like a fixed sum in a bank account. The amount varied with each man, but with enough withdrawals the balance would eventually read zero. When that happened, the most stalwart man was reduced to a child beset by night terrors.

Even those who emerged from battle seemingly unscathed often developed odd habits. One officer of his acquaintance had been forced to shut a gate under heavy fire and for the remainder of his life could never be in a room without first making sure all of the doors were shut. Another compulsively washed his face at least a dozen times daily after being splattered with his best friend's brains. The slight tremor in Pennywhistle's right index finger warned him his own balance was running low, but he told himself it was enough to make it through today's fight.

He walked calmly and deliberately in front of the line, as leisurely as if promenading with his lady in Hyde Park. His epaulettes gave him legal authority, but the far more important moral authority had to be earned with men who did not know him. He positively grinned toward the enemy, as if they were a regiment of clowns rather than soldiers.

He felt a puff of air near his ear. He paid it no mind: merely a sharpshooter practicing his craft. He mentally dared the enemy to bring him down. He wanted the Americans to publically expose their ineptitude to his men. If they could not hit a single man almost asking to be shot, they likely could not hit anyone else.

He forced optimism into his mind as the *zip zip* of bullets passed close to his head. The sound reminded him of dozens of people quickly sucking in breaths through their clenched teeth. He would trust in the belief that all bullets were bound by the sacred geometry of fate and that today was not his day. One day he would be dead wrong.

He faced the company, drew his cutlass, and flourished it about. Well-chosen words delivered with utter conviction at just the right moment were mighty weapons. The time-honored exhortations that coursed through his mind had proven their worth on dozens of battlefields and had summoned forth brave deeds that transformed ordinary farmland into hallowed ground. "Forward, my brave heroes! Seize the heights above! Smash them, smash them! They will not stand!"

To his surprise, smiles burst forth upon the hard faces of cynical veterans and their lungs erupted in deep shouts. "Hip hip, huzzah! Hip hip huzzah! Hip hip huzzah!"

It moved him that the ancient slogans still called forth such gallant enthusiasm. His eyes moistened slightly. He pivoted smartly, pointed his sword at Barney's guns, and shouted at the top of his lungs, "Follow me!" The advance was completely suicidal yet he had never felt more alive.

For a brief moment, nothing mattered more than conquering those heights. If he died accomplishing that, he would have no regrets. This was the true madness of battle. A hundred-yard patch of meaningless turf at the top of a small, unremarkable hill possessed far more value than all the treasures of King Solomon's mines.

Drums thudded, whistles blew, and bugles blared. The men stepped off smartly, shoulder to shoulder, and advanced up the hill at the usual marching speed of 75 paces per minute. He could have ordered a faster pace but he wanted to conserve their energies in the baking heat. He also wanted to give the Americans the idea he had no need to rush because professionals had only contempt for rabble. Still, he determined to limit the time in the lethal zone to well under ten minutes.

The men were experienced enough to know the long odds they faced, but that deterred them not at all. Training, discipline, and pride cancelled out all thoughts of personal safety. They came on menacingly--slow, determined, inflexible. It was the classic thin red line of legend moving as an indomitable battering ram.

*****

Tracy had heard the earlier huzzahs and had locked his glass onto the advancing wall of red. He saw what he expected, one brave officer inspiring an entire line. He just never thought it would be his own brother. It was inevitable they would meet. He had both wished it and cursed it.

Tracy knew his duty. He grasped his Pattern 1803 Harper's Ferry Rifle to carry out its strictures. He would let the Englishman advance a further hundred yards to be sure. As the British came on with an icy inflexibility that stood in sharp contrast to volcanic heat of the day, he grudgingly acknowledged their discipline was magnificent.

His target was out of range, but he put the rifle to his shoulder, trying to prepare himself for a duty that was as necessary as it was distasteful. After thirty seconds, and almost against his will, he lowered the weapon. He was a hard man, but he could not do it. It was his brother. Let him at least take his chances with the normal flow of battle. He slung the rifle and simply said, "Steady men, steady, wait for my command. Remember: aim low!"

*****

Two figures raced out of nowhere and took place alongside Pennywhistle. It was a grave breach of discipline and it astonished the regulars. The men were Gabriel and Isaac, former slaves he had helped to liberate. The two men had been acting as guides for the army and with that duty discharged, they wanted to fight.

They had taken the King's shilling and wore the red tunics of Colonial Marines. Two hundred marched with Ross's Army. Composed entirely of American runaways and well-trained in Bermuda, the black marines had proven a successful experiment and were showing themselves particularly valuable as light infantry.

"You take care of us, give us back our manhood, Cap'n," said Gabriel. "You help us, believe in us, we do the same for you. Those folks ahead all be friends of my old Masstuh. We British now, no longer muricans! We show them what stupid field hands can do!"

The black men marched smartly and he doubted whether he had ever seen more sincere and deep smiles. He admired them greatly as it was an impressive show of new-found dignity, but he wondered if they understood its implications. They had just begged for death. Their former owners would find blacks in British red hugely offensive. Moreover, they were as conspicuous as dark rocks on a white beach. They had spoken to him of wanting be treated like men. They would certainly die like it.

John Tracy let out a shocked, "Shit!" It was one thing to have sympathy for Negroes but quite another to allow them in the front line of battle. Perhaps in the rear, if at all, but the front was a place of honor. It was just too much! His brother was dangerous like all the English, a completely uninformed European gentleman unused to New World racial loyalties.

He would explain it to him, in short order. He fired expertly, and Isaac's skull exploded, showering Pennywhistle and Gabriel with grey gobs of mush.

Gabriel froze, unbelieving. He stared mindlessly stunned at the headless corpse of his best friend, now just a large rag staining the ground with blood. Pennywhistle calmly produced a silk handkerchief and wiped the porridge of Isaac's brains from his face. He did the same for Gabriel. He understood the shock Gabriel was experiencing as it was the normal reaction of a sane man to an insane situation. Nevertheless, he could not allow a common reaction to induce paralysis. On the contrary, this was an occasion to show your enemy you had plenty of bottom. He touched Gabriel gently on the shoulder, and said quietly, "Steady there, don't lose heart, just follow me!"

Gabriel wilted briefly then stiffened to attention, taking inspiration from the Englishman's words. "Don't you worry none, Cap'n. I ain't goin' nowhere. They took my momma, they took my poppa, but they ain't gonna take me. I come here to fight and I aim to do so. If this be my great gettin' up mornin', that be fine. I meet Jesus with an open heart and an honest spirit."

Time slowed for Pennywhistle. The men marched steadily forward and the glowering line of cannons loomed larger and larger, but he had no idea of how much time was passing.

Time in battle acquired the elasticity of a spring, sometimes coiled tightly, other times loose and expanded. Critical moments unfolded with the painful slowness of a drunken turtle, while rote actions raced by so quickly you could scarce remember performing them. It reminded him of Hooke's Law: the degree of expansion or contraction of an object, in this case battle, was directly proportional to the degree of tension applied or removed.

He heard fifes and drums playing *Rule Britannia,* which cheered him slightly. A few pipers joined the tune a minute later. The advance seemed to grind on interminably but progress was being made as he could almost make out the faces of the hilltop artillerists. The British battle step was disciplined and the line maintained its integrity despite the numerous humps and dips of the ground. He wondered why the cannons had not opened up on them. He reminded himself that Barney's men were trained as naval gunners and the most destructive broadsides were delivered when ships were within a cable's length of each other: six hundred feet.

Two hundred yards to the top. "Quick time!" He bellowed. The pace quickened to 105 steps a minute. They were already in the lethal zone for cannon and rifle fire and would soon be in that of muskets. He became very aware of the sound of his heavy hessian boots, one foot after the other quickly brushing through the three-foot-tall grass. He could hear the steady tread of the line behind him. His ears blanked out the pounding of the drums and the warbling of the fifes and he focused all of his consciousness on the hill ahead. There was firing in the distance from Brooke's men, but his little corner of the universe was devoid of any sound of violence.

The air was choked with a baleful residue of gunpowder mixed with high humidity. A cloud of vomit-inducing smoke hovered five feet above the ground and advanced on his men as a small breeze sprang up. Several soldiers wretched as the cloud passed through them but the men's footsteps did not stop.

He looked ahead and saw the gunners bring their glowing portfires close to the vent holes of their 12- and 18-pounders. He braced himself. One hundred fifty yards now. "Double quick-time," he shouted. The line speeded up to 120 paces per minute. In painfully slow motion, he saw the gunners lower their arms and saw their portfires kiss the vent holes of the five cannon.

Boom! Huge thunderheads of acrid white-grey smoke billowed up. The 18-pounders fired first, followed ten seconds later by the 12-pounders. The cannons shot backwards more than a dozen feet in obedience to Newton's Third Law. There was a loud *swoosh* and he heard the sound of hundreds of hissing snakes speeding past him. He felt tugs at his sleeves and coat tails, but his luck was in and he was wholly uninjured.

Crump, crump, crump! A wave of solid shot from the 12-pounders ripped through the humid air crushing men and equipment. It was followed by shrieks, moans, and pitiful lamentations. He turned to survey the damage.

A quarter of the line had been blown down. The forward momentum had stopped and there were large gaps. Men rolled in agony on the ground, others lay completely still. The dead lay in small groups, almost like recently cut sheaves of wheat. He glanced to his side and was gratified to see Gabriel still stood, completely bewildered-- natural enough after such a storm--but alive.

He saw the head of a column of blue poke its head out of a nearby ravine. US Marines! They were about to be counterattacked. The gunners at the top of the hill wormed and sponged their pieces.

"Close ranks! Close ranks!" He shouted. Discipline held. The men stepped over their fallen comrades and the gaps in the line immediately healed. "By the right wheel. March." The commands were instantly obeyed. The line swung like a hinged barricade to face the sea of blue now forming into line eighty yards distant. "Halt. Make ready!"

*****

"Make ready!" Tracy shouted, at the exact moment as Pennywhistle barked the same command. His men had also formed a long two-rank deep line. It was a race to see who fired first. The Marine line was considerably longer than the British and overlapped it.

"Fire!" Tracy and Pennywhistle shouted simultaneously. Sheets of flame erupted and scythes of lead flew in two directions. Men fell on both sides, but the US Marine fire was more effective simply because of the greater number of muskets.

Boom! The cannon on the top of the hill roared again. A hot, giant hand of lead cuffed out like a Titan swatting flies. Pennywhistle's line already had large gaps from the Marine volley. The blast of canister hit the line at right angles and widened the gaps. The men were off-balance and wavering. "Steady boys, steady!" yelled Pennywhistle. "Reload in quick time."

Barney's shellbacks saw the British discomfiture and the holes in their line. The sailors cheered, grabbed their cutlasses, and raced down the hill. "Board 'em! Board 'em! Board 'em!" They shouted with mad glee.

"Let's show them American steel!" Tracy shouted. "Charge!" The Marines dashed forward at the run.

"Fire!" Yelled Pennywhistle. British muskets roared out but there were too few to do more than put dents in the onrushing line of blue.

He made up his mind in an instant. He was outnumbered and caught in a rapidly closing vice. He could see reinforcements coming across the river. Better to yield ground than yield men. He would return when the odds improved. Logical, but it was very hard to give the order. He shouted for the bugler to sound the retreat, waved his sword, and pointed toward the rear. "Retire! Retire! Reform at the bottom of the hill!"

The men obeyed instantly. They did not run as green troops would have, but calmly faced about and began a steady jog down the hill. He turned to confront the onrushing US Marines and walked slowly backwards down the hill. He had no wish to be captured, but he would be damned if he would show the Yankees even a trace of fear.

"They run, they run! Egad! I told you they wouldn't stand," shouted a triumphant Tracy. The men cheered, but he knew the truth. He could see red-coated reinforcements moving across the river so even with the charging sailors, he had too few men to sustain the counterattack long. Damn! If only he had several hundred more marines and sailors he could have punched through to the river and ripped the British Army in two.

Boom! Barney's guns fired again, aiming carefully so as not to hurt any Americans. The canister was less effective against scattered running men. Nevertheless, a few more redcoats met their Maker. Barney's volume of fire throughout the battle had been impressive but it had depleted his supply of ammunition. The Commodore sent a runner to the rear to summon the reserve ammunition trains.

Pennywhistle leveled the Ferguson. It was stupid, but he could not resist the temptation to squeeze off one more shot, before he shed dignity entirely and made a run for it. He saw Tracy clearly, knew he could take the man's head off. He lined up the shot, but at the last second swung the piece slightly right and killed a nameless running subaltern instead. He slung the rifle rapidly and raced down the hill as fast as his long legs could carry him.

Tracy saw Lieutenant Coffee fall. It dismayed him, but he knew the round was originally intended for him. Why had the English captain demurred at the last second? The answer was obvious. The Briton had performed him the same kindness he had vouchsafed Pennywhistle. Perhaps they did indeed have things in common, although he was uncertain if it was related more to training than blood.

He laughed to see his English brother running down the hill and knew ignominious retreat must be a novel experience for him. The redcoats were gone. Time to halt the men. The local success would be lost if the men ran wild and galloped at everything. If they continued too far down the hill, they would forfeit the support of the big guns.

With a lot of shouts and the repeated waving of his sword, he got the marines to halt and form a line. They obeyed him, but reluctantly. Their spirits were high, their blood was up, and they wanted to savage the British. Marines were trained to metaphorically kick in doors and follow that up with quick action. Retreat came ill to them. Their courage and will were steadfast and admirable, but it was up to him to see that those qualities were employed wisely.

He convinced the sailors to retire back up the hill, and his men returned to the gully in which they had sheltered earlier. It gave excellent cover and there was no reason to expose his men to fire until the last second. As long as Barney's guns held firm and their militia support did not waver, a second counter attack could definitely be managed.

*****

Brooke's men advanced steadily while Tracy completed his clever little victory. Brooke had methodically worked his way round the American left. He was nearly in a position to enfilade Barney's guns and capture the ammunition and supply trains. Two militia regiments fled before the bayonets of his men.

Winder galloped into the rapidly swelling mob of running, shouting, screaming fugitives. He completely misread the situation on the left of his line as hopeless, which it was most certainly not. Some of the militia men were indeed running, but whole regiments were standing firm and eagerly awaited the opportunity to greet the British with strong volleys.

Winder dismissed the remonstrations of Colonel Walter Smith who said his District Militia had come to win, not run. Winder issued an order for the entire American left to withdraw from the field. It was met with confused looks but was slowly obeyed. Winder had decided the fight had been a reverse, but a quick withdrawal would save it from becoming an unmitigated disaster. Just as the Russians had done against Napoleon, he too would cede ground to spare men. He was most concerned that President Madison be notified. The President would want the government evacuated and would naturally be concerned for his wife's safety.

Lieutenant Colonel Scott had studied Napoleon like Winder, but had absorbed a completely different lesson. Rather than surrender the initiative, he would do as Napoleon had instructed his marshals and march toward the sound of the guns. On his authority alone, his Regulars advanced in a carefully measured battle step toward Brooke's men. He resisted the natural urge to fire too soon after waiting so long. He wanted their first volley to be close and destructive.

"By the left wheel, march." The line swung round like a heavy pinwheel in a light breeze. He shouted, "Halt!" when the men were within one hundred yards of the redcoats. The blue line was at a perfect ninety degree angle to the end of the red line.

The blue line halted expertly, expectancy in every eye. The Regulars were tired of allowing their country's fate to rest in the hands of lazy, pot-bellied militia, time to show the arrogant lobster backs what professionals could do. "Forward march!" The Regulars knew it was wise to shorten the distance to make the volley even more lethal. Scott's men moved forward confidently. Their elbow-to-elbow alignment was so tight that they no longer seemed individuals, but rather one seamless entity possessed by one overwhelming urge--the complete, total, and absolute annihilation of the enemy.

Major Colden White of the 44th Foot saw their parade ground perfect evolutions and exclaimed in surprise, "Those are regulars, by God!" He smelled a hotly contested firefight coming. "Close up, close up, close up those ranks!" he shouted to his men. The redcoats responded with vigor and precision.

At forty yards, the Regulars halted and the front rank kneeled. "Fire!" bellowed Scott. A necklace of red blazed out and a mailed fist slammed into the flank of the oncoming 85th

Foot. The deadly accurate fire staggered the British and temporarily halted their advance. The Regulars cheered and Scott placed his hat atop his sword and waved it in celebration. "Huzzah, my brave hearts! Reload and let's finish the business!"

Winder galloped up. "Colonel Scott what is the meaning of this? You had no orders to attack. You must withdraw."

Scott's temper boiled up. "My meaning is very plain, General." His hard blue eyes shot javelins into Winder's insipid brown ones. "I mean to fight, sir, and fight hard, drive those British bastards off the field in dishonor and disarray. A few good volleys will finish them as a fighting force. The damned redcoats are seconds away from collapse! Withdraw? Are you mad, General?"

"You are speaking to a superior officer, Scott! Blast your impudence! You damned Regulars think you know everything! You have no idea what I have in mind. Do your duty and obey your orders. Withdraw and be quick about it. I have to inform the President."

Scott bit his tongue and desperately wished a stray British round had Winder's name on it. As a Regular, it was his duty to set an example and obey orders, no matter how stupid. He choked down a curse involving what Winder could do with his mother and forced out a terse, "Yes, sir." He then snapped a smart salute. Winder merely nodded and galloped off, seemingly satisfied.

The Regulars heard the contentious conversation and exchanged startled glances. Throwing away an incipient victory and casting honor onto a rubbish heap made no sense. Still, they were good soldiers and obeyed Scott's reluctant order. They withdrew in good order, but a low buzz of grumbling hovered over the column like a storm cloud, most of it having to do with wishing Winder a quick death and a painful stay in the nether regions.

As Scott unwillingly marched his men toward the rear and observed the retreat of his supporting militia units, he realized Barney's men were holding firm while their flank was being uncovered. He wondered if Barney's men had received the order to withdraw. Winder could not have failed to inform him. That was inconceivable. Or was it?

*****

Barney saw the retreat and let a stream of curses that would have shamed the most hardened sailor. What was that idiot Winder playing at? The entire American left was disappearing like goose down in a high wind. Colonel Beall of the Annapolis Regiment galloped over to Barney, and said that he had orders to withdraw.

"Damn it, Beall," Barney shouted in complete exasperation, "I have heard nothing about a retreat. That cursed poltroon Winder has the mind of a jackrabbit! No brains, no guts, but long legs for scampering away from trouble! To hell with your orders, Beall! Stay and fight. If you withdraw, you will leave my left naked, floating in the air."

Beall enjoyed a reputation as a brave man who had fought honorably in the Revolution, but the bewildered eyes in his parchment face proclaimed his moral resolve had departed with the spryness of his skin. He was a complete novice as a regimental commander. He was used to mindlessly obeying the limited orders given the subaltern but unfamiliar with employing personal judgment to determine the viability of more wide-ranging ones issued by a senior commander. He wavered. He found Barney's determination admirable, but in the end he knew he had to obey lawful orders. The word "disobedience" simply was not in his lexicon.

Barney did not remonstrate with him. Beall was simply doing his duty as he saw it. The orders issued might be almost criminally foolish, but they were lawful orders, lawfully issued by a legally constituted commanding officer. And they likely were issued with the President's full approval since he was close by.

Barney would fight on as long as he could. He guessed Winder was making the invidious distinctions of an attorney and had felt no duty to inform Barney of his plans since Barney and his men were Navy personnel that fell outside of Army jurisdiction. If he had been a praying man, he would have begged for a miracle, but he was just an old shellback with a will of iron. He hoped the deity would smile upon his enterprise, but he placed his real faith in the skill and determination of his men.

*****

General Ross saw crisis of the battle was at hand. He had been warned Barney's men would remain steadfast and unyielding. The Americans were withdrawing, but Barney's men showed no disposition to follow. "Take the hill," he told Thornton. "Move forward when you see Colonel Brooke begin to advance." Brooke's men would come in from the north, directly behind Barney. Once Barney was finished, the way to Washington lay wide open.

Pennywhistle received his orders with satisfaction. Two-thirds of the Americans were running. The one steadfast island of American resistance had taken heavy battering and the much greater number of British veterans could certainly overlap its shores, if the will was there.

Ross was no reckless gambler, but he knew a beaten army when he saw one. He followed boxing as many gentlemen did and understood his opponent was on the ropes and ripe for a knockout blow. He had an impeccable sense of timing from his years in the Peninsula and was throwing in nearly all his reserves, save a few units kept fresh to execute an immediate pursuit. The Americans at the top of the hill were brave, determined and well-led, but they had not been fighting the cream of French soldiery for six years. They might sell their lives dearly, but the result was inevitable.

*****

A company of Royal Marines under Lieutenant Athelstan Stevens advanced to Pennywhistle's direct support. They had an admirable combat record and because of that, had been held in reserve for the key moment. Pennywhistle conferred briefly with Stevens and the marines formed up behind the light company. He smiled in satisfaction. With the Royal Marines involved, the chances of carrying the hill had just doubled.

As the Reserves formed up into the neat ranks that would form a red tidal wave, Pennywhistle noted two of the sad costs of doing business. A badly wounded man crawled painfully toward the imagined shelter of a pile of rocks. Just like dogs, dying men sought a place of privacy for their final moments. Another soldier held his firelock high above his head and marched crazily in circles. He had observed birds flying spastically in circles when fatally hit by buckshot. The man collapsed like a discarded scarecrow a few seconds later.

An American rifleman fired repeatedly at him and several balls passed close. The man guffawed loudly after each shot, as if each bullet were a source of unique merriment. The insanity of battle turned reason upside down and played havoc with men's emotions. Hysterical laughter was a not uncommon side effect.

Unearthly screams erupted from three wounded redcoats a hundred yards away to his right. "Help me!" One shouted frantically. British wounded were usually quiet and stoic, but these men had been hit in the legs and were desperately trying to crawl away from one of the small grass fires rapidly advancing on them. The grasses had been ignited by smoldering wads from Barney's guns.

It would be the most natural thing in the world for some to break ranks and dash to their rescue. Amateurs might do so, professionals never. The flames were moving very fast and destroying the protective integrity of the line in the interests of humanity was as foolish as it was stupid. In line, a man was part of a seamless entity that could defy any summoning from Old Nick--alone, he became a mere victim.

Pop pop pop pop pop pop pop pop was followed by brief howls of agony then silence. Flames had cooked off all of the cartridges in the men's cartridge boxes.

Tears clouded many redcoat eyes but it was not for men but for an animal, that by all rights should be dead. The flames that just killed the three redcoats licked out toward a black artillery horse that lay on his belly. The explosion of an ammunition chest had blown his front legs entirely away. His exposed red-grey triceps undulated with each rasping breath. The lower part of his jaw was missing has well. He had but one eye. It pleaded pathetically for someone to help him out of a situation he did not comprehend.

*****

Tracy saw Beall's men withdraw and it disgusted him. The guns would need very close support. Reluctantly he gave the order to move out of the gully and back up the hill. It might well come down to a hand-to-hand struggle. The numbers were certainly against his men, but they would do their duty and more. They loaded their weapons and waited.

Marine and Naval artillerists grunted, grimaced, strained and swore as they manhandled their cannons back to their original positions. Because of the tremendous recoil, the heavy cannons had to be pushed forward as much as fifteen feet after each shot. It was backbreaking, man-killing work in the torrid heat and choking smoke.

Gunners rammed home double rounds of canister and carefully checked the elevations of their barrels. They were not sure how many rounds they could get off before they were overrun, but knew the final round was often the most decisive. Fired point blank in the enemy's face, it often destroyed a charge just when that charge was within a hair's breadth of success.

Pennywhistle briefly explained to Manton a small variation he had in mind. Manton nodded in agreement. Gabriel asked respectfully if he could march next to Pennywhistle. Pennywhistle merely nodded, knowing Gabriel aggressively courted fatal trouble by twice marching in the same position. Yet he could hardly fault a man, held so long in subservience, who put himself front and center to oppose his former oppressors.

Pennywhistle had the company dress ranks, then walked along the line using the flat of his cutlass to periodically to check for a straight alignment. He looked behind him and his heart glowed with pride at the ocean of red supporting his advance.

Despite historians discoursing long and loud about clever maneuvers, battle often devolved into a simple, straightforward slugging match of the sort Pennywhistle faced now. It was a test of character and training in which mind mattered little but mindset a great deal. Confidence that you would prevail counted for much and victory lay with the side that supported that belief with the most resolve. The victors were always those who could take a licking but never quit punching until the enemy fled or died where they stood.

A horrid, indescribable cry rent the air. AAHHHHHHHGGGGGRRRRIIK OOOHHEOOOH! It was an awful, shrill and keening noise that was part whinny, part snort, and part scream. The animal's death cry curdled the blood of even the most heartless. The flames had reached the legless horse and had quickly enveloped him.

The men looked in horror toward the writhing equine figure. Hard men they might be, but humanity had not entirely deserted them. Men understood, but animals only trusted. They were briefly mesmerized in shock and pity.

"No!" Pennywhistle demanded, his sword held high. "Eyes on me, my lads! We will take the hill ahead and nothing made in heaven or hell can stop us! Bugler, sound the advance!" His eyes blazed as his voice vibrated with confidence. The men of the 4th forgot the horse and remembered their duty. He flourished his sword several times and shouted one simple command, "Forward! March!"

The thin red line tramped determinedly forward. Weapons were loaded, but Pennywhistle felt the business should be decided not with lead but the bayonet. He had told the soldiers and marines to reserve their fire until they were literally in the faces of the Americans. "No man can do very wrong if he withholds his fire until he is within pistol range," he said calmly. He did not want to get into a contest of volleys which would lengthen the time in the lethal zone. He meant to close the distance as swiftly as possible, then take the Yankees in one mad rush. He would lead from the front, but he would let Manton resume command at two hundred yards.

His skill with his Ferguson Rifle enabled him to do what few others could do. It gave him the opportunity to quickly target the gunners. Kill the operators, and the cannons would be rendered inert. He might even be able to manage a shot at the indefatigable Barney. That seemed a trifle unsporting, he greatly respected the man's toughness, yet without Barney's will, his command could be broken far more easily.

Manton had readily agreed to the bargain. From long experience, he understood just how good Pennywhistle was with his rifle. Pennywhistle had saved his life in Spain with that skill. Manton knew himself as a good, solid officer, but not an especially clever one. Manton was a fiery creature of the moment, but saw only his limited surroundings whereas Pennywhistle was a thinker who saw infinite possibilities and could cold-bloodedly conjure the future.

Boom! Barney's five big guns thundered out at three hundred yards. The 18-pounders fired canister, the 12-pounders solid shot. The ear-shattering noise was an evil symphony combining the high pitch of whipping, whizzing, tearing exclamations from canister with the base percussion of thumps, crumps, and rumbles from solid shot.

The battery fired a little high and the gale of lead missed Pennywhistle's front rank, but loud screams and ululations announced the volley had done solid damage to the closely-packed ranks supporting his advance. A quick glance over his shoulder revealed the bouncing solid shot had mown down two files like super-energized bowling balls shattering human pins. The canister had peppered the ranks leaving numerous clots of bloody, misshapen flesh twitching feebly on the ground and giving the still standing wounded the appearance of men afflicted with measles.

Close the distance, thought Pennywhistle. The marine ordered the step increased from 75 to 90 paces a minute. He needed to conserve the men's energy, wanted plenty in reserve for the last dash.

He would have preferred a faster pace, but some of the men were showing sure signs of heat exhaustion: fire-red faces, heavy sweating, cramps, and vomiting. Under normal circumstances, he would have halted the line immediately and made sure every man drank his fill of water and then rested in the shade.

But battle was anything but normal. His duty required him to demand the impossible and push his men until they were ready to drop and then push some more. They just had to last thirty minutes. The 'God of Battles' was propitiated only with cruel sacrifices. A good officer had to be prepared to ruthlessly surrender the lives of those he held most dear, his men, if victory demanded it. If the survivors cursed him to eternity, so be it.

Tracy watched the gunner's reload. They did it quickly and expertly. Tracy felt like he was standing in the 12th circle of hell as the constant firing of the big guns had likely added twenty degrees to a temperature that had already topped the century mark.

Tracy knew the distance was still too great for musketry, but some of the officers would soon be in range of his Harper's Ferry Rifle. He walked along the line of his men and told them to have patience. They merely nodded. They needed no instruction, no words of inspiration. They were tough, experienced campaigners, and their expressions showed they trusted him completely.

A number took advantage of their respite by dropping their trousers and defecating on the spot. It was a common enough practice when men were forced to stay in ranks, but it gave the line the reek of a kitchen midden. Tracy paid it no mind because battle compelled a man to check any notions of dignified privacy at the starting gate. He kept his face a neutral mask of command but smiled inwardly at the steadfastness of his men.

*****

Brooke's men formed on the north end of the Washington Turnpike. The militia was now entirely gone. His brigade was poised to move against the ammunition trains. The most destructive guns in the world were mere blobs of metal without ammunition. He would wait until Thornton's men got just a little closer before launching his main attack.

For now, Brooke ordered a line of light infantry skirmishers forward to soften the Yankees up, unbalance them. *Pop, pop, pop.* Sparks of red flew from British muskets. Some of the flotilla men turned with alarm when they realized the shots had come from behind.

A skirmisher's bullet sliced off the top of young Bill Adams head as he ran forward with a shot case. Jake barked in confusion, expecting the boy he had adopted to rise. A second later, a round bounced in front of the dog, kicking up bits of gravel that blinded the little animal. Jake whimpered in despair but no one heard the small sounds in the thunderstorm of battle.

*****

Boom! Barney's guns thundered out. Two flecks of canister blew off Pennywhistle's hat and his right epaulette, but again left him unharmed. The line behind him showed huge gaps, but file closers moved up from the rear and patched them rapidly. He ran his fingers absentmindedly through his sandy red hair to be sure he was unscathed. His brain measured the distance to the guns at just under two hundred yards. Here came Manton, right on cue. They exchanged quick salutes and made the handoff of command.

Pennywhistle could see British light infantry to the north firing. *Woosh! Woosh*! Four more Congreve's soared aloft and as usual did little damage, but contributed much as distractions. Manton shouted a command and the heavily sweating redcoats unhesitatingly quickened their step to 105 paces a minute.

Pennywhistle spotted a small gully twenty yards ahead. He dashed forward and plopped himself down in its shelter. He carefully loaded the Ferguson from his prone position--easy with a breechloader that required no ramrod, supremely difficult with a muzzle loader that did.

You needed three elements for a good shot: unobstructed view, bone support, and natural point of aim. You had to maneuver carefully to ensure a clear line of vision and then rest the weapon on the steadiest natural surface available. Boulders or logs were good but human bone was most readily available. Muscles and tendons vibrated slightly, no matter how much you willed them to remain rock steady. The barrel had a tendency to rise with each inhale, so after you had zeroed your sights on the target's largest lethal area, you fired at the bottom of your exhale.

He drew a crude 'Y' shaped piece of wood from his haversack and jammed it hard into the ground. It was a perfect substitute for an elbow, a kneecap, or toes. He rested the barrel of the Ferguson on its center.

Boom! Barney's guns fired again, but he hardly heard them. His disciplined brain calmly blanked out the thousand and one thunderous noises oppressing the battlefield. Everything was about focus and concentration. Background details of no moment vanished from his consciousness until only things that served his deadly purpose remained.

His eagle eye watched the hill with detachment. The heavy smoke made targets visible only at intervals. He would limit his focus to individuals that could sway the battle's outcome. Usually that meant officers, but he was always on the alert for private soldiers whose exceptional courage might enable less gallant hearts to fight on.

Every fiber in his body sang with a hyper-alert readiness. He focused his heightened attention on a spare, graying older man, a naval lieutenant who likely would never make captain. He had to be one of the flotilla's senior officers. The tall naval officer waved his sword aggressively and shouted slogans. His men responded with huzzahs. He was the epitome of gallantry and definitely worth a bullet. He lined up his sights on the man's chest, exhaled, and softly squeezed the trigger. The officer stood stock still a second. A ragged roundel of crimson blossomed on his chest and then he fell gracelessly to the ground.

Pennywhistle reloaded the Ferguson in ten seconds. Scanned the line, saw a gunner with a slow match poised just above a 12-pounder's venthole. He blew out the man's left pectoral and the impact punched the gunner back against the breech of his piece. The ricochet caused him to rocket forward and bounce off another 12-pounder before he fell to the ground like an abused rag doll. Pennywhistle had just spared the men behind him one volley of canister.

He felt a deep satisfaction in the precision of his shots. Whatever God ruled in heaven had given him a talent for inflicting death. Why a supposedly benevolent God would give such a gift puzzled him. Yet God did not give gifts He did not wish to see used and the Old Testament was rife with cities put to the sword with God's apparent blessing.

The Bible often used the phrase "angel of death." He preferred to think of himself as a child of the Enlightenment but perhaps his highest purpose was to function as an earthly emissary of that baleful angel. It disturbed him that for all of his education and commitment to high-flown principles, the only task he had consistently shown a talent for was wrecking things.

He centered his sights on the yellow facings of a Marine Sergeant Major and squeezed the trigger. The man collapsed like an eggshell hit by a hammer.

The savage part of his nature protested about his disdain of its importance. It reminded him that it, not reason, gave him the strength and energy to be a warrior. While others vacillated and shirked responsibility, it allowed him to decide and act. It instructed his subconscious in its usual disciplined way that now was not the time to wax philosophical. *Do your duty and spare no one who stands in your way!*

He fired again and his round connected solidly with the chest of a blue-jacketed petty officer.

His animal cunning had full control now and it thrust his humanity aside. His internal energy levels were spiking and he was living completely in the moment. A queer image flashed into his mind that startled him, a shimmering city, like nothing on earth. He remembered the phrase from the

Sermon on The Mount: "You are the light of the world. A city set upon a hill cannot be hidden." This city certainly commanded attention but it was nothing from the Bible. It represented ideals that were older and rawer, primal and pagan. It was Valhalla.

The place of warrior's reward was a realm of brooding, eerie light and soaring columns, towering tapestries and vast parquet floors. Stern, dark majesty issued from every surface with a dread, fantastical beauty that inspired awe rather than repose. Gigantic statues of heroes locked in epic struggles with all manner of men and beasts lined the unending halls. Seraphim and cherubim clad in bloody armor smiled with savage sweetness from a gloriously painted ceiling of ancient battles that stretched to eternity. Booming spectral choruses of triumphal, lusty song coruscated through its immeasurable corridors.

Then everything suddenly vanished in an explosion that far eclipsed any supernova: *Die Gotterdammerung*. A sepulchral voice that was him, yet not him, warned that such was the final fate of a warrior's efforts; glorious yet futile.

His mind acknowledged that the paths of glory lead but to the grave, but his will thundered that Charon would most assuredly not collect his coin today. He was in his element and no longer a man, but a carefully calibrated mechanical engine of death. Paradoxically, his body sang with vibrant life, glorying in the arrogant power of playing Atropos's trusted surrogate.

He experienced a hot flash of self-recrimination, wondered what kind of monster he had become, but the comforting coldness returned a moment later. The only thing that mattered was efficiently taking down his targets and making every death a work of art.

The marine spotted a gunner sponging out a 12-pounder and shouting encouragements that seemed to be steadying his mates. He focused his attention on the gunner while calmly noting the redcoats were advancing. He heard bugles shouting and observed Manton pointing his sword confidently toward the big guns.

The redcoats speeded up to 120 paces per minute, the fastest step short of an outright run. All of their actions were admirable and important but irrelevant to his immediate purpose. The gunner was his universe for the next few seconds. He made his calculations and the final variables locked. The equation completed, he squeezed the trigger with a feather-light touch.

*****

Tracy saw the gunner flinch as the Ferguson's round caught him in the stomach. His brother again! The redcoats advancing on his front had moved to a fast jog and commenced yelling like banshees. "Aim!" he bellowed. The Marines leveled their weapons and sternly narrowed their right eyes. "Fire!" A torrent of flame lashed out.

Boom! Barney's guns crashed out a second later. Their combined efforts tore ragged holes in the British line. But the red line kept coming. Barney called for more ammunition. The heavy firing had left each gun with only one remaining round of canister. He needed the reserves brought forward at the double quick.

A messenger frantically dashed up to Barney. The civilian commander of the ammunition train had seen Brooke's men advancing on his wagons and had panicked. "God damn it! We are undone!" shouted the apoplectic Commodore. The reserve ammunition trains were on their way off the field as fast as their galloping horses could move them. Barney's big guns fired their last blast of canister and then fell silent.

Tracy dashed over to Barney to find out what had happened. The two men conferred for half a minute and reached the same conclusion. Without artillery, the position could not be held. The battle was lost and the best that could be managed was a rearguard action to allow the rest of the army to escape. Both men made the hard choice--sacrifice some that others might be saved.

The battery had almost 200 horses to transport the big guns, but there was no reason why some could not be used as rides for Tracy's Marines. Tracy hastily mounted his men and told them to ride with all speed for Washington City. The men's faces looked downcast but they understood they would get a chance to serve the Republic another day. Barney mounted half of his flotilla men and the sailors departed with equal reluctance.

The remaining Marines and flotilla men stood firm and determined. They would just have to fight twice as hard and make the redcoats pay dearly for every foot of ground.

*****

The redcoats broke into a flat-out run, every face a mixture of feral madness and disciplined purpose.

Pennywhistle jumped up, slung his weapon, and drew his cutlass. He sprinted forward and joined the redcoat line, thirty yards from the American position. A group of Royal Marines spotted him and raced forward to provide him a ferocious escort. Men in red shouted reckless cries of bloodlust while men in blue volleyed back with ear-splitting yells of defiance.

Pennywhistle expected to be met with a stiff pasting of canister but strangely none was forthcoming. He put on a burst of speed and punctured the American line with his blade extended. He skewered a Marine Corporal then yanked the blade clear.

Blue sparks filled the air like clouds of restless fireflies as cold steel collided with cold steel. *Clang, Clang, Clang,* echoed through the air, sounding like the peels of old, cracked church bells. Soldiers and Royal Marines forced their way into the mass of flotilla men and US Marines, slashing, cutting, gouging, and gutting with their bayonets.

US Marines returned the savage lunges of their red-coated marine counterparts with precision and ferocity; the two forces were equally matched in skill. Sailors drew cutlasses and hacked, slashed, and thrust vigorously at their red-coated attackers. Artillerists clubbed and swatted frantically with rammers. It was a raging, swirling cyclone of madness, but it could not last more than a minute or two. There were just too many men in red. Despite great heroics, Americans fell fast and quick.

Pennywhistle sensed rather than saw a sword thrust at him from behind. He instinctively sidestepped and ducked. The blade whizzed by where his head had been a second before. He spun on his heels as if executing an about turn, rising like a coiled spring and jabbing with his cutlass. His cutlass entered the diaphragm of a baby-faced petty officer. The man silently mouthed, 'no, no' as the marine spitted him with the full force of his powerful legs.

Pennywhistle spied Barney out of the corner of his eye and saw a round tear into his upper thigh. He sagged against a 12-pounder but did not fall. He saw his own brother duel briefly with a British sergeant, sidestep a bayonet lunge, and expertly slash at the sergeant's neck with a distinctive Mameluke sword. Blood squirted from the carotid artery and the sergeant dropped noiselessly to the ground. A stray bullet ripped off an epaulette from his brother's uniform, but he did not falter.

And then it was done. Barney, propped against a cannon barrel, frantically waved a white handkerchief from the end of a stick. He was a brave man, but not a fool. Resistance was futile against such numbers. Pennywhistle realized he would have done the same, although it was the hardest order a commander could give. The fighting abruptly ceased a few seconds later with both sides staring at each other in disbelief, not quite able to credit that the madness had ended. A British corporal advanced to accept Barney's surrender, but Barney shook his head and spoke some gentle words to the man.

Pennywhistle instantly understood it was about the Commodore's dignity. He sheathed his sword and walked briskly over to Barney. "Commodore, it is a great honor to meet you. I am sad to see such a fine warrior wounded. Thomas Pennywhistle, Captain, Royal Marines, at your service, sir."

Barney's face was ashen grey. He had lost a lot of blood. He spoke slowly with great deliberation. "Your people have been after me for a long time, and now you have finally got me. I appreciate your assistance, Captain. My sword is my honor and I hated to give it to an underling."

"You fought hard and ably, Commodore. I should be most distressed to take your sword. Please retain it and accept my compliments as admirer of gallantry wherever it may be found. I shall have one of our surgeons attend to your wounds at the earliest possible moment."

"What do you intend to do with me, Captain?"

"It is not up to me to make that determination, Commodore, but I am certain that it is not in the interest or the honor of the Prince Regent to keep a brave officer under confinement. I should imagine you will be paroled in short order." Pennywhistle heard horses approach from behind and turned to see a very concerned General Ross and Admiral Cockburn rein their mounts in. They dismounted and walked over.

"I told you, General, that Barney's people would be the only ones that would fight."

"You were certainly right, Admiral, he made it quite a contest."

Cockburn nodded briefly to Pennywhistle. "Good to see you, Captain; in the thick of the fray as usual." Pennywhistle introduced Ross and Cockburn to Barney.

Barney smiled and said, "Well Admiral, folks call you 'cock burn' hereabouts. My countrymen think you are the devil incarnate, but I see just a man. What do you intend to do with me, Admiral?"

Cockburn hated the American's deliberate mispronunciation of his name: the 'ck' being silent; but Barney's cheeky response amused rather than offended him. He admired brave men with spirit. "I am most concerned with your wounds, Commodore. I shall see you receive an escort to the rear so they may be quickly attended to. As soon as you are able to travel, you will be paroled and allowed to go wherever you will. It is the least I can do for such a gallant opponent. I will let Mr. Pennywhistle here make the arrangements."

Four of Barney's men trudged over with the rolling gait of men used to ships at sea. They were tough old shellbacks with weather-beaten faces and flinty expressions. The sea aged men fast and Pennywhistle doubted the oldest was more than thirty-five. Yet all of these hard men had moisture on the edges of their eyes. Two were lightly wounded and one displayed a poorly bandaged arm. Loyalty to one man trumped any concerns of pain, either physical or psychological. All were eager to be stretcher bearers.

Their naked sincerity moved Pennywhistle, Ross and even touched the heart of the supposedly heartless Cockburn. More than a few of the surrounding redcoats felt mist glaze their eyes. They might be all leathery toughness on the outside, but many had deeply sentimental streaks at their cores.

"Commodore, I shall pass the word immediately for the Fleet Surgeon to attend you," said Cockburn with unfeigned compassion. Barney understood the honor. The Fleet Surgeon was actually a full-fledged physician, a rarity who was a member of the Royal College of Physicians and Surgeons in London.

Cockburn and Ross exchanged a few words of admiration and condolence with Barney and departed. Barney was a tough old bird, but his skin grew greyer with each passing minute as the blood loss was more severe than anyone thought. Complications from this wound would claim his life two years later.

His men got him into a crude litter and moved forward. Pennywhistle marched alongside. Manton walked up briskly. His presence presented Pennywhistle with an opportunity. He conferred briefly with Manton who found the arrangement congenial.

"Commodore, please allow me to present Lieutenant John Manton. He is a gallant soul like yourself and enjoys my full confidence. I will be turning you over to his good offices. I have a..." he hesitated, " a close relative who fought with you today and I confess I should very much like to see how he fared."

Barney looked up. "My men's welfare comes before my own, Captain, and I quite understand the concerns of family. Might I inquire who this officer is?"

Pennywhistle should have expected the question from the inquisitive, direct Barney, but it caught him off guard. He had not told anyone save Manton. He wanted to be discreet about the relationship since even he was unsure of what it meant or portended for the future. Still, it seemed farcical to wonder about social niceties when blood and death lay so heavily around him. Who really cared anyway, save the two principals involved? It was not as if anyone who found out would have doubts about their loyalties. "Captain John Tracy of the United States Marine Corps."

Barney smiled. "I must be more tired than I thought. I should have seen the resemblance earlier. It is quite marked. I suspect the family resemblance extends to heroic deeds on the battlefield. Please Captain, see to him by all means, and present my compliments for his steadfast conduct today."

He snapped Barney a crisp salute which Barney returned weakly. "Thank you, Commodore. I doubt our paths will cross again, but I feel privileged to have met you. I wish you a long life and a speedy recovery. I trust the unpleasantness between our two countries will be brought to a quick and mutually satisfactory conclusion."

"Thank you, Captain, I heartily second your last thought. As long as the British have men like you, there is hope it will happen. Good luck to you, sir!" He sighed and fell back into the litter. The sailors walked briskly with their burden because their commander clearly needed a surgeon immediately. Pennywhistle saw the Fleet Surgeon and several of his mates dashing across the field toward the litter and breathed a little easier.

Chapter Five

Pennywhistle checked his watch and blinked in surprise. With all of the noise, smoke, and confusion, it was always difficult to gauge how long a battle had lasted. The battle had taken a little more than two hours, but it had seemed a lifetime.

He walked back up the hill, but his temporary relief at the battle's cessation dissipated with each passing step. He really had no idea at all what he wanted to say to the half-brother he was about to face.

Part of him wanted to keep it briskly efficient and business-like, just paying a courtesy call on a fellow officer who happened to be a relation. They could compare professional annotations of the battle just fought; detached analyses from seasoned soldiers. It would be painless enough to play the stolid, unemotional British officer, he was very experienced at that, but the result would be highly unsatisfactory. They shared a father that he obviously knew less well than he thought, and a sibling he had only met on the battlefield. Above all, he was simply curious. His brother was a fine soldier, but he wanted to know what the inner man was like. He was determined to subtlety probe his character.

That might not be easy. He himself was a guarded individual, one who had trouble expressing feelings directly and kept his emotions hidden behind a mask of courtliness. He had no reason to assume his brother was of a more effusive temperament. But his brother had had a completely different upbringing; perhaps with a loving mother who encouraged the open expression of honest feelings. Maybe training was stronger than instinct.

His own mother had been completely unsuited for the role and had displayed far more maternal instinct for her pianoforte and music then she did for her only child. When she had passed five years ago, he felt sad, but the bitterness remained. He should have forgiven her neglect, but he had never quite been able to summon the graciousness of soul to do so. It bothered him that her coldness of heart might be hereditary.

Perhaps talking to Tracy was a way to expunge his bitterness by telling a relative the good news that they were blessed with a father who did have a good heart. If Tracy had had a doting mother he might see in Tracy the man he might have been had his own mother understood children. He shook his head angrily. He would find out soon enough and it was pointless to speculate. He had no idea exactly what he would say but would trust to the inspiration of the moment.

The battlefield he walked was the usual mess. It distressed him, and you never really got used to it, but he had seen too many to be moved to tears as any sane man should be. Mostly he felt an overwhelming sense of waste, good lives blown to tatters for a fleeting military advantage.

His right index finger began twitching badly. He clamped his left hand on it and squeezed. It stopped, at least for now.

Corpses littered the ground in various states of disrepair. Some bodies lacked arms, some legs, some heads. Canister and musket volleys were unforgiving and many of the remains looked as if they had been shoved through a fast rotating coffee grinder. Strips of skin, shards of muscle, yards of crazily unraveled viscera, and bloody clods of flesh dotted the landscape at intervals. Streams of bile leaked from many of the bodies. A few stomachs had already started to swell with gas because of the extreme heat and by evening, many would burst.

Some corpses had only fragments of faces and looked like unfinished, misshapen china dolls. Of those that had faces intact, most seemed rubbery and distorted with staring eyes and mouths agape in expressions of pain, astonishment, and fear.

The rotten egg smell of spent gunpowder permeated everything and mixed foully with the sickly sweet smell of incipient putrescence. The reek of excrement and urine added to the vomit-inducing stench as dying men voided their bowels and bladders.

The wounded writhed and moaned on the ground and the eternal cries of "water, water, for the love of God, water," assaulted his ears. Two crows landed on a corpse next to him and began their natural functions as carrion eaters. They generally started with the eyes. Flies buzzed about in abundance. They swarmed the faces of the dead and crawled in and out of mouths, nostrils, and ears.

Clouds of mosquitoes continued to annoy the living.

One carrot-topped private of the 4th, as short of stature as he was innocent of years, squatted in the grass and lovingly stroked the hair of a corpse that seemed nearly his twin. He looked up as Pennywhistle passed and grabbed his arm so hard the marine winced. Such an action against an officer could be considered an assault: a death penalty offense. The great distress in the boy's face suggested grief had unmanned his reason.

"He were my cousin, captain. We were raised together and enlisted alongside one another at Reading. He done everything right and never acted but by our sergeant's leave. Sarge said he was up for promotion to corporal. He didn't curse or use tobacco and read his Bible regular, too. Why, sir, why is he dead?" His quavering voice, a second away from sobbing, pleaded for Pennywhistle to supply some officer-like wisdom that would bring him solace.

"I don't know," said Pennywhistle without thinking, caught off guard as he met the youth's bewildered eyes with weary ones of his own. For all of his intellect, he could supply no direct answer to a cosmic question. 'Things just happen' popped into his head, as good an explanation as any for the sheer randomness of violence but it was hardly comforting.

"What was your cousin's name, Private?" He knew he could not go very wrong if he allowed the grieving boy a chance to publically give the empty shell an identity.

"Obadiah Masterson, sir. Just like the Obadiah in the Good Book what had the big vision."

Pennywhistle understood the boy wanted consolation, not a philosophical explanation of a life's ultimate purpose. Christian platitudes would serve far better than logic. In times of grief, people cleaved to the safety of the simple and the familiar. His father had once compelled him to listen to an itinerant Methodist preacher, not for his salvation, but that he might learn what a braying ass sounded like. The preacher's drivel had apparently lain dormant in his brain like a tick hiding in a fold of skin.

Pennywhistle respected the power of faith but had turned cynical about organized religion after witnessing its employment for anything but godly purposes. In Spain, he had seen two captured French soldiers boiled alive and two others castrated, skinned, disemboweled, and decapitated by partisans who claimed to be acting in the name of Jesus. Such atrocities were not isolated. They were quickly followed by horrific French retaliations that God was again called upon to justify.

The polymath Blaise Pascal had once asked whether Christianity was a religion of love or reason, but had missed a frightening third possibility. A Spanish bishop had told the marine, "I am a good Catholic, *Señor Capitan*, but I never go abroad without a knife tucked under my belt."

Pennywhistle's view of the deity was that of an Enlightenment being of awesome complexity, logic, and intellect who had gifted man with the most God-like power of all, the ability to think. The capacity to discover the universe through empiricism rather than superstition was of far greater moment than the fire Prometheus had stolen from the gods.

He forced his face into an expression of sincerity that he hoped was convincing. "Son," he began--a patronizing form of address the preacher had favored--"The Bible tells us that Man cometh forth like a flower and like a flower is cut down. Your cousin died well. You and I are alive to have this talk because of the actions of men like him. Remember John 15:13: 'Greater love hath no man than this; that he lay down his life for his friends.'

"He has honored both the Prince Regent and God with his conduct. I have no doubt that he is walking the halls of heaven at this very moment, likely with Our Savior's hand upon his shoulder."

Christ! He was laying it on with a very heavy trowel, but then subtlety was never the strong suit of lay preachers. The words felt stale and hollow, yet they had the intended effect. The boy looked up with intense eyes that shouted desperately that they wanted to believe. "Truly sir?"

Pennywhistle gripped his hand strongly. "You may wager your life upon it." He was turning into a very polished liar. The things he did for England!

"Thankee, sir, thankee," the lad smiled in relief. He released his grip, sighed deeply, and dropped back into his squatting position. His eyes fluttered briefly and he slipped into the deep sleep of post-battle exhaustion.

Pennywhistle walked brusquely onward, embarrassed he could not think of something better than embracing the mantle of the religious huckster to beguile the grief of a good lad.

The wind blew a bloodstained piece of paper onto his boot. He picked it up out of curiosity and began to read. It was an unsent letter from a lieutenant James Dobbins to his fiancée, a Miss Claudia Collins of Baltimore. He rambled on about how much he missed her and talked of plans for their wedded life. He was convinced the campaign ahead would be short and decisive and he promised and that he would soon return to her. The campaign had indeed been short and decisive for him.

Pennywhistle wondered where his corpse lay and doubted whether it would ever be returned to her. After looters stripped a corpse and left it to bloat in the sun, there was very little way to identify who it had once been. Not content with stealing a man's humanity in life, war also did so after death.

Dobbins would likely end up in a shallow burial pit with dozens of other anonymous corpses.

The first wave of looters were already about their business: chiefly seeking coins, watches, rings, and anything containing valuable metals or precious stones. The second wave would relieve the corpses of clothing. Boots and shoes were particular targets since hard marching killed footwear. Cartridges were taken as well.

Most of the looters were soldiers but a goodly number of civilians had materialized as if by magic. He noted one old woman calmly sawing off a swollen finger that bore a ruby ring.

Another kind of looter was also in action. He spied a man prying a tooth from the fly-filled mouth of a corpse; a local dentist. Human teeth were highly prized in dentures. A complete set of teeth from an upper jaw could fetch as much as thirty pounds. Most teeth came from executed criminals but battlefields were a better supply source since all specimens came from the mouths of young men in their prime. When battlefield teeth were set in denture frames crafted from hippopotamus ivory, the price could well top one hundred pounds.

Pennywhistle spied several wagons driven by civilians approaching in the distance. He had seen similar ones in Edinburgh during his time in medical school. They were not ambulances for the wounded but the conveyances for the dead. They belonged to "Resurrectionists," professional body snatchers who sold corpses to medical schools for dissection.

The trade had no legal legitimacy, yet such was the need that these men escaped prosecution and earned a good living. Most had written pricelists and carefully factored in considerations such as the age, sex, size, and mortification of the body. They usually selected people called 'friendless,' people with no family or known associates. A good many battlefield casualties would forever remain unknown, so battlefields became sources of bounty to those plying this nasty trade.

He stopped when he came to a smashed sutler's wagon, emptied of its contents. Sutlers were merchants who followed armies and sold everything from small necessities to luxury goods. They invariably carried an impressive stock of expensive food, fine wines, and spirits. Their prices were highly inflated to compensate for their risks. They were both loved and despised by armies and their wagons were the first things looted by battered troops.

He pawed through the wagon idly and was surprised to discover a bottle of Martell Cognac that the scavengers had missed. Looters were usually thorough but perhaps a stray patrol had frightened off those searching the wagon. He looked at the bottle and was pleased to note it was 1811 vintage, the best year in living memory and tremendously expensive stuff. At least one Yankee had sophisticated tastes. Most Americans seemed only concerned with the amount of alcoholic kick in a beverage.

French vintners said the mighty comet that appeared in the skies that year had done something magical to the grapes, but they were just using the exotic to explain simple luck. He was bound to discipline men for looting, but decided it would do no harm to take the bottle. The damage had already been done and the bottle might come in handy to soothe things when he confronted his brother.

Two well-fed Irish Wolfhounds prowled the field slowly and sniffed the ground carefully. Their heavy coats were clearly a burden in the baking heat. He hoped they might find their master alive.

Compassionate men did as the hounds and sought fallen comrades. Some cried when they found friends beyond earthly comfort, while others shouldered those still alive and headed to the rear hoping to find a surgeon. He guessed the surgeons would only have time to patch the walking wounded. They might be able to manage a few quick amputations for a few more. The severely damaged would probably be left behind. At least the Americans were reasonably compassionate in that regard.

He passed an improvised surgical station of the 44th: two crudely cut beams ripped from an old house sat atop two sawhorses and formed an operating table. A cheap tin bucket stood alongside ready to receive discarded arms and legs. Both stood in an open field under the blazing sun. Most of the wounded had been escorted or carried there by fully ambulatory friends but a few had just crawled the distance. Unlike the French Army, the British had no system of battlefield ambulances and the wounded trusted to luck and friends.

It surprised him that the surgeon was making a mighty effort to save what he would have considered a hopeless case. The stocky, fair-haired surgeon looked young. He likely had not had much battlefield experience judging by the fact he appeared fully sober. He had probably not yet forfeited his idealism and wanted to save everybody. That would change quickly.

His patient of perhaps twenty years had two bandaged leg stumps and a mangled right arm. He had spat out the lead ball he was supposed to bite on for the pain as the surgeon clearly had no laudanum or rum to blot out the agony, and was screaming his lungs out. The surgeon sawed manfully through the shattered bone of his left arm. The young private of the 44th would soon be nothing but a branchless trunk. Mercifully, his departure for the Great Beyond probably lay only a few hours away.

The battlefield looked a bloody chaos put into suspended animation, but officers moved about purposefully and began herding men back to their units to await further orders. It was clear that the army would not linger long but would exploit their victory and quickly push onto Washington. The Americans had been soundly beaten, but it was important not to permit them any time to rally.

The 21st and the Royal Marines who had remained unengaged would spearhead the advance into Washington. Fresh troops could easily brush aside any stands made by beaten ones. Bonaparte himself averred fresh troops outweighed used-up ones at a factor of three-to-one.

A line of drummers had formed in the distance and began to loudly beat The Parley. The distinctly cadenced drumbeats represented a tradition stretching back centuries. It was a formal summons to negotiate, a rhythmic subpoena. War was barbarism personified yet men still worked to limit its depredations.

When Badajoz, Spain repeatedly refused terms and the city fell in March 1812, after a bloody final assault, British redcoat's exacted retribution with a three-day orgy of drinking, killing, looting, and raping. Their behavior was so mindlessly destructive that the stern disciplinarian Wellington had been forced to admit that his army was completely beyond his control. Four days later, after most redcoats had sobered up and a few had been hanged, the army returned to its duty.

It was a black mark on the honor of the British military and the memory of it haunted senior British commanders.

Because of Badajoz, the British were going out of their way to ensure Washington received reasonable treatment. Surely someone of importance would hear and the Americans would send out plenipotentiaries to spare their capital misery. Or was the panic on the American side so widespread that they were beyond any rational appeals? Pennywhistle viewed the American Experiment with a certain admiration and had no wish to see its capital or its citizens harmed.

He heard piteous howls and noticed the two Wolfhounds had stopped. They had found their master. They licked the corpse in hopes that they might wake him, not yet sure his sleep was eternal. With no one to care for them and they being expensive to feed, they likely had not long to live.

"Cap'n, Cap'n, there you is. Been lookin' all over for ya. Killed me two of the muricans; used my bayonet just like Sergeant Dale taught me. Muricans done run off real fast. I say it was de Bladensburg Races!" Gabriel sounded happy and proud. By all rights, he should be dead. Yet battle was quirky above all things. One man might take few risks and perish, while another took ridiculous ones and lived. It reinforced his sense of fatalism. Today had just not been Gabriel's time.

"Bladensburg Races?" He repeated the words under his breath. Others had made the same observation and he guessed the label might stick. It certainly was the greatest debacle suffered by American Arms. He looked in disgust at flies crawling over the unseeing eyes of a nearby corpse.

He faced Gabriel with a sad, resigned expression. "A battlefield is a terrible place, Gabriel. I truly hope this will be the only bloody field you will ever walk. Look around you; see, hear, and smell it. Does anything about this scarlet pasture seem glorious? You told me you embraced the Bible. Is it not like hell, save that here the virtuous are punished along with the guilty?"

Gabriel nodded, but there was a hint of puzzlement in his expression. He had expected the Captain would be cheerful over the great victory.

"I understand your satisfaction in smiting your former oppressors, but I assure you that emotion will be fleeting. When your passions have cooled and the triumph of victory has faded, the truth will come home. Lying in bed one night, you will see the faces of the dead and it will not be pleasant. Take pride in your bravery, but do not take pride in the infliction of death. Any fool can kill. The greater lesson is to restrain yourself from doing so when every instinct shouts that it is right and proper. Don't ever allow killing to become easy and casual and don't let anger and hatred change you into your old master. You are a good man, far better on your worst day than your old master was on his best. I wish you to remain that way."

Pennywhistle saw Gabriel's disconsolate expression and realized he had probably confused him. Gabriel looked up to him, expected him to speak about the warrior's calling. He had spoken as a man, not a soldier, had let his personal feelings intrude upon his duty. He had been over-familiar, treated Gabriel as worthwhile man, not a mere battlefield asset.

He became the officer again. It was Private Prosser, not Gabriel. "Private, you have done well and the Colonial Marines and General Ross are well pleased with your conduct. I would wish you to return to the Marine column I see forming up in the gully over yonder. I assume it will accompany Patterson's Brigade and advance into Washington. Think of it, Private, you will be marching past the Capitol as a free man and a proud warrior!"

Gabriel snapped to attention and favored him with a crisp salute. "Aye aye, Cap'n. Right away!" He returned the salute and Prosser pivoted smartly on his heel and marched away.

It was ironic that Gabriel would march into his nation's capital a free man only because he wore a red coat; a former non-citizen of a nation that shouted loudly about freedom and liberty, yet denied it to millions simply because of skin color. The sight of armed blacks in red parading down Pennsylvania Avenue would occasion great hair pulling among the Yankees.

America had numbers of free blacks, chiefly in the larger cities, but they were compelled to keep their presence unobtrusive and display subservience to whites. London had free blacks, too, but no black man walking London's streets needed to carry a special piece of paper proclaiming his freedom.

Before he had arrived in the Chesapeake, he had never encountered slavery personally and so had never considered it deeply. The idea of measuring a man's value by the color of his skin made little sense to him. Lifetime involuntary servitude was opposed to the universal ideals the Americans had espoused in their Declaration of Independence as well as *La Revolution's* of *liberté, égalité, fraternité.*

His viewpoint on slavery had evolved considerably seeing the reality of 'the peculiar institution.' As he talked with more and more runaways, heard stories of mindless beatings, families split and sold apart, and men treated as less than beasts, he became convinced slavery had no place in the Enlightenment ideals he had studied at university in Edinburgh.

His time in the Service had taught him the real worth of a man was measured in achievement. He had seen men of great birth fail utterly in battle and men of obscure birth perform brilliant feats of arms. Worthiness was found in the most unexpected places and a distinguished pedigree was no guarantee of a courageous soul.

He found plenty of brave hearts and noble characters among the runaways. That inner merit merely needed cultivation and direction. He felt slavery's days were numbered in America, although given what he had seen of the mercurial American temperament, it might well require some violent and bloody upheaval to banish it completely. It would not happen with a whimper as it had in Britain.

He stopped and shook his head. He was procrastinating, ruminating upon the future of a cruel institution, rather than begging his imagination for guidance about what to say to his brother. Oh hang it all, time to stop thinking and just get moving. He put his head down and walked quickly toward the small area where the American marine prisoners had been herded.

He spotted his brother easily because he might as well have been staring into a mirror. His brother had platinum blonde hair and china blue eyes while his own hair was sandy red and his eyes emerald green--other than that the man might have been his twin. He even had the same tall, rangy build. His brother looked surly and his right shoulder was crudely bandaged.

Their eyes locked in recognition, briefly fired volleys at each other, then relaxed into an expression neither wore often: confusion. His brother was as bewildered as he about what to say. He broke the ice uncertainly. "Greetings, brother.

I am sorry to see you wounded. I trust it is not serious." His customary nonchalance deserted him. "I have some excellent cognac here that might ease your pain." The heartiness he forced into his voice went wrong and his carefully chosen words came out sounding brittle and artificial.

Tracy glanced at his bandaged shoulder dismissively. "Trifling; no real damage." He felt dead tired and his emotions were ragged. His voice came out much more gruff and grim than he intended. "So you figured things out."

Pennywhistle nodded. His brother had likely understated the seriousness of the wound. The Englishman tried to keep his reply matter-of-fact, but did not quite succeed. "There was only one explanation that obtained after I had eliminated agreeable theories based on wishful thinking."

He shrugged his shoulders and extended his arms with palms upturned in sadness and acceptance. "Every son wants to believe his father is a demigod, un-cursed by the faults and foibles of mere mortals. Discovering that your parent's feet of clay reduced him to merely human stature is painful. I think if he were here now he would admit his faults with ready candor, yet speak as Macbeth did, "I dare do all that becomes a man: who dares more is none."

Tracy looked him deep in the eye, but it was with respect, not disapproval. "I have found you to be a formidable opponent. I surmised you would do as I did and eliminate pleasant, improbable theories conjured by a heart that was loathe to accept the only factual verdict that made sense. I gather the conclusion shocked you as much as it did me. I... well... damn it." He drew in a deep breath as if gathering up profound reserves of determination, "Let me be blunt. I felt, no, I knew, this meeting would happen. I have looked forward to it and dreaded it as well."

Pennywhistle saw the fatigue in his eyes, the deep worry lines in his powder-blackened face and the compulsive patting of the ground with his left hand. There was the tiniest hint of wetness in his eyes. He was having trouble controlling his emotions and his tongue just as Pennywhistle was.

"I need some answers about my father and his family. I would prevail upon your honor as a gentleman to supply them. I am trusting that your heart is as generous as your battlefield conduct was gallant. We Virginians value family above all things. You and I are bound by a tie that knows no allegiance to flags. I know I was born on the wrong side of the blanket and realize that my existence must distress a proper gentleman such as yourself. Yet I am gambling that you also value earnestness and character." He stiffened his posture and cleared his throat. "I am prepared to throw myself upon your mercy to obtain those answers."

Pennywhistle saw the pain in his eyes. That a man of honor and proven fortitude was prepared to abase himself to know the truth moved him deeply. He understood that that which he took for granted from childhood might have incredible value if hidden from a man as an adult.

"It is your birthright to know the truth and my privilege to acquaint a gallant officer with his heritage. Our earliest progenitors were Saxon knights raised to prominence by Alfred the Great. Pennywhistles were prominent when the ancestors of the present Hanoverian dynasty were living in peat hovels. You and I need bow down before no man. However, before I furnish you the full particulars, would you first grant me the honor of satisfying my curiosity about your own back-ground? Please be frank, I am not here to judge, merely to understand...my...brother." He let out a long sigh, aware that his heart had at last accepted the truth.

Tracy's mouth curved slightly upward at Pennywhistle's use of the word brother. He would be simple, direct, and factual, the way he guessed the Englishman would write up a scouting report. "I grew up an only child, never knowing my family past. My mother died when I was five, before she could tell me much. I was farmed out to her brother and his wife who were unable to conceive. They treated me as their own and grew up on a fine plantation on the James River next to Westover with lots of fine, dark bottomland, good horses, and an anchorage where ships could land goods direct from England.

"My adoptive folks were upstanding people who loved me, educated me well, and took me to church regular. It was a good childhood. But they would simply never, ever speak of my father. I tried hard, pressed them often as I grew older but they always found a way to change the subject. I came to feel they were protecting me from an awful secret, yet I still wanted to know." He stopped for a second as if puzzled by his loquacity.

"I can understand that it must have been difficult not to know who you really were. You have my most sincere sympathy," said Pennywhistle. He walked over and sat down next to Tracy. He opened the cognac and took a healthy draft, then passed it to his brother who did the same. The velvety fire calmed tensions, but the gesture itself was of far more importance.

The Englishman's tone and the cognac caused Tracy to smile fully for a brief second. He squared his shoulders and continued. "My uncle and aunt always evinced dark countenances when I asked after my real father, as if even saying his name was an incantation that might summon legions of dark imps to our doorstep. I had no idea if my father was a murderer, a gypsy, a brigand, or a day laborer. I did not know if he was dead or alive. I thought the worst and sometimes cried myself to sleep, whispering. 'Oh father, why did you not want me? Why did you not stay?'

"When I was fifteen, my adoptive parents finally ceased their prevarications and said, 'You shall know the truth upon your majority. It will be a hard burden for which you are not yet ready.' But they died only six weeks apart when I was twenty. I inherited a plantation but no answers. I left the College of New Jersey, sold the plantation, and decided I wanted some adventure. The Corps offered me a chance to see the world. I determined to prove myself worthy and show the father that lived in my imagination that he had made a great mistake by rejecting me.

"To find out after all these years, that I was not alone, that a living link to him existed, stunned me, yet I felt great joy. I would have an answer to the mystery. Even if the news was bad, it would still be better than not knowing at all. The fact that you are a King's officer opposed to me professionally made things difficult." He took a deep swallow of the cognac.

Pennywhistle saw a wealth of emotions flow and ebb across his brother's face in under a second. He felt his pain and confusion. He understood he was hearing deep things that Tracy had voiced to no man. Nothing hurt as deeply as pains from childhood.

"Let me guess. You wanted to meet me as a brother to supply answers, yet were mindful of your duty to destroy me as an enemy of the Corps and your flag." He laughed in relief. "I confess I had similar conflicts about you. There is so much you probably desire to know about your forbears, yet I would guess you would wish to learn first about your father."

Tracy released the breath he had been holding in expectancy and nodded. "Was he a good man?" His voice wavered slightly, indicating he was almost afraid to finally hear an answer he had sought for years.

"Yes, a very fine man," said Pennywhistle. "You and I have his looks and I like to think his character. His name was Tobias."

"Tobias, Tobias, yes, yes!" Tracy murmured quietly. A first name was the start of an identity. His father was becoming real.

"He was a deep man, and in many ways, a sad man. Yet well beloved by those he commanded, feared by those opposed to him, and deeply respected by those who worked alongside him."

"Tell me more about his character." Tracy's hard face had softened to a child-like vulnerability.

Of course! Tracy would first want to know about their father's essence, rather than a long recital of events and deeds. Tracy handed the bottle to Pennywhistle and he took a healthy swallow. The smooth and mellow elixir was an excellent anodyne to both the stresses of battle and the revelation of secrets.

"He was a man who always did his duty, John, if you will permit the liberty of using your Christian name."

Tracy looked gratified. "It is how brothers should address each other."

"Agreed, please call me Tom."

"My honor, Tom."

"Our father was honorable and upstanding, always willing to fight for his principles: a gentleman as much by character and conduct as he was by lineage. He served in Parliament for several years but declined to stand a second time because the corruption disgusted him. When he died fourteen years ago, people of every occupation and station from miles around came to his funeral. Nobles, gentlemen, yes, but plenty of humble folk as well and lots of soldiers from his old regiment. After the funeral, people I had never met told me stories of his kindnesses, the little things, quietly done for people in need. His charity was of the finest sort, private and never spoken of, known only to God and the people he helped.

"He schooled himself to become a staunch warrior, but it went against his deeper nature. At his heart, he was a scholarly, gentle man who would have been far more comfortable teaching natural philosophy at university than pursuing the profession of Mars. As the eldest son of a family that had faithfully defended the English crown since before The Conquest, it was simply expected he would assist the House of Hanover in its fight against American rebels.

"My people," Pennywhistle corrected himself. " No... *our* people," he looked Tracy directly in the eye, "were marcher lords, rough-hewn frontier barons, rather a rum and ruthless lot who were far more skilled with swords than sonnets. I refuse to sanitize the past by calling them *keepers of the peace* as they liked to style themselves. In Wessex, they matched the savagery of Viking invaders with equal savagery. Later, they established themselves in the far north and kept the Scots out of England with a brutal violence honed to perfection by centuries of practice.

"They were the King's vanguard on the ragged edge of the realm and had a license to raid, burn farms, slay peasants, and steal cattle, coin, loose jewelry, and anything valuable that was not bolted down. Lovely young maidens constituted a favorite form of booty. Not all of our female ancestors were willing partners!

"The family was exiled into societal wilderness in the 17th century because James Pennywhistle opposed the installation of the Dutchman William of Orange on the English throne. He had regularly played cards with James II and simply liked him as a man. He was politically naïve and could not grasp the difference between private and public character. He did not understand that once James refused to hide his Catholicism, the Stuarts had to go.

"Our great-grandfather, Nicholas Pennywhistle, revived our fortunes by pursing an unsavory occupation in India. The maharajahs and princelings of the many small independent states constantly squabbled with each other and wanted modern firearms to carry out the wars that resulted. Astute bribes and kickbacks to certain East India Company officials persuaded authority to look the other way and allowed Nicholas to pursue unmolested a highly lucrative gun-running trade. As I am sure you know, those who sell arms profit far more than those who wield them." Tracy nodded with cynical understanding.

"His advice on war was much sought in India because he had been a successful gentleman adventurer in the armies of Louis XIV. He had a facility for languages and easily insinuated himself into local courts where he flattered and encouraged the worst instincts of their rulers. He was a death merchant who actively exploited regional tensions and fomented wars to enhance his business. Someone once said behind every great fortune is a great crime. In the case of our family, it is sadly true.

"He commissioned Nicholas Hawksmoor to build him a fine mansion in the English baroque style and became a patron of local charities. I suspect his charity work sprang not from an honest seeking after atonement but from desire to appear respectable. From what I have heard of him, his private credo apparently was, 'with enough money respectability can always be bought.' He did a good job burying his past and spread the lie to his neighbors that he had become a successful nabob through the spice trade. He was not a good man, but he was an able and clever one."

Pennywhistle frowned. "I wish I could portray a more pleasing vision of our past but I feel certain you value honesty as much as I do. Instead of allowing beguilement by romantic fables, it is far better to look men and events hard in the eye and call them by their rightful names."

Tracy nodded with a look of sad resignation that suggested disappointed idealism. He wanted a heritage that was fairy-tale noble in spite of a natural cynicism that suggested the majority of men usually acted from less than pure motives.

Pennywhistle continued. "Our father did his duty in the American War but I am certain he never desired to live a martial life. But whatever task he set himself, he never did anything by half-measures. He always resolved to make himself master of any new undertaking. He became an expert soldier simply because it was his nature to thoroughly understand any task set before him.

"He never really recovered from his service here. I think he was a man too sensitive for his own good and reaped the whirlwind. He suffered nightmares which gradually deepened into a melancholia that eventually took his life. He called it

'The Black Vulture' because he felt it was constantly circling his consciousness, always looking for an opening.

"He commanded the 23rd Royal Welch Fusiliers when they surrendered at Yorktown. He took a mortar fragment in the skull during the last moments of the siege and was quite insensible for several weeks. A kindly fellow Mason, a French major named DuMotier, nursed him back to health. He told me memories of that period were incomplete at best. It is just possible he literally had no remembrance of your mother.

"Our father never did anything for trivial reasons. When he joined with your mother, he must have felt something important for her. He never spoke much about what he did here, but said the entire war was a great mistake and a dark stain on British honor. He told me he first saw the Americans as renegades but in the end viewed them as family members who could simply no longer remain in the old home. He was an idealist, John, and I think the war destroyed something in him that he never got back. He always had a smile and a kind word for everyone, yet mankind's general venality greatly saddened his heart.

"He never wanted anything to do with soldiering once he returned home, always said it was time to practice the arts of peace. He died before I entered the marines. I am not sure he would have approved of either of our careers. Still, he always had a ready ear and a good meal for old veterans who dropped by the house. One broken-down old private stayed with us for a full year. He came here intending to suppress rebels and outlaws, but came away thinking you Americans might actually be honoring the Enlightenment ideals he believed in. Perhaps your mother had something to do with that." He smiled kindly.

Tracy's eyes welled up and he spoke with great emotion. "I do not imagine my mother was popular for loving a prominent officer whose soldiers occupied our lands. I do remember just before she passed she said she loved my father very much. To discover he was a man of honor, a gentleman doing his patriotic duty and pursuing the right as he saw the right, gladdens my heart beyond measure. To feel an orphan for so long, then to find..." He bit his lip to hold back the tears. He took another swallow of the cognac. He touched Pennywhistle's arm gently. "A brother who is... a gentleman of honor.."

Pennywhistle felt a wave of emotion engulf him. His voice quivered a bit. "Don't worry about it, John. My intuition and your battlefield conduct tell me that you and I are very alike. We claim to be cold-hearted, pragmatic realists, but at our hearts we are unredeemed sentimentalists. We have seen much other men could neither endure nor understand. We have been through the fire and have become grimmer and harder men because of it.

"We listen to the braying of patriotic orators with skeptical ears and view the actions of saber-rattling politicians with jaundiced eyes. We purse our lips in distaste when corpulent preachers thunder from their pulpits about *good wars*. We are of the same blood, but more than that, we are of a kind: soldiers. We are clever, men look up to us, and we take that trust and lead them to their deaths.

"I'll warrant that you sometimes have the same sort of nightmares as I. You see the faces of the men you have killed as well as faces of your own people who have died from your mistakes. You worry you have become a little too good at the business you are about, a little too far removed from the sentiments of civilized men. We do not share our feelings easily. Even now, we both understand this exchange would not be taking place but for the battle we have just survived and the blandishments of Lady Cognac. Our tongues are not ordinarily so relaxed and easy."

Tracy smiled and nodded in understanding. He took another pull at the cognac. It was a relief for him to drop the mask men needed to see in a crisis: calm, confident, imperturbable, and completely unacquainted with pure, naked fear. "Yes, you are right," sighed Tracy. "I sometimes feel I am an outlaw of civilized and proper feelings, a distasteful tool fit only for battle and unsuited to the sweet ways of anything like a *Pax Romana*; a godsend in war, a curse in peace."

Pennywhistle nodded in sympathy. "I expect all professional soldiers of experience and merit feel the same way. Our presence makes civilians uneasy. We represent dark impulses trained and hardened that they would rather pretend did not exist. They avoid us until they need us. Given the proclivities of civilians who claim to love peace but who constantly find ways to prevent its outbreak, we will always be in strong need. You and I will simply do our duty, serve our foolish civilian masters, and hope for the best. But more pressing matters command my attention. You are a prisoner of war, as are your men. I cannot answer for your men, but it would be my honor and privilege to arrange your parole."

Tracy looked astonished. "You would do this for me?"

Pennywhistle replied, "You are an officer and deserve to be treated as such. Moreover, you are my brother and a fine warrior. Your word is enough for me and my commanding officer.

"The terms would be standard. You agree to serve no more in this war until properly exchanged for an English officer of equal rank. I would be honored if you would accompany me into Washington City. I would assume you would want to report to Captain Tingey at the Naval Yard and explain your condition and your duty. We can give you an escort under a flag of truce. There will likely be brigands and looters infesting the roads that care nothing for the honor of paroled officers."

"I am touched and accept your terms, brother." He stood to attention and saluted crisply. He then reached into his jacket and extracted a small leather portfolio whose gold wax seal looked to have been recently broken. "Now I must further presume upon your good offices as both a brother and a gentleman. It pertains to the contents of this portfolio. What is inside is embarrassing to my country yet it also may hold the potential to stop some greater national folly. I regret the documents allow no easy or clear-cut choices. I share them with you because the papers are prizes of war and would soon be confiscated in any event. I feel that as a man of reflection you may be persuaded to put them to a better use than would your intelligence officers. I ask much on short acquaintance but I believe you and I both want this ill-conceived war brought to a proper conclusion. However, I would not think less of you if you declined to become involved and simply followed standard military protocol."

"I am curious to discover precisely what you mean, John. I can make no promises save I will listen carefully and give the matter my utmost consideration. I know you would not make such a request save for the gravest of reasons. We are alone for the time being. Let us sit upon the grass and talk." They made themselves comfortable and Tracy passed the cognac to Pennywhistle who took a small swig. Pennywhistle handed it back and simply said, "Pray begin."

Tracy took a quick sip and then a deep breath. "During the battle just concluded an attempt was made to assassinate President Madison who was present upon the field. I stopped it by firing first. The killer was an American not a Briton. Whatever our differences, I know his Majesty's Government does not suborn the murder of leaders of state. The assassin was part of a group of traitors known as The Knights of the Golden Horse Shoe."

Pennywhistle blinked in surprise. "I had heard Madison was unpopular but I had no idea that someone would attempt to kill him. I thought you Yankees were so proud of your system of government; *vox populi* and all that. Assassination of a leader is something I'd expect in the Barbary States rather than in a civilized country. We Britons do actually consider America civilized if rather rough around the edges."

"The Knights have opened secret negotiations for a separate peace with your people," said Tracy disgustedly. "They also speak of an upcoming convention in Hartford. I suspect it may have to do with detaching New England from the Union. Exposing them would likely stop the negotiations and ruin designs of secession.

"Yet publishing the names of traitors might also undermine American morale and exacerbate simmering regional tensions. Faint hearts barely supporting the war would be apoplectic knowing that such important men had lost faith in our Republican government. The power of a government is only as strong as a people's belief in it.

"The Knights don't seem to know much about security. I took this portfolio off the assassin; that he was carrying such important information on his person suggests he was an insider, not a hireling. His sorry performance was consistent with an amateur.

"I've only had a chance to briefly inventory the contents. It contains the names of quite a number of knights written in plain text. They are all New England men of influence and property. There is nothing here to directly link them to the assassination but solid circumstantial evidence to suggest they were behind it. The tie to the secret negotiations is clear and unequivocal. I debated whether to burn everything before the battle but my anger told me to wait and expose them publically, pass all of the information onto a well-established newspaper like the *National Intelligencer*. But the matter rests with you now."

Pennywhistle paced back and forth, lost in thought, and did not speak for a full minute. "As far as I know, the only official peace negotiations are being carried on in Ghent. But there is an ambitious man on our side who lives for conspiracies: Sir John Sherbrooke, the Lieutenant Governor of Nova Scotia. He has been a great headache to the military authorities in Halifax always carrying out plans without authorization from London.

"I met him once; he is a self-serving empire builder and just the sort who would endeavor to treat with disaffected Americans on his own hook. I suspect he has gotten carried away with his own grandiosity and far exceeded any general guidelines supplied by the Foreign Office. Sherbrooke would undoubtedly profit personally from a breakup of the Union but it most assuredly would not be in the interest of His Majesty's government. We have no wish to transact business with a balkanized America of virtually independent states all yelling and squabbling like children. America under the Articles of Confederation was a nightmare that we have no desire to see repeated."

Tracy shook his head and spoke in a voice that rippled with contempt. "The Knights are men too clever for their own good who are playing with fire. I suspect every one of them, at his heart, is motivated by profit, not principle. Greed is a rotten dish but garish talk of patriotism becomes a sauce which covers up its stink.

"These men have also called upon religion to sanctify their base proceedings, claiming they act as rescuers of God's Grand Design for our Republic. Many are very prominent members of their churches. How murdering a President has anything to do with what the Good Book teaches is quite beyond me.

"I was raised to trust in Jesus Christ as my Lord and Savior and still believe thus. These Knights seem to worship a different Jesus than the one I know. Their Jesus disdains the poor and promises prosperity to all who follow him, at least in a certain very particular way. Wealth is worn as an honorable badge signaling divine preferment whereas poverty is regarded as a black stain announcing moral weakness. I recall very vividly the instruction Jesus gave the rich man who wished to join his band. 'Go and sell your possessions and give the money to the poor and you will have treasure in heaven.'

"Their Jesus says nothing about summoning up the fortitude to bear hurts nobly, but instead promises an easy path free of pain and strife. Jesus' blessing apparently is not an admonishment to work toward the good but a special dispensation to act in any manner the recipient sees fit. I say, if you seek to discover who a man wishes to be, speak to his priest but if you want to find out who he really is, speak to his bookkeeper."

"Act as if the documents never existed. Burn them," said Pennywhistle decisively. "The negotiations will never amount to anything. A separate peace is a chimera. This is about a fool on our side playing even greater fools on yours. The only lasting peace will come from Ghent and that peace lies in the province of diplomats.

"These tarnished Knights are amateurs and I doubt they will try another assassination attempt. Grandees of their sort are good for one big push and then their efforts collapse as fast as hot air balloons punctured by lightning. They become like a committee convinced it can invent a perpetual motion machine. They will plot and plan and fail.

"Sometimes the hardest course for soldiers trained to act is to simply stand aside and allow Machiavellians to destroy themselves by their own arrogance and folly. Be what you are John, an honorable warrior. We are best at fighting soldiers, not conspiracies."

Tracy removed the documents from the portfolio and gave half to Pennywhistle. The American walked over to a campfire, ignoring several surprised redcoats, and tossed the papers into the flames. Pennywhistle threw in his contribution a few seconds later. Both watched quietly for a minute as their role in the conspiracy went up in flames. "History will probably remember all of them as upstanding Americans; solid servants of the Republic," said Tracy disgustedly.

Pennywhistle smiled wryly. "How did Gibbon put it? *Corruption is the most common symptom of constitutional liberty.* It's just as true today as it was during Cicero's time. Besides, much of history is simply a series of lies agreed upon and sanctified by the victors. The victors naturally cast their motives in the best light."

"*Wealth corrupts all rich men*: that's rule number one of history," said Tracy resignedly.

"What's rule number two?"

"Good men can't change rule number one."

"Well, no one can alter human nature. *Plus ça change, plus c'est la meme chose*," said Pennywhistle sardonically. "Now that we have discharged our responsibilities to history, let us have some more of this excellent cognac and celebrate that we are alive to get know each other better."

"As one of my sergeants said to me after a nasty skirmish, 'Life can sometimes be hell, but it's so much better than the alternative,'" Tracy observed with a wintery half-smile.

Pennywhistle laughed then turned serious. "I will confess to you something else. I have spoken of it to no one, but it seems strangely appropriate to discuss it with you." Fatigue, the cognac, and a brother who had trusted his honor were pushing aside his usual circumspection about matters of the heart.

"My older brother Peter died two months ago. Half-brother actually. The transatlantic posts being what they are, it took time for the letters from his solicitors, sorry, lawyers to you, to catch up with me. I received word only two weeks ago. I am the last male to bear the name Pennywhistle and have worried that an ancient line would die with me. Discovering your existence unsettled me but I was secretly pleased that you might be able to carry on our line even if you did not bear our name."

Tracy looked genuinely sad. "My condolences, sir... uh, uh, Tom. It must be a difficult time for you."

Pennywhistle spoke with sadness but there was an undercurrent of disparagement. "Peter and I were never terribly close and frequently at loggerheads. He worshipped money, I worshipped knowledge. Since he had no male heir and the estate was entailed, everything passes to me. He left some funds for support of his wife and two daughters, but I will increase their portions so they need suffer no degradation of condition. They can continue to live in the home in Berwick. I love those girls even though my brother thought my peculiar notions about class were a bad influence on them. One of my adopted sons lives with them."

Tracy looked surprised at the mention of stepsons, as if he expected Pennywhistle was unmarried.

A mask of melancholy briefly covered the Englishman's face. "She died three years ago," he said simply. "I miss her greatly."

He cleared his throat, wiped his eyes dismissively, and continued. "As the owner of large mills, my brother privately had a small opinion of my minimally remunerative patriotic duties. 'Smart men fight for profit,' was his private philosophy, much like your Knights I should think. Peter was ambitious and our PM Lord Liverpool gave him a mid-level post in the cabinet. Oh, he was always eager to tell his government friends that his dear brother was giving his all to fight the Corsican Ogre, but I think it was a very calculated public pose designed to advance his career.

"He lived a prosperous, safe, sedentary life and always expected me to die first, since my career is one of hazard, but Fate has a sense of humor. I lost one brother who understood little about me and have just now gained another whom I do not know, but who instinctively understands much about me. Just when we believe we have life under control, Fate steps in to show us the unexpected is really our lot."

Tracy spoke earnestly. "We do think alike. My side has been abysmally led. I am proud of my men, but much distressed by my government. Your late brother sounds as if he would have been right at home with Mr. Madison's cabinet.

"I did notice one thing with your people that bothered me. We are having such a frank and unfettered conversation that I feel I can push the strict limit of good manners just a bit. You have armed Negroes. That is a very dangerous thing. I understand the British are not acquainted with them and are perhaps convinced they have hidden talents as a race, but I must tell you that is not so. I do not believe in their mistreatment, but they require a more mature people to watch over them. They are like children in many ways. Children should never be mistreated, but they should also never be given weapons and allowed to make decisions beyond the scope of their limited intellects. The white race has a responsibility to look out for and protect them--sometimes protect them from their own foolishness."

Pennywhistle's face turned hard. He liked his new-found brother, but his insights on race sounded patronizing and misguided, if typical of those of his countrymen. He did not want to sow discord, but could not let the remarks pass unchallenged. "I must disagree with you strongly. I think blacks are only like children if you legally compel them to remain so. I have no doubt you would treat those around you with kindness, but I have heard stories from the runaways that tell me many masters were bad parents and treated them less as children than spaniels to be schooled by the stick. Tales of families ripped apart and sold down river repel me. I have particular problems with females used as unwilling concubines and brood mares for more batches of slaves. Hardly the actions of sound parents!

"We have had good outcomes turning runaways into soldiers and the Colonial Marines are a notable success. We have had no desertions and no problems with drunkenness. They have responded well to training with most showing up for morning drill with smiles betokening a true eagerness to learn. They have behaved admirably under fire. I noticed a considerable number of blacks among your flotilla men. Surely, you will allow they fought well?"

Tracy responded quickly. "You will get no argument from me about the flotilla men but I would say they are the exceptions rather than the rule. Every race has outstanding individuals, but I think it a severe mistake to generalize about the rest based on the actions of a few. The sea tends to attract the hardiest and most enterprising souls so anyone who would brave its dangers is unusual to begin with. Even an inferior equine line may occasionally produce a prize stallion. The law of averages tells us that millions of seeds sown under the most adverse conditions will still produce a few healthy plants."

Pennywhistle said thoughtfully, "I think you have it wrong. These are men we are talking about, not horses or seeds. I believe it mistaken to judge the possibilities of Africans when they have never had the opportunity to display their gifts minus the chains and sundry burdens imposed upon them by the white race. These people have been stripped of their dignity, families, and any connections to their language and home, all things most white folk will never have to endure.

"Blacks pretend to be stupid sometimes, and are actually quite clever at it, because it is what you expect of them and they do what they must for survival. Don't mistake studied performances for reality. It would be like breaking a man's leg, then asking him to run a footrace. When he fails to perform well, you say he had no ability to run in the first place.

"I assure you, I have no plans to join the abolitionists. I simply say the jury is out on the black race and that it is folly to reach a verdict based on insufficient evidence. Admiral

Cockburn had an attitude similar to yours when the Colonial Marines were first formed. He was skeptical that any military value might come of such a formation and thought the whole thing a Whitehall political stunt chiefly useful for its propaganda value. Observing them training and then under fire, changed his opinion of the black race entirely. He told me he informed Lord Bathhurst, the Secretary of State for War, *that they are brave, dependable fellows whom I would commend to anyone seeking good fighting men.* You Americans may consider Cockburn a monster, but I think you will allow he is no fool when it comes to battle."

Tracy sighed pensively. "I think some of what you say could be true. Females unwillingly pressed into sexual service distress me as well, but you can find weak men who abuse power at all levels of society. I observed a few Negroes marching with Ross the other day. I must admit that they looked smart. But the military is always a special case and discipline is ever present. Your perspective is that of a tourist who only sees brief highlights of life here and is not compelled to discover the day-to-day reality. It is easy to judge from afar, far more difficult when you must live with the results of such moralizing.

"I would never call slavery a good thing as some have. Our Founders knew its abolition would be a fatally divisive issue when our Constitution was written. They prudently chose to accept the reality of an established institution rather risk an action which might wreck the Southern economy and spark a second revolution.

"Slavery has made this country prosperous and the slave trade has certainly enriched the owners of Blackbirder fleets in Bristol and Liverpool. It has made possible the large crops of cotton which fuel your mills in Manchester and Birmingham.

Even some of our pious New Englanders who have railed against slavery, the Cabots in particular, have relatives who are secret shareholders in ships bringing Africans to these shores. The people who speak boldly about abolition constantly refer to ideal circumstances and better worlds that will likely never exist. They do not appear to have considered the practical ramifications of large scale manumission. Have you ever considered what changes such an event might cause?"

Pennywhistle shook his head.

"I thought not. It is all very fine to speak as Mr. Wilberforce and his Clapham saints do when the number of blacks in England is a mere 25,000 and they are seen mostly as exotic novelties. Negro bandsmen, footmen, and carriage drivers add, forgive the pun, a touch of color, to the lives of aristocrats, but do so only because they are relatively rare. They have an insignificant effect on the economy.

"But how would Mr. Wilberforce handle millions suddenly given their freedom and dumped precipitously upon society without any preparation for the responsibilities of citizenship, let alone managing their lives without supervision? It would be chaos. In the end, it would be far more harmful to all concerned than the present institution. I am not sure what the future of slavery is. It will probably change over time, might even end someday. But it is something that must happen in its own time, it cannot be forced by proclamations or decrees. My people are simply not ready to accept its direct and immediate demise."

"I admit I had not considered what you say," replied Pennywhistle, "and manumission on such a scale might cause great disruption to the established orders of things. Still, the life of one black man in England has shown we might look upon their future freedom with hope. Fellow's name was Ignatius Sancho and he was born on a slave ship near Greenwich around 1730. He worked as a servant for the Duke of Montagu. The Duke was so impressed with his exemplary service, intelligence, and quick wittedness that he taught him to read and write. The Duke freed him and set him up with a small grocery store in London. Sancho became a supporter of Charles James Fox and became the first black to vote in an English election. Sancho was not only a man of letters, corresponding with numerous literary luminaries, but something of a composer. Three books of his compositions were published. An obituary notice for him appeared in '*The Gentleman's Magazine*' yet no mention was made of his race-- clearly he had gained real acceptance.

"I first heard of him as a boy. My tutor, Ogilvie, said he had come across a biography of a 'remarkable negro' and that it was worth my while to read. Said the fellow was an example of virtue triumphing over incredible odds. The work contained not only Sancho's life story but a compilation of his letters. I have not thought about the book in years, yet it convinced me long ago to never underestimate the power of will."

Tracy looked dubious, yet Pennywhistle realized it indicated his words had sown doubt and that he was at least open to new perspectives.

Pennywhistle smiled a gentle smile of resignation. "But as soldiers we must deal with practicality, not vague theory and the fate of weighty issues will always lie in the realm of politicians rather than military men. And yet, I believe all problems, even thorny ones of long standing, have an eventual solution if men of sense and good will work together to solve them. You and I cannot today fix several hundred years of muddle. On more congenial matters, I have noticed you looking at my rifle with curiosity. It belonged to our father. Here, take a closer look." He handed the Ferguson to Tracy.

Tracy smiled and carefully inspected the piece, almost like a jeweler surveying a rare gemstone. It was not just a fine weapon, but a link to his father. "I confess I have not seen its like." He worked the breech loading mechanism a few times. "It's very ingenious, so much faster than a muzzle loader. How many rounds can you get off per minute? Five? Six?"

Pennywhistle replied, "Generally six, but I have managed seven on a few occasions."

Tracy relaxed visibly as he discussed professional concerns; so much easier to deal with fact not emotion. "It's a Ferguson, is it not? Based on Chaumette prototypes, correct? I had heard rumors of them, but thought perhaps it was all just fanciful talk."

Pennywhistle nodded. "Our father was Patrick Ferguson's second-in-command when he formed an experimental rifle corps of a hundred men in the last war. All of the men were armed with his invention. Father told me that Ferguson had General Washington in his sights at The Brandywine but declined to fire because as he put it, 'it is not the business of officers to assassinate enemy commanders.' The unit was disbanded after Ferguson was wounded and most of their weaponry disappeared."

Tracy continued to examine it and took careful note of its features. "I know a gunsmith who could probably make a good copy. I would love to have a weapon like this. What kind of range does it have? Three hundred yards?"

"Roughly that, under ideal circumstances," responded Pennywhistle, "although the ideal rarely occurs in battle as you know. Practically speaking, two hundred is much better, similar to the Baker and your Harper's Ferry piece. I made a slight modification to the rear sight myself and have been most pleased with the improvement in performance. When you fully extend the folding sight, you will see the ticks marking various distances."

Pennywhistle saw Sergeant Dale approach with two horses in tow. Dale's expression said he had come on important business. He was sure his brother understood the value of a good NCO. It would be pleasant to make the introductions.

Dale stopped and saluted. His stolid face betrayed surprise for just a fraction of a second when he saw the uncanny resemblance between the two men and noted how easily they conversed. Their accents were wildly different yet the timbres of their voices matched closely.

Pennywhistle saw Dale's confusion. "Good to see you Sarn't. Relax. He has given me his parole. Let me dispel the mystery. Allow me to present Captain John Tracy of the United States Marine Corps. He is my brother." He turned to Tracy. "This is Sarn't Dale, the best NCO in the Service. He has saved my life on occasions too numerous to mention."

Dale was far too discreet to inquire after more particulars. He snapped Tracy a quick salute. He knew his duty. The man was an enemy but a proper officer for all that.

Tracy returned the salute. "I am glad my brother has such a stalwart fellow as you at his side, Sergeant."

Pennywhistle inquired, "I presume you come with new orders, Sarn't?"

"Aye, sir. Admiral Cockburn's compliments and would you please join him at the earliest possible moment? He has need of 'your particular talents.' That's how he put it, sir. I rounded up these two mounts for us."

Tracy's eyebrows shot skyward. "So you know the evil genius Cockburn, brother? I confess I have been most curious to know if he is really the demon our papers proclaim him."

"He may be the scourge of your country, John, but I assure you he is no monster and far from a barbarian. He is a clear thinker who devises very practical plans. He simply makes war harshly, without compromise. He is ruthless, but not devoid of principle or sensibility. He wants to force this war to a speedy conclusion and believes severe measures are far more humane in the long run. I actually think you might like him. If he had been in charge of your forces today, I might be in your position right now."

A thought struck him. Cockburn admired brave men and was always curious about the enemy. Why not bring Tracy along? Would it be scandalous? Maybe with civilians, but not with Cockburn. He knew what kind of fight the Marines had put up today. He would of course wonder how a brother ended up on the enemy side, but was worldly enough to accept the explanation Pennywhistle would offer. He was a sailor after all, had only married a few years back. He certainly had known his share of women before settling down. His brother needed an escort into Washington City anyway.

"Come with me, John, I will introduce you myself. Sarn't, do you think you could rustle up another horse for yourself?"

Dale nodded. "Not a problem, sir."

Tracy smiled. "I would like that very much. I would far rather meet Cockburn right now then General Winder. I can at least admire Cockburn as a skilled and clever foe. General Winder is fit only for the firing squad." There was real anger in the last sentence.

"It's settled then," said Pennywhistle. Tracy handed him the cognac and he took one last gulp. He then handed the bottle to Sergeant Dale. "For your troubles and exertions, Sarn't."

"Thank you, sir!" Dale smiled broadly. He guessed Dale had never had cognac before. Dale was an abstemious man, but a few quick shots would probably be very welcome right now. It would make a very hard day just a little easier.

Chapter Six

Sammie Jo sat up very slowly as the mental mists in front of her gradually dissipated and consciousness returned. She moved her head gently from side to side and gingerly touched her jaw. It hurt. She looked around the room for a few seconds and remembered where she was. Her eyes flashed and her lips contorted as if she had just bitten down on a row of porcupine quills. Damn the man!

She massaged her jaw and considered Pennywhistle's actions. The hint of a smile played at the edges of her mouth. The man was clever and had devised a neat solution to an unusual problem. Passion had been indulged followed by a practical way to keep her from her deadly business.

The Englishman could have killed her, maybe should have killed her. She was not sure exactly why he had not carried out his threat, he certainly was a man of his word, but likely his carnal thirst had simply overpowered his better judgment. He worked hard to conceal his feelings, but he was a man of powerful emotions. Might he have deeper feelings for her? It was probably too much to hope for. Lust was at least a starting point. His face flashed into her mind. Her skin flushed deeply and her breath caught for a few seconds.

Samantha Josephine Matthews had lost her virginity at seventeen. It was a black mark as polite society reckoned things and enough to curse her with slim prospects for a good marriage. That had never bothered her much because even with her beauty, polite society considered her a woman of small breeding and less fortune; a fine marriage had probably never been in her future. Yet unlike prim, upright ladies of quality, she saw her womanly desires as a gift not a punishment. Love making was something to be savored and it made no sense to close your eyes, shutter your feelings, and will your spirit to be elsewhere.

She had been with a few roistering, boastful country boys who had promised heaven but delivered something far less uplifting. She had enjoyed each act of passion, but instinctively knew things would be far better with a more experienced and worldly partner. Tom Pennywhistle proved her instincts were deliciously right.

Upon closer examination, the Englishman had turned out to be much different than he had seemed during their initial encounter. What she had seen at first was a glamour; a projected image akin to stage scenery standing in for real objects. His polished veneer of agreeable manners was a tarpaulin over his actual essence and made him seem far more personable than he actually was.

He was a serious, deeply private man who masqueraded as an affable public one. He was skilled at gently deflecting any inquires that got too close to the truth away from real answers and toward pleasant expectations that he surmised a questioner wanted fulfilled.

He perfectly satisfied the traditional expectations of a stalwart officer--a lion in the field, a lamb in the parlor, yet his true essence was much more complex than either. People thought they had been welcomed into the courtyard of his heart when they had actually been turned away at its gate. He was a difficult man to know, yet many thought they knew him well.

For a few brief minutes, the stresses of battle had opened a pathway into his soul. It was a good if impure soul, deeply mottled with pain, sadness, and regret. He was lonely too, a cerebral man whose mental quickness made it hard for others to keep up. But then the portal closed abruptly, like the door of a bank vault slammed shut.

She saw him as a man who liked his world to function with the precision and predictability of his expensive Swiss time piece. Undoubtedly, the messiness and uncertainty of raw emotion annoyed him. He seemed prone to analyze even trivial things to death and she wondered if he ever permitted himself the luxury of simply having fun.

She guessed that his mind placed people, events, and emotions in tidy mental drawers similar to the compartments found in gentlemen's writing desks--everything categorized, labeled, and ordered, but ready to be trundled out as a situation required. A new drawer probably bore the marker "Sammie Jo."

Unlike the country boys she had grown up with, he had no need of loutish gestures or fiery words to prove his manliness. He was the soul of self-assurance: a gentleman of impeccable comportment, direct speech, and steadfast calmness. His voice was as resonant as an orator's yet he spoke softly and never yelled, save when giving a battlefield command.

His quiet manner proclaimed strength far better than the bluster of most men. His mouth might smile and his words might soothe, but it was his eyes that mattered. They were restless, probing, and ironic. They warned those with the wit to see that they were being assessed. To the perceptive, he gave the impression of a sentinel: constantly observing, analyzing, and patiently logging threats.

His might was veiled in a manner that reminded her of something he had told her about his time with Wellington in Spain. The Duke typically concealed his strength and dispositions from the French by positioning his men on the reverse slope of a low hill. The French knew a powerful, dangerous force lay to their front but they remained uncertain about how to attack it.

He could convey more strength in a quick glance than most people could do with a torrent of violent words. She had once seen him stand rock silent and use the sheer force of his gaze to overawe an angry marine into wilting like old lettuce in a hot sun.

When he moved to carnal matters, he became a different man entirely. His disciplined passions completely slipped their shackles and a beast of raw Nature emerged that was gifted with fire, strength, and a complete lack of inhibitions.

Sammie Jo quieted her racing heart, gathered her clothes, and dressed quickly. She went to the window and looked out into the street. A few bodies lay there, but mostly it was quiet and deserted. She could hear the chattering of sporadic gunfire across the river. She was in an eddy of calm, just outside of the storm. She smiled when she noticed Pennywhistle had not taken her rifle or her possibles bag; very sentimental of him, but very stupid. Of course, most women would have taken a punch to the jaw as great encouragement to quit.

She would not stop. She might be a woman, but she was a hunter at her core. She had been a few seconds away from killing the monster Cockburn. She had the scent. She had him in her sights once and could do it again.

She was honest enough with herself to understand it was not really about patriotism. It might have started that way, but it had changed along the journey. It had become a test of her talents, a trial of her character. She had often made men jealous of her skill as a hunter, but she had never really met an extended stalk that she could not easily master.

This was different. She was not sure if she could do it, but she had to know. She might well die in the attempt. The omnipresence of death made life incredibly sweet and vital. Pennywhistle was right when he told her killing men was far different from killing animals. Animals never fired back and were completely predictable. The fury of battle had not repulsed her, but thrilled her. It was not the death, but the sheer fast-paced uncertainty of it all. She had always felt rejected by polite society, the perpetual outsider, but the roiling chaos of battle welcomed her, made her feel a powerful insider. Battle made her blood grow hot and ratcheted up her senses to a degree of awareness she would never have dreamed possible.

Her quarry was not a dumb animal but a clever man. He was well protected. It would be difficult to get close. Her pa had told her, whatever you aim to do, be the best at it. He was right. This was her chance to find out if she was the best at her craft.

She had two major assets. No one would expect anyone to do what she was about to. They might foresee a few random shots from fleeing soldiers, but would not anticipate a methodical, determined stalk carried out by an experienced hunter. She knew he would be headed to Washington and she had but to follow the advancing British to find him. She was attached to no army and served no commanding officer save herself. Her designs were impossible to anticipate because they were devised on the spot. No spy or traitor could betray her.

The British were trained to defend themselves against regulars and militia, but were not prepared for a determined single operator, particularly a woman. Women were regarded as frail creatures, save when it came to matters of home and hearth, where they were expected to be hard-working, tough, and resilient. She had used the imagined frailty and ingrained male chivalry to her advantage before, and she would do so again.

She looked out across the river once more. She saw only indistinct blobs of red, rapidly fading from view as was the chattering of gunfire. It was clear the Americans had lost. Still, one man's disaster might be another man's, she chuckled, or woman's, good fortune.

Washington would probably be in chaos as the responsible and well-born fled the city. It would mostly be deserted and those remaining would be concerned only with easy looting. It would be about self-centered greed; human jackals scavenging without regard to patriotism. The enemy would be focused on maintaining order and dealing with obvious miscreants.

As long as she kept moving and avoided crowds, she would attract little attention. There was always the danger of rape, but if she concealed her looks a touch, it was no real difficulty. Besides, with her height, strength, and skill with a knife at close quarters, any man choosing to try conclusions with her would be in for a very lethal surprise.

Men of high stature but low intent had chased her three times before. She had simply outrun Reverend Hammond who said it was God's will that he know her in the biblical sense. When Deacon Robertson tried the same stunt a year later, she declined to play the victim. She had by then attained her full height and knew the forest well. She concealed herself and when he passed her hunting knife did all the necessary talking.

James Chesterton was a slobbering, jowly merchant who thought because he owned much of the countryside the same applied to its womenfolk. He had cornered her in a livery stable when she had been inspecting a horse. No one else was about so he thought her screams would remain unheard. She played the fearful maiden because she wanted him close in and vulnerable.

He thought he was in control--men always did. He dropped his trousers, proud of his manhood and eager to acquaint her with its prowess. She sliced off his scrotum in one swift stroke. She silenced his screams with a few hard kicks to the head and covered him with straw. The locals found him the next day, bled out. No one ever spoke of it directly, but no man ever bothered her after that. The country people simply called it 'rough justice' and the sheriff was unwilling to initiate inquiries.

She needed a horse. The buggy might be identified and connected with her earlier imposture. The pregnant lady gambit would probably work again, but she doubted it would be necessary to employ disguise. There would be a sufficient number of displaced civilians on the road to blend in. No one would pay attention to a nameless fleeing woman. Everyone would be focused on their own limited horizons, simple survival instinct. It could definitely be done. She gathered up her belongings and bounded down the stairs, full of distinctly un-girlish enthusiasm.

*****

Capital's Punishment

Daniel Parke wearied with each passing mile, but a stubborn part of him refused to fall out of line and rest. He could have done so without censure, plenty of human castoffs already littered the gullies on either side of the road, but he tried to hold onto some imaginary reality of a last stand. If he allowed himself the luxury of sitting down for a few minutes, he might not get up for many hours. He was damned if he would be part of the human detritus of battle.

The chaos increased as each passing mile brought them closer to the Capitol building. Rumors abounded a last ditch defense would be organized there. He had attached himself to some District Militia who had come to fight and had then been commanded to abruptly reverse course and plod on home. They had advanced in good military order, but during the retreat they had degenerated into a shambling progression of disgruntled day laborers. The men marched poorly, files were sloppy, and the column bristled with angry murmurings and seditious talk.

Horsemen dashed back and forth along the cluttered roadway, barking orders from unseen commanders, which appeared to have little effect on anyone. Militia simply trudged back toward the capital; confused and discouraged, not knowing where they were going or what awaited them when they got there. The presidential party had dashed by him two hours ago, headed back to the White House at a fast gallop. He understood the need to warn Dolley and preserve treasures, yet it was hugely demoralizing to everyone who had seen it, a clear declaration of irredeemable defeat. At least he had gotten a first-hand view of the President. His fleeting impression was of a gnome-like man in black, a beaten-down old parson on his way to a funeral. He decided that it was as true metaphorically, as it was physically.

What truly angered him was the betrayal by Winder. He wanted to fight and would have, as would every man in the 5th, but they had been denied the chance. It was not the men who failed, not even the junior and regimental officers. It was the high command and the government. He wondered what happened to the rest of the army after the 5th had fled from the field. Had anybody stood and shown the British some backbone and bottom? This was a black day for everyone who loved the Republic.

He was aware the militia regiment he marched with was gradually disappearing. It reminded him of water evaporating from baking hot winds. Several hours ago the regiment had numbered around six hundred. The exodus had speeded up greatly after the President rocketed past. It had been at least five hundred then. Now, just as Capitol Hill loomed in sight, he guessed it was down to two hundred. If its ranks got any thinner, he decided he would seek out his friend, Mark Weir, in Georgetown and ask shelter for the night. He wondered if he was at home or had fled, like most of the other civilians.

They halted just below Capitol Hill. The major in charge marched up to several mounted regular officers and conferred with them. He came back red-faced and angry. Neither the promised rations nor the ammunition were ready. A chorus of derisive cries and angry hoots erupted from the troops. The stream of curses swelled louder and louder like the noise of a rising hurricane. Parke stood silent, but the men on either side shouted violent epithets directed toward everyone from the President to God.

Then a chain reaction set in. One man slammed his musket to the ground and walked away in disgust. Another followed. "God damn that cur Madison and every one of his cowardly toadies!" shouted a third. It was the effect of a fingertip pushing against a line of dominoes. The anger spread like wildfire. In two minutes, the regiment ceased to exist. Parke stood alone with the major and a few die-hards.

The major's anger changed to laughter. "What a pretty turn of events this is: who would ever have expected it? All the millions spent to build a lovely capital, and not a dime to buy supplies for its defenders!" He looked at Parke and the other ten men with a mixture of compassion and resignation. "Thank you for standing with me. Your patriotism and devotion do you great honor. But now it is time for you to think of your own welfare and those of your families. There is nothing more to be done here. Go to your homes and see to the lives of those you care most about."

He stood at parade ground attention and snapped a smart salute. There were tears in his eyes. "Be well and Godspeed." The last word was so choked with emotion it was barely audible.

The forlorn ten saluted. Most, like Parke, also had tears in their eyes. They all walked away in sadness, dejection, and anger. Parke had tried his best at redemption, but his failure to achieve it had nothing to do with him. No one seemed concerned about rescuing the Republic just now. It was just four miles to Weir's house. He could make it by sunset if he maintained a brisk pace.

He already saw looters smashing windows and entering unoccupied homes. It disgusted him. He saw carriages speed past, filled with what he guessed were government documents. He would tell his children about the night he saw the Republic disappear.

He stopped at the President's House when he saw someone had placed tubs of water and bottles of wine on the front lawn. People dashed in and out in a great frenzy, carrying objects, papers, and paintings judged to be of great importance. He had no idea if Dolley was behind the water and wine, although she had a reputation for hospitality at all hours of the day.

His parched tongue took control and guided him to one of the tubs. The water tasted surprisingly cool and fresh. He relaxed for a few seconds, forgot the cares of war, and reveled in the simple pleasure of liquid refreshment.

He looked up at the President's House. It was indeed a noble structure, meant to reflect the honor of the Republic. He wondered if the British would see it so and spare it from destruction. He decided it mattered not at all what his opinion was, the British would act as they saw fit. Refreshed and rejuvenated, he plotted a course to his friend's house. Archie's face flashed into his head which he decided was a good thing. It would save him from the despair he felt closing in about him.

He loved his country but could do nothing for it, save pray to a Divine Providence whose will he little understood. He had done his duty and tried earnestly to get himself killed but God seemed to have other plans. Maybe in the end, family was more important than country. He could make a great deal of difference to his mother, to Archie, to his children, if only he could survive. He suddenly felt a surge of energy. If he could just find a horse, he could make it home. Everyone there loved him for just what he was and cared nothing for his martial imperfections.

*****

Pennywhistle grew tired of listening to the incessant drumbeats of mounted drummers beating out the parley. It seemed clear the Americans were not going to respond but he understood why Ross had instructed the drummers to keep trying. His thoughts drifted as he rode and Sammie Jo's face appeared unbidden in his mind's eye. He hoped she was out of his life, but with someone like that, you could never be sure.

"Mad, bad, and dangerous to know": the words spoken about the tempestuous Lord Byron applied equally to her. He should have finished her. The popular term, 'weaker sex' was a grave misnomer in her case. She might have caused other deaths besides the subaltern. It was ironic that he might have helped her, having carelessly furnished advice on shooting when she had barely missed him. And yet, at a deep level he admired her spirit. The Americans had a word for it: 'spunk.'

Cockburn, Ross, and several aides lay a few yards ahead, in animated discussion as they rode. He moved closer, but kept silent. He had definite opinions, but would not volunteer them unless asked.

"General, I appreciate you sentiments," said Cockburn forcefully. "They are those of a civilized man, but the Yankees have brought this mess upon themselves. We have been beating the parley for hours and given them plenty of chance to respond like men of probity and good will but it seems clear the city has been abandoned to anarchy. Since the Americans have not shown themselves gentlemen and have spurned the chance to even listen to the highly reasonable terms you were prepared to offer, I believe they deserve the most severe chastisement. Restraint would be a mistake and would be perceived as weakness by these ruffians. They gave no thought to delicacy or mercy when they torched York. The civilians who lost their homes were shown no consideration. It was wholesale destruction. It absolves us from the obligation to display anything but simple, brute force.

"The looting has already started. The good people have already fled and only jackals, villains, and scoundrels remain. Firing the city might be doing everyone a favor. It would burn out a nest of vermin as well as eliminate anything of military value. I think the men should go in quickly, apply the torch widely and without restraint, then withdraw and head back to the ships. Gordon has been delayed, but I am in great hopes his vessels will arrive by nightfall. A great bonfire will teach the Yankees a never forgotten lesson and certainly push their negotiators in Ghent to accept whatever terms we dictate."

Ross looked pensive and replied diplomatically. "We might be justified, Admiral, but what you suggest would hardly be a measured, thoughtful response. If we behave as they did, how can we claim any moral superiority? Is it not the mark of a civilized nation to act out of cool, mature reflection rather than the un-thinking heat of the moment? I would ask, how will history remember us? Will it be as devotees of Alaric and Attila, or as disciplined representatives of a responsible, modern nation? When I served with the Duke in France, we were careful to comport ourselves with honor, discretion, and restraint. We spared people and property wherever possible. It had the most beneficial effect on the people of France. The French civilians came to trust us far more than the destructive soldiers of Bonaparte. Indeed, they hid supplies from the French army and instead sold them gratefully to ours."

"But this is not France," replied Cockburn with some asperity, "this is America. The Yankees can be quite dense about things unless the lesson is taught to them most forcefully."

"Still, what you suggest makes me uneasy," said Ross. "Here comes your man Pennywhistle. You know and trust him and I have come to understand his value. Let us ask his opinion." He motioned to Pennywhistle, who gently urged his horse forward. "Mr. Pennywhistle, draw closer. I gather you have just heard our discussion. We should very much like to hear your opinion on the matter." Ross and Cochrane both looked surprised to see an American Marine riding alongside Pennywhistle.

Pennywhistle knew both Ross and Cockburn preferred bold honesty to subtle temporizing and frank words to honey-tongued talk. He did what came naturally and introduced one gentleman to others. "General Ross, Admiral Cockburn, allow me to present Captain John Tracy of the United States Marine Corps." He paused for a few seconds. "He is my brother."

Ross and Cockburn betrayed no disapproval and nodded acknowledgment. Pennywhistle continued, "He has given me his parole and you both know how well the Marines fought in the battle just now. I did not know of his existence until a few days ago and it is only in the last few hours that I have had a chance to speak to him at length. He is an honorable gentleman and I am pleased to call him friend as well as brother."

Cockburn noted the strong resemblance between the two and remembered Pennywhistle's father had rendered distinguished service in the first American war. He had obviously not been a monk. "Your Marines fought very well, sir," he said to Tracy with characteristic directness, "A handsome performance, sir, most handsome. My compliments to you and them."

Tracy responded gallantly. "Coming from such a distinguished warrior, that is a very fine accolade, sir." He continued boldly. "It would be a grave mistake to burn the city, Admiral. It will only anger and stiffen the resolve of my people. It will not cause us to lessen our efforts against you, but will rather inspire us to redouble them." Tracy looked Cockburn directly in the eye and made no effort to adulterate the strong words he had just spoken with a gentle voice.

Cockburn unexpectedly laughed. "It took courage to say that, Captain. Your sentiments do not surprise me, but I fear you give your countrymen far too much credit. If they had been as bold and resolute a few hours ago as you are just now, we would not be having this talk. At any rate, I should very much like to hear your brother's opinion."

Pennywhistle responded directly. "I take the long view, Admiral, and think the burning of a capital city, no matter what the provocation, will look very dark in the history books. It would be far more consistent with Tartars and Cossacks than good-hearted Britons. No one knows who started the fire that consumed Moscow but the French certainly reaped every possible calumny as the invading party. I counsel against temporary satisfaction and advantage achieved at the expense of our reputation among forward-looking nations.

"The rest of the world looks to us for leadership. It is we who built the coalitions which drove the Corsican usurper into exile. It is we who will change the face of Europe for the better when the Congress of Vienna assembles in the autumn. We have outlawed slavery and will likely seek to ban the trade entirely at the Congress, but burning an enemy capital will discredit our efforts, show us not to be the civilizing influence we claim.

"We have built a commendable reputation for graciousness and magnanimity in victory. Lord Castlereagh has shown wise mercy toward our late Gallic foe and I think we might draw inspiration from his actions. Surely the mere occupation of the enemy capital, even for a few hours, will achieve the same long term result as its destruction!"

Pennywhistle willed himself to relax as he had grown far too emotional with the last few sentences. "I would ask for one more hour of beating the parley in the city proper before any action is taken." He doubted it would do much good but the Yankees were unpredictable and might have a last minute attack of common sense. "I know the Yankees have taxed our patience but patience is a virtue and it would be good to show the world that we value it over precipitate action."

General Ross nodded in silent agreement. The little group cantered forward and Capitol Hill came into view. Cockburn spoke. "Your arguments are reasonable, Mr. Pennywhistle, perhaps all too reasonable. I am willing to stay my hand for an hour and continue the parley, although I think the result will be same. If I felt the Americans more amenable to logic and reason I should be inclined to entirely forego any effort to teach them such a violent lesson. But they are not. We must do something to chastise them for York. To not do so, would send the message that we allow injustice to go unremarked and become soon forgotten.

"Strong action is in order but I am not without compassion. I do worry that the innocent will suffer and I am particularly concerned for Mrs. Madison's safety. I have heard fine things about the First Lady and it is wrong she should be imperiled because of her husband's foolishness. All manner of brigands, blackguards, and renegades appear when a city falls and I propose to give her a small escort under a flag of truce to see that she exits Washington safely." Cockburn smiled wryly. "I realize such a gesture will damage my reputation as a heartless monster."

"I agree about Mrs. Madison," said the ever diplomatic Ross. "Let me propose a compromise. Give the Yankees the additional hour to respond and then if we must act, spare all homes and businesses, respect the private property of civilians, and punish only the foolish government that brought about this cursed little war. We can establish a curfew and deal harshly with any looters, American or British and show we respect the rule of law. It would cast us in a good light and shame their government for so hastily abandoning its people. Burning only military installations and governmental buildings would certainly punish them for York, but would show that Britons value the lives civilians have worked hard to build. Would such a course be acceptable to you Admiral?"

Cockburn pondered. "My heart says otherwise, but your arguments for judicious punishment certainly serve the cause of reason. I would like one exception made: the offices of the *National Intelligencer*. They have printed scurrilous lies about me for the past year and I should like them stopped once and for all. Beyond that, I find your compromise acceptable. And," he said turning to Tracy, "it would be my honor to spare the Marine Barracks on account of the gallant conduct of you and your men."

"I thank you, Admiral," said Tracy. His neutral face betrayed just a hint of surprise that the American *bette noir* had a human side after all.

"Excellent," said Ross, "let us consider matters settled. I..." His horse suddenly stumbled and fell, pitching the general onto the hard packed dirt. He picked himself up and brushed off the dust. A second later Captain Rottley, his aide, clutched his chest and fell from his horse.

Damn! *thought Pennywhistle,* snipers at the worst possible time. They were not military. This was no well-staged ambush, merely opportunistic shooting by civilians who had not been anywhere near Bladensburg. He swiveled his head quickly and discerned the shots came from an open window on the third floor of an elegant Georgian residence. He doubted it was the owners.

"Let me handle it General!" Ross was startled by the marine's outburst, but Cockburn shouted "Go!"

Pennywhistle dug his spurs into the horse's flanks and she dashed ahead. He held on for dear life, wished he were a better rider. He was thunderstruck when Tracy galloped alongside.

"Don't worry," shouted Tracy, "not going to break parole. Figured I could lend a hand. Damn bushwhackers. Shot grazed my hat! Those folks shame real soldiers. I'll follow your lead."

Brotherly love indeed! It pleased him; his other brother would not have lifted a finger. The double door of the residence ahead had a high clearance and was slightly ajar. He guessed a wide hall and stairs lay immediately beyond. It could be done, and the surprise and momentum were welcome allies. He glanced at Tracy and pointed. Tracy smiled and nodded back.

Pennywhistle heard rather than saw a flurry of shots behind. They sounded a volley, maybe a hundred reports, and from the direction of the sound, had to have been fired from inside the Capitol. *Damn fools,* thought Pennywhistle. *Probably militia under no coherent control.* They had just fired the most 100 expensive shots in Washington's history. All considerations of mercy would be banished and Washington would burn.

Pennywhistle's mare bounded up the stone steps and crashed through the doors into a spacious hallway. He yanked violently back on the reins and brought her to a quick halt. In an elegant economy of motion, he freed himself from the saddle, grabbed his loaded weapon, and dashed up the stairs.

His brother followed a few seconds later. He still had his sidearm, no one had thought to relieve him of it, a .44 rifled pistol that was a smaller version of the American Long Rifle. He reached the third floor landing just after his brother disappeared into a room at the end of the hall.

Pennywhistle caught the two of them turning round. They were thin, scruffy scarecrows. One in dirty blue overalls had huge buck teeth that gave him the appearance of a malicious beaver. His mate sported a ratty little mustache that distracted attention from a weak chin. His small frame was overwhelmed by a large buff coat. Both looked and smelled as if they were complete strangers to bathing and were badly out of place in such a fine home.

Beaver had already re-loaded and Buff Coat was beginning the process of doing so. Both wore the expressions of deer suddenly hit by a bright light.

Bang! The report of Beaver's rifle sounded unnaturally loud in the small room. Pennywhistle felt something tug at his elbow, saw torn fabric, but knew he was untouched. He fired the Ferguson from waist level, knew he could not miss at three feet. The impact smashed beaver in the chest, lifted him as if he were made of straw, and swatted him harshly against the far wall. He crashed to the floor mewling and scrabbling with his fingers at the rapidly spreading crimson floret on his sternum. His chest heaved violently for a few seconds as scarlet bubbles dribbled from his mouth. A quarter-minute later, he lay still.

Buff Coat snarled a string of curses and slowly advanced against the marine. The American put down his gun and drew a huge, beautifully crafted knife. He looked like he was going to enjoy ripping Pennywhistle apart. The blade was uniquely American: a foot and a half long curving downward from the razor sharp tip into a quarter-circle. Later generations would call it a Bowie knife and it could be used for either hunting or skinning. Buff Coat waved it menacingly, if amateurishly. "I'm going to wrap your guts around your neck and strangle you with them, redcoat," the man sneered. His fetid breath reeked of cheap rum.

"Ha, ha, ha!" The marine's booming laughter filled the room. It was absurd, a superior knife wielded by a distinctly un-superior man. He could see his reaction angered the scarecrow. He felt calm and mostly curious about how short a time it would take to send this man to the next life.

The outcome was not in doubt. He had been trained in adolescence by his French tutor in *savate*, Parisian Street Fighting. His opponent was merely a bellicose amateur with more Dutch courage than sense, an intoxicated mouse facing a wily cat.

Buff Coat narrowed his eyes fiercely and again waved his blade. Pennywhistle pegged him as a barroom tough that had learned his trade in gambling dens and back alleys. The man screwed his face into what he obviously thought a terrifying expression but a second later it turned to puzzlement as the Englishman continued to smile. The scarecrow abruptly feinted left then shot his knife straight at the marine's belly.

Pennywhistle flashed ninety degrees to port at the last possible second, his supple body a slim memory of the fat target it had presented the instant before. He felt the *woosh* of air as the knife shot by. He grabbed the scarecrow's extended knife arm with both of his hands at the wrist and just below the elbow. He jerked the arm stiff, pulled it high, and brought the elbow down smartly on his raised and bent knee. The noise of breaking bone sounded like a tree branch shattering after a spring ice storm. The knife clattered to the floor. His anatomy training had taught him men were most vulnerable where they were jointed.

AAAAAAAGGGRRRRH! The man lurched forward in pain. Pennywhistle shot his two arms out, locked his fingers behind the man's neck, and pulled him violently down. Buff Coat's face smashed into his upraised knee like a wave on a rock. As the man's face ricocheted backwards, the marine punched his thumb forcefully into the tough's right eye, as if plunging it into a soft peach. He pushed hard and twisted sharply upward as it penetrated the brain. He released pressure a few seconds later and the corpse thudded into the floor.

Tracy saw his brother needed no help, but heard movement in an adjoining room and dashed into it. A very tall man in a floppy hat and bib and brace overalls turned to face him. Tracy did not hesitate, but leveled his pistol and fired. Just as his finger pulled the trigger, it struck him that the he was a she.

She dove at him in the last second and the shot caught her not in the chest but in the top of her left shoulder. She hit the floor and rolled slowly, clutching her shoulder. She did not moan or vomit, but let out a string of violent curses that would have been right at home in a waterfront tavern. She most certainly was not dead.

His brother dashed through the door thirty seconds later. "Tom, Tom? Is that you?" the woman wheezed as she looked up. "This sumbitch shot me." His brother looked appalled, but there was something else he could not place. Maybe it was just shock, but the English had very antique sensibilities about the fairer sex.

"You know this woman?" Tracy asked with a combination of shock and outrage. Something intellectual in him said he could not possibly, but something intuitive said he did, and well.

Pennywhistle ignored his question, bent down to the woman, and offered her water from his canteen. His look was tender and concerned, his voice strained and husky. He stroked her hair gently. "Christ, Sammie Jo, you little fool, why didn't you go home?"

"Sorry, Sugar Plum," she said quietly. "Couldn't let you go without a proper good bye. Knew if I followed you, the big brass would turn up sooner or later. I missed on purpose this time, just wanted to get your attention. I had the Admiral dead to rights. I wanted to finish him, really I did. But decided it came down to you or him. Something took control, an odd feeling that didn't make no sense. *Kill for your country and the Englishman will hate you forever*, says a little voice inside. Those other two fellars in the next room were just pikers compared to me. They weren't no good with rifles. I could see that direct. Just back alley buzzards who wanted to knock off a few English lords who were too stupid to take cover."

What the blazes did she mean by that, wondered Tracy. He sensed a very peculiar chemistry between his brother and the woman. Sammie Jo? His refined brother would *never* be associated with a crudely attired, countrified hoyden speaking in a backcountry dialect barely discernible as English. No, the possibility was simply too fantastic to credit!

But he had known plenty of women and recognized the warning signs. They were all there. His brother had been with her! He could not even speculate how it happened, but decided it was no more fantastic than him having an English brother serving America's most hated enemy. He could see the strange earnestness in his brother's face and decided he would help if he could.

Pennywhistle's left arm supported Sammie Jo's back as he had her sit up. The fingertips of his right hand remembered medical school in Edinburgh and gently and expertly probed her wound. There was minimal damage to the musculature. The bullet had passed clean through flesh and entirely missed bone. It was painful, but not terribly serious. There was surprisingly little blood. She would probably not be shooting anytime soon, which was a good thing, but she should make a full recovery. Maybe Providence had just done what he could not; taken her out of the fight once and for all.

A cold part of him shouted, leave her, you have done enough. But his heart would not listen and gently whispered he must get her to safety. He laid her down gently. "Give me a minute, Sammie Jo. I need to discuss this with...." he hesitated a few seconds, "my brother."

Sammie Jo's eyes widened. She suddenly sat up, fully alert. "Y' all said your brother?" she said loudly in surprise. She looked at Tracy. "Well, don't that beat all, he does look a heap like you. Not nearly so fine, though. How come he..."

Pennywhistle put up his hand in restraint. "I know; a thousand questions, Hawkeye, but save them for later. We need to see to your wound."

He rose and walked over to Tracy. Tracy also had a thousand questions, but was perceptive and compassionate enough to reduce things to one simple interrogative. He looked at Pennywhistle kindly. "Do you love her, Tom?"

Pennywhistle's brother was direct and cut to the heart of a matter whose answer he did not want to know. Part of him wanted to lash out in anger and focus on the rash indignity of the question; point Tracy anywhere but at the bedrock truth.

He made ready his mental carronades to unloose a broadside of imprecations at his brother, but all that came out was a quiet, "Yes I do, God forgive me." He frowned a second later. "Damned if I'll tell her though."

Tracy took his brother's hand gently and squeezed it. "No explanation is necessary, Tom. One question, do you trust the honor of United States Marine Corps?"

Pennywhistle smiled. "Based on your conduct in the last battle, and the steadfast actions of your men, it is one of the few things in America in which I do repose confidence! Have you a suggestion?"

"I can get her to the Marine Barracks at the Washington Navy Yard. She will have good medical care and plenty of protection. She is an American after all and marines believe in the defense of women and children. Although..." he looked her up and down, "she looks like she can take care of herself quite well."

He shoved the rest of his negative assessment to the back of his mind, not wishing to offend his newfound brother. He continued in a gentle voice, "The wound can be properly dressed and rioters, looters, and vagabonds will be kept out. I know Captain Tingey in command of the Yard. He will have to destroy it and the ships under construction, I am sure you understand, but certain things can be protected and the destruction will serve to keep away unwanted visitors. After that loud volley I heard on the way in, I assume Washington will be put to the torch but your Admiral said he would spare the Marine Barracks. Have I your assurance he will be as good as his word?"

Gratitude overwhelmed Pennywhistle and waves of untamed emotion crashed over the rock that was his trained rationality. Christ, he did care for Sammie Jo! "You may wager your life on it, John. He never gives his word idly. I know you Americans think him a monster, but he has a well-developed sense of chivalry and is always happy to honor the actions of brave men. You have your written parole, is that sufficient? I can pen some further protections if you like."

"Don't think that will be necessary, there's plenty of loyal men happy to protect a wounded woman if I give the word. Once in the Yard, we will be fine."

"Would gold help? There may be roadblocks and ruffians in time of chaos. I have a small purse here." He reached into his pocket and struggled to bring forth the purse. "Gold guineas and ...."

Tracy put his hand on Pennywhistle's arm. "Not necessary, but thanks, brother. I will manage things and keep her safe. I am not without resources and have always kept certain funds in a safe place. I will send word of her safety through the lines under a flag of truce. I will direct the message to Suter's Tavern, a well-known public house."

"Excellent," responded a greatly relieved Pennywhistle. "I have seen the place on my maps. We are agreed then. Keep her safe, please, John. She can be very headstrong."

"Yes," said Tracy straining hard to maintain a neutral face. He could not resist allowing the logical part of his nature a brief voice, "Although others might use a somewhat more earthy word than 'headstrong.'"

Sammie Jo wobbled to her feet, shook her head slowly, and planted her feet wide apart that she might remain standing.

She glowered at the two men like a Valkyrie told Valhalla was a joke. It annoyed her they had been discussing her as if she were not there. "Don't I have no say in the matter?"

Pennywhistle and Tracy looked at each other and then at her. "No!" They chorused in perfect unison.

"For once Sammie Jo," growled Pennywhistle with exasperation, "Don't pull a tartar! Please! Let someone," he searched for the words, "rescue you from your own stupidity. Just... shut up!"

She rocked back on her heels, and surprisingly said nothing, temporarily cowed by the Englishman's forceful directness.

Tracy smiled gently and moved close to Pennywhistle so that Sammie Jo could not hear. "Rest assured, I will make sure she receives the best care, although the much more difficult task lies ahead."

Pennywhistle looked puzzled. He was only focused on her immediate survival.

Tracy's face assumed a gentle cast. "You must decide exactly what to do and I do not envy you the task. Your heart and your honor tell you one thing, your common sense and your intellect counsel quite another. I wish you great good luck sorting things out." It felt strange to be having such a weighty conversation, but a part of him welcomed it, made him realize how lonely he had been most of his life. A sibling in moral perplexity made him feel connected to a family other than the brotherhood of the Corps. He had always felt an outsider and sensed his brother was a bit of one too.

Pennywhistle hated to admit his brother was right. He had no idea what to do. It was best if she were gone from his life yet that outcome distressed him. He shook his brother's hand to seal the bargain. His brother's palm felt warm and welcoming, although he decided it was mostly his imagination speaking.

"I will never forget this," said Pennywhistle. "I shall always be in your debt."

Tracy sighed inwardly and wondered if love was a blessing or a disease. His brother was definitely smitten with a woman that was likely the opposite of what his English family would want. "A brother and a friend can never be in debt."

CHAPTER SEVEN

The night sky over Baltimore formed an eerie burgundy dome straight out of Hades. A lurid band of scarlet marked the horizon and giant crimson-black thunderheads blotted out most of the stars. The pungent scent of wood smoke coruscated through the hot night air. Mary Pickersgill continued to sew the huge American flag that would soon fly over Fort McHenry but the bright heavens worried her. For a fire blazing forty miles away to illuminate the sky as it did meant something very bad had happened to Washington.

Daniel Parke riveted his attention on the blazing Capitol Building, a mile distant. Even at that remove, the fire's heat made him feel as if he were standing near a small oven. Fine particles of ash swirled in the air and gave the landscape a misty cast straight out of a Turner painting.

A growing crowd watched the spectacle with fascination; sighs, lamentations, and indefinable murmurings rose from the gathering at irregular intervals. The far from finished building consisted of two separate wings connected by a wooden walkway over which a dome would someday rise. Each wing was stately and impressive but also evidence of a much grander design yet to be realized and a solid belief that a great future lay ahead for America. Now that belief was literally being tested by fire.

He should ignore the spectacle and continue to Weir's home but he could not help himself. It was a disaster for the Republic, yet disasters have the power to compel unswerving attention.

A fusillade of shots had issued from the building two hours ago and a minute later it had been stormed by British soldiers and marines. There had been gunfire and a lot of shouting. The fires started half an hour later.

The blaze had grown slowly at first, small fires here and there, but they quickly merged into a general conflagration. The Senate Wing went first, followed fifteen minutes later by the Wing of the House of Representatives. The garish flames illuminated the entire city and he guessed they could be seen for miles.

The terrible display awed even the most jaded. The British were certainly thorough. People around him talked in hushed whispers, shook their heads, and looked skyward with a mixture of fear and disgust. He heard several lordly-looking gentlemen quietly curse President Madison. He understood their sentiments represented those of the crowd, but wondered why they had not bestirred themselves to have joined the fight at Bladensburg. That they were nowhere near the fight was obvious by the pristine state of their expensive clothing. But that was bitterness talking as a few extra men would have made no difference. An entirely different leadership might.

He looked at the President's House half a mile away and surveyed Pennsylvania Avenue. Two columns of redcoats marched down it in good order. It was obvious where they were headed. They encountered no opposition as most of the civilians had fled and those who remained wisely stayed indoors.

There only looked to be about 300 redcoats. There was also at least one company of blacks in British uniforms marching with the second column. That astounded and disgusted him because the British seemed determined to add insult to injury. He decided the rest of the British were probably encamped behind the Capitol. The British General at least did not seem to desire wholesale destruction since he could have turned all of his troops loose in a free-for-all of plunder and rapine.

Winder was such a fool. Even after the Bladensburg disaster, the Americans had far more troops in the vicinity. If they could be concentrated and put up some kind of a show, the British could probably be forced out by the sheer intimidation of numbers.

But the government had fled and Winder had as little backbone as he had judgment. Local superiority of numbers made no difference. It was superiority at point of contact that counted and the British clearly had that. Parke wished the American leaders had been half as good as Cockburn and Ross.

*****

Cockburn and Ross rode at the head of the column and talked quietly. "I am a little worried to be honest, Admiral. We are still badly outnumbered. I had expected Gordon's squadron would be here by now and give us the means for a speedy evacuation. The Americans may be fuddled and disorganized, but sooner or later they will recover and mount some action. We cannot stay here more than a day. I fear much hard marching lies ahead."

Cockburn's hooded eyes blazed satisfaction and confidence. "I appreciate your prudence, General, but I believe we have little to worry about from the Yankees. We should not tarry unnecessarily, but I don't think we need to rush things either. We must be thorough in the destruction of their government offices and leave nothing official standing.

"I thoroughly enjoyed the mock legislative session our men staged in their Senate before setting fire to the Capitol. It was good to see the men have a bit of sport. It serves the rascals right for their damned impudence in Canada. Our men piled up a huge amount of combustibles in the center of each capitol wing then added in powder from the Congreves. I am surprised the building is burning as slowly as it is. It appears of sturdier construction than anyone would have guessed.

"We definitely need to do something about Little Jemmy's Palace ahead" said Cockburn with a menacing glint in his eye. "I wonder where he is right now. I understand his wife was among the last to leave a few hours back. Strange his wife showed far more presence of mind than he. Perhaps she should be President." He laughed derisively.

"I am quite curious to see if its interior matches the pretentiousness of its exterior. It hardly seems fitting that the chief officer of a government that claims to eschew the trappings of royalty should live in such a splendid structure. But we can attend to it a bit later. I confess I am hungry. I see Suter's Tavern just yonder. I understand the food there is quite good. I think we should pay a visit."

"You are quite right," replied Ross. "I have not eaten since morning and some hot food would be in order. I wonder if they serve any of this fried chicken and sweet potato pie that is so much talked of by the locals. I heard an American prisoner mention something about grits. I should be curious to discover exactly what they are. Let us send a detachment ahead to secure Madison's residence from looters. I have orders to write for the morrow, but I should first like the pleasure of your company for supper."

"I intend to pay an extended visit to the Palace, General, perhaps take away a small souvenir to remind me and my heirs of this night. I have a ledger book I took from the Capitol. It is Mr. Madison's account book of 1810 with the government's expenditures listed in detail. It is a small item, but personal to Little Jemmy and so, is an amusing thing to possess. That I have it shows me how clearly their government has collapsed."

"I see some flames to the southeast. It looks like they have begun wrecking the Navy Yard. We need to send a detachment there."

Pennywhistle rode just behind Cockburn and heard most of the conversation. He urged his horse forward and drew alongside. He had his own reasons for wanting to get to the dockyard. It was time for some impertinence.

"Admiral, I wonder if you and the General would mind if I rode ahead to the Dockyard and did a little scouting to prepare the way for the detachment you will send. I should be very curious to see what ships their much vaunted Navy had under construction. They have been so bold trumpeting their successes." It seemed a reasonable explanation and much more acceptable than his highly personal one.

"That would be fine Mr. Pennywhistle," said Cockburn. Ross nodded his agreement. "But, I have a duty for you before that. I should like you to proceed to the President's Home first. I should like a representative of the Naval Arm present. I shall join you in an hour."

"Aye aye, Admiral, I will see to it." Pennywhistle said agreeably. He saluted Cockburn, turned and did the same to Ross. Ross and Cockburn made a good team. Joint outings of the Army and Navy were often plagued by professional jealousy but there was none here. Ross needed Cockburn's fire even as Cockburn's impetuosity needed Ross's restraint. Despite their differing outlooks, there was a true unity of command, a sharp contrast to the confusion on the American side.

Pennywhistle departed, admittedly curious to see what lay inside the President's Home. It looked impressive as he approached. It would probably not look that way by the time Cockburn finished with it.

*****

Manton's company rested four hours on the field before departing Bladensburg. He only left six wounded behind and they were turned over to a kindly group of Quakers under a flag of truce. His company bivouacked on the capitol grounds and was as awed by the spectacle of its destruction as everyone else was. Manton performed the usual tasks of roll call, equipment and ammunition checks. He made sure the walking-wounded received proper medical attention. He sensed his company would have only a night's respite before they marched again.

He was very pleased when a few of his men brought in a fully loaded sutler's wagon. Its owner had been just a little too slow because he had been a little too greedy. He had wanted to leave nothing behind and had instead lost everything. It was full of food as well as a variety of other military goods. Most dangerously, it was stuffed with bottles of fine wines, brandy, and whiskey.

Despite their hunger, his men would have aimed themselves straight at the liquor if he had not swiftly intervened. He thought the legendary affinity of British troops for alcohol was exaggerated, but tired, hungry troops, fresh from a smashing victory, usually wanted to celebrate with more exuberance than judgment.

Amidst cries, groans, and lamentations, he had most of the bottles smashed. Some troops threw themselves on the ground and tried to lap up the rapidly disappearing contents with their tongues. He was not without a heart. He ordered a number of bottles saved.

He called the company together and said each mess of six would receive three bottles of wine. They could distribute it as they wished. The bottles were small enough--500 milliliters as the new Metric system reckoned things--to ensure a little merriment, but no lasting damage. Besides, they had plenty of food for a change to slow the absorption of the alcohol. The men were overjoyed and gave three loud cheers.

He arranged things carefully with the Color Sergeant and the food was distributed equitably. The men had not eaten well for days, but tonight they would dine as well as the finest gentlemen. They rapidly consumed Smithfield hams, several bushels of apples and pears, fresh bread, and apple, peach, and blueberry pies. A good meal with plenty of fine wine was far preferable to jewels, silver, and gold.

While the men ate, he and two subalterns from the 4th's grenadier company helped themselves to clothing. The wagon contained four very fine white shirts of the softest cotton which were close to his size. He stripped off his own filthy shirt, impregnated with dust, grime, and powder residue, and tried on one of the new ones. It felt splendid.

He pawed through the rest of the clothing and found a pair of flint grey trousers. They featured silver buttons and the wool was luxurious. His own were patched from harsh service. He tried the new pair on and they were a good fit, although cut for rather more generous buttocks than his own. No matter, they would be all the more comfortable for marching. They were a slight departure from regulation cut and color, but not outlandishly so.

Ross, like his mentor Wellington, cared less about regulation clothing than keeping his men healthy and full of vigor. As long as they fought well, he did not care much if variegated colors and patterns appeared in their clothing. Besides, officers had always been allowed a certain eccentricity in their attire.

Manton's hessian boots were in rough shape from hard marching and he was pleased to discover the sutler carried a supply of jockey boots: favorites of American officers. He tried on five pair. The last one was not a great fit, but an acceptable one. The leather was of excellent quality and would probably see him through the remainder of the campaign. He laughed, a very nice outfitting all done at Yankee expense!

He sat down for a leisurely supper with the two other subalterns. They ate the same delicious fare as the men with the exception that they shared a very delightful bottle of French Brandy. It had been a very long day, but exhaustion retreated as they realized they had done something remarkable.

The two lieutenants speculated about what was next. Manton felt that Gordon's squadron on the Potomac would arrive soon and transport them back to the main fleet lying in the Patuxent. After some rest the next target would be selected, likely Baltimore. Cockburn might be hot for immediate action, but Ross would restrain him. The other lieutenants had seen far less service than Manton and argued boldly that Ross should press on directly to Baltimore. The Yankees were on the run and could be knocked out of the war with only a few hard blows.

He smiled and knew the brandy was fueling their overbold tongues. He told them he had served with Ross and that Ross knew better than to push a good thing too far. Ross, like the Duke, was a careful man and risking the entire army for a possibly Pyrrhic victory was not in his makeup. They acknowledged that he certainly knew Ross better than they, and in the end, reluctantly agreed prudence was probably a good thing.

Supper broke up at ten and the other officers retired. He stayed awake until midnight, mesmerized by the outlandish and terrible beauty of the burning capitol. It seemed rather a shame to burn such a fine building.

Washington and the surrounding District of Columbia numbered but 13,000 souls. It had been hacked out of a wilderness yet it followed a very well-conceived design. Major Pierre Charles L'Enfant who laid it out, had drawn inspiration from the Saint Louis development that had been specifically built to service the 20,000 folk living in Versailles Palace. Saint Louis Town was the first example of modern urban planning based on mathematical principles. The Americans clearly had a grand future envisioned for the city, judging by the spacious avenues that awaited future buildings. It was in fact often called, with some derision, *'the city of empty avenues.'*

As someone who had confounded the barriers of class through luck and ability, he had a certain sneaking affection for the American Experiment. He wondered if their new sort of Republic would actually work in the long term. It had certainly served them poorly in the last few days. Mr. Madison was the laughing-stock of both armies.

Yet he liked the idea of a society where a newly minted gentleman might fashion whatever destiny he chose. People here cared far less about lineage than his countrymen, although arrant snobbery was far from unknown in America. Merit was appreciated and welcomed. He talked with the accent of a gentleman at least. No one here would trouble himself to find out whether had always spoken thus.

He was undecided about his own future after the war. For now, he just wanted to survive the campaign. He had some money saved, but once the war ended and he sold his commission, he was not sure Britain was quite the place for his new family. America was a rough-and-tumble land and everything seemed to be perpetually in the midst of construction; not just buildings, but society, government, and manners. It might be a place to make his fortune, perhaps establish a dynasty of his own.

America was a tumultuous place, and he had only seen the more settled parts. The frontier was supposed be hugely perilous, but he was a professional who had faced down Napoleon's best. He could handle himself and feared little from violent amateurs whether they were pasty-faced ruffians or war-painted Indians.

He shook his head, realized he had gotten carried away. He needed sleep badly. It was altogether a fantastic idea that he considered becoming an American after he had just finished killing them. He lay down and thought of Juanita and the baby. He hoped it would be a son. He was fast asleep in less than a minute.

CHAPTER EIGHT

Pennywhistle entered the President's Mansion. It was a beautiful structure with a grayish-white exterior reflecting the legacy of Andrea Palladio. The interior did not disappoint and mirrored the classical influences of the Adam brothers of Scotland. Graceful white neoclassical columns rising from its herringbone parquet floors and painted pilasters featuring Roman motifs such as vines, urns, and vases put Pennywhistle in mind of Syon House outside London.

Gold, yellow, and blue were the dominant colors and were reflected in the draperies, swags, and ribbons, as well as the chair seats. Most of the mahogany furniture showed the influences of Hepplewhite and Sheraton, but the heavily gilded rococo design of several tables and chairs suggested they had been brought from France. He recalled that Mr. Madison's predecessors, Jefferson and Adams, had spent considerable time there and the First Lady was rumored to enjoy all things French, particularly in matters of fashion.

He was not the first to arrive. Other officers wandered about and he followed a major and a captain into what looked to be the principal state dining room. He estimated it to be eighty feet in length and close to forty in width. It was dominated by a large portrait of President Adams positioned over the mantel of an outsize marble fireplace. Two twelve-foot-tall ornate gold mirrors shimmered at the east and west ends of the room. A huge chandelier of gold and crystal hung from the elaborately decorated ceiling. It held at least a hundred brightly burning candles which brilliantly illuminated the room. The candles gave off almost no smoke and were likely made from spermaceti.

It was called the President's Palace with good reason since everything was of the finest quality. This magnificent room would have been at home in Versailles.

The twenty-foot-high ceiling featured plaster frieze American eagles clutching arrows in their right talons and olive branches in their left. Each eagle was surrounded by a laurel wreath punctuated at intervals with tobacco leaves and ears of maize. The eagle's heads were all inclined in the direction of the arrows: the reverse would certainly have been better considering what had just happened at Bladensburg!

The long Sheraton mahogany table in the center of the room was set for forty people. Bottles of well-iced wine stood ready on nearby sideboards. The blue china place settings, featuring silverware emblazoned with the American Eagle, were the most formal imaginable. The plates had all been recently heated.

"Looks like we spoiled their victory dinner," said the major.

"We certainly did," laughed his companion. "It would be a pity to let all this fine food and wine go to waste." He noticed Pennywhistle standing behind him. "Don't you agree, sir?"

Pennywhistle nodded. "It would indeed, sir, but this may just be Mrs. Madison's usual festive presentation. She has a great reputation as a hostess and is renowned for her splendid dinners and gracious hospitality. I understand the President is a very studious and reserved man and that she is quite the opposite: vivacious, charming, and able to put people of every station instantly at their ease."

"Sounds like she is far more personable than the positively grim little Jemmy," the captain chuckled. "I heard she is four inches taller than he. I wonder how far away he is right now? I understand he has a very fast horse."

The captain and major laughed uproariously. Pennywhistle found the occasion sad. He felt less a witness to a triumph than a member of a gang of scavengers pawing through a recently deceased grand dame's possessions.

As if by some hidden prearranged signal, officers began to sit down at the long table; first one group, then another and another. Each officer was permitted a manservant and they appeared as if by magic. The servants did as they were trained, decanted the wine and poured it for their officer. The President had a fine cellar with plenty of splendid clarets as well as some diverting white wines from the south of France. Not a glass remained empty for long. Conversation grew animated and loud.

Pennywhistle yielded to the inevitable despite his distaste for the proceedings. He was famished and there was no point in remaining so when plenty of good food was available. Maryland oysters on the half-shell were served first. They were followed by a rich and thick lobster soup: the tomatoes blended in gave it a very distinctive, creamy flavor. The roast trout with asparagus and potatoes that graced the table next was splendid dish. The fish, lighter in texture, flakier, and more piquant in taste than its British counterpart.

A side dish known as Hoppin' John signaled a change from the water's harvest--it was a tasty mixture of rice, black-eyed peas, onions, and bacon. The beef ragout that served as the main course possessed a delightful spiciness that was neither too bold nor too docile. Pennywhistle guessed it came from an astute mixing of red wine and several varieties of peppers, all thoughtfully interblended to make the chief virtues of both the grape and the fruit shine forth.

The meal seemed at variance with the usual blandness of American food, but he had heard the President employed an ex-French soldier as his chef and that likely accounted for it. Molasses cake and baked rice pudding rounded out the meal, thus somewhat different from the nuts, fruits, and cheese that usually concluded an English formal dinner. Someday he could tell people he dined at the President's House, although he was not sure if he would tell them with satisfaction or embarrassment.

Pennywhistle subdued a satisfied burp with a silk serviette. He leaned back in his chair and reveled in his stomach's complete contentment: something he had never expected to feel after a bloody battle fought under a terrible sun. Many officers beside him lit up cigars in satisfaction and poured hefty draughts of brandy into deep glasses. He did not smoke and drank little, but appreciated his fellow Britons were in a triumphal state requiring a healthy celebration.

Pennywhistle realized he had grown used to a ready supply of good food because America was a land of plenty. Everything here, from grains to meats to various fruits, seemed tastier than their European counterparts. Prosperous harvests appeared the usual, not the extraordinary. The Jonathans were an agreeable people in many ways, willing to ignore political allegiances if a buyer with hard coin could be found for their produce and poultry.

With the help of Sergeant Dale, a born deal maker, he had enjoyed several prime sirloin steaks during the campaign.

Dale said the steaks were unusually tender because the cattle here were fed on maize--corn the locals called it--rather than hay as in Europe. The steak was usually accompanied by new potatoes, carrots, and peas from nearby fields. Hot apple pie topped with cheddar cheese often concluded his feasts. Such meals were a welcome anodyne to the baking heat and had spoiled him for ship's food. He worried he was evolving into a voluptuary.

A Lieutenant of the 21st Fusiliers raised his glass high. "To peace with America," he paused slightly, "and war with Madison!" A wave of cheers echoed through the room. Some pounded the table with fists in agreement. Everyone drained his glass. Pennywhistle did not feel their exuberance but it seemed pointless to play the killjoy at the party and he emptied his glass as well. He had to admit Madison had superior taste in clarets.

"A toast to Dolley, the planner of this wonderful meal!" Everyone smiled and drank the toast. Chivalry was not dead and there was a genuine admiration for the pluck and courage she had shown. She had departed several hours before the British arrived, but the officers had talked to civilians who had seen her careful efforts devoted to rescuing valuables.

An odd feeling came over Pennywhistle. He had a good idea what was about to follow this strange but jolly dinner and thought one person might have prevented it.

Cockburn, for all of his ruthless ways, had a soft spot for charming and sincere ladies. Dolley Madison was certainly that. If she had stayed and begged Cockburn to spare the mansion, there was a good chance it would have been left intact. But of course, Cockburn had an extremely dark reputation thanks to the *National Intelligencer* and based on that, she had followed the wisest course and departed.

Several more toasts were offered and Pennywhistle decided to add one in recognition of his brother. "To the United States Marine Corps! Enemies by law, but by gallantry, brothers!" He saw outraged looks on the faces of two officers but each appeared to be a staff *éminence grise* who likely had done no fighting at Bladensburg. The ones with powder grime on their faces endorsed his toast heartily.

There was a stirring at the table and everyone suddenly rose to their feet. He glanced over his shoulder and saw Ross and Cockburn enter the room. Ross looked pensive, Cockburn very pleased.

Cockburn gestured with the palms of his hands. "Gentlemen," he said heartily, "Please be seated, and resume the meal. You have earned the right to enjoy yourselves. General Ross and I will help ourselves to some Madeira, make a brief inspection and return in half an hour to organize," his tone turned sepulchral, "the final arrangements." He poured glasses from the sideboard for himself, Ross and their aides, and then the lot of them departed on a tour.

Pennywhistle knew Cockburn well enough to understand he was not only enjoying his triumph, but was genuinely curious about the home and its late inhabitants as well. He drank his claret and decided to join Cockburn's entourage.

The family quarters of the mansion proved as impressive as the public rooms. It was clear Cockburn's party was not the first through. The President's personal items were mostly intact, but there was clear evidence others were missing. Officers were not immune to souvenir hunting, particularly when they had a chance to take them from the home of a foreign head of state.

One aide of Ross helped himself to all of Madison's spare white shirts. Another aide took the President's sword. A third made off with the President's portable medicine chest. A naval aide contented himself with the President's chapeau de bras even though it was far too small for his own head.

A fusilier captain found a cache of love letters from the President to Dolley. He read one aloud and laughed. The President sounded like a love besotted newlywed. The fusilier was about to pocket the lot, when Ross gave him a gravely disapproving look and said, "No, let intimate thoughts stay that way." Pennywhistle had heard he wrote often to his own wife and undoubtedly believed that such correspondence should never go further than the two principals. It was such routine acts of chivalry that inspired the men to aim for his high standards of conduct.

The exploring party returned to the dining room and Ross called everyone to attention. He gave his orders quietly. He clearly found them distasteful, unlike Cockburn who relished their outcome. "Gentleman, I want two companies inside on the double, with axes. I want the furniture and curtains chopped to bits. I want everything combustible stacked in a pile in this room. We will then withdraw outdoors and finish the business by the application of torches."

Admiral Cockburn stepped forward and addressed the assemblage. "I have detailed sailors under Lieutenant Pratt to attend to the second floor rooms so do not concern yourselves with those." He smiled malevolently. "Let us make it an entertaining contest between soldiers and sailors to see which accomplishes their task more efficiently."

The officers saluted and quietly set about their business. Sailors on the second floor liberally doused beds and bedding with oil before setting them alight. The two companies of the 21st pitched into their task with great gusto. They were usually threatened with grave penalties for destroying private property, now they were being ordered to do so.

They hacked apart curtains, tables, chairs, sideboards, desks, and bookcases in several ground floor rooms, then brought the debris to the dining room, and piled it all into a wide mound that nearly reached the ceiling. They added plenty of miscellaneous books, documents, and oil paintings to the pile.

Pennywhistle sadly realized some of the titles were quite rare, noting a first edition of *Candide*. Likely all of them belonged to Thomas Jefferson, a legendary bibliophile.

"Stop! Stop! Now!" Pennywhistle shouted frantically at a very startled private. The private had in his hands a very old, very heavy volume. He was tugging hard on both covers, trying to tear it in two. From his gleeful expression, he was having a fine old time engaging in wanton vandalism.

Pennywhistle recognized it for the treasure it was and he simply could not allow it to be destroyed as it was far more than a book. It was the finest monument ever created to the English Language.

"I'll take that, if you don't mind," said Pennywhistle authoritatively.

"As you wish, sir," said the private cynically. "Don't make no difference to me if an officer wants a souvenir." He handed the volume to Pennywhistle.

"Thank you, Private," said Pennywhistle matter-of-factly. "Please, resume your duties."

Pennywhistle gently caressed the heavy book, almost as he would a lover. He removed two long silk handkerchiefs from his pocket and covered the volume carefully, both to protect it and shield it from unappreciative eyes. Keeping it safe was not a just a passion but a sacred responsibility to future generations, one that transcended the parochial considerations of the present war.

Shakespeare's First Folio was the first authoritative assemblage of all of the Bard's plays, replacing earlier pirated and inaccurate versions of some of his works, while presenting twenty plays that had never been printed at all. Only 750 copies of the book had been printed because it had been an expensive thing to create. Its 630 pages were printed on the finest quality paper imported from France and had required an army of type setters.

Only 200 copies remained, all in the hands of wealthy men. The book had originally sold for 24 pounds, a considerable sum in 1623, but the bidding of avid collectors for this copy would likely start at around 10,000. Lesser men might think of the book as a nest egg, but Pennywhistle cared only about saving the art it contained. So many things were dying tonight, not just a President's palace but the ideals it stood for. It was wrong that Shakespeare's legacy should be among the casualties.

The process of readying Mr. Madison's home for destruction took an hour from start to finish.

When the pile of chopped-up goods was deemed finished, the soldiers sprinkled it with powder from some Congreves and then repaired to the outside of the building. Sailors lit fires on the second floor before dashing into the night. Long, lovely Palladian windows on the ground floor were smashed and legions of torches were lit and tossed inside. Redcoats watched the blaze grow with a mixture of uncertainty and fascination, like civilians watching the first firework at a celebration of the King's Birthday.

The companies then formed up in front of the house to watch the extended results of their handiwork. Within fifteen minutes, the President's mansion was a raging inferno that caused all of the witnesses to immediately recoil from the unexpected heat generated by very rapid combustion.

The sight awed Pennywhistle just as it did everyone else. He had seen plenty of destruction in his career, but he had never seen a palace burn. It impressed him fully as much as it bothered him. He felt as if he were watching the Vandals sacking Rome. He realized he was getting soft, thinking too much when he should not be thinking at all. The President's home was a casualty of war as were many more ordinary hallmarks of civilization. At least it was empty of people.

He understood the reasons for torching it, perhaps some military advantage could be derived, but he stood by his original recommendation. The British would forget it all soon enough, the Americans never would. Humiliation of an enemy brought only temporary satisfaction. He remembered the first part of one of the toasts, 'Peace with America.' Yes that was what he earnestly desired. Clearly others among his fellow officers felt the same way. It could not come soon enough.

The man of peace inside him was tired of the man of war. The man of peace said the President's Mansion represented a republic spawned from the Enlightenment ideals he so highly prized. It was not just a building of grand design and beauty; it was a symbol of something much greater, the triumph of reason over superstition and of the arts over armaments. Tonight war had overmastered peace, and destruction had trumped creation.

Stop it! He was being maudlin and sentimental. This was no time to play Hamlet. He forced his conscience into submission and listened to the voice of duty. He had to get to the dockyard before the naval detachment arrived. He had received no word yet from Tracy but perhaps the runner had gotten lost in the chaos of the night.

Boom! Boom! Boom! The noises startled him for a second, but he quickly realized the Americans had begun the process of wrecking the dockyard. They apparently intended to have it done before the British arrived to salvage anything. He wondered if Tracy had gotten Sammie Jo through. No, it would be quite impossible for his brother to fail. He had given him his word and they shared the same strength of will. Sammie Jo was safe for the time being.

A wave of fatigue swept over him. He had been through a tough battle and had not slept since yesterday. His Blancpain said it was just after midnight. He craved rest, if only for a few hours.

He mounted his horse and rode slowly up the deserted Pennsylvania Avenue. It was nearly as bright as day because of the flames and their heat added to the discomfort of the muggy night. He stopped briefly at Suter's but there was as yet no word from his brother.

He proceeded two blocks farther and found a deserted boarding house with a 'rooms to let' sign on the door. He dismounted, tethered the horse, and walked in. He shouted a few times to rouse the inhabitants, but no one answered.

He felt as dirty as a chimneysweep and scouted out a washbasin and a mirror. He found some soap, scrubbed his face thoroughly, and dried himself with a heavy cotton towel.

It lightened his mood until he looked in the mirror. The creature that stared back startled him.

He looked a survivor of the Black Death, his face old, lined, and haggard. There were dark circles under the usually energetic green eyes and his cheeks appeared hollow and ravaged. His lips were the grey of a corpse and the rough stubble on his cheeks and chin were remarkably like what was found on the faces of the poorest East End beggars.

His right index finger started jerking, as if in a spasm. He glared at it and willed it to stop. To his surprise, it did.

He angrily soaped his face and vigorously applied his straight razor. He looked again: better.

He trudged wearily up the stairs to the next floor and found a clean room with a bed. The sheets were fresh, crisp, and smelled of lemons. The mattress contained straw not feathers, but it was comfortable enough. He eased himself down on the bed, merely intending to get a feel for it. The cheap mattress felt soft and welcoming, a paradise of easy comfort. He lay his head gently on the pillow, thankful at least it was filled with feathers. He thought he could stay here forever.

He bestirred himself to sit up, take one last glance out the window. The obscenely red sky glowed even more brightly than it did an hour ago. The smell of smoke drifted in through the open windows. It was dramatic but other than the danger of stray sparks setting the building alight, he had little to worry about. Anyway, he was too tired to care. He plopped his head on the pillow. He thought of Sammie Jo's face briefly then drifted pleasantly into a deep sleep.

CHAPTER NINE

Tracy reached the Navy Yard around ten. He had narrowly avoided British patrols and stopped from time to time to make sure Sammie Jo drank plenty of water. She rode in front of him on the horse. She complained loudly for the first five minutes but then the pain caused her to lapse into surly silence. As the miles wound by, she drifted in and out of consciousness. He observed some slight suppuration from the dressing his brother had applied to the wound. He was worried. She looked very pale.

He had stopped at several buildings with signs indicating physicians, but they had all fled. There was still a semblance of order at the Yard, even though the laborious process of destruction had begun. He explained his parole and his female charge to the guards at the gate, who were most sympathetic.

With the help of a Marine lieutenant, he found an unused room in the Bachelor Officers Quarters of the Marine Barracks. He laid her gently on the bed and she quietly drifted into a deep sleep. Her breathing seemed steady and regular, but he realized he was no physician and needed to locate one quickly. The dressing at least displayed no more blood than it had been there the last time he checked.

No British had yet appeared at the dockyard, but he knew that it was just a matter of time. He posted two guards on the room. Normally he would not have worried, but the orderly process of destruction could transition easily into chaos. Chaos did peculiar things even to disciplined people and caused them to act with strange, self-destructive illogic. Sailors on sinking ships sometimes broke into the liquor stores and drank themselves insensate even as their ships foundered. Of course, sailors were not marines, but it was as well to make sure Sammie Jo was protected.

It took him an hour of searching and methodical questioning to locate a ship's surgeon. Several sailors had been injured when a cannon exploded they had been attempting to spike. Surgeon Ames had just performed two emergency amputations. Ames was sympathetic to his plight and agreed to come with him.

Ames administered two teaspoons of laudanum to Sammie Jo. Laudanum was either mixed with wine as a liquid or administered in balls to be sucked like lozenges. The powerful opiate was highly addictive but it was nevertheless used to subdue pains arising from maladies as varied as rheumatism and ringworm. Wounded soldiers given too much of it for too long found they could not live without it. Their affliction came to be known as "The Soldier's Disease."

Ames probed the wound, then cleaned and dressed it carefully with fresh linen. He pronounced it free of infection and said there was no damage to bone or musculature. He explained rest was the best medicine and counseled against moving her.

On the contrary, Tracy knew that it was imperative she be moved. He hoped Cockburn would honor his promise to spare the Marine Barracks but he could not be sure the Admiral would be as good as his word. He would need a safer place for Sammie Jo to convalesce. He was stretching the limits of his parole by helping his brother but Sammie Jo was an American and as such was part of the country he had taken an oath to protect. It was a rationalization, he knew, but he was willing to embrace it because he was caught up in the thoroughly novel sensation of having a brother.

He dispatched a marine corporal to Suter's Tavern under a flag of truce, but he would not know for some time if the man had gotten through. It probably did not matter. Pennywhistle was smitten and if he had to, he would move heaven and earth to reach the dockyard.

Once that obligation to his sibling was discharged, he faced some hard decisions. He was still a marine officer, you never really stopped being a marine until you died, but he was professionally neutered and out of the war. It troubled him, but he was a gentleman of honor and would scrupulously observe his parole. There was a faint possibility a cartel of exchange could be arranged with the British so he could return to duty, but that would not happen for many months.

For the first time in years, he had no idea what to do. He had been a lonely man but he had seldom had a free moment. Now he was merely lonely. His orderly existence had just been turned upside down, even as the city around him spiraled toward insanity. He could not picture himself as a gentleman farmer enjoying rural life. He had seen too much of the world and tasted too much danger to covet an existence bound to animals and agriculture.

He had decided Three Tuns Inn ten miles downriver would work as an improvised hospital. It was owned by a retired marine officer whose new wife had compelled him to settle down and adopt a more responsible existence. He owed Tracy a favor and was far too discreet to make any detailed inquiries.

He wished he could evacuate her immediately, before things became too unsettled at the dockyard, but necessarily had to wait for his brother's arrival to apprise him of his plans. There was always the possibility his brother had met with some misadventure, but he was far too clever to allow that. His brother was a survivor like himself.

He deeply questioned his newfound sibling's choice of woman, but it was not his place to tell him directly. His tongue was sometimes far too frank and he worked hard to shackle it. She was beautiful certainly, but completely wrong for an educated, refined man. Moreover, from the information he had coaxed from his brother it remained to be seen whether she was aggressively patriotic or simply murderous.

A union based upon passion might be fine in the short run, but as the years wore on and her body coarsened, her hair grayed, and her crow's feet deepened, her lack of polish would begin to grate. The conflict between reason and passion had created a dissonance in his brother's thinking that was obvious to anyone who paid attention, but he hoped reason would enjoy an eleventh-hour triumph.

For his own part, when he selected a wife he would make sure she was of the proper station and brought with her a suitable marriage portion. It was just as easy to love a wealthy woman as a poor one ...it merely took longer to find her.

He mopped Sammie Jo's brow as she slept, gently held her hand, and settled in to wait. *Boom! Boom!* He wondered what part of the yard had just been destroyed. He stood up and walked over to the window. There was a frenzy of activity below, men darting to and fro like fruit flies bred on coffee.

*****

Pennywhistle awoke with a start, one second fast asleep, the next fully awake. He checked his watch: 2:30 a.m. as expected. His internal clock had not failed him. The two hours of sleep had refreshed him. He looked out the window and realized little had changed. Well, several more buildings burned now, but he decided those fires were the result of renegade sparks rather than being set by men's hands. He washed his face and dressed.

He heard footsteps downstairs. Damn it, probably looters. It was to be expected. He was not in the mood to deal with them, but he did not have much choice. He picked up his Ferguson, cautiously opened the door, and slowly and carefully descended the steps.

An outlandishly dressed man appeared around the corner at the bottom of the stairs, his arms full of bread. He glanced up at Pennywhistle in complete shock, dropped his cargo, and froze. A few seconds later he slowly put his hands up, uncertain if it was expected but apparently wanting to play it safe.

Pennywhistle laughed. The man's elaborate costume was so wildly out of place that he could not help himself. No, it was not a man at all but a boy, probably not more than twelve with a frame slightly above five feet. The black lad sported a gigantic white turban far too big for his small head. It had gold cross belts in front and a large crescent where the belts crossed. It was topped off by a foot tall aqua-blue peacock feather. His crimson tunic was vaguely military, but the arms sported elaborate bullion piping, seldom seen on even officer's uniforms. He wore a curved oriental scimitar at his side, although the hint of rust round the hilt made him doubt that the owner had ever used it. His real weapon, if it would be called that, was strapped to his back. It was a trumpet.

The black lad was a bandsman. Elite units in both British and American armies featured black musicians dressed exotically as Turks. It was a fad that had started in Europe ten years before and every important army on the Continent had them.

The musicians were expensive to outfit and paid for out of a commander's private funds. They were always the best players of their respective instruments. Since a musician of ability might have numerous men of means bidding for his services, music furnished a good living to many free blacks. Most professions were closed to them but entertainers rose or fell on talent alone and race meant little.

"Don't shoot me, mister." The boy pleaded. "I don't mean no harm. I'm just hungry. Ain't had nothin' to eat since yesterday."

He had no reason to doubt the boy's sincerity. He looked closely and saw powder stains on the boy's baggy, Prussian-blue pantaloons. "Were you at Bladensburg?" He spoke gently.

"Yes sir, I was. My band played all through the fight. I think we done a lot of good. We just needed better generals." There was real pride in his voice. "I saw you there, sir. You towered above everybody else. Some of our boys said 'why can't our officers fight like that?'"

"What unit where you with?"

"5th Baltimore City Regiment."

It made sense. The regiment was a gentleman's outfit with a lot of money to spend. Its officers were smartly turned out and its private soldiers sported impressive attire as well. Unlike many militia units, they had fought well.

"What happened to your regiment?"

"I'm not really sure, sir. There was a lot of shouting and bullets were flying everywhere. An officer galloped up on horseback and yelled something to our commander and then everything just fell apart. Everyone started to run. I saw redcoats coming up the hill with bayonets and I ran too." The boy's voice quivered over the last few words. He fought it, but started to sob gently.

Pennywhistle understood. Battle was sheer chaos and utterly confusing. Most survivors of a first fight had no idea of what really happened and carried away only fleeting impressions and raw emotions. It was hard enough on a man and far worse for a boy, particularly when the boy had to endure fire but had no way to fire back. The lad was clearly worried his courage had been wanting. Pennywhistle noted that he still had his instrument, a sign that he had not panicked. Panicked men generally discarded their weapons to run faster. A trumpet that could inspire men to stand firm was a weapon of a kind. "Have you a name, lad?" He inquired kindly.

"Rufus, sir. Rufus Randall." He choked out the words, but arrested his crying.

"I am glad to know you, Rufus Randall. I am Captain Pennywhistle of the Royal Marines. Despite the wild rumors you have probably heard, we British are not monsters. Please be at ease, I mean you no harm. So, you don't know what has become of your regiment? Have you a place to go?"

The boy wiped the tears from his eyes and pulled himself erect. "I have no idea where they are, sir. Everyone scattered when we reached Washington City. My uncle was a free man who ran most things for Miss Sally, the old woman who owns this boarding house. I came here hoping to find him. And I did find him, out back. Dead, shot right through the head. Why would anyone do that, sir? He never caused anyone any harm." The boy began to sob quietly again. "I ain't got no one else."

It was likely scavengers. His uncle had probably tried to reason with them and got shot for his trouble. He had seen many orphans of war, but this boy's plight touched his heart. Little Molly, caught up in a former battle, had too, and his foolish arrogance had indirectly caused her death. Maybe he could get it right this time. The boy was just so damn earnest! He made his decision instantly.

"It's definitely not safe out there, Rufus. All manner of brigands are about tonight. My manservant died a few months back and I have not a chance to replace him. Would you be interested in the position, just for the next few days, until we can sort things out? I will pay you a shilling....." He tried to remember American coinage. "I will pay you a dime a day as wages. I promise you will not have to do anything that would harm your countrymen. There might be danger. I would ask you entertain my men from time to time with your trumpet. Do you know any British tunes?"

Rufus looked at him with a puzzled look that said he could not credit his ears.

"I am quite serious, Rufus. You are not dreaming, but I do require an immediate answ..."

"Yes, yes, yes, I will do it, sir." The boy's face split into a toothy grin, half surprise and half excitement. "And you won't be sorry, sir. I give you good service. I know lots of British tunes. Everybody say ain't no tune I don't know." He reached behind him, enthusiastically brought the trumpet to his lips, and began to play *Britons Strike Home*.

He was good--*remarkably* good. If the Archangel Gabriel had a human counterpart, it was Rufus. He was easily the equal of the best musicians who entertained at the Vauxhall and Ranelagh Pleasure Gardens in London. He could have listened for hours, but needed to get moving. He motioned for Rufus to stop after four minutes. Rufus looked worried. "You misunderstand, Rufus. You are very talented but I have duties that require my immediate departure. I have a horse outside and you can ride behind me. Gather your gear and follow me."

The two of them walked out into the smoky, red night. The horse was still there, thank goodness. He had been careless, but his luck had held and no vagabond had stolen her. The mare looked as if she had enjoyed her rest. He would push her a little harder and see if he could make the dockyard within the hour. Other than a few red-coated officers exploring about because of sheer curiosity, the fires had largely emptied the streets.

Rufus recovered quickly from his earlier discomfiture and seemed to treat the whole thing as one grand adventure. Washington aflame was a sight never to be forgotten.

He made his first port call at Suter's Tavern, two blocks away. To his surprise, a United States Marine stood outside, chatting pleasantly with two British privates from the 4th Foot. Once battle ceased, English and American soldiers usually forgot political differences and got along well, warrior-to-warrior. Similarities of military life and a common language far outweighed their differences.

The US Marine spotted Pennywhistle out of the corner of his eye. He abruptly ceased talking, executed a smart about turn, and snapped to parade-ground-perfect attention. Pennywhistle rode up next to him. A second later, the two British privates also snapped to attention. Well, perhaps 'snapped' was the wrong word. Their evolutions were more leisurely, likely the effect of liberal quantities of alcohol.

The marine saluted perfectly. "I am here under a flag of truce with a message for Captain Thomas Pennywhistle. Would you be that gentleman, sir?" His tone was crisp, his voice respectful, and his words un-slurred. Unlike his two British compatriots, he had remained steadfastly sober.

"I am indeed, Corporal. I trust you bear a message from Captain John Tracy of the United States Marine Corps."

"Yes I do, Captain. I am instructed to convey my captain's regards and inform you that your friend has received proper medical examination and is doing well. Your presence at the dockyard is urgently requested."

Pennywhistle nodded. "Thank you, Corporal. You have done well. You look to have seen action recently... Bladensburg?"

The marine looked embarrassed but his voice remained steady. "I was there, sir."

"A great and a terrible day," said Pennywhistle thoughtfully, "The conduct of you and your comrades brought great honor to your nation even if the results went against you."

Pennywhistle reached in his jacket and tossed the man a silver half-crown. The private instinctively caught it in flight but his face looked puzzled.

"I admire gallantry wherever it is found, Corporal. Please go inside and have a whet at my expense. You have earned it."

The marine smiled, then frowned. "Thank you, sir, but I must decline since I was instructed to return with a reply."

"I think I can speak for Captain Tracy when I say you have done more than your duty and are entitled to some refreshment before you return to the dockyard. I will give my reply to Captain Tracy personally. Consider yourself ordered to enjoy a round at the inn."

The marine broke into a broad smile. "Very good, sir. Most understanding, sir."

Pennywhistle smiled back at him and the American's two inebriated new friends slapped him on the back and merrily led him inside.

Pennywhistle put the mare into a fast trot and set out for the dockyard. He passed the President's Mansion after five minutes. It burned vigorously, but the walls were largely intact. He was both eager to get to the dockyard and dreading it. He would enter under a flag of truce, but there was nothing that would prevent him using his eyes and ears to observe and satisfy his curiosity. He was however, compelled to keep those observations to himself as part of the conditions of the flag of truce.

His heart and personal concerns were steadily eroding the sense of duty that had always been his lodestar. His mission was to make sure the expeditionary force got back safely to the ships at Bartram's Cove. Nothing could be allowed to impede those efforts. Since Gordon's ships had not arrived, having been held up by tricky shoals in the Potomac, the army would have to move by land.

He began formulating a plan. It would require improvising a fortress involving a place where the British could regroup after hard marching in this obscene heat. It would have to stop any Yankee pursuit cold. Mount Prosperity Plantation came to mind; the estate of one Daniel Parke, an American militia colonel, would serve perfectly. He had billeted his men there earlier in the campaign. He had noted the ravines and hedges presented excellent defensive possibilities and had filed the information away for later use.

He would also need the assistance of some of the Colonial Marines who had been left behind to guard the supply depot at Bartram's cove outside of Benedict. He cudgeled his brain for the order of battle at Benedict. Ah yes, one company of Colonial Marines was available. A hundred and twenty determined, trained, and battle-blooded black men would strike great fear into amateurish white militia called upon to oppose them. He would need light, portable ordinance as well.

Most of all, he would need the full assistance of his own ingenuity to pluck much from little in a very short time. He had some infernal weapons in mind that would push the limits of respectable warfare. If his plan was to work, messengers on fast horses would have to be dispatched before dawn.

He would pay Tracy to take Sammie Jo to some sanctuary. He would never have to make a real decision about his feelings for her. They would part ways, now and forever. She would return to her former life and he would return to England. It was better thus.

War unbalanced your judgment on matters of the heart. He had been fighting twelve years and had forgotten what the absence of conflict was like. It made far more sense to reconnect with the relaxed joys of peace and make a decision about adding a woman to his life after a leisurely, relaxed, and thoroughly pleasurable exploration of possible candidates. A pity his brother no longer lived to arrange suitable meetings. He had always disdained his brother's counsel on women but at least it was based upon cool, measured reason which was so different from the mad, foolish illogic Sammie Jo stirred in him.

Discovering the right mate should be like a Royal Society expedition, well organized, thoughtfully planned, and completely systematic. His disciplined mind was skeptical of trusting raw emotion as the pilot of his future.

The problem was Sammie Jo. She was not an abstract variable of the kind he liked, but a very sensual woman. Seeing her again would probably result in the complete defenestration of well-ordered thinking. The powerful physical attraction between them had overmastered his reason in their previous encounters and there was no logical reason to expect a change. Her injured condition would likely stir his chivalric instincts. He would have little defense unless he could come up with an alternative.

Mount Prosperity Plantation, the key to his plan, lay within a few miles of where Sammie Jo said her home was. Her brothers had gone off to war, but perhaps like other demoralized militia they had returned home. Let her plague her own family.

His plans grew more detailed with each passing moment. He based them on a few chance remarks that a worried Ross had made. The Americans were inept but they were also angry. America did not lack for patriotism and Ross had been told by exploring officers that plenty of Americans were coming forward in the crisis to serve the Stars and Stripes. Ross had been badly outnumbered at the start of the campaign and things would grow worse with each passing day. Even great professionalism could be destroyed by amateurs if the numbers were great enough.

Ross needed to march away quickly; a well-fortified bastion of defense a day-and-half march away would be a godsend. Pennywhistle's subconscious calculated variables as he rode, moving from the general to the particular. He formulated a mental checklist of what he would need and where he could get it: supplies, entrenchments, artillery, and man power. He needed to make a local version of the Lines of Torres Vedras outside Lisbon.

His design depended on accurate, up-to-date intelligence. Gabriel likely had that information. The underground network of slaves maintained a constant surreptitious flow of communication among the plantations and would be happy to assist Gabriel. They would give Pennywhistle access to hundreds of reliable eyes and ears and he would be notified of any major movement long before it arrived.

He would need a boat. The 30-foot Brenton Yawl he had used earlier in the campaign was perfect. A detachment of Marines was necessary and his Special Reconnaissance Group had the skills, experience, and initiative upon which he could absolutely depend. They would have to be informed immediately.

He looked at the innocent Rufus. A twisted idea sprang into his mind, one that could only erupt from a debased nature used to exploiting the lowest impulses of men. He thought back to the talk with his brother about black men. His brother was more amenable to change than the majority of his countrymen, but he had deduced that Southerners hated the idea of black men armed with guns above all things. The splenetic reaction to black Colonial Marines entering Washington had confirmed his surmise. American prejudice against blacks could be made to work in his favor.

Rather than employ Colonial Marines in a static defense, he could use them actively as a lure. They could entice American forces toward the plantation and compel them to approach along pathways of his choosing. He might be outnumbered, but he could make the Americans fight his battle, not theirs. It was similar to something he had learned in medical school: draw pus toward a boil and then lance the boil.

His planned use of the Colonial Marines would be risky. They would be outnumbered, although with the cooperation of the slave network the odds against them could be reduced. He sternly reminded himself his overriding duty was to secure victory for the Crown. Personal concerns over the welfare of men recently freed from bondage had no proper place in his calculations. These men had accepted the King's shilling voluntarily and had not signed up to be bandbox soldiers.

His humanity protested against treating men as mere chess pieces, but his animal nature knew the hard truth. His soul had to sleep that his ruthlessness might awake.

He felt a surge of confidence in his plans, bordering on arrogance. He knew he could outthink anyone in the Yankee command and it gratified his ego. He had no false humility about his talents but arrogance was dangerous and set you up for a fall. His arrogance had killed the beautiful innocent Molly. She had been a charming blonde girl of but seven years and the embodiment of untarnished goodness and hope.

He resigned himself to committing more sins in the service of the King and finally decided that a few more misdeeds would probably do nothing to increase the blackness of his soul.

He dug his spurs into the side of the horse and pushed her into a gallop. Rufus manfully hung on as the boy had an even more amateurish seat than he. Racing along dark, unknown streets was usually not prudent, but the illumination of the fire helped him see far more than was usually possible.

*****

Daniel Parke woke up at almost the same moment. He had found his friend's home deserted and let himself in. His friend had left in a hurry. He was both sad and pleased. He wanted someone to talk to, wanted to deliver some kind of apologia for the conduct of the American Army yesterday. He needed to tell someone he had at least tried. At the same time, he knew he could barely control his raw emotions and did not want to break down in front of a friend.

He looked at the clock and realized he had been sound asleep for six hours. He fixed himself a cold supper from items in the pantry, poured himself an ample glass of beer, and considered his options. There really was only one choice that made sense: return home to Mount Prosperity and sort things out there. He had no idea where Winder and the rump of the American forces were, although he heard a rumor they were just beyond the Georgetown Heights.

In the stable out back there was one tan horse. It was old and cranky, but he managed to get a saddle on the beast. Mounting up, he trotted up the Georgetown Pike intending to skirt the field of Bladensburg. Care would be needed to avoid British patrols and he had a long ride ahead of him. His entire focus now, just to go home.

CHAPTER TEN

Lightning illuminated the red sky in spectacular split-second spurts. Some bolts collided violently with the ground, while others crashed into roofs and set them afire. Peels of booming thunder, louder than a fleet naval battle, followed seconds later. Obscenely bright flashes reflected evilly off low, glowering clouds, and convinced pious Americans that God was very angry at the British. The wind kicked up violently and the rain arrived in driving sheets.

The suddenness and violence of the storm caught Cockburn unaware. He and his three aides had been prowling the city on horseback, observing the destruction firsthand. Cockburn wondered if such violent, infernal storms were common to America. He took one last look at the President's Mansion, shook his head in disgust, and spurred his mount into a gallop. His aides followed. It was high time to seek shelter.

Cockburn swore under his breath. The powerful sheets of rain doused most of the fires in just a few minutes. The blaze at the President's Mansion sputtered out, and the one at the nearby Treasury Building died a short time later. He glanced ahead toward Capitol Hill and saw not flames, but rising plumes of steam. If Cockburn had believed in such things, he would almost have called the storm providential. What the American's could not do, nature had done for them.

The damage to the President's Home and the Capitol was severe, but the outer walls of both stood strong and defiant. He hated to admit it, but the damage could be repaired. He could go back later and order the blazes restarted, but that would be risky. Ross wanted the army to evacuate the city before nightfall today.

Ross had warned Cockburn that even with the losses at Bladensburg, the Yankees still had more than double their numbers. After the shock of seeing their capital in flames, numbers of indignant militia would turn out and make the odds closer to three-to-one. He emphasized that it was almost a miracle they had captured the enemy capital with such small numbers and that it was unwise to push their luck. It was far better to accept a substantial if incomplete victory than linger about and risk disaster. Speed was of the essence now.

Just as Cockburn reached the Patent Office, the rain suddenly stopped. It was yet another example of the freakish weather that had plagued the campaign from the start. He noticed a band of soldiers brandishing torches. A group of well-dressed women was arguing with a captain of the 21st Foot who appeared to be in charge. Cockburn brought his horse to a halt and dismounted next to the officer. "What seems to be the problem here, Captain?"

Before he could open his mouth to reply, a well-dressed older matron intervened. "Sir, these soldiers mean to burn the Patent Office, but there are many models inside that belong to civilians. My husband's is among them. Destroying the Office will cause great hurt to a great many private citizens who have applied for patents. Please, I beg of you, tell these men to put away their torches."

Cockburn stroked his chin in thought. "Your request is not unreasonable, madam," he said with great courtesy, "And we British have no interest in harming resourceful men blessed with mechanical genius. I shall grant your wish." He bowed gallantly then turned to the officer of the 21st. "Extinguish your torches, Captain. You won't be needing them."

The well-dressed woman burst into a broad smile, as did the five women at her side. "I thank you sir, for your consideration and my countrymen will not soon forget your kindness. It is a great pity that ogre Cockburn is not so fine a man as you. Might I have your name sir, so that others might know of your magnanimity?"

Cockburn smiled wryly. "Why madam, I *am* the Ogre Cockburn." He purposely pronounced his name in the American fashion: 'COCK BURN'.

The ladies looked as if as they had all been lashed with a cat-o-nine tails. One started to swoon.

Cockburn spoke with unfeigned warmth. "I assure you ladies, I mean you no harm. You are far safer under my protection than that of your President, Little Jemmy."

Cockburn mounted his horse and graciously tipped his hat to the stunned ladies. He and his party cantered on for ten minutes until they reached the shelter of Suter's Tavern. He could stay for a few days if given his head, dare the Yankees to do what they might, and make sure all of the planned destruction was carried out as planned. But Ross had the last word on land and he had pushed the man all he dared. Any further prodding would come across as importunate and might ruin the excellent relationship they had established.

At least he had destroyed the presses of the *National Intelligencer*. He made sure of the typeset first, starting with the letter "C". Mr. Josey Gales, the editor, would print no more lies about him. It was a small thing, but it greatly pleased him.

*****

The usually placid Anacostia was in a proper fury. The sixteen-foot jolly boat pitched violently and yawed madly each time a wave slammed into her hull and sought to rip off her mooring rope. The pounding waves made things difficult for Pennywhistle and Tracy. They had to wait a full hour after Pennywhistle's arrival for the storm to abate sufficiently to even begin the attempt.

At least, the explosions in the yard had stopped. The fury of man had stepped aside out of respect for the fury of nature. Sensible men had all taken shelter and the path to the quay was deserted. Pennywhistle and Tracy seized the moment to carry Sammie Jo to the boat. Rufus did not understand exactly what was happening, but tried to help as well. They had fashioned a crude stretcher from two muskets and canvas. It was necessarily slower than one of them just carrying her over his shoulder, but both agreed this was a safer and more comfortable method of transport.

They laid her out, mercifully unconscious thanks to the laudanum, and carefully covered her with tarpaulin. There was water, salt pork, and ships biscuit in a small storage locker. Pennywhistle and Tracy agreed it should be more than sufficient for the short, but arduous journey ahead. Tracy laid his rifle and two muskets aboard, all carefully wrapped in canvas to shield them from the elements. Pennywhistle checked to make sure the shot locker contained plenty of dry powder and ammunition.

They examined the mast and sail together. It would be dangerous to employ sail in this vicious weather, but Tracy assured Pennywhistle he could manage things and it would certainly speed their progress.

"It's utter madness being out on a night like this," shouted Pennywhistle, "you know that, don't you?"

Tracy had to yell to be heard above the shrieking wind. "It certainly is. I could not have asked for better weather! The river will be clear of traffic and every scout on either shore will have retired indoors. The storm will blow itself out in short order. I know the route and the currents."

"Thank you," said Pennywhistle gratefully. "One way or another, I will meet you at the Three Tuns before midnight tomorrow. Tell the owner he will be amply compensated for the brief use of his facilities. I will instruct my men to practice the utmost restraint."

"I understand, Tom. For now, I am a soldier without a war and I am glad to help one of my countrymen, particularly one so comely and so...uh...strong-willed. Are you quite sure you can get Ross and Cockburn to agree to all of this? You are gambling a lot that they will fall in with your plans."

"Agreed, but I enjoy Cockburn's confidence and he has a very high," Pennywhistle laughed, "and misplaced opinion of my odd talents. He knows I will have thought things through, even if Sammie Jo appears nowhere in the story he will hear. He has had to push Ross to get him here and Ross will be glad of a contingency plan, a bolt hole if things start to go bad."

"How long will you have to get things ready?" Tracy yelled between howling blasts of spray.

"I'd guess forty-eight hours, maybe a little more. It's a deuced short time to get a lot done."

"Will Gordon cooperate? My story will sound like fantastical fiction."

"Don't forget John, he is my cousin. We served together and I was best man at his wedding. Your resemblance to me will argue your case powerfully as will the uniform you wear so honorably." He handed Tracy a map case. "I have written things out in detail on the document inside. Emphasize I need the Brenton Yawl. He will be surprised of course, but you will find he is an active campaigner who likes designs of bold initiative. I know he is disappointed that Ross has beaten him to Washington. He will have seen the fires and will be glad of a report of the situation here. Again, you have my thanks. This would not be possible without you."

"I won't deny I feel a conflict," said Tracy, "but since I am forbidden from fighting I prefer to make myself useful assisting a brother. I am a non-combatant now, but far from a civilian. What I am doing will change the course of the war not at all but might possibly spare a few lives. You know of course, if bullets begin flying, I shall have to retire, much as that runs counter to my nature and training."

He nodded and handed Tracy a heavy purse. Tracy looked to protest, but Pennywhistle waved a hand and shook his head. "Take it. There may be expenses," said Pennywhistle sharply. "I can hardly ask you to pay for things that in no way serve your cause."

Tracy sighed and accepted the purse. "You said you wanted the Brenton Yawl." He spoke with curiosity. "I know of most types of small boats but I have never heard of that particular craft. What is that exactly?"

"A craft designed for coastal raiding by a captain who was well practiced in the art, thirty feet long, fast, sleek, maneuvers well, and is especially good in shallow water. Carries up to 35 men and also packs a nasty punch. 12-pound carronade on runners stowed in the floorboards amidships. There is one assigned to each squadron."

Tracy looked deep into his brother's eyes and stepped into normal whispering distance, although he still had to shout loudly above the raging winds. "Tom, I want to let you know you are making the right decision about the girl, difficult though it is. I will see her home. I will make every effort to find her brothers. Failing that, I will leave her some coin from my own purse. She strikes me as pretty self-sufficient. She will never go hungry."

Pennywhistle looked pleased then chagrined. "Thank you for that, but I am taking the coward's way out, John. I am not sure I would be able to cast her out if she was conscious and talking. She summons madness in me. I fear the sound of her voice would unman my resolve and cause me to adopt a hasty, foolish course of action."

Tracy's expression turned unexpectedly harsh. The strangely innocent look on his brother's face banished the little tact he had. "You are doing the right thing, my brother, putting your duty first. You are a soldier Tom, first, last, and always. I entreat you to be one for just a little bit longer. You barely know this woman. You would have been well within your rights to have hanged her in the first place. I would have without hesitation. I will have no truck with bushwhackers.

"You spare her and how does she answer your kindness? She returns and nearly kills your commanding officer! And you would consider a lifetime with her? Think man! Think! Be a cold-blooded rationalist just a bit longer! She belongs out in the woods with her murderous instincts, not in your world of polite talk, gentle women, and polished manners. I think you have some charitable urge to reform her, to make her into a lady. While I appreciate the generosity of sentiment, I think it is the height of folly.

"Has it occurred to you that if she had not been deeply flawed you would never have even met her? Sometimes it's not the polished ladies but the quirky birds and odd ducks that command our attention. You are bewitched by her beauty and the sheer novelty of her. You take pride in your logic, but Sammie Jo is testing your devotion to it."

Tracy's voice turned low and cynical. "So you slipped from your honorable pedestal and enjoyed a round of bump-and-tickle. So what? She is nothing but a bumpkin bitch that showed you a good time! She gave you a chance to purge some of the tensions of command and you sensibly decided to not be a monk. What officer wouldn't have jumped at what she offered?

"You joined with her under extraordinary circumstances that perhaps only veterans would understand. Don't think a few minutes passion is an invitation to spend a life together. A wooden cup should never be mistaken for a silver chalice.

"Put it down to the insanity of war, just a wartime firework that had a brief flash in the sky then faded away as it was meant to. Forgive me, but I heard real sorrow in your voice when you mentioned the mother of your stepsons. You said you missed her greatly. My intuition says she was...well... *the one*. I would ask you, does Sammie Jo compare in any way?"

"No," Pennywhistle said in voice choked with emotion, "No, she does not. Carlotta had my heart and I had no doubts. The fact that I cannot even make up my mind about this woman speaks volumes. I thank you for pointing that out." He shook his brother's hand. "You better get going. I will see you later tonight."

"Count on it, Tom," said Tracy. He stepped into the boat and sliced the mooring rope in half with his cutlass. He hoisted the mast and ran up the sail. The screaming, angry wind threatened to tear the sail from the halyard, but he braced the driver round to the proper angle and it drew strongly. The boat raced off into the night.

Chapter Eleven

Parke spotted the British patrol well before they saw him. He guided the horse into a small alley and waited patiently. Howling winds had nearly blown him from his horse twice during the three miles already covered. The wind slackened a bit as dawn approached but the going would be slow until the storm stopped. At least the lack of traffic aided his journey. There was another thirty miles to cover before stopping and it was uncertain whether the old mare was up to it.

The patrol continued past the alley. He pulled his soggy slouch hat down lower to protect his face against the constant pelting of the rain, and after waiting a full five minutes, gently put the spurs to the mare. She moved ahead at a fast trot, but he had to be careful to conserve her energy. This route passed the steaming ruins of the President's House and surprisingly the walls were still intact. He had originally taken the Georgetown Pike, seeking to avoid the city, but changed his mind when he realized that route would require him to cross the field of Bladensburg again. He had no wish to see stinking corpses. That route also directly paralleled the main British supply line.

The best would be to strike directly south, heading toward Fort Washington, eight miles ahead. There was a back road from there directly to Mount Prosperity.

He rode on another ten blocks and veered left, keeping to the back streets. The storm gradually dissipated. It was mostly a fine, gentle mist now. He passed the Navy Yard and continued on following the Anacostia.

OOOOMPPPHHH! A giant hand cuffed him on the back of the shoulder and violently drove the breath from him. He slumped forward, but righted himself a few seconds later. He instinctively put his hand to his shoulder and felt a small hole in the fabric of his duster. He withdrew his hand and stared stupidly at it. It was covered in blood.

"Get him," yelled a British sergeant as he lowered his smoking musket. Three soldiers dashed toward Parke. Why had they shot at him? Had they nothing better to do? Then he realized no other civilians were about at this early hour and they probably thought he was some kind of spy.

The pain was minimal and when he touched the wound again, there was not much blood. It was unpleasant but far from incapacitating. He swiveled in the seat and saw the threat. The closest soldier was less than half a block away. Strangely, he did not spur the mare into a gallop, but instead waited.

The rush of blood in his veins fueled anger rather than panic. He was tired of running, tired of being a victim, tired of never having the chance to strike back. He had a large horse pistol in a holster on the left side of the saddle. The heavy .69 caliber piece was useful only as a close range weapon. He was a good shot against targets, but had never fired any weapon against a man. He would have to wait until they were nearly upon him.

He was terrified, but the anger kept that in check. He was not going to let such an opportunity slip. He drew the piece and pointed the horse toward the onrushing British. Time slowed to a crawl. He felt detached, as if he stood outside his body, and watched someone else carefully level the pistol. The British private's chest came into clear view at five yards. He gently squeezed the trigger.

The shot hit the private in the sternum. He collapsed like a soufflé punctured by a spatula. His comrades yelled in anger.

Parke pirouetted the horse neatly, he had a way with animals, and drove his spurs violently into her flanks. She shot ahead with a speed for which he would have hardly given her credit. The angry shouts quickly faded to whispers as she galloped ahead. He turned her into another alley and slowed her to a trot. He stopped at the alley's end and looked behind. No sign of pursuit. But then British soldiers could not be expected to know the city byways as well as he did.

He commanded his panting breath and his racing heart to slow, both with indifferent success. He felt really good, which was most peculiar. He had done it, faced death. He had not wilted, but stood his ground. Instead of fleeing, he had inflicted death on his attackers. At least one enemy of his country would trouble it no more. What he had done was of no interest to anyone and unlikely to influence the war in even a tiny way, but it was a defining moment for Daniel Parke. For the first time in two days, he could face his reflection in a mental looking glass and not flinch at what he saw. He checked his wound once more and decided it was not serious. The elation of the moment banished any pain. He had a long way to go, but for the first time, his heart knew he would make it.

*****

The jolly boat did not like the stern discipline Tracy applied. She corkscrewed violently through the grey-green waves, and madly fought his efforts to keep her bow into the wind. She was a headstrong child having an unending tantrum. The wind and waves slammed harshly against her hull, tried to turn her sideways. If that happened, she would swamp in short order. He kept a firm hand on the tiller, interrupted only when he had to rise to adjust the sail.

The sensible thing would be to furl sail and ride out the storm, but the wind, while dangerous, drove the boat at a very fast speed. It was a dangerous and constant test of his seamanship to keep her on course, but if he could, he would reach the British squadron in just a few hours. Time was of the essence, the wind was at his back, and the outer edge of the Frying Pan shoals lurked just ahead. He loved it!

Several waves burst over the gunwale and deposited a few gallons of water before departing. He was already soaked and could not spare the extra effort to bail. The water reached his ankles, but he did not mind, the boat was safe enough.

Sammie Jo, wrapped like a mummy in tarpaulin, stayed dry. She awakened once, when a violent swell hurled her against a gunwale. She blinked in puzzlement, opened her mouth to speak, then lapsed quickly back into unconsciousness as the laudanum continued to weave its spell. Just as well, what they were experiencing would terrify any landsman and she would be spared the nausea of seasickness.

The wind slackened as the storm blew itself out over the next hour. The rain stopped, the sun peaked through the overcast, and the wind settled into a steady, stiff breeze out of the northwest. It reduced speed, but progress was still steady and respectable.

He rehearsed his story. It sounded implausible and he would have had a hard time believing it if he were the recipient. Still, there was the physical resemblance and his brother had told him several details of Gordon's wedding that should help.

As the waves gentled, he began to make calculations. Mount Prosperity lay thirty miles inland from the Potomac. At least by the roads the British had taken. He could cut the distance by ten miles if he used the landing that lay fifteen miles south of the Three Tuns. Mr. Carson had a ramshackle stable at the landing with plenty of second-rate horses.

Pennywhistle had said just get the boat to the Three Tuns. He would march his men there from the Dockyard. He said he had a brief stop to make before he arrived. Tracy guessed that would be at Fort Washington. His force was too small to capture it but large enough to manage a demonstration. He hoped he was not aiding the enemy, but decided the garrison at the fort had sat fat and comfortable while he and his men had fought and died at Bladensburg. Garrison troops always stirred his contempt. Perhaps a little excitement might show them what real soldiers faced on a regular basis.

He adjusted course neatly to avoid a clam bed that was notorious for grounding ships. There was one more bad spot two miles ahead, but from there on, it was clear sailing. He hoped his guess about Gordon's position was correct. The winds were good for him, but contrary for Gordon's Squadron. They might even be grounded as that part of the river necessitated a good pilot and he had the idea that Gordon had not been able to obtain one. Apparently some mariners possessed a sense of patriotism.

He relaxed slightly, as the clam bed dropped swiftly astern, but began to worry about his own actions. The confidence with which he had spoken to his brother had vanished with the storm. He was aiding the movement of British soldiers and about to inaugurate a parley that in no way served his country. It was one thing to help a brother, quite another to give aid and comfort to the enemy.

His duty demanded he sheer off immediately, but the loneliness of a life without a family got the better of him. He told himself his actions would in no way affect the outcome of the war, although his conscience knew that determination was not his to make. Brotherly love had put him in dangerous waters, literally as well as figuratively. War had always been so simple and direct!

He would get Sammie Jo home then take his leave. A myriad of things could still go wrong. Steady, he told himself, one wave at a time!

*****

Pennywhistle found Cockburn and Ross at Suter's as expected. He joined them for a quick and exiguous breakfast. Ross insisted he try some of the hominy grits he had found delicious, particularly served with the Maryland accompaniment of shrimp, but he was too keyed up to have much appetite. The shrimp was excellent but the grits tasted like mush soaked in gun oil.

He explained his plans to Ross and Cockburn in detail. They applauded his initiative and thought his idea sound. He appeared to have plans accounting for every contingency. The written orders issued by an aide twenty minutes later opened with the usual, 'You are hereby requested and required to...' and directed him to proceed with 128 men to secure the Dockyard. He would leave Spottswood in command with 100 men after he branched off with his special group and marched south. The redoubtable Sergeant Dale would accompany him.

Dispatch riders on extremely fast thoroughbreds soon departed with orders for the marines and quartermasters in Benedict. The captured Yankee horses were fast and the riders were well armed with generous amounts of coin to purchase replacement mounts from cooperative locals. By changing horses regularly, the riders would average ten miles an hour and cover the fifty-plus miles to the British base by early afternoon. Men and supplies could be moving toward Mount Prosperity by late afternoon.

He realized his brother was in a precarious moral position. The conditions of parole sometimes generated unexpected and less-than-clear-cut choices about honor. He would not think less of Tracy if he left the little expedition early; in fact he would urge him to do so. He understood honor was a shy, evanescent thing that vanished swiftly at the first sign of moral compromise. When bullets flew, men screamed, and battle cast its heavy shadow of moral bewilderment, honor was often the only ethical beacon you had.

It took him forty minutes to make contact with Spottswood and his men and an additional hour to reach the Dockyard. They arrived at the gates just before 8 a.m. The Americans had done a good job of destruction in the time available, but a surprising amount of the Yard remained untouched. A nearly complete frigate and schooner had been burned to the waterline but the sail and rope lofts were intact, as was the nearly finished brig *Lynx*. He made a thorough survey and instructed Spottswood to pay special care to the preservation of the Marine Barracks. He told him the priority was weapons and powder. He saw quite a number of cannons that remained un-spiked.

Spottswood assured him the company would attend to it. Several over-eager privates began to dismantle a small monument commemorating the heroism of sailors and marines in the Barbary Wars. They laughed and jeered as they did so. Spottswood angrily stopped them. He said the Yankee Army might be a joke, but America's sailors and marines most certainly were not. They had done valorous service against the Algerian Brigands which deserved respect. He informed them the great Nelson had commended Captain Decatur as having performed 'the boldest exploit of the age' when he had burned the *Philadelphia* in Tripoli Harbor. The marines obeyed and some hung their heads in chagrin.

Spottswood approached Pennywhistle five minutes later, a grin on his face. "The Gods with their quirky sense of humor have again smiled upon you, Tom. I know you thought all of the yard's boats destroyed but one of my marines discovered a whale boat at the bottom of the mast pond. She is a 28-footer and has a hole near the cutwater, but a marine who once worked as a shipwright tells me she can be hoisted out and the hole patched in a couple of hours. I could load her with all the spare powder and shot she can carry and have her rendezvous at the Three Tuns tonight. Corporal Thistle knows his way around boats and with the storm abated, he can handle the Potomac."

"It's a shame that boat wasn't available last night. It would have made things so much easier."

Manton handed a small notebook to Pennywhistle. "Here is a quick inventory I made of the contents of the central magazine."

Pennywhistle quickly flipped through the pages and his eyes brightened. "Excellent, Peter. I see they are well stocked with canister. Good! Plenty of musket cartridges. Good! Their cartridges will work with a Brown Bess even though ours won't work with a Springfield. Since we shall oppose numbers with firepower this lot is a godsend. Can you have the ammunition stowed and the boat ready to sail by early afternoon?"

"Better than that, by noon. Thistle and the boat should be waiting for you when you arrive at the inn. I like the economy of it. Yankees beaten by their own ammunition. I will see to it directly." Manton saluted and briskly walked off, already considering how to stow things to give the boat its best trim.

Pennywhistle assembled his marines five minutes later and briefly explained the highlights of his plan and their immediate destination. The men listened closely and without emotion. He had their absolute trust and confidence. They knew that hard marching lay ahead and it bothered them not at all.

He said his new manservant, Rufus, would play as they marched. He could see in their eyes they wondered where he had found such an exotic creature. They seemed unable to credit Rufus' musical ability. Englishmen were uncertain about black people, although far less prejudiced against them than Americans.

A demonstration was in order. He turned to the young black. "Rufus," he said loudly and confidently, "My marines do not seem to realize they are privileged to have so gifted a musician in their company. Perhaps even an American Mozart. I should be much obliged if you would give my men a rendering of..." he thought for a minute and tried to come up with a familiar song that was difficult to play, one that showed expert command of a trumpet, "*To Anacreon in Heaven.*" The tune was a well-known drinking song that had come from a

London glee club. Three weeks hence a lawyer named Francis Scott Key would appropriate the tune to accompany a poem he had penned and the duo would later become the American National Anthem.

Rufus flashed a bright, broad, confident smile. "Suh," he said to Pennywhistle, "You'uns just need to prepare for dee-light." He put his lips to the trumpet and blew. He and the instrument became as one and magic happened, notes burst forth that seemed from a heavenly author. The skill of the prodigy brought smiles to everyone. Music truly did have the power to soothe the savage breast.

Private Crouchback interrupted Pennywhistle's reverie. "Excuse me, sir, sorry to disturb your enjoyment but I spotted two crates that I thought you might want to take a look at. They were labeled *Chamber's Patented Repeating Swivel Guns*. Not sure what they are but I know you have a liking for new-fangled weapons."

"I commend your initiative, Private, and a repeating swivel gun does indeed sound interesting. These Yankees have an undeniable talent for invention." Pennywhistle followed Crouchback and soon came to two long pine boxes. Pennywhistle handed Crouchback a crowbar and he pried off the lid of the first one.

Pennywhistle brushed aside the storage straw, took out one of the swivel guns, and carefully inspected it. His face beamed with delight. The heavy weapon had a four-foot length like a standard swivel gun but it had seven barrels bundled together, which would fire in sequence once the flintlock set off the first barrel. He estimated each barrel was of .75 caliber although the balls it would use would be of much smaller diameter.

He made the requisite extrapolations. The piece could discharge 120 balls in a single blast and be very useful in a close-quarter fight, although probably impossible to reload after the first firing. No matter, it was the shock of the initial volley that counted. These weapons would come in very handy for the plan that was shaping up in his mind. He recalled Manton's inventory and noted with satisfaction that it contained plenty of small canister charges for swivel guns.

He opened the second box and found that it, like the first, contained five similar weapons. Although not readily portable in a firefight, ten of these contraptions would give the defender of a fixed position a real advantage. A blast of 1200 small balls at point-blank range would go far to canceling out any disparity of numbers. They were also small enough to be easily concealed with brush and branches and could be unmasked in a trice to give an invader a nasty surprise. The two pine boxes and their contents could be easily transported by mules.

"I think you have just saved a great number of lives, Crouchback," said Pennywhistle enthusiastically. "Now would you be so good and see if you can rustle up two beasts from those stables over yonder to transport them?"

The eternally dour Cockney betrayed just hint of a smile at the praise. "Aye aye, sir. I will have mules here in just a few minutes."

"Capital!" said Pennywhistle merrily. Nothing brought him joy faster than discovering an ingenious way to confound the enemy. His smile departed and his brows knitted in fierce concentration as be began to calculate where he would place the swivels to defend the main approaches to Mount Prosperity. If only there was a way to give them mobility! He would be outnumbered, perhaps by as much as five-to-one.

He might be able to control the enemy's avenue of approach but only the clever application of firepower could compensate for his lack of numbers.

Infernal devices and poison would also assist in swinging the fight his way. Those things would be condemned by gentlemen fighting in the honorable way but a close reading of Greek and Roman warfare had told him the ancients from Archimedes to Caesar had employed such weapons on a fairly regular basis. Poisoning water supplies and arrows, leaving behind toxic honey, hurling infected animal carcasses into besieged cities and devising contraptions that fired barrages of arrows worked but were always excluded from official accounts. Then as now, fine talk counted for nothing, while victory counted for everything.

Crouchback appeared with the mules just as Pennywhistle had completed his calculations. He and Pennywhistle bound the boxes stoutly to their saddles with naval rope, even as both mules loudly brayed their disapproval. Crouchback volunteered to guide the sulky beasts.

A supply building remained untouched. Pennywhistle instructed his marines to fill their haversacks with biscuit and salt pork and top off their canteens. Every man carried three canteens, since he had ordered them to take extras from the Bladensburg dead. He knew there was a considerable stock of wine inside the building as well as large puncheons of fresh water, but he trusted his men to make the appropriate choice. A few might take quick swigs from wine barrels, but they were experienced enough to know that water was far more important for the hot march ahead.

He looked at the clearing sky. The storm had brought little relief from the heat and it would be another oppressively sultry day. He checked his watch: 9 a.m. If they marched within the quarter hour, they should make the Three Tuns by midnight. He briefly wondered about Sammie Jo's health and then angrily exiled the thought from his mind. He needed his full concentration for the task ahead.

Chapter Twelve

"No, damn it, I don't need more troops," shouted a harried General Winder, "I can't even feed the ones I have. Most of the new ones arrive with hungry bellies and no weapons."

"But general," said his aide Major Franklin March, "Are you not heartened by the outpouring of patriotic fervor? Surely you don't want to send these men away? They are willing to lay their lives down for the Republic and I feel certain we can find some way to employ them."

General Winder had established his new headquarters at Montgomery Court House, fifteen miles northwest of the capital. Survivors of Bladensburg filtered in slowly, a thin but steady stream. Newcomers swelled his ranks to 9,000 men, more than he had during the recent battle.

"We could move some of them closer in, at least feint toward Washington," said March hopefully. "The British would be unaware of the musket shortage if we armed them with pikes and at a distance it would be hard to tell what they carried. Any kind of demonstration would put heart into our side and unsettle the British. It's a matter of numbers, sir. If the British see large forces moving towards them, they will make the requisite calculations and withdraw from the District."

"Washington is lost," said Winder with a mixture of anger and despondency. "There is nothing we can do for the city. We have to think ahead, anticipate the next British move. They will proceed against Baltimore, I am sure of it. We have to move our men toward that city, get between it and the British. I have to meet with General Smith who is in charge of its defenses. We need to keep our forces concentrated, not adulterate our power by engaging in pointless distractions."

March knew he served a fool, but hoped against hope that he might still persuade him to take some action. "General, permit me the honor of leading an armed column into the northern environs of the city. 3,000 men would be a suitable number, just a fraction of the forces available. We could avoid a pitched battle, but still serve notice on the British that our forces are active and determined. It would put heart into even the ones remaining in camp and would inspire confidence in you, let the men know you will never give up."

"Blast it March, you take too much upon yourself, and your ideas border on impudence. I require obedience only, I don't want advice. We need to reorganize our men, find food and supplies. I suggest you drop your fanciful ideas of personal glory and instead concentrate your efforts on mundane military necessity."

"If you must do something, send these newcomers out to forage for arms and supplies. Hungry men usually find something to fill their bellies. I understand Sprague's Regiment just arrived from Annapolis. That would be a good place to start. For now, I must depart. Several of these damned Militia Colonels have demanded meetings. They are all so hot for action they simply do not understand cooler judgment must prevail. I am also in hopes the President will soon grace us with his presence, although I am not certain of his whereabouts just now."

"Very good, sir," said March with resignation. "I will arrange foraging details." He struggled manfully to choke off a tart response and it was only with supreme effort that he prevented his boot from kicking Winder out of his camp chair.

March was a fighting soldier and hated playing nanny to a ninny. He decided it was time for some French leave, what would be labeled AWOL by future generations. In the continuing confusion at headquarters, he would not be missed for a good while.

He had no intention of leaving the war but every intention of taking the fight to the enemy. It was important the Americans do something, anything, and not let the British think they were no better than whimpering dogs after a bad whipping. The militia men were eager for a scrap, spoiling for a chance to show the British the Americans had grit. As a Regular, he had experience and training. The militia lacked both and he believed they would rally to his leadership. He would show them how they could be heroes of the Republic rather than the equivalent of military paperweights.

Josiah Beems was much spoken of as a firebrand who constantly preached the gospel of armed resistance to the British. Men were turning out in great numbers in response to his message. He would seek him out. He had his doubts about working with an amateur but none of the professionals seemed disposed to dispute Winder's judgment. Beems would have to do.

*****

Twenty miles away General Ross and Admiral Cockburn considered their options. "I am greatly distressed to hear of the burning of the Library of Congress, Admiral. It was never my intent to destroy repositories of knowledge and learning. I am mightily shamed that we may have wrecked the precursor to another Library of Alexandria! Alas, it is far easier to begin the process of destruction than it is to control it. We have done more than enough, now it is time to think of our safety. Would you not agree, Admiral?"

Cockburn's cobra-like visage betrayed just a hint of doubt. "You are probably right General, but I confess I do not like to leave a job only partly finished. I think we have seen the best the Yankees can throw at us. But then, it is your decision, General, and I have come to have great confidence in your judgment and foresight. This has been a most successful expedition."

"It has been a very happy coincidence that I have you as a colleague, Admiral," said Ross with his usual tact. "We need to evacuate before eight tonight. I plan to feint toward the Foxall Foundry in Georgetown since the Yankees will expect us to go after a cannon factory. It should command their attention admirably. The Marine Brigade will depart first in the opposite direction, toward Bladensburg, and the 2nd and Light Brigades will follow."

"My man, Pennywhistle, will have everything ready at the rendezvous," said Cockburn confidently. "The messengers left hours ago. But while I think it good to have such a place, I doubt it will be necessary. After Bladensburg, the Yankees have no stomach for a fight. If they could not lick us in the open field, they will certainly not try to attack us behind fortifications."

"Probably true, Admiral, but if I learned anything from the Duke, it was to never bet everything on a single course of action. Recall the situation of the early days in Portugal. When

Marshal Massena advanced against His Grace in great numbers the Duke calmly retired upon the elaborate *Lines of Torres Vedras* ringing Lisbon."

"He had wisely thought ahead and ordered their construction ten months earlier. He left scorched earth behind him and Massena starved in front of those impregnable forts while the Duke was amply supplied by the Royal Navy. Mount Prosperity can be our *Torres Vedras*. I will rest the men a bit before we depart. The Yankees will not expect a night march and it will give our men some respite from this awful heat."

*****

Pennywhistle's men soldiered manfully on through another day of punishing heat. They kept silent, maintained a brisk pace, and ignored the clouds of mosquitoes and gnats which plagued them constantly. They sweated heavily and their red tunics absorbed the grime and dust roiled up from the surface of sandy roads. No one fell out of line, straggled, or missed even a step. Two scouts preceded the column and two followed slightly to the rear. Two men acted as flank guards on either side of the formation.

Pennywhistle marched just behind the advance scouts, having dispensed with a horse since they hoped to shortly transfer to boats. Gabriel, acting enthusiastically as the expedition's guide, walked alongside, whispering to him from time to time about the stretch of road immediately ahead. Dale marched behind the rear scouts.

Rufus kept step with the troops surprisingly well. Pennywhistle decided it was because of his unusually well-developed lungs. He played a pleasant variety of songs as he marched and greatly boosted morale. *Yankee Doodle* and *Rule Britannia* both caused the men to smile, although for entirely different reasons. People in the vicinity might hear Rufus' music, but since it was a trumpet rather than a fife or drum, he doubted they would assume it signaled the passage of a military force.

The tiny column stepped in loose, open order, each man's mind silently keeping cadence in the absence of a drummer. The lack of idle chatter marked them as unbreakable professionals; just the steady *thud, thud, thud* of disciplined footfalls. Soles, as well as souls were tested by the heat. Several men had worn holes in their shoes from the extended hard marching, but none slowed his pace. Their faces were fixed in expressions of patient resolve, soldiers used to privation and demanding service.

Pennywhistle stopped for ten minutes each hour, standard march procedure, and then stretched one stop into thirty minutes so the men could drink and eat. Rufus showed amazing energy and continued to entertain with his songs. It was a small relief from the heat and dust, but it was welcomed. They reached the marshes near Fort Washington about two in the afternoon, having made better time than expected. Rufus finally stowed his trumpet. Pennywhistle had the men take cover in the marshes below the Fort.

Spottswood's assessment made several days before was still accurate. The fort was designed to command the river approaches to the capital but no one appeared to have given much thought to a land-based attack. The marshes should have been drained and the tall reeds destroyed long ago. He unfurled his glass and methodically surveyed the Vaubanesque brick work looming above. He observed a few lookouts, but they seemed focused far downstream in the direction of Gordon's Squadron. There was an air of listlessness about the place, as if the man in charge didn't care.

To his surprise, a small group of about 30 men emerged from the south sally port ten minutes later. They marched carelessly onto the open ground a hundred yards away. An officer followed closely behind and barked an order. The column stopped and formed into line. The men came to attention and the officer walked slowly down the line, pausing now and then to inspect muskets.

Pennywhistle panned his glass down the line noting postures and men's faces. The stances were slack and many faces showed traces of resentment. It was understandable, far better to shelter in the shade of a cool casemate than fry in an open plain. Not a patrol at all, but some sort of training exercise. The officer probably wanted more extended marching than was possible on the parade ground inside. He felt sympathy for the hapless soldiers. He guessed their training so far had been spotty and an afternoon of drill in the hot sun would do little to improve their mood.

The officer in charge looked annoyingly ebullient. The young spark acted very full of himself and apparently relished the joys of command. It seemed a shame to spoil his fun. Unsporting or not, it was too fine an opportunity to be missed. He had intended a demonstration against the fort and this was the perfect opportunity. He wished he had more men. There was a real chance he could gain entrance to the fort if the pursuit was close enough. He reminded himself this was merely a sideshow.

He made his dispositions quickly, chiefly through well practiced hand gestures. They would echelon right, attack the north flank, and get between the men and the fort. No shots, strictly the bayonet. They could cover the hundred yards swiftly, one silent rush to decide the business.

Something was off. Everything suddenly stopped, as if nature held her breath. The hint of a breeze vanished abruptly. The heavy atmosphere acted like huge tapestries, throttling the flow of air. The sky turned a sickly, yellow grey. Dark clouds, shaped like walls, had moved in a few minutes back. Two of them swirled in viciously concentric circles and began a gradual descent.

What had Gabriel said to him about such clouds? Yes! They were funnel clouds, breeders of cyclonic activity. 'Mastuh call them tornadoes, we folk call 'em twisters.' Whatever the label, they were trouble. And yet, he could use them. He estimated touchdowns at a point a half-mile distant. He knew their courses might be wildly erratic, but thought they would head in the general direction of the fort.

As if to berate him for thinking he could use her creations, nature slammed down sheets of violent, driving rain that made it barely possible to see more than twenty yards. It was also perfect cover for his men. Powder was useless, but not cold steel. Now or never! "Charge!" The marines rose up like misty wraiths and dashed toward a line of men they could no longer see.

The American officer in charge had his back to the funnel clouds but his men saw them. Several soldiers shouted alarms at the officer, but the driving rain made it difficult to hear. At just the moment he grasped their intent, the redcoats burst out of the gloom.

Men normally run when attacked by bayonets, but these Americans did not. It happened too fast for them to react. One minute nothing, the next redcoats among them slashing, impaling, and gutting with bayonets. Most never got a chance to even club at their attackers and were slaughtered where they stood. Two made a run for it toward the fort. One made it to the gate. The twister sucked the other into space.

The business with the soldiers was done in less than a minute. The second twister had not dropped where Pennywhistle expected, but plopped itself down only fifty yards away. The damn things were notoriously unpredictable. The noise was ear-splitting, like a thousand naval broadsides fired simultaneously ten feet away. Pennywhistle felt himself being pulled violently toward the swirling vortex. Gabriel said all you could do was flatten yourself in the nearest ditch and hope for the best.

"Run! The marshes!" He yelled louder than he ever had before, but it sounded a whisper in the thunderous roar of wind. Discipline as well as instinct took over and the men raced toward cover. They jumped into the reeds, lay flat, covered themselves, and those who were religious prayed. The twister veered away from the marsh at the last second, but directly in front of Private Carnegie, the slowest runner who had not yet reached safety. Pennywhistle would never forget the puzzled look on his face as he spun like a top and was whisked into the dark funnel; a flailing marionette sucked heavenward until only a dot of red remained visible.

The great roaring, sucking sound rose to a horrible crescendo and he felt a giant hand tug at him, but just as suddenly, the funnel's momentum carried it past and the pressure disappeared. The rain stopped a few seconds later, as if someone had just toggled a cosmic off-switch.

The men smiled at each other, glad to be alive. It was one thing to fight Yankees, quite another to fight Mother Nature. Pennywhistle cursed himself inwardly for his arrogance in believing he could outthink nature, but he had only lost one man and that could just as well have happened in battle.

Gabriel crawled over to him. "Glad ya is alright Cap'n. Weren't it just like I told ya?" Pennywhistle nodded emphatically. "Got me one of them Yankee bastards," he said proudly.

Rufus crawled over to him. "Are you safe, sir?" There was real concern in his voice. "I thought I might play, *The World Turned Upside Down*, when we resume the march." Pennywhistle smiled at the appropriateness of the title in light of what had just happened. "Please do, Rufus."

His force was intact, and although shaken, they would be fine in short order. He ordered a thirty minute rest and the men broke out food and canteens. They talked quietly among themselves about the madness and the miracle they had somehow survived. It would shortly pass into legend, Pennywhistle guessed. The size and power of his force, the enemy, and the tornado itself would increase with each retelling. They would dub it 'Pennywhistle's Tornado' as if he somehow had the power to summon nature.

What the Yankees had seen probably confused them. He was glad one man had survived. It would confirm that the British were at the heart of the maelstrom that had wiped out their men. The garrison would bother no one for the rest of the day.

He reviewed the map: only another seven miles to go. They would make the Three Tuns by ten. He wondered how the storm had affected Tracy and Gordon. He normally felt God was far too rational and busy to respond to individual entreaties, but his worry caused him to make an exception just now. The prayer for Sammie Jo was short and silent.

Chapter Thirteen

John Tracy departed the Three Tuns with satisfaction. He had completed a solid arrangement with his old colleague Richard Coleman for the use of his Inn. He had been fully forthcoming about everything, including his relationship to Thomas Pennywhistle. Coleman was dubious at first, but the gold coins helped quiet his concerns. The Inn had been completely deserted since the British arrived because people were sensibly staying home.

Sarah Coleman's concern for Sammie Jo had clinched things. Sammie Jo was an American after all and had been injured fighting the British, although Tracy was careful not to mention who had inflicted her wound.

Sarah Coleman took an immediate shine to her, told Tracy she reminded her of a recently deceased sister, and admonished her husband they must do all in their power to aid her journey back to health. They carried Sammie Jo to a second floor room which overlooked the Potomac.

She had awakened briefly. "Where is Tom?" She asked groggily. "Is he well?" It surprised Tracy the woman's first thought was for his brother. He could not decide if the concern sprang from the heart or was merely delusional raving. He thought it best to humor her and kept things simple. She was in no fit state to hear a complicated explanation of events.

"He is fine," he said soothingly, "He should be along by tonight. You will see him then. Until he arrives, please rest and let these good folk take care of you."

She smiled wanly. "I worry about him. Where am I?" She revived a little and tried to sit up. She touched the bandage on her shoulder and flopped back down on the bed. "It hurts, how bad is it?"

Tracy tried hard to be a good nurse, but it did not come easily to him. "You are safe in the Three Tuns Inn. We are south of the city. Mr. and Mrs. Coleman are my friends. I have left them funds for your care, food, and board. The surgeon says you should recover fully given plenty of rest and a quiet convalescence. I think you should begin that directly and go back to sleep." He realized she probably could stay here safely for a quite a while. It made more sense than trying to get her home.

"Here, take your medicine." He gave her two teaspoons of laudanum. "The Surgeon said you should take some twice daily for the next five days. There now, be a good patient." She would likely be as bad a patient as she was a human being, but he nevertheless kept a pleasant expression on his face.

"Thanks, I'm grateful to you for gettin' me patched up." She slurped up the medicine. "I need to get home though. Don't want to stay in a fancy place like this on someone else's dime. I can take care of myself, have to....." Drowsiness passed over her like a magician's spell and she faded back into sleep.

Just as well. He was in no mood for an extended conversation, since he felt she was bad news for his brother. Her untutored charms had no effect on him.

*****

He had been on the river two hours since he talked with her. The breeze swelled and the sail filled. The wind was two points off the quarter, and he kept the course straight and steady. The jolly boat ploughed along at the respectable pace of four knots. With luck, he should sight the British Squadron within a few minutes. The voice of duty whispered he was pushing the limits of his parole past the breaking point, but he was committed and there was no going back.

His luck vanished in an instant. The wind dropped as if sucked into a giant carpetbag and the sail sagged like an old woman's bosom. Forward momentum continued because of the current, but the boat slowed greatly and the tiller became sluggish. It became eerily, irredeemably still. The air swam with moisture, the waves diminished to mere suggestions of motion, and the sun vanished as if during an eclipse.

The line of dark squalls approached with the speed of greyhounds. The two funnel clouds gave him pause, but darted over and past his position. The rain came in pounding sheets, followed seconds later by a giant burst of wind that ripped the sail from the mast. He jumped forward to stow the mast, but the wind snapped the stout pine as if it were a cheap twig. The top half flew off into space with a sharp, *crack*!

The water turned an angry, vicious grey and rolled skyward in great swells followed by enormous troughs. Waves crashed into the gunwales and he had to fight to keep her into the waves. He had done the same thing hours earlier, but this storm was far more violent. He still had oars, but rowing toward the shore half a mile distant was as futile as trying to anchor with a rope made of paper. He would just have to tough it out. It would be a mighty rough ride.

*****

It was just as rough back in Washington City.

"Get inside, Go! Go! Go!" Lieutenant Manton waved his sword toward the red brick row house half a block away. His men grabbed everything they could carry and ran pell-mell, less a company than simple fugitives from nature's wrath. Manton had seen violent storms at sea, but he had never encountered this sort of fury ashore. He was under orders not to molest civilian property, but he decided the present emergency necessitated an exception. This was about survival.

The storm drenched everyone well before they came close to the front doors, but they had all made certain the flaps of their cartridge boxes were closed and their powder stayed dry. When the first man neared the front steps Manton dashed to the front door, founded it locked. He drew his pistol in one quick motion and put a bullet into the box lock. He kicked the door violently with his boot and it flew open. It was a miracle the pistol even fired in this horrendous rain. He waved the men through. When the last was through, he ran inside, slammed the door violently shut, and took a deep breath. He wondered how long the storm would last or if it would delay their evening departure.

It lasted two hours and he and the men watched out the windows with awe. Homes were battered like nails hit with Thor's Hammer. Whole roofs wrenched themselves free, windows blew inward, and several ramshackle outbuildings collapsed as if smashed by giant fists. The wind and rain came in rapid, unpredictable bursts. During each brief respite, he had a chance to assess damage caused by the previous spasm. Boards, shingles, and bits of unidentifiable property flew down the streets, making it exceedingly dangerous to remain unsheltered.

He saw two fools on horseback try to thread their way through the storm. The first was dashed from his horse by a flying piece of clapboard. He lingered in his saddle a fragment of a second, then was blasted down to the cobblestones. The second made it a few hundred yards further and was unhorsed by a sudden gust of wind. The gust lifted him from the saddle and swatted him into the side of an apothecary shop. He lay an unmoving heap of clothing.

Manton had received orders from the brigade major about an evening withdrawal. He was amazed by the storm's power, but thought it would work to his advantage. It would add to general confusion and as long as it blew itself out before evening, it would help mask the withdrawal.

*****

Daniel Parke was well clear of the city when the storm hit. The horse struggled against the waves of billowing rain and could only manage a very slow walk. Parke saw a barn and headed toward it. He doubted the owners would mind.

He got the horse inside, dismounted, and shut the doors. The storm pounded the barn angrily as if demanding entrance. It frustrated him, having to wait. The urgency of the storm matched his own to reach home. He removed his dripping duster and plopped himself in the hay. He decided to make himself comfortable. There was no point in arguing with nature.

He had taken a bottle of champagne from his friend's home, intended to open it in celebration when he reached Mount Prosperity. He threw caution to the wind, appropriate given the storm outside, and inexpertly popped the cork. It shot into the air and some of the contents of the bottle sprayed him. He laughed hysterically for no reason he could fathom. It just seemed the silliest thing to be having such a festive drink under such dire circumstances. He took a large gulp from the bottle, utterly without elegance or dignity.

Fatigue, stress, and an empty stomach caused the alcohol to work its magic quickly. The champagne stopped the annoying throb of the wound. Suddenly, things did not seem so bad. All problems could be worked out if you just had faith that they could. He could fix things when he got home. He wondered idly about his children and then about Archie. He realized he could have one or the other but not both. It was too much to consider right now.

He drank and thought. He had killed a British soldier, had reason to be proud of himself. His wound would be something of a trophy, tangible evidence he had done his duty. They had probably heard about Bladensburg but would take his wound as proof that at least he had personally put up a scrap. They would never discover the wound and the battle were unrelated.

His pride in himself swelled as the bottle emptied. He finished most of the champagne in an hour. The storm rose to a thunderous peak outside, but his inner self waxed peaceful and content. He laid the bottle aside, and gently deposited his head on the hay. Yes, it would all work out. He was fast asleep in ten seconds.

*****

Commodore James Alexander Gordon, on HMS *Seahorse* in the middle of the Potomac, saw the fast approaching squall line with alarm. He quickly ordered all sails furled. Other captains gave the same orders on their ships. This would be something for the squadron to ride out under bare poles. He was just a little too slow. The squalls had far more speed and force behind them than even his experienced eye could discern.

The wind tore through his little fleet. He saw the three topgallant masts on HMS *Eurylaus* crumple and fall overboard. A few seconds later, the wind crushed her jib boom, making her very difficult to control.

The roaring wave hit the bomb vessel, HMS *Meteor*, squarely in the side and drove her aground on yet another hidden clam bed.

Waves crashed over the bow of the *Seahorse* and grey water cascaded over the deck. The scuppers filled but did their job and drained the water. All of the men were instantly soaked to the skin. She was not a small ship but she pitched and yawed like a tiny cork in a great bathtub. Gordon ordered two more quartermasters to the wheel which was struggling to fling the helmsmen off.

They got her under control, but barely. Gordon had suffered a very tough week making it to his present position. He briefly toyed with the idea of withdrawing but then angrily dismissed it. He had come this far and was so close. He was utterly damned if some storm was going to stop him!

It was hard to see much in the driving rain, but he unfurled his telescope anyway to get a better view of the rest of his squadron. He could see the other ships in flashes, between the gaps in the bursts of rain. They were all in distress but none was critical. For a brief second he thought he saw a man in a jolly boat waving a white flag at the end of a long stick. It couldn't be. The river was clear of traffic. Everyone had fled at the approach of the British squadron.

Another gust shook *Seahorse*, then there was a brief respite and he saw the boat again. Whoever was in it continued to signal violently. The waves crashed over its hull and it looked in real danger of foundering. It was insane to attempt a rescue in the present weather but duty and discipline took over. He would not contravene the iron law of the sea: a boat in distress demanded rescue. His men were well trained and would respond without hesitation.

Moreover, he was curious about the man in the boat. He looked to be wearing some sort of uniform and the boat was clearly American Navy issue. The white flag was being used to signal truce not distress.

"Helm, bring her a point to starboard, gently now. Stand by with boathooks." The jolly boat was losing its battle with the waves. He hoped he was not too late.

Chapter Fourteen

The diminishing waves of rain swept Pennywhistle's little column like a powerful liquid broom seeking to banish dust mites. The men ignored it and determinedly staggered forward. Progress was slow, but it was progress. The men were soggy but cartridge boxes were shut and their contents bone dry. The unpleasant weather was an advantage in a way. It shielded their advance and eliminated the possibility they would run into any armed opposition.

The rain ceased as abruptly as it had begun. The howling winds dropped to a slight but steady breeze. The storm had at least cooled the temperature and the column welcomed the relief. It was probably in the mid-seventies on the Fahrenheit Scale. Pennywhistle halted the column for a twenty minute rest before the final push to the Three Tuns. The men ate, drank, and talked quietly as usual.

It was almost dark. Pennywhistle guessed they had two hours' march left and would reach the Inn well before ten. He would make sure the men had a proper meal and a good rest. He would depart with the dawn and hoped the usual morning breeze from the northwest would manifest itself. If not, the men had some heavy rowing ahead.

*****

Sammie Jo awakened, feeling greatly refreshed. Her wound hurt, but much less so. A pleasant evening breeze drifted in the window. It took her a minute to remember where she was. She had only met the Coleman's briefly but they seemed good people. She sat up, felt just a bit dizzy, and lay back down. She decided a good night's rest should see her up and about on the morrow.

Sarah Coleman entered the room. Sammie Jo's cheeks had turned from grey to rose-colored and it made her smile. "Are you hungry, Sammie Jo?"

"Powerful hungry. Obliged to you for helpin' me. Y'all got any huntin' food?"

"Huntin' food?" asked Sarah. She had grown up in Alexandria and the colloquialisms of country folk were foreign to her.

"I mean good solid food that sticks to your ribs, gives you plenty of energy for huntin'. Steak, chops, chicken, stuff like that. Not fancy party grub, none of them peddyy fours."

Sarah nodded. Sammie Jo was certainly direct. "How would ham and biscuits sound?" She tried to play the good hostess but she had a lot of questions about Sammie Jo.

"I'd be mighty pleased to sink my teeth into them vittles," said Sammie Jo with unabashed pleasure. "It's been a while since I had a proper fillin' meal. All that chasin' after those damn redcoats done left me feelin' like a piece of old shoe leather marched over by a passel of armies."

Sammie Jo was a big girl, very athletic. She did not look like she wanted lady-like portions. Sarah was being well paid and would make sure she ate her fill. The girl might be ill-bred and uncouth, but someone clearly cared about her welfare. It was certainly not John Tracy. Her husband said he liked elegant, refined women. Tracy seemed to regard her with suspicion and disdain, yet was very particular to make sure she received good care.

For all of her crudity, Sarah sensed a great strength of will in Sammie Jo. She also sensed something dangerous about her, something she could not quite put her finger on. It felt a bit like being in the same room with a wounded panther. Her bad side was probably a very bad place to be. She would treat her well and very, very carefully.

Sarah forced a smile onto her face. "You just rest now, Sammie Jo. I'll have the food ready right quick and I promise you will not go hungry."

*****

Tracy estimated he was less than an hour from the Inn. The yawl was very responsive and needed only a feather-light touch on the tiller. His meeting with Commodore Gordon had proved both easier and stranger than expected. He was a strong swimmer, but would not have answered for his chances in the river when his boat went under. Gordon's men plucked him from the angry fury of the Potomac at the last second.

Gordon saw to his welfare before he even spoke a word. He was taken directly to Gordon's cabin where he was given dry clothing, food, and most welcome, a stiff tot of Jamaican Rum. Gordon stayed on deck until the storm blew itself out, but came below directly when it finished.

Gordon was a big man, a fraction of an inch below six-foot-four. He walked stiffly, for his left leg just below the knee was made of wood. His booming voice matched his frame. His tone was friendly, almost jolly. "As I live and breathe, I have seldom been more amazed than when we brought you aboard. You are the spitting image of my dear cousin. Maybe a little older, but the resemblance is striking. I confess I almost willed the storm out, so I could solve this very piquant little mystery. I have speculated in all manner of ways for the past hour, but have realized the best thing to do would be to simply ask you to explain yourself. All I know is that you are a United States Marine Officer who must be on an important errand. No one else would have been on the river in this kind of weather."

Tracy smiled broadly. James Alexander Gordon might be an enemy, but he was a very hard man to dislike. Tracy explained his background and recent events quickly.

"That's the most extraordinary tale, Captain. I would scarcely credit it were you not sitting here. It is a remarkable thing that the tides of war swept you and your brother into the same eddy. It is even more remarkable you are in the same profession. I also thank you for your frank and honest description of the battle of Bladensburg. That must have been painful for you. We have seen the fires in Washington and guessed the outcome, but had received no first-hand accounts."

Tracy explained his brother's idea and his need for a boat. "I confess, Commodore Gordon, I am acting out of filial loyalty and testing the limits of my patriotism. I wish to violate neither my parole nor my oath to my country, but feel assisting a brother and saving a few lives is acceptable in the grand scheme of things. My conduct will not change the outcome of this disagreeable campaign, but it may ameliorate the suffering of soldiers who are not so very different from the professionals I was honored to command. I don't think I am betraying any secrets when I say the American command has made a foul mess of things. My brother clearly knows it and so do you. I should be very surprised if they mount any pursuit at all.

"The most I can do to retrieve American honor is to make certain my conduct is above reproach. I intend to see the girl my brother rescued safe home and will take my leave of both when her farm draws near. I will miss him. I have become quite fond of him in the short time I have known him."

At that moment, there was a knock on the cabin door. "Come," said Gordon. It was the First Officer.

"Sir, you said you wanted to be called when the boatswain had an assessment of the storm damage to the rigging. He has it ready but he said he'd like to speak to you personally about one or two concerns."

"Very good, Mr. Lindsey. I shall join you on deck in a minute." He turned to Tracy. "Forgive me, sir, but duty calls. I shall return in a few minutes to continue this very interesting conversation. In the meantime, please make yourself comfortable and feel free to sample," he reached into a small wine chest and brought forth a bottle, "this very delightful port."

"Your hospitality is overwhelming Commodore. I cannot thank you enough."

"My honor, Captain." Gordon nodded then bustled out of the cabin, his amiable face changing to a professional mask of command.

For all of Gordon's generosity, Tracy felt uneasy. He was still a serving officer in the US Marine Corps, even if a non-fighting one. Here he was in the cabin of a commodore, commanding an enemy squadron and he was not there under duress. It was one thing to assist a newfound sibling, quite another if that assistance turned him into the errand boy of a foreign power and imperiled his primary duty to his country. Sticklers for honor might even call any assistance to an agent of an enemy government, no matter how reasonable the circumstances, a clear violation of parole.

Because he was so conflicted, temptation ambushed him like an assassin in the night. He needed to balance his assistance to Pennywhistle with something that could help his own country and his alert eyes spied a way to do it. It was a dishonorable idea and a blot on the conditions of truce, yet it might ease his conscience.

Under a flag of truce, anything you heard, saw, or read that was not related to the strict purpose of the truce was to be kept confidential. Truces were meant to resolve thorny issues in a gentlemanly way, not allow one side to plant a spy in the enemy camp. Gordon trusted him and had left a sheaf of papers on his desk with no attempt at concealment. They might or might not be valuable but any insight into the enemy's plans or frame of mind could prove useful to the United States. And after the disaster of Bladensburg and the fall of Washington, the young Republic needed all the help she could get.

Seahorse lurched violently as a liquid aftershock of the storm ploughed into her. The papers flew off Gordon's desk and wafted across the cabin to land at his feet. My God! You really did have to be careful what you wished for! Maybe this was some heaven-arranged test of his honor. If so, he was bound to fail since it would be foolish to look a gift horse in the mouth.

He would have to be quick, Gordon could return at any minute. He shuffled the papers into a sheaf and began systematically inventorying them. He scanned each document as fast as he could for any words, phrases, or names that sounded important. After a minute that seemed a lifetime, he struck gold. The word 'Baltimore' jumped out at him.

It was no surprise to him that Baltimore would be a British target, but the document indicated no attack on it would be forthcoming for another three weeks. That was important because Baltimore was unfortified and if the British launched an attack in the next few days it would almost certainly fall. Three weeks would give the Americans plenty of time to construct earthworks, turn out the militia, and make Baltimore a much harder nut to crack than unfortified Washington had been.

He heard the *clump, clump, clump* of a peg leg approaching. He jumped up and raced over to the desk. He tried and failed to remember how the papers had been arrayed and made a crude attempt at shuffling them into their former order, or rather lack of it. He shot back to his chair, wiped the sweat from his brow and tried to assume an air of relaxed nonchalance. He prayed Gordon would not look that carefully at his desk.

"Sorry for the delay, Captain. Weather will not be denied no matter how much sailors might wish it. Ah, I see you have not touched the port. It would be truly bad manners on my part if I allowed you to depart without tasting this really splendid libation. Please, have a glass."

Gordon poured two, one for himself and one for Tracy. Tracy smiled woodenly as he accepted the glass, glad of a drink to calm his nerves.

Gordon sat down, the picture of genteel relaxation. While Tracy was worried sick about compromising his parole, he clearly enjoyed Gordon's complete trust.

"You have been propelled onto a difficult and treacherous sea, Captain," said Gordon, "but you are navigating it most expertly and honorably."

Tracy felt shamed by Gordon's words but nevertheless managed to summon a gracious response. "I am doing my best to balance honor and duty, Commodore."

"Please convey my felicitations to your brother when you see him. How soon do you need the boat?" Gordon smiled. "I can have one ready to sail in twenty minutes. Please also convey to your countrymen we sailors are decent folk, a long way from the monsters your people have made Cockburn and his helpers out to be."

"I will certainly let people know of your graciousness, Commodore." *And I will do my utmost to hide my own treachery,* he thought. "Time is of the essence, Commodore, and I should be obliged if I could have the boat forthwith. The only monsters I see in this conflict are bloodthirsty civilians who write newspaper articles speaking of the joys of battle yet have never been anywhere near a real fight. They incite the innocent to think war is the most glorious thing imaginable."

"I was most impressed by the dignity with which your people treated my commanding officer, Commodore Barney. It is a great pity the arts of peace cannot be practiced with the same success as the courtesies of war."

It was also a great pity that after truth, personal honor was the second casualty of war.

*****

Manton's men reached the field of Bladensburg an hour after Tracy had docked at the Three Tuns. They had covered the distance from their camp in ninety minutes. Manton was glad to be shed of the enemy capital. The men were tired, but discipline held and there was little straggling.

The bright moonlight gave an eerie cast to the battlefield. Only a few of the dead had been buried. Some bodies appeared as white islands because they had been entirely stripped of clothing by zealous looters. There were details of slaves from nearby plantations digging hasty graves as the troops passed. The blacks paused in their labors to gape at the British.

Manton spoke briefly with a young woman named Elizabeth Jarndyce who had approached under a flag of truce. He had seen her calmly driving a hearse labeled "Capital Arrangements" and stopping from time to time to examine bodies. She explained she had come from Washington seeking the remains of one Lieutenant Colonel Joseph Sterrett who was reported to have fallen at Bladensburg. His family had commissioned her to place the body in a lead-lined coffin that it might be brought home for a proper burial.

Manton was astonished a woman would be involved in such a calling, particularly one who was so comely and well-spoken. He was equally surprised that his lantern revealed she was wearing a dress of the brightest red, in startling contrast to the traditional black of her profession.

"It was the family business, Mr. Manton. My father had no sons, so he trained me. As a young girl, I helped spruce up dead folk instead of playing with dolls. I learned that I had nothing to fear from them. By the time I reached 21, it was second nature to preserve 'em, primp 'em, and plant 'em. I continue to do it because I like working with people."

She saw his eyebrows arch in surprise and half-smiled in embarrassment at the unintended irony of her words. "I just meant I feel I help assuage the grief of good people by giving their loved ones the best sendoff I can manage. I treat bodies as sacred works of art created by our Maker and I take pride in giving them the best care, and the most life-like appearance, I can manage."

"Forgive my impudence Miss Jarndyce, but could you tell me why you wear a red dress? The color is most... ahem... unexpected." Manton struggled to be tactful.

To Manton's surprise, the undertaker laughed. "Black is just too depressing! It is easy to succumb to melancholia in this job, so anything that brightens your day--or night--figuratively or literally, is worthy of being heartily embraced. The color red is the color of life and it reminds me that while I care for the dead, my chief task is to assist and comfort the living."

"That makes perfect sense. A sanguine cast of mind is always an asset and on a bloody field like this, almost a necessity. Just how will you find Sterrett, Miss Jarndyce? Many of the bodies have been stripped of uniforms."

"A birthmark, Mr. Manton. He has a very prominent triangular one on his right forearm."

"That has to be awful work, closely examining corpses that are already...well...uh... ripening."

"It is why I always anoint my person with expensive French perfume. I favor *Eau de Lubin.*"

Manton smiled. "I noticed the scent when you arrived. The smell of roses and fruits is a welcome relief from the noxious odors abounding here. It goes well with your red dress but it is in stark contrast to the leather tanner's apron you are wearing."

"There is no rule that says the practical and the pretty cannot be mixed, Mr. Manton. Sometimes a little bit of gentility goes a long way to mitigating the effects of events that sneer in the face of civilization."

"May I say, Miss Jarndyce, your genteel manner conveys the essence of civilization even in a place that is its nemesis."

"Thank you, Mr. Manton! I do have a reputation for discretion and possess a considerable skill with makeup. Many members of Congress have trusted me to make the final arrangements for their loved ones."

"I think right now many Americans wish their congressmen were in a condition to merit your tender ministrations."

"That is very true, Mr. Manton. This war was a mistake although it is good for my business. 'Tis an ill wind that blows nobody good.' I work hard to maintain a respectable household and have accumulated substantial savings." The pride in her voice turned to exasperation. "Alas, I am a poor marriage prospect since many eligible gentlemen call me 'the death maiden.' My presence reminds carefree young sparks of that which they would prefer to forget and is naturally a strong impediment to romance. Gentlemen also do not think it proper that a woman should work at all and if she must, well, what I do is hardly a suitable calling for," she sighed deeply, "the weaker sex."

"Weaker sex? Ha! I think you exhibit a strength of character as striking as your beauty, Miss Jarndyce. You do something most men have no stomach for and you do it well. I admire you. Were I unmarried and living in happier times, I would ask for permission to call upon you."

"What a kind thing to say! But for now I must proceed with my sad business and take my leave of you. You may be the enemy of my country but I am certain your courtesy brings comfort to good-hearted women everywhere. I wish you a long life."

"I wish the same for you, Miss Jarndyce!" He smiled and bowed. She smiled back and acknowledged his gesture with a nod of her head. Her face turned grim a second later as she tugged at the reins and the hearse began to move.

War was so damned odd! Manton mused. To encounter a vision of loveliness in a field choked with death defied logic. It was like spotting a diamond perched atop a mound of dung; the beautiful surmounting the obscene.

Manton knew what the bodies looked like and was glad the darkness cloaked the details from his men. He remembered walking among the corpses after Salamanca, a battle also fought in baking heat.

The bodies at Bladensburg would display the same results. Most would be bloated into grotesque parodies of the humans they had once been, their faces rubbery with elephantine features. The flesh on the faces would vary from fish-belly white to piss yellow, from midnight purple to coal black depending on the time of death and the force of impact of the fatal projectile. Some bodies would be swollen to at least twice their normal size and a number of them would have burst and released all manner of stinking gases.

Manton's soldiers said nothing as he got them marching after a short rest stop, but he knew revisiting Bladensburg was demoralizing. He thanked God that at least the night prevented his men from recognizing any friends.

The numbers of dead at Bladensburg were trifling in comparison to what he had seen in Spain and France and at least here there would be no desecration. In Spain, angry peasants had sometimes relieved French corpses of their private parts in retaliation for the atrocities they had visited upon isolated villages. The war in America was relatively civilized as Elizabeth Jarndyce had just shown him. He shook his head at the irony of his thought. War and civilized were two words that never belonged in the same sentence.

Mercifully, as the men marched and the minutes passed, olfactory nerves anesthetized themselves to the putrid stench in the air. He gave the orders to the NCO's to increase the pace. The faster they got clear of Bladensburg, the better.

*****

Tracy adjusted the tiller slightly starboard and returned to the present. The top of the sun dipped below the horizon, but a sufficient glow remained in the sky to see the quay at the Three Tuns clearly, two hundred yards ahead. He checked his watch; just a few minutes before nine. Good. His brother was due anytime in the next hour.

He was running late because he had stopped off to send a message. He had given the information about Baltimore to a retired Congressman who had been a friend of his stepfather. The man was integrity personified and would see the message swiftly reached the highest levels of government. He fervently hoped it would help because he had sacrificed a piece of his soul to obtain it.

*****

Pennywhistle spotted the outline of the Three Tuns a few minutes before ten. He breathed a sigh of relief. The men were almost asleep on their feet and needed rest. He halted the column and told Dale to take charge until he returned.

Corporal Thistle had arrived two hours earlier and had lashed the whale boat to the dock. Pennywhistle made a quick inspection and was gratified to see the boat was packed to the gunwales with powder and shot.

Tracy met him at the inn's door. His first question surprised himself as it was the opposite of military. "How is she?"

"She is fine, asleep right now. She asked the same thing about you just a bit ago." His brother's tone was disapproving but resigned.

"Good, good," said Pennywhistle somewhat absent-mindedly. "Did you get the boat?"

"I have the yawl. Commodore Gordon sends his best wishes and says you must dine with him and Lydia when you return home. He is a good man. You are lucky to have such a cousin. I envy you your family ties." He inwardly winced when he thought of his betrayal of Gordon's trust.

"You are part of that family now, John, don't forget that. No idea what we can do about it until after this foolish war is over, but together, we will figure things out. I need to get the men fed and bedded down for the night."

"Sarah has a giant pot of beef stew ready," said Tracy pleasantly, though his stomach lurched at the realization he was feeding men he had fought at Bladensburg, something hardly consistent with his parole. Feeding men properly was often more challenging than leading them in battle; most looting was occasioned not by greed, but by empty bellies. He told himself he was doing a good thing by forestalling foraging, but it worried him that he was becoming skilled at offering up rationalizations for questionable actions. His parole was becoming more and more like a sieve with each passing hour.

"When do you want them in the boat?" asked Tracy, now not the brother, but the professional interested in operational details.

"We sail at 4 a.m.," said Pennywhistle calmly. "I want to catch the flood tide." He hoped the rising tide would mirror similar fortunes for the little expedition.

Chapter Fifteen

Manton ordered a halt just as dawn broke. The men had marched all night and kept up a good pace. Fatigue had begun to play a greater and greater role as the miles passed. Straggling increased and some men simply staggered out of line and went to sleep. A few could not be roused, despite the most dire threats and sincere entreaties to remember duty. He knew Ross was right to push the men, put some distance between them and Washington in the shortest time possible.

Everyone in the long column was close to exhaustion when they stopped. Most of the rankers simply dropped where they stood. There was no attempt to arrange things in the usual orderly manner. More prudent redcoats sought a shady spot under the pines before they plopped onto the grass and instantly passed into the deepest sleep. He needed sleep badly himself, but with greater rank came greater responsibility. He had a myriad of annoying tasks to perform, military housework of a sort, and wearily forced himself to concentrate.

His company was down to fifty-five men out of the ninety he had started with. He guessed one or two might have deserted, although it was far less a problem with his men than in some other companies, but more likely they lay sleeping somewhere miles back and would rejoin when they had mastered their fatigue. Nature enforced a discipline even more stringent than that of the army.

He kept his men going with talk that an advanced supply base lay only a day ahead. He said there would be plenty of food and drink. They could rest, compose themselves, and then make the final push back to the ships. He knew Pennywhistle had been detailed to take charge and it filled him with confidence. Confidence was infectious and it came through directly when he had addressed his men.

He sat down, opened his canteen, and looked skyward. Damn it! Another scalding hot day. He swore Maryland was not part of the United States but the infernal regions. How did the Yankees cope with such a blasted unfriendly climate? He swatted at a cloud of mosquitoes, they never seemed to take a rest, and began making entries in his pocket ledger.

*****

The yawl departed the Three Tuns just as the top of the sun broke over the horizon. Thistle followed in the whale boat. The launch was tightly packed with food, water, powder and shot and thirty-two people. Pennywhistle manned the tiller, and Tracy positioned the sail; logical since they knew the most about sailing. Dale acted as lookout on the bow.

Sammie Jo sat with her back braced against the stern sheets just to the right of Pennywhistle. She looked much better than when he had seen her last, although she wore her right arm in a sling to take pressure off the injured shoulder. She was unexpectedly silent which Pennywhistle put down to the effects of laudanum. She swiveled her head frequently and almost furtively, like a forest animal not sure if it should stay put or attempt escape.

When he arrived the night before, she had merely smiled and said, "Right glad to see you, Sugar Plum." She had squeezed his hand in what felt like relief and drifted back to sleep.

He had wakened her an hour ago and asked if she was fit to travel. He told her she would be perfectly safe where she was and that she might remain until she was well and truly healed. She puckered her lips, narrowed her eyes, and shook her head, "No, ain't nothing gonna keep me from comin' with you. I kin manage jus fine."

He was dubious but her expression was that of a child about to throw a tantrum if refused. He had neither the time nor the inclination to argue and also realized sheer willpower could often overcome any defects of health. And Sammie Jo had willpower in abundance. Even in her injured state he still desired her but his duty spoke loudly. It made him more determined than ever to attend to reason and follow his brother's counsel rather than succumb to the demands of his loins.

The wind was strong and stiff this morning and he was grateful. Dale acted as leadsman and pitched the lead over after they were underway for half an hour. He pulled it in and read the markings--five knots. Pennywhistle did the calculations and at this speed they would be at the landing site by seven, well ahead of schedule.

Pennywhistle was betting a lot that the careful instructions he had sent ahead to Benedict were being exactly followed. He checked his Blancpain and noted the Colonial Marines should be arriving at Mount Prosperity about now assuming they had made a hard night march.

The marines would fight well enough but their white officer, Lieutenant Barrington Chivers, stuttered at critical moments and was not over-gifted with initiative and smarts. It was why the twenty-year-old had been left behind at the supply depot. Chivers was well-connected, friendly, and brave enough, not a bad chap by any means, but he had a history of bungling assignments. He was the sort of fellow habitually labeled 'hapless.' His delicately handsome, almost feminine face wore a perpetually perplexed expression that told people that this was a fellow routinely plagued by unfortunate happenings.

Ordinarily a senior NCO would have been commissioned to supervise the marines since the unit was not really suitable as a gentleman's command, but as the perpetual supernumerary who served no apparent function, it had been dumped in Chivers' lap. Pennywhistle had tried to make his orders exact and detailed so they would be useful to someone who was a stranger to initiative.

Quartermaster Lieutenant Hamish Peebles was a far more experienced officer who was known for his ability to bring order out of any chaos. He would likely accompany Chivers to make sure the supplies got through and would undoubtedly supply him with lots of sound 'suggestions.'

Scotland was the most literate nation in Europe with over 90% of her population able to read and write and as the son of an Edinburgh bank clerk, Peebles had entered the army far better schooled than the average private soldier. He was quickly talent-spotted as a man with a head for paperwork and a knack for organization and advanced rapidly to the rank of sergeant. After twenty solidly successful years as an NCO, he had finally been offered a commission out of respect for his ability to routinely perform miracles with a minimum of staff and supplies.

At forty two, he was old for his rank and would never advance any further but his reputation was such that rank really mattered little. Colonels and generals listened closely to his counsel and frequently deferred to his experienced judgment. Pennywhistle reposed the utmost confidence that his pack mules would bring everything he had requested.

Pennywhistle reviewed the other things he needed for his plan. Mount Prosperity's cellars contained plenty of wine; most excellent vintages although hot, thirsty men would likely care not at all. He had recognized a local variant of the highly toxic aconitum flower, wolfsbane, growing in profusion at Mount Prosperity. It could be ground into a powder and mixed with the wine. It was unsporting to make hospitality into a lethal gift but anyone who took things at face value in war was a fool.

He talked with his brother about the horses as they neared the landing site. Tracy said Carson, the ostler, typically kept around sixty animals of widely varying quality. He said farmers bought them as personal mounts rather than for the plow. They were a long way from thoroughbreds, not very fast, but sturdy and dependable. Most were docile animals, congenial to farmers who were not practiced riders. That was excellent, because his marines were certainly amateur riders.

His brother's and Gabriel's knowledge of horses would be very helpful in making intelligent purchases. He could simply commandeer the horses as prizes of war but he had enough gold to purchase the entire stock. A well-paid man was unlikely to shout an alarm that the British were in the neighborhood. Animals not used as mounts would be used as pack animals to hurry supplies forward. He turned to Gabriel, sitting just ahead, who seemed to be thoroughly enjoying the voyage.

"You helped us before with your knowledge of horses, Gabriel. Might I presume upon your knowledge now to assist my brother in determining a fair price for some mounts we will likely purchase?"

Gabriel burst into a huge laugh and slapped his knee. "Horses, Cap'n? Ain't nuttin I don't know bout 'em. Grew up with them, worked in mastuh's stables for nigh onta fifteen years. What you wants to know?"

Pennywhistle explained his problem and Gabriel listened attentively. "In addition to determining reliable beasts, could you control and guide animals being used as pack horses? Could you keep them moving and prevent them from being spooked or stampeded?"

"Ain't no problem, Cap'n. Horses be fine creatures but they is real dumb. They think wit their feelins, not their heads. They always follows the strongest, the leader. Long as I rides the leader, I can handle things jus fine. Only trick is to find the leader. Folks like ya can't, meanin' no disrespect, Cap'n but you is a fine, upstandin' gent and takes someone like me willin' to spend years down and dirty g'ttin' to know the beasts. Don't ya worry none, I do a great job for ya, Cap'n!" He spoke the last sentence with a pride Pennywhistle found as touching as it was reassuring.

Pennywhistle began to review the layout of Mount Prosperity. He would have to choose positions wisely. Even with the addition of the Colonial Marines, his force was small. His greatest ally was surprise. Nobody had any reason to suspect he was there but it was foolish to assume news of a British presence would remain a secret for long in a roused countryside. American militia might be amateurs, but even professionals could be beaten by the sheer weight of numbers.

He would part ways with Tracy and Sammie Jo just before he reached the plantation. He trusted Tracy to guide her home. She still had not said exactly where she lived, merely that it was 'not far' from Mount Prosperity. He was both sad and relieved at the idea. He hated emotional farewells and would try to keep the whole thing brisk and business-like. He and his brother had exchanged addresses so they might correspond after the war, but he would simply allow Sammie Jo to fade from his consciousness.

That seemed less and less likely with each passing hour. A lustful part of him wanted her just one more time and a sentimental part said there might be hope for her in a different world. It would require a supreme effort of will to part, but he would find the strength. He remembered his brother's reference to Carlotta and he thought of her memory. That had been true love and his heart still ached for her. Sammie Jo could not compare, but a part of him whispered she should not have to.

He realized the loneliness that he had battled for so long had clouded his judgment. Was Sammie Jo merely a substitute for a lost love, or was she something new and remarkable in her own right? Carlotta had been strong-willed, but she had been worldly and civilized. She was never the wild, dangerous elemental that was Sammie Jo. It angered him that his heart was as foolish as his brain was wise. His brother was right. Be a soldier, be Machiavelli's disciple for just a bit longer and see the thing through to a cold, logical conclusion.

Dale shouted, "Land ho!" Pennywhistle unshipped his telescope and took a good look. A long dock lay half a mile dead ahead. He made his final preparations. He scanned the banks for any signs of scouts or lookouts, but could discern none. He was reassured, but only to a certain point. American scouts were practiced at concealment and he might well have missed some.

The yawl and whale boat landed a quarter of an hour later. His men emptied the boats of their contents and people in five minutes. It was all done in silence and with a practiced economy of movement, since every man knew his task. He kept an eye on Sammie Jo but for once could not read her expression. Her face looked surprisingly bland and impassive, possibly a side effect of the laudanum. She moved without a word of comment or protest.

It was a five minute walk from the dock to the stables. His brother greeted Carson as an old friend and handled the negotiations expertly. He asked Gabriel for his opinion from time to time and the two often nodded in agreement. Pennywhistle had no idea what a fair price for a horse was in these parts, but his brother certainly did and could be trusted to wring the maximum hard bargain out of the proceedings.

In the end, his gold guineas purchased sixty animals, rather more than expected, but the increased numbers would certainly speed the resupply. He was delighted to still have five coins left.

It was comical watching the marines confront their beasts. Amidst a great deal of swearing and cursing, they managed to mount up. His brother and Gabriel helped greatly. They went down the line and gave each marine advice about how to stay in the saddle and a quick primer on horses in general. He selected a small grey mare for his mount. She seemed a friendly enough animal, although she compared unfavorably to Lightning in Spain.

The animals not used for riding were docile and quite willing to be used as pack horses. Barrels of powder and cases of canister from the whaleboat were lashed to their saddles. Pennywhistle also realized that the horses might have another use once a battle commenced.

It took an hour to organize things but everyone was ready to move by 9 a.m. He was pleased. Things were going better than planned.

There was one problem but he had no way of knowing about it. One of the stable boys, a thin, reedy-voiced beanpole of fourteen observed the proceedings. He knew someone who would pay very well for the information he possessed. Jed Hastings, as the boy was called, was not especially brave or patriotic but if a profit could be turned by causing trouble for the British, he was game to take action. He knew the local militia commander might be able to do something about a small group of redcoats. The lieutenant colonel had missed the recent ambush by the lobster-backs and desperately wanted to show he could fight with a talent his predecessor lacked. Men had come forward in large numbers after Parke's defeat and had more than made up for the losses at the Battle at Waterman's Farm.

There was also a more personal reason. His mother had never told him the name of his father but had implied on several occasions that it was one-and-the-same lieutenant colonel. His name was Beems and he was a famous fire-and-brimstone preacher in private life. Perhaps this information could provide him an entrée into his putative father's life.

His boss might wonder where he was under normal circumstances, but today was hardly normal. A few minutes after the British departed, old man Carson would probably break out his stone jug of moonshine in celebration of his good fortune and be insensate for the rest of the day. Jed would slip away unnoticed. The boy chuckled to himself at his cleverness and began to daydream about ways to spend his upcoming wealth.

*****

"I say, Peebles old man, you are being simply beastly to the men." Chivers pointed to 90 Colonial Marines a quarter mile away. The black men were clad only in trousers and their backs were drenched in sweat. They were industriously wielding shovels and throwing up great piles of dirt as zigzagging lines of earthworks were beginning to take shape. Mount Prosperity Plantation was changing from a farm to a fortress.

"Now look here, Peebles, demanding these men dig ditches in this blasted heat is just... unconscionable! I saw you out earlier shouting at them like some disgusting overseer. We should at least allow them to rest after their long march and wait until the heat abates before shoving them into heavy manual labor. These fellows just left slavery, now it seems you are thrusting them back into it. I simply won't have it." Chivers crossed his arms and shook his head to emphasize his point.

The short Scots quartermaster rolled his eyes and spoke with a tone of patient resignation, as if trying to reason with slow child. "Mr. Chivers, you may be senior to me, but I beg that you heed my words. Understand I mean no disrespect but your naiveté will kill far more men than any Yankees we may encounter. I must play the assassin of your innocence so that you, I, and our marines stand a fighting chance of walking out of here in one piece.

"I do not know you personally, sir, but I have met many of your type. You are an aristocratic sprig only just arrived from England with a head full of mush and a character besotted with glory from battles fought solely in your imagination. You are the second or third son, not going to inherit, so your father decided buying a commission was a fine way to provide for you as well as make a man of you. I am guessing you have read plenty of books and understand the theory of war but have never heard the whine of a bullet or the ripping sound of canvas when a cannon ball passes close. You haven't much training and have relied on sergeants to put men through drills. Likely the hottest actions you have seen have been chasing wayward milkmaids or disputing outrageous bills with your tailor.

"You wish to make your mark on the world but are not sure just what that mark is. Thus far, I am informed it is that of a bumbler." Peebles smiled gently. "However, that need not remain a permanent state of affairs. Allow me to help you become the soldier you wish to be. You naturally seek honors and distinctions and are willing to run all manner of risks to secure a mention in dispatches. The problem is that the road to glory is paved with the corpses of good men."

Chivers stared in shock at Peebles, as if he possessed a supernatural ability to read minds.

"I was fighting the French, sir, when you were still sucking on your nursemaid's teat. I have opposed Bonaparte's best on three continents and under the banners of both Scots and English Regiments. I wear the trousers of the 4th now but I started my service in the kilts of the 42nd. I have seen every manner of battle and every manner of man. Believe me when I say my actions spring from experience, not caprice or cruelty.

You have a lot of growing up to do, young sir, and if you will follow my guidance I believe I can be of great assistance.

"Mr. Pennywhistle is depending on us, as is the entire Army. He will be arriving this afternoon and will expect us to have things in place. His instructions are so specific and detailed that I wonder if he missed his calling by not signing on with the Royal Engineers. We have a lot to accomplish in a very short time, so rest is a luxury we can ill afford. We shall have to push these men until they are ready to expire and then push a little harder. In war, men die. You cannot change that. What you can do is sell their lives dearly and make sure every death brings victory a little closer. And for your information, Mr. Chivers, I was not shouting at them, I was singing with them."

Chivers looked thunderstruck. "Singing? Singing? Whatever do you mean?"

"I mean, Mr. Chivers, these blacks are even more musical than the Welsh. They are used to singing when they work, much the way merchant sailors warble sea chanteys when setting sails. Their music is of God and the spirit but its joyful melodies and lively rhythms are far different from the doleful psalms sung in the Cathedrals of Britain. I sang with them to encourage them and... well... I like to sing.

"It may astonish you Mr. Chivers, that though their labor is backbreaking, they are more than willing to continue in their work. I simply told them they would get a chance to take a solid bash at the white folk who had once been their owners. Revenge is considered a bad thing in the Good Book, but it is a mighty powerful motivator in war."

Chivers looked perplexed, uncertain of whether the adoption of a new perspective was a good or a bad thing. A few seconds later, he struggled manfully to screw his face into a dignified expression he thought befitted a King's Officer. "Well Peebles, I'm not sure I hold with a lot of what you say but I grant you have more experience. I suppose I have to allow for a certain eccentricity from a man who once wore skirts into battle. I have a gambler's heart, sir, and I have never been able to resist a long shot. I will take chance on you, so *lay on Macduff* and tell me what we need to do."

Peebles smiled, pleased that his words had gotten through the Englishman's thick skull. "One word Mr. Chivers: *DIG!*"

A chorus of voices swelled in *Swing Low, Sweet Chariot* and the Colonial Marines continued to do just that.

Chapter Sixteen

March viewed the column swaggering past his horse with great satisfaction. He had spent the previous day forming 1000 stout-hearted men into an *ad hoc* regiment. Frustrated by his meeting with Winder, he had prowled the Montgomery Court House grounds like an angry panther denied food. He soon discovered a number of company-grade officers grumbling loudly and freely about sitting inert while the British pillaged Washington. The lack of any coherent plans emerging from Winder's headquarters had created an atmosphere of cynical discontent. What good was patriotism if the higher-ups disdained to put it to any use?

March found ten especially hot-blooded captains who were just itching to fight the British. Their passion furnished him a heaven-sent opportunity and he convinced them that he could use their companies to scratch that itch. Since Winder had no interest in using their men, he saw no reason why he might not borrow them for a while.

They would still be in charge of their companies but now they would be leading instead of supervising; real soldiers rather than *de facto* nannies. All of the officers expressed disgust for Winder, derisively referring to him as Granny, Scooter, and General Windbag. As word spread, March ended up turning away troops rather than soliciting them.

March was not sure if he was filibustering, making war independently of the government, but the lawfully constituted government had fled and strange times called for unusual actions. He was absolutely certain that it was disgraceful to do nothing while the national honor lay rotting like a forgotten corpse. He needed to find like-minded leaders to organize a greater effort and the name Josiah Beems kept recurring in his talks with officers. He had been nicknamed, "The Fighting Preacher."

Two officers who had attended Beems' sermons gave him glowing endorsements. They averred that he had an irresistible personal magnetism that enraptured a man almost against his will; later generations would call it "charisma."

"When that man speaks, he puts the fire of God into you," said the shorter officer. "Once you hear his words, you can never go back to being what you were before," said the taller officer. He was always spoken of with respect and more than a little awe. Beems had spread the word far and wide that he was hell-bent on fighting the British anytime, anywhere.

March found Beems' lack of a military background worrisome but his success as an evangelical preacher would be very useful in rousing the countryside. Beems' skill in working crowds added to his own military knowledge would likely create a winning combination. Besides, when time was of the essence one could not be too particular about allies. Beems at least possessed great energy and will, two things that Winder lacked and which counted for much in war.

Beems was reported to be assembling a large body of troops at the Charles County Court House and so it was the logical destination for March and his newly-formed command. If he had heard of Beems' efforts there was a possibility that other patriots had as well and the Court House might prove a center of an American military renaissance. The Court House was some distance but nearly astride the chief British supply route and the quickest way to bring an enemy to heel was to sever that lifeline.

There was an air of cheerful expectancy among the troops as they marched; a feeling that they were actually doing something to prove the Republic had men of zeal who would take bold actions rather than prattle bold talk. Much might be done against the British if men with patriotism in their hearts and fire in their bellies worked together.

*****

Daniel Parke greeted the dawn with a mixture of relief and pain. He was badly hung over and his tongue tasted like old sawdust, his stomach shot fountains of bile, and the light speared his eyes like demonic lances, but he was pleased he was making steady progress toward home. The horse had far more stamina than he had guessed. He had pushed her harder than he should, but the urgency to reach home outweighed other concerns.

He had awakened three hours after the storm ended and had decided to ride through the night. He normally would have waited, but he was giddy from the champagne and completely unafraid of any obstacles. The false confidence of alcohol convinced him he had almost supernatural good luck that would see him through. Mostly, he kept seeing Archie's face. He had to know how his recovery progressed.

He was ashamed that he had thought of him before his children and his mother, but he could not help himself. He knew his involvement with Archie had to end, but he had no idea how to bring it about. He hoped he would discover the will somewhere in himself, but right now he could only think of holding Archie in his arms.

Archie was a thoroughly decent fellow. He had been far too harsh in his earlier assessments. The ambush of his regiment was actually no one's fault, just one of the accidents of war. He had let fear and grief unbalance his judgment and had blamed his second-in-command. He hoped Archie could forgive him. A part of him said it was all the foolish sentimentality of wine, but his subconscious would not listen.

He wondered if the British had done any further damage to the plantation. Much repair would probably be necessary, but he had to admit they were usually far better behaved than American troops would have been in similar circumstances. Whatever the damage, he would sink his teeth into the repairs straightaway. He needed something to put his back up against, take his mind away from his unnatural urges.

His wound started throbbing again. He needed to have a physician look at it. All the more reason to get home quickly and have it properly dressed. It did not seem any worse and the slow bleeding had ceased. Still, there just a hint of an odd scent when he poked his finger on it. Odd and unpleasant, like cheese slightly past it's prime. Maybe the champagne had affected his sense of smell. He drove his spurs into the horse's flanks and she surged violently ahead.

*****

Manton's men resumed their march. He had inspected the troops before starting and had to leave two of his men behind. It amazed him they had made it as far as they had. One private had been shot in the thigh, and had hobbled the entire way using his musket as a cane. When it came time to fall in, he simply could not get up. The crude tourniquet round his thigh oozed a steady flow of pale blood. His color looked poor. The other soldier had been wounded in the upper arm and shoulder and the wounds reeked. The smell was distinctive, the outcome potentially lethal-- gangrene.

They both needed medical attention, but the surgeons were already overworked and the column could not stop its march because of the distress of two men. He spoke to a mounted officer carrying a flag of truce. He had been detailed to inform the Americans of men in need of medical attention. Manton felt some slight relief. Whatever the Americans were, they were not barbarians and treated British wounded with the same solicitude their own received.

Pop, pop, pop...He felt rushes of air pass his face. Damn it, American militia again. Probably just a squad or so. There had been no organized pursuit as far as he could tell, but small bands of militia had appeared at irregular intervals to lob a few pot shots at the column before vanishing into the woods. He yelled "charge bayonets" with what remained of his energy.

The men advanced slowly and deliberately, their bayonets thrust forward at waist level. He heard a lot of shuffling in the woods. By the time the redcoats reached the trees, the militia had fled. It was a typical result. They had no stomach for British steel. Still, the constant nipping at the column by such squads wore the men down. Each time they had to perform pest control, they lost a little more energy.

The redcoats resumed their march and the miles ground slowly by. The men said nothing and plodded on with grim determination. Their uniforms were filthy and the brick red of their tunics had faded to a dusky reddish brown. The driving rains had wilted the fronts of their tall black shakos and they looked like low, misshapen, mud chimneys battered by a hailstorm. He told his men from time to time that solace and succor lay just a day ahead at a plantation that had been specially prepared for that purpose. It seemed to cheer them. He hoped he was not lying.

A small regimental band struck up the jaunty *Lilibolero*. The drummers pounded a dramatic accompaniment. Pipers from the Fusiliers lent their stirring skirls. Smiles appeared on a few faces and the marching cadence improved. For a least a few minutes, the soldiers forgot the powerful sun and the choking dust.

*****

Peebles gave a sharp salute to Chivers which Chivers returned in a leisurely fashion. "First patrol just reported in, Mr. Chivers. No sign of Yankee activity."

"A good sign, I think, Mr. Peebles. Perhaps we overestimate the patriotism these Jonathans boast so loudly about. Just how many patrols do we have out?"

"We have fifteen two-man patrols covering every possible approach to Mount Prosperity. Most of our men have woodland experience in addition to their light infantry training. In addition, four of the men have relatives on neighboring plantations, so that multiplies our eyes and ears considerably. Not a grasshopper moves in these parts here that the local blacks do not know about. It's almost as if we have spies planted in the enemy camp."

"I wouldn't count the Yankees out just yet, Mr. Chivers. They are probably calling out the militia as we speak and it will take time to concentrate their forces."

"I have to admit, Peebles old man, that these fortifications are shaping up nicely. Those blackthorn hedges are short but almost as thick and impenetrable as those in the Bocage country of Normandy. With the trenches dug below them they give the men excellent concealment. Those other things, however, seem rather barbaric." He wrinkled his nose in distaste. "What was the term he used?"

"Tiger pits, Mr. Chivers. They are widely used in India. It turns a harmless looking field into a series of traps. I gather you object to the punji sticks embedded on their bottoms?"

"Yes, it seems a horrible way to go, spitted like a roast pig."

"We lack numbers, Mr. Chivers, so we have to make up for that with cleverness, even if it is a bit diabolical. At least we aren't covering the sticks with excrement as is done in India.

"The bits of metal and pipe Mr. Pennywhistle has asked us to collect are part of that ingenuity. He says in his instructions that when he arrives he will assemble them into infernal devices packed with explosive charges. A flintlock will be attached to each one for ignition. The flintlock will be activated by either a pressure plate or a trip wire. We can plant them all over the avenues leading to Mount Prosperity. It will give any attackers a series of nasty surprises and will soften them up just as effectively as if we had a battalion of the 95th acting as skirmishers."

Just then a squad of marines rolled two large wine barrels by. Peebles smiled in satisfaction. "Please note, Mr. Chivers, that I feel utterly safe in trusting those black men not to sample the contents. I could not make the same boast with white soldiers."

Chivers shook his head slowly and pursed his lips in distaste. "Adding wolfsbane powder to the wine when the barrels are opened does not seem right. Killing men when they merely seek to slake their thirst? Horrid, sir, horrid! So is our use of infernal devices. Both are far outside the bounds of fair play I learned at Eton and definitely not in any of the books I have read about warfare. I feel like we are become lethal versions of Capability Brown, designing gardens of death instead of pleasure." He sighed deeply. "Still, when you've drawn the short end of the stick, I suppose you must seize any advantage you have."

Peebles spoke gently and philosophically, "Mr. Chivers I can appreciate your concern for some modicum of civility in war but I would ask you this: would you rather be alive to feel guilty or dead and unburdened by any guilt?"

Chivers gave a rueful half-smile. "When you put it that way, there really isn't much of a choice."

"I do put it that way, so please grant your conscience a long rest."

*****

Pennywhistle, Tracy, Sammie Jo, and the mounted marines cantered along for a solid hour before they reached a literal parting of the ways. Sammie Jo rode well and boldly like a seasoned horseman. She had a natural seat and disdained all of the sidesaddle nonsense apparently inbred in polite women. They halted their horses at the spot where the trail branched in two directions: one north toward Mount Prosperity, the other south toward Sammie Jo's home. The trails would take their lives in two different directions as well.

Pennywhistle found himself choked up and it angered him. He forced steel into his voice but it came out in an odd, husky tone, barely above a resonant whisper. "I saw you didn't take your laudanum earlier. Are you well enough to proceed on home? Just how far is your place, Sammie Jo?"

"Don't need the potion no more. I like a clear head and a little pain keeps you alert. 'Bout five mile, right straight ahead, Sugar Plum. I could stay, you know. No reason I gotta go." Her face softened for just a second, and she looked him right in the eye. She held his gaze for perhaps a second.

Her half-smile changed to a frown and her face hardened. "But I can see in your face, you don't want that; duty, honor, serving the crown and all that folderol always trump regular folk in your mind.

"I understand you better than y'all think. First time we met, you purred at me oh-so-polite, but I could see in your eyes you were hornier for me than a three-balled tomcat. You tell yourself a woman ain't got no place in your soldiering, but that ain't it at all. I think you're hiding. Regulations, oaths, and duty signify mighty big to you because you use them like quills on a porcupine to prevent any risk to your heart. Ain't no man nor beast you're afeared of, but damned if the word 'passion' don't make you quiver like a whipped hound dog.

"I know I'm just no-account country bushel buby to you but I speak my mind and don't hide my feelins behind fancy talk and high falutin notions from some old-timey books. You got fine ways from good breeding but deep down you're the one that's a bumpkin of the heart." She shook her head. "Damn shame, damn shame! It coulda been..." she struggled for a word he would understand. "Glorious!" She laughed with bitter resignation.

Pennywhistle kept his face stoical and refused to offer any soothing words in mitigation. She had read him well, but he could not let even a hint of it show. He gave her both barrels, metaphorically, right between the eyes. "Sammie Jo," he said brusquely, "I have no time to argue with you. You are quite right, I have my duty. You might think it trifling but I most certainly do not. Duty is my watchword. The feelings you speak of so carelessly are the sort that get people killed on the battlefield. Only by remaining dry-eyed while others weep, can

I preserve the lives of my men. I have done all I can for you. I wish you the best. Our association has been most interesting, pleasant in many respects, but do not for a second mistake it for something it is not. You have tested my patience, my mercy, and my oath to the King. Others who have done so have suffered fatal consequences. Take some well-meant advice. Go home. Hunt, fish, and trap. Never play soldier again, no matter what. Find yourself a man of your own background who appreciates your many unique gifts."

The last sentence sounded a bit wistful. That would never do. His voice became crisp and military. "I wish you a long and fruitful life."

Sammie Jo glared at him and her voice cut like a skinning knife. "Fruitful life? Where did you pull that phrase from, your arse? This ain't no drawing room and I ain't no delicate flower! I reckon you and I are like two stray shoes that have seen a lot of hard use. We belong together as a pair. We may be covered in scuff marks, but there ain't no kind of ground we can't handle."

"Shoes?" Pennywhistle said in surprise. *An odd analogy yet it fit like...well-made shoes.*

"Damn it, Tom, not everything in life has to be based on tradition and always doing what quality folk expect! Don't you get it? I'm jawin' with ya about lookin' into the feelings that make life worth living. You don't gotta be kept on a leash by the silly manners en mores that you A-RIS-tos get all fussed about! For once, try listenin' to yer heart. Jesus, Tom! Do you even know you have one?"

He heard her clearly, but acted as if he did not. "My brother will see you home. Trust him. Hard as it is for you to obey, follow his instructions exactly. Have I your promise to do so?" He looked her sternly in the eye.

"Shucks, Sugar Plum, I'd never think of not doing what y'all ask." She had a dangerous twinkle in her eye that was the opposite of amusing. She smiled brightly. "Promise I'll go right straight home and never bother the British again." She crossed her heart and laughed cynically.

He could see she was thinking and plotting. Her thoughts likely presaged trouble. He turned to his brother.

"John, it has been a privilege to know you. You have my Berwick and Edinburgh addresses. I want our association to continue after the war. I think peace may furnish many pleasant prospects for the both of us. Life is so strange. I lost one brother, but have gained another. Take care of yourself and....how did you put it? Don't take any damn fool risks!"

Tracy edged his horse close and extended his hand. He angrily wiped a solitary tear from his left eye. "My enemy now my friend, a brother who is new yet a part of me; the world turned upside down! You have given me more than you can know; not just a family but a legacy. I will most certainly write. Be careful, I have known you too short a time to lose you to some addle-pated notions of gallantry!"

The Englishman recognized his own sentimentality in his brother. This was getting entirely too emotional, time to spare him embarrassment. He snapped the crispest salute he could muster. It was briskly returned. "Good Luck!" He pivoted the horse and dug his spurs into her flanks. She burst into a gallop. He raised his right hand and brushed the tear away.

Focus, damn it! Do what you always do. Put Sammie Jo and Tracy in a mental lockbox and don't let them out until the job is done.

*****

March was pleased that his men chatted merrily as they marched. Spiral columns of dust marked their progress and rose high above the tall pines that fringed the road. Ordinarily evidence of poor discipline, he took chatting as a good omen. Cheerful, optimistic men looked at the future with confidence and would have faith that they would prevail upon the battlefield, even against the experienced British. He checked his watch and estimated his men would reach Charles County Courthouse within the next two hours. He was very eager to confer with Colonel Beems.

"What do you think, Gaius? Maybe 700?"

"No Titus, I'd say closer to 1,000."

Gaius Gates and Titus Taylor lay sheltered behind a stand of oak trees and a line of ferns that marked the left edge of the road to Charles County Courthouse. They had been shadowing March's men for twenty minutes. The column was noisy and conspicuous, while they had been the opposite. The two colonial marines wanted to be sure of numbers and destination before they reported back to headquarters at Mount Prosperity.

"Where do you think they are headed?"

"Charles County Court House. One of the field hands at Boyd's Bluff Plantation told me his mastuh had been talking about big doings there. He also said his mastuh was fixin' to call out the militia from Blake's Hundred. Put two and two together, Gaius. There is some kind of rally going on there. I want you to get that information back to Mr. Peebles while I continue to follow them."

"But Mr. Chivers is in charge!"

"He's just an old granny with a young swell's manners and body. He don't know nothin'. Talk to Peebles. That old boy's seen lots of action and will know what to do with your report."

"Do you think it will come to a fight, Titus?"

"Did you get a look at their faces? Every man jack in that column was as hungry for a fight as a dog spotting a steak bone. We're going to be tussling with them soon, real soon." A fierce smile bloomed on Titus's face. "I can't wait."

*****

Pennywhistle pushed his mount and his men hard and reached Mount Prosperity at noon. Nothing had changed since his last visit. The large, two-story plantation house of red brick and tall windows was a tribute to the classical influences of the Adam style: Federal Style in the local parlance. Long porches on both floors encircled the main structure and twenty four Doric columns of marble supported the mansard roof. From the rocking chairs on the second floor, one had a view of tobacco fields stretching as far as the eye could see.

The home was set a quarter mile back from the main gate which was framed by low hedgerows. The approach to the gate came through a long alley of soaring oak trees and perfectly manicured grass. Shallow ravines bordered the edges of the oak alley. A better killing field could not be imagined.

Pennywhistle immediately assumed command from Mr. Chivers who perfectly lived up to his reputation as a silly, well-meaning aristocrat. He probably cut a dashing figure in a drawing room and set ladies hearts atwitter but was out his depth on a battlefield.

Mr. Peebles came along a minute later. He and Chivers listened to Pennywhistle's plans, although it was clear that only Peebles grasped them completely. The businesslike Scotsman was a man after the marine's own heart and concerned with even the smallest details. Peebles took him on a quick tour of the fortifications. Pennywhistle was impressed his instructions had been followed exactly and that much had been accomplished in a short time.

The entrenchments were formidable. The only problem was an insufficiency of soldiers to man them properly. With Pennywhistle's men added to the Colonial Marines, the defending force would still be fewer than 150. Still, one man behind earthworks was worth five in the open and all of the British had training whereas the majority of their opponents would likely have little.

The lines zigzagged to provide enfilade fire although the general shape of the fortifications was that of a cone. Wide at the top, narrow at the bottom, the lines were designed to funnel attackers into a narrow avenue of approach which could be swept by concentrated volley fire. A compressed approach would also limit the number of muskets an attacker could bring to bear, reducing the impact of a disparity of numbers.

Patrols came and went as he spoke with Peebles. A very active defense was in play and they would have plenty of warning of an attack.

He spoke with a returning scout at length and was struck by how zealously the marine had performed his patrol duties. Gaius Gates exhibited intelligence, an attention to detail, and an impressive knowledge of local trails. He was also eager to meet his former owners in battle and give them hot lead and cold steel as payment for years of floggings and mistreatment.

"Capital use of cover and initiative, Private Gates. I think your instincts are right. Get some food and water and then head back toward Charles County Court House. This time take a section of Marines with you. Link up with Taylor and continue to shadow those militia men. If they make any move toward this locality, send a messenger and open a distant, running fire on them. Nothing hot or headlong, mind you, merely a swarm of bees annoying a large flabby animal. Provoke their ire and their stupidity and draw them toward Mount Prosperity. They would likely find their way here anyway, but I'd prefer them to arrive worn down and off balance."

"Aye aye, sir. It'll be a pleasure, sir." His wide smile confirmed the sincerity of his words.

After leaving Peebles, he told his men to establish bivouacs just to the rear of the lines so they could stand to at a moment's notice. Once that was accomplished, he had them trundle carts full of metal oddments from the barn to their encampments. He turned command over to Dale as he went to confer with Gabriel about reliable field hands on neighboring plantations. The more raw intelligence he had, the better.

The marines were puzzled as to why the bits of metal were valuable. Dale was happy to explain. "We're going to start a bomb factory, lads. Don't look so surprised! You know Mr. Pennywhistle has more tricks up his sleeves than a card sharp playing a table of beginners. You don't have to understand how they work, just follow the drawings the captain made. Four men to each group and let's see if we can have these things ready for the insertion of explosives in the next five hours. After that we will plant 'em where Mr. Pennywhistle says they will do the most damage."

Corporal Barker spoke for many. "This ain't exactly proper warfare, is it Sarge? Soldiers won't be able to shoot back at these things...these uh...uh..."

"Mine's the term you are looking for, Barker," said Dale harshly. "Since when did Mr. Pennywhistle fight fair? He plays to win and because he does, a lot more of you will be alive after this fight. I have a feeling in the years to come, infernal devices and odd mechanical contrivances will dominate the battlefield."

The men smiled and nodded, pleased they were participating in a foretaste of the future and believed their chances of survival had increased considerably.

March reached the Charles County Courthouse and smiled in satisfaction at seeing impressive numbers of militia already camped upon the green. His 1000 men were tired after the long trek from Montgomery Court House but they were delighted to have put a good distance between themselves and the perpetually misguided Winder. His men wanted to fight and if Colonel Beems lived up to his reputation, they would get that chance very soon.

He saw a grinning Beems galloping toward him; a smile something he hardly expected since the man was as renowned for his lack of humor as he was for his hatred of all things British. Beems' expression said he had received the message March had dispatched via a fast dispatch rider and wanted to do something about it.

Taylor saw it all and knew that his friend Gaius had been right to have him follow the column. Trouble was brewing for the British and it would all start from the village green that lay 400 yards beyond the tree line that he was using for concealment. The only question was when it would begin. He hoped his friend would be back soon with reinforcements so he could cause these folks some devilment. He began a careful counting of the American militia. He moved around to various locations to be certain he did not miss a man. Twenty minutes later he had a number: 2,200.

*****

Pennywhistle began a detailed inspection of the perimeter of the field works. He paid close attention to sites that would give the Chambers Revolving Volley Guns good concealment while affording them clear fields of fire. He wanted the Americans caught in a ring of fire.

Dale thought his commander could use some feminine comfort about now. He was amazed at his commander's strength of will in ridding himself of Sammie Jo. She was bad news but could certainly provide some diverting moments. His officer was ruthless in command of men but seemed to have a blind spot towards women. He should have rogered Sammie Jo vigorously and then ditched her. Alas, his officer was cursed with something Dale lacked: chivalry.

*****

The arrival of Pennywhistle's marines and the general bustle about Mount Prosperity had been observed by two American scouts hidden in the tobacco fields. They were dull men and had been assigned the duty because no one had expected anything to come of it. Private Parsons was slightly less dull than his companion, Private Hewett, who could actually read and cipher. He and Hewett were here waiting not for the British, but for Daniel Parke. He had disappeared and no one thought he was stupid enough to reappear, yet the possibility existed.

The new militia commander, Beems, had sent them. Beems had told Parsons and Hewett that Parke was an incompetent, a coward, and most darkly: a pervert. He had a lot to answer for and he could only be brought to justice if his whereabouts could be established.

294

Private Parsons took a chaw of tobacco from his pocket and stuffed it into his mouth. The chaw would help him stay alert. He had slept soundly through the steamy night and was surprised when he awoke to flashes of red dimly glimpsed through the morning mist. British? But these men were black! What were they doing here, of all places?

He thought they were just passing through but they soon commenced digging. He continued to watch in amazement as fortifications began to take shape. He observed through the late afternoon when white redcoats marched in. He carefully counted numbers. This redcoat incursion was a complete surprise and Beems wanted the fullest information as soon as possible. The men back at Charles County Court House were spoiling for a fight and the British presence at Mount Prosperity would give them an excellent place to start one.

Since the county militia regiment under Colonel Parke had been wiped out in an ambush four days ago, events in Prince George's and Charles Counties had tumbled toward insanity. Parke had disappeared and the lack of an official account had given rise to all manner of outrageous rumors. People congregated in large numbers in the many small towns and gradually those gatherings moved toward mobs. People wanted simple answers and quick action, but events were too complicated for either. Town mandarins who counseled patience were met with jeers and derision.

When reports of Washington in flames and the government on the run began filtering in, the existing fear, confusion, and panic had morphed into full blown hysteria.

Local governments fractured as town alderman and county commissioners fussed, fumed, and speechified but clearly had no idea what to do. "Committees of Safety" were formed to deal with the emergency. Every able-bodied male with a musket was called out, not just the usual sixteen to sixty, but old men and boys as well. Some did not even have muskets, merely pitchforks and angry intentions.

Ad hoc mounted patrols, often based on local fox hunts, roamed far and wide seeking any sign of a British presence. They wanted someone to pay for what had happened to their country and any British unit would do. A few patrolman also favored stringing up Daniel Parke should he be discovered.

Militia musters were held on numerous village greens. While patriotism and determination swelled, training and discipline remained poor. The locals firmly believed that sheer numbers and the desire for retribution would supply them the strength to face down Regulars.

Chaos often gives rise to the most unexpected of leaders and the upheavals in the Chesapeake were no exception. Beems had stepped forward and boldly took charge while others dithered. He fancied himself a later day Cromwell.

Cromwell had been a - forty year old country squire of limited means before the English Civil War lifted him from obscurity. He combined religious zealotry with an unexpected brilliance in soldiering and eventually became England's first and last military dictator, styling himself 'The Lord Protector.' The Founding Fathers had seen Cromwell's legacy as a bad one and had worked hard to separate church and state. Beems admired the Founders but saw no reason why church and state could not work in tandem for the greater glory of the Republic.

Beems instinctively understood the military principle of concentration and had ordered the scattered militia companies to march forthwith and hard for a central county assembly point. Charles Court House was chosen because it was close to where Beems thought the British were, or at least might be.

Beems had read a lot of books on soldiering but had no formal military training. He did however, look the part of the heroic leader and had plenty of skill in manipulating men. He was four inches over six feet with the thin, almost emaciated body of an aesthete. He had a noble head capped with long flowing silver locks. His face was craggy with long fissures and reminded people of an outcrop of granite.

He had great physical presence and radiated energy and strength of will which came in very handy in his Pentecostal pulpit. The good reverend was a fire and brimstone orator as famous for his jeremiads as he was for his stubborn refusal to learn the art of compromise. It was said his booming voice could easily be heard at a mile.

The Old Testament was far more congenial to him than the New because judging and smiting came far more readily than understanding and mending. Humor was unwelcome in his reality and it seemed almost blasphemous for anyone to crack a smile in his presence.

He made a great show of public dedication to his mousey wife Charity, whom he beat in private when she was not suitably obedient, but marriage alone could not sate his powerful sexuality. Two of his female parishioners made regular calls to the parsonage for special "counseling." His wife was always out on an errand when that "counseling" took place.

Most of the militia thought Beems the perfect man to administer a little fire and brimstone to the British. They were lambs to the slaughter when Beems made extravagant promises about how he would grind the British into dust when he met them on the field of honor. No one thought to ask him just how he would accomplish this.

Parsons had seen enough. He told Private Hewett to stay put and continue to observe Mount Prosperity. Hewett sleepily agreed. He was rather slow on the best of days. Parsons dashed to the edge of the field and untied his horse. He mounted up, and put his spurs to her. Beems would be pleased. He had very good news. Lots of redcoats would die in very short order. The Americans would finally have vengeance and victory.

CHAPTER SEVENTEEN

"We won't need your plantation for more than a week, Amity," said Pennywhistle patiently. He was gently putting the old woman in her place by casually using her first name. "I am happy to talk with you but things under me will be no different than under Mr. Chivers. Other than the earthworks, we will cause it no damage and as long as my soldiers remain unmolested by the militia, it will stay that way. We kept our promises the last time we were here and will do so again. I will give you a few guineas for the use of your place. You and your children will naturally remain under confinement, pleasant and easy, unless you give us reason to make the terms more harsh. I must rely on you to do nothing untoward. Have I your word, Amity?" Pennywhistle's manner was courtly, but his words brooked no compromise.

"I don't like it, don't like it one little bit, but there is not much I can do about it either, is there? I won't cause you any trouble. I have to admit, you were as good as your word last time. But really, I am only the temporary mistress of the household. My son, Daniel, will be home soon. This is his plantation. You will have to talk to him."

Pennywhistle doubted that would occur anytime soon, but he noticed the old woman had a child-like faith that her son would find a way home. He had discovered the hapless colonel had survived the ambush and had gone back to join the American forces, but for all he knew, the man had met his end at Bladensburg. He respected a man who sought active atonement for a mistake.

He left the house and slowly walked the grounds. Chivers had sensibly consented to Peebles' guidance and the Scotsman's initial dispositions were good. Peebles in turn had consulted with Dale and the result further improved the troop deployments.

Logic told Pennywhistle the Americans would not come. Their government was in shambles, their high command in disarray, and their militia disorganized. Supplies were low, the weather was torrid, and they were still punch drunk from Bladensburg. Attack was impossible. *Therefore, that is exactly what they will do*, screamed his intuition.

Americans might lack sense and experience, but revenge mixed with patriotism was a powerful motivator. The Americans would find a way to bring the fight to him. He felt it in his bones.

There were two avenues of approach. Ross' men would arrive by the Acquesco Road. The Americans would use the Charles Road.   As soon as the American approach was detected, the wolfsbane would be dumped into the wine barrels placed by the side of the road. Thirsty soldiers and wine were like magnets and metal filings.

Parke had planted hedgerows on either side of the gate. They were only about three feet tall, blackthorn hedgerows took years to mature, but they were thick and gnarled. They were perfect defensive positions and allied to the earthworks dug beneath them, they were well-nigh impregnable. The road leading to them was wide and afforded an excellent field of fire. He could see any armed force coming well in advance of musket range.

There were two large tobacco barns that flanked the main house on the left, three hundred yards from the mansion. They would form the second line of defense if the first was breached. The space between the two barns was short and could be covered by fire from the upper floors. The barns would be formidable obstacles. Barns often formed islands of resistance that disrupted the linear fighting favored in Europe. Heavily defended buildings were very, very difficult for raw militia to handle.

His last line of defense would be the house itself. The walls were thick, stout brick and there were plenty of windows to fire from, both on the first and second floors. His father once mentioned the Chew Mansion at the Battle of Germantown in the Revolutionary War. A small group of soldiers had turned it into a fortress and the American's fruitless attempts to take it had wrecked their entire battle plan. Artillery in skilled hands was necessary to root soldiers out of a house; small arms were not sufficient. He wished he had field pieces but the Chambers Volley guns would be reasonably effective understudies.

More than anything, though, war was about psychology, rather than sheer force of numbers. Predators hunted the weak, the wounded, and outliers from the herd. He needed to convince the Americans that the British were anything but easy pickings. To that end, he would be aggressive in his defense as he had seen Wellington do in the Peninsula. He was taking a risk attempting the most difficult coup in all of warfare: a double envelopment. Yet the risk was less than it seemed for he had an excellent insight into the mentality of the enemy. Racial prejudice was not just a perspective, it was a weapon. He wanted to make the Americans perform the equivalent of sticking their heads into a long sack then pinch that sack off at the neck.

The one thing he was not certain about was the horses. He had never understood the beasts and he had no idea how they would react to their first exposure to gunfire. Once they were launched, he probably would have little control over what course they would follow.

Gabriel had spent the day unloading the pack horses and distributing the powder and shot. He worked under Dale's guidance and Dale was impressed by his intelligence as much as his zeal. It occurred to Pennywhistle that such a man might prove useful to him after the war ended. If Gabriel had been born white, he would have gone far in the world.

As the redcoats made their preparations, he had Rufus play a few more tunes from his seemingly inexhaustible repertoire. The soldiers enjoyed it greatly and it pleased him too. He had always loved music. It was one of the few good legacies from an acerbic mother obsessed with the piano. Rufus belonged in a formal orchestra. If they got out of this fight, he would look into that.

He watched Gabriel unload four swivel guns that had been sent forward from Benedict. With the Chamber's weapons, he would have fourteen pieces of light artillery. He debated where to use them. Forward or rear. He would compromise. Two would go forward with the repeating volley guns and two would defend the house.

He posted lookouts on the Charles Road, but told the rest of the men to eat and rest. Four Colonial Marine patrols were still actively scouting and he had reinforced the small reconnoitering force under Private Gates.

Rufus had spent the morning entertaining the troops with his playing. Pennywhistle told Rufus to stop playing and go inside lest heat stroke hit. It was insanity to indulge in excessive movement in the blazing midday sun. Marylanders had no formal analogue to the siesta he had known in the Adriatic and Spain. Dale had the keenest eyes of anyone and had been an extremely successful poacher in a former life. He settled into a comfortable hide half a mile beyond the plantation gate. He unfurled the Ramsden that Pennywhistle had lent him and scanned the horizon carefully. Nothing. That would change. The Americans would come. It was just a matter of time and he was a patient man.

*****

Daniel Parke rode hunched over, but the effects of the hangover were steadily retreating. He had just reached the northern fringe of his 5000 acres. The road to the main house lay just around the next bend. His shoulder hurt badly and the smell worsened with each passing mile. He had an idea what it meant, but hoped he was wrong. He would send word for Dr. Crawford straightaway.

The fields were still in good shape. The British had left the tobacco crop untouched. The hot weather was actually good for its growth. It put heart into him and he quickened his horse's pace.

The road had been unoccupied but he spotted a lone rider materialize from the bend three hundred yards ahead. The rider spurred his horse forward, first into a fast canter, then a full gallop. The man headed directly for him. Who was it? He did not recognize the horse or rider, but it was too far to make out a face clearly. He halted his own mount, transfixed with curiosity.

The distance between the two of them closed quickly. When the face came into view at twenty-five yards, he did not recognize it, but it was angry and determined. The man on horseback seemed to recognize him. The stranger drew a large pistol from the saddle, leveled it at him, and crashed his spurs into his mount. His horse shot forward like a spear of lightning.

Parke saw the lethal intent at the last second and providentially ducked. It was hard to hit a target from a fast moving mount. Pistols were inaccurate in the best of hands, and the other rider most certainly did not have them. His shot passed no closer than a foot from Parke's shoulder and then Parsons blazed past.

Parke recovered quickly. He was livid and he had a pistol too. Unlike Parsons, he had good hands, a fine eye, and a lot of anger.

His shot hit Parsons in the back of the shoulder and shoved him hard against the horse's mane. He screamed in pain. He was bleeding badly, but he did not quit. He cruelly rammed his spurs into his horse and galloped off.

Parke smiled slightly, in satisfaction at his shot. Damn the man! Why did a stranger want him dead? It made no sense. He touched his own shoulder and winced from the pain. He urged his horse forward and tried to think. Something was badly wrong. Whatever it was, it was very dark and his well-ordered universe had begun to un-ravel. Every one of his fears returned in an instant. He had to get home; his mother would undoubtedly know what to do with the situation.

It would almost be better for everyone if he died of his wound. His life might end, but the stories about him would remain unsubstantiated and his family and legacy protected. A wave of despair washed over him.

No! He had too much to live for. He had to see Archie again. He had to make sure Archie lived, had to hold him in his arms one last time. He had to hug his children as well. He rounded the last bend and what he saw took his breath away.

Redcoats! What were they doing here? He wasn't going to turn back now. Hang the consequences! He was going home!

*****

Manton's men marched on, mile after steamy mile. The redcoats pushed their physical exertions to the edge of collapse and their pace continued to slow. The cruel Maryland sun showed no mercy. It amazed him they did it all for a shilling a day. They plodded grimly forward, held together by pure heart and iron constitutions. There had been no further militia attacks and each mile passed lessened the chance any pursuit would overtake them. The killing pace paradoxically increased the column's safety. Manton had seen a few mounted American scouts at widely spaced intervals, but no sign of any organized infantry movements.

Despite his best efforts, straggling had increased. The open march order of his company had gradually become very loose indeed. He would never have permitted it under ordinary circumstances, might have tightened the order to the half-distance. His company resembled a line of bread dough being pulled longer and longer and growing thinner and thinner. He also knew several men had deserted. That bothered him. He felt it a personal failure of leadership.

But he knew it was not just his problem. The provost marshal had been sending out parties to retrieve deserters. A captured few would be made examples, pay the ultimate penalty. He understood the necessity, but it was also hardly fair. Men could only take so much.

He recalled a rest halt lay just ahead. He remembered Pennywhistle telling him that it was moment's like these that truly tested an officer's ability. It was a time to move men beyond their limits, convince them that even though they were ready to drop, their officer reposed sufficient confidence in them to be utterly certain they possessed the hidden reserves of strength to conquer that one last mile.

It was never done with the flat of a sword smashed against a backside or dire threats bellowed with fire, but with words of quiet encouragement administered at just the right moments. It was a trick, a game, an artifice but one that if well played, saved lives. It was not as if the men did not know what was happening, they had keen eyes for truth, but faith in a good officer allowed them to see beyond mere reason.

He walked slowly down the line, quietly telling the men a very cold, fresh brook awaited at the next rest stop. Just a few more miles to sanctuary, he joked, just a walk in the park. His tongue carried him away, and by the end of the line, the stop sounded like a second Eden. He hoped it was true, but really anything short of the Sahara would seem a paradise.

Chapter Eighteen

Private Parsons almost fell off his horse. He made it to Colonel Beems headquarters on the Courthouse Green on sheer willpower alone. One of Beems' aides, Captain Packard, a Baptist deacon turned militia officer, saw his plight, and caught him as he slid sideways. "Got to talk to the colonel. Right now. Important. Redcoats. Parke. Please!" The words came out barely above a whisper, but Parson's urgency was clear. He noticed Parsons was bleeding, but the man did not seem to care.

He got him to Beems in short order. The unnaturally thin colonel was demanding, wanted action. Parson's words would probably bring it about. Beems seemed surprised at Parson's zeal. The captain knew he had never expected much from Parsons.

Packard handed Parsons a flask of whiskey. He thought one quick jolt might perk him up. Parsons took a deep gulp and smiled. And then he started to talk. It just poured out of him, in short, almost breathless gasps.

Beems listened skeptically at first, but as the tale progressed, his mouth widened into a broad, if not particularly benign smile. He hit his fist against his open palm smartly. He had Parke. The traitor was almost in his grasp. The boy, Jed, had alerted him about the redcoats, but he had no idea about their destination. But redcoats and now Parke in the same place! God truly was on his side. It would advance his reputation splendidly! And of course, his country's.

He would hang Parke very publicly, right after burning his plantation with all of the redcoats in it. He questioned Parsons energetically for the next few minutes about the redcoats; numbers, positions, everything. Parsons took sips of whisky between answers and slowed a little each time.

Packard worried the alcohol was too much for a man in his condition, but Beems did not seem to care and pressed him relentlessly. Finally Parsons just stopped talking in midsentence and his eyes lost focus. Packard stepped forward and pressed his hand to Parson's neck--as expected, no pulse. Packard felt sorry for him, he should have gotten him medical attention although he was probably too far gone when he arrived for it to have made any difference.

Beems seemed to read Packard's thoughts. "He would have died anyway, but at least this way he helped his country. He was never very useful when he was alive. The world has lost a useless dullard, but we have gained important information." His tone was cold, almost reptilian. Beems started to pace.

Packard knew from church experience, the colonel wanted to talk, wanted an audience. His *Premillennial Pentecostal Holiness Church* regularly drew huge crowds and his revival meetings always sparked great emotion.

"A pervert and a traitor protected by nigrahs with guns!" His voice thundered and he flailed the air with both hands. "What is the world coming to? It seems the British are not content with promoting immorality. They seem to be trying to provoke a race war as well as demolish our Republic. Parsons said there are only about a hundred redcoats at Mount Prosperity. It sounds to me like they are guarding some sort of supply dump which usually only second-rate troops draw that kind of duty. We should be able to wipe them out, every last cursed one of them."

"Packard, how many men do we have camped outside just now? I have not had a chance to review the morning's muster sheets."

Packard responded quickly. "Twelve hundred present for duty, Colonel. That's way beyond the usual county levy. We need to do something about food. We will exhaust our supply today."

"Good, good. With Major March's command, that gives me 2,200 men! God is showing me that I am become his own right and righteous hand! March has agreed to place himself under my command and hold his men as a reserve to follow up our victory. Once I have smashed the enemy into kindling, fresh troops allow me to scatter the chips. I can instruct March to have his men forage in the meantime although I think the Lord will provide the food we need by giving us the strength to make the British supply it. It will be an added incentive for the men to press home the attack with vigor."

Packard looked dubious. Beems sometimes got carried away by his own oratory and saw reality through the dark lens of religious fervor and personal grandiosity. "Colonel, a lot of our folks are just old men and boys. They don't have much training. Some only have pitchforks and knives. Maybe three-quarters have a musket or fowling piece and most have only shot at varmints or deer. We have perhaps 500 bayonets among our men. We are a lot stronger on paper than we are in reality."

Beems responded imperiously. "Nonsense, nonsense, Packard! We are strong in spirit, patriotism, and grit. Those far outweigh any defects of training. The French Revolutionary Armies had no training and were badly outnumbered, but they had heart and patriotism. They overwhelmed the best professional armies of Europe! And they were Godless! Something we most certainly are not! We can certainly master a few score redcoats shielding a pervert and traitor! Get the men assembled, Packard. We march within the hour!"

*****

Tracy wondered how much of what Sammie Jo had said was true. He sensed she and truth would not be on intimate terms if she could wring advantage from avoiding its embrace. They had been riding for hours and still no sign of her farmstead. He repeatedly asked "How far now?" She would evasively reply, "Just a few miles more, don't get all lathered up, we will get there." They conversed as they rode. Mostly he asked her questions and she responded with answers he found ambiguous and unsatisfying. She talked a lot and easily, but actually revealed little.

He got an idea of her background, but only a very general one. He decided for all of her corn pone country girl talk, she had a very sophisticated sense of people. She read them well and used her naive persona as a weapon of manipulation. His brother was a perceptive man and it surprised him he had missed her essential deviousness. Her looks undoubtedly had a lot to do with it. Her beauty was a far more lethal weapon than the rifle she used with such skill.

She was flat out dangerous. The air of thinly caged violence annoyed rather than attracted him, but that was probably not the case with most pmen. She would bring grief to any man foolish enough to trust her. She reminded him of a wild animal, recently domesticated. The trouble with such beasts was that they reverted to their former behaviors at the most unexpected moments, frequently savaging the people who had given them their trust.

Sammie Jo felt better with each passing mile. She needed to get rid of Tracy. She had no real plan to win Pennywhistle, but she would figure something out. She wondered how she would explain his brother's absence. An old hunting cabin lay just ahead. He would have no idea that it was not the family place. No one would find him for some time. No, she would not kill him, although it crossed her mind. Pennywhistle would never forgive her. She just needed him out of the picture for a day or so, enough time for her to work her magic. "We are almost there, Captain. There have been some bandits and robbers about and I ain't been back for a spell. These are bad, strange times and lots of folks are out to steal all manner of stuff. Bandits sometimes stash their loot in cabins like mine, use them as hideouts. You better let me go first."

She took her arm out of the sling. It hurt less than she thought, probably just the excitement. She touched her rifle sticking out of the saddlebag. Her intention was clear. She watched him carefully, wanted to see if she had provoked the chivalrous reaction she expected. He was a gentleman after all. He would not appreciate the imputation about his courage or his competence. "There, that little cabin ahead that's it. Ain't much but it's where I grew up." She forced sentimentality into her voice, utterly false but just what he expected. "I have a lot of good memories."

She reined her horse in and quickly dismounted at the door of the nondescript little cabin. She held her rifle at the ready, poised to step across the threshold. "Wait, Sammie Jo!" said Tracy with perfect, misplaced chivalry. "Let me go first, my brother would never forgive me if you were attacked. If there are any brigands about, I will deal with them. I have a lot more experience with such people than you do. Leave it to the professionals."

"Thanks very kindly, Captain, I am right grateful." She laughed inwardly. He might be a professional soldier, but he was a thorough amateur in reading hidden motives.

He brought his horse to a halt, grabbed his rifle, and dismounted from the saddle. He calmly walked up to her and clamped a restraining hand on her wrist. "Stay here, I will go first."

She summoned her best smile of gratitude. It was as bright and false as fool's gold, but it would fan the flames of his heroism. She looked him dead in the eye. "Thanks, just ain't used to havin' a fine man lookin' out for me. Been on my own too long, I guess."

He smiled quickly back. Helping was part of his code. He leveled his weapon and advanced slowly toward the cabin. He carefully swept his rifle left to right, focused on the potential danger ahead. She followed close behind, waited for him to halt at the door.

He never saw a thing. She struck him solidly with the butt of her rifle, just below the right ear. He hit the ground with a dull thud. She bent down and examined him. He would have a bad headache when he awoke, but the injury was far from fatal. Guile and indirect methods always worked best. Men always dropped their guard when their desires or egos took control.

She mounted up and took one last look at the prostrate Tracy. She shook her head. He was old-fashioned and had paid the price for it.

She wasted no time and spurred the mare to a gallop. She had an urgent feeling that Pennywhistle was in danger. She was no stranger to sexual desire, but she was experiencing feelings well beyond that, feelings that puzzled her. She had always scorned sentiment and laughed at all the fluttery woman talk of the heart.

She had once traded deer hides to a sea captain for a book by 'A Lady' titled *Sense and Sensibility.* The women in it had seemed plum silly at the time, but now she felt a pang of sympathy for the lovesick Marianne. A frightening wave of compelling, powerful emotion crashed over her as she rode. She told herself it could not be love. Potent womanly drives were far different from something so fine and selfless. Besides, love made you weak and vulnerable and she wasn't having any of that.

She thought love a cruel illusion and was proud that it had never once knocked at the doors of her heart. Her widowed father had been cold and unemotional and her brothers had the same temperament. The current sensation was extraordinary and demanding, almost a drug. The feeling was a strange beast that had to be stalked and treed to discover just what it was. She could think of no more satisfying thought than spending a lifetime at the Englishman's side.

She urged the horse to go faster. She had to know! She cared for nothing save to see him once more.

*****

Pennywhistle had just finished anchoring the final Chambers Swivel into a cart when he saw the lone rider. Nothing was directly visible to anyone approaching along the road to the main gate, but the ten Chambers guns and two ordinary swivels arranged in a semi-circle could sweep the road with a lethal barrage of canister. All were good at only very close range so he needed to wait until the last possible moment before firing.

The rider was clearly a civilian. He had definitely seen Pennywhistle, but had not veered off. Most civilians would have speedily turned tail at the sight of a scarlet coat. It made Pennywhistle curious. He walked down the road toward the rider. Two privates leveled their pieces to cover him, but he motioned for them to stand down. The rider seemed to intend no malice.

At twenty yards, Pennywhistle noted the rider was both well dressed and wounded. He hailed him directly, "Who are you, sir, and what is your business?"

A strong voice replied, "I am Daniel Parke, sir, the master of this place. Whom do I have the honor of addressing?"

Pennywhistle continued walking and stopped five yards short of the man. If the rider had wanted to open fire, he would have done so already. A whiff of unpleasantness hit his nose. Gangrene had an unmistakable smell. "Thomas Pennywhistle, Captain, Royal Marines, at your service." He flourished his hat and gave a quick bow.

The rider touched his top hat in acknowledgment. "I see you have made yourselves comfortable on my plantation. I cannot say I approve, but I will cause you no trouble. I have come home to be with my family."

Pennywhistle appreciated his courage and directness. "You are wounded I perceive and in need of medical attention. I regret to say I do not have a surgeon present, but perhaps a local physician could be summoned. I have no interest in seeing civilians suffer. You have my word you will not be molested if you proceed to the main house and stay sequestered with your family. I have talked with your mother and she makes it clear you are a thoroughgoing gentleman. Have I your word you will cause us no difficulty?"

Parke was very, very tired. The Englishman seemed honorable and civilized. No artifice was necessary, just the unvarnished truth. "You have my most sincere assurances, Captain, I will cause no trouble. I merely entreat you to leave my place intact, so that I might provide for my family."

"I fully appreciate that, sir. I have met your children and found them very agreeable. They will be protected, whatever happens. Please proceed, Mr. Parke. You look like you could use rest. If you will select a trustworthy house servant, I will permit him to pass through the lines and summon a surgeon."

Parke sighed and said, "Thank you." He spurred his horse toward the main house. He had to see Archie.

Pennywhistle watched him pass and silently wished him luck. He wondered if Parke knew he was the man who had ruined his well-ordered life. Probably not and his mother would likely say nothing as she had come to realize her loose tongue had played a key role in her son's discomfiture.

He walked back to the main gate. So far, his presence had gone unnoticed by the Americans. Parke could not have told anyone. He sensed an air of resignation about the man, someone who had given up and merely wanted to bow to the inevitable gracefully.

There was a badly wounded gentleman in the house who was very close to death. He had heard rumors about Parke and guessed he had feelings for the man. He did not understand that type of love, but such things had existed since the dawn of time. The scientist in him said perhaps the phenomenon could be studied someday. He rebuked himself. Feelings could not be studied under a microscope. That was his problem, he was entirely too clinical about emotion.

It did not matter. All he had to do was defend the place for one day; hold until relieved. He wondered how far away Ross was. Then his mind wandered. Sammie Jo had a lovely mouth.

*****

"Hold your fire until you can see the warts on their faces. Two volleys, then make a run for the rally point. I want the white folk to get a good look at us, know it was black men who killed their mates. They'll come after us like hounds chasing hares and that's exactly what Mr. Pennywhistle wants."

Gates gave the order quietly and the 15 colonial marines nodded their assent as they full cocked their muskets. "Remember your training, but think of this as your repayment for all those times you were whipped and beaten. Aim low and make 'em howl."

Taylor sighted his musket on a tall, older American with pinched cheeks and a jutting chin. His face reminded him of his old mastuh and that was enough to make this shot something personal.

Beems' men marched carelessly, seeming to pay little attention to keeping proper cadence. The column of 1200 resembled a happy procession of day laborers sauntering home from a day at the county fair rather than anything approaching a military formation. There was plenty of enthusiasm in their steps, but little discipline. There was lots of loud talking, boastful sloganeering, and even some jaunty singing.

"Hope there's some food at the end of this march."

"Wish I had a bayonet."

"Beems will give it to 'em good and hard."

"Redcoats ain't gotta chance."

"One white man can lick ten Nigrahs."

The rear of the column spontaneously erupted in a chorus of *Hail Columbia.* The singing was as enthusiastic as it was loud and off key. Fifers and drummers joined in accompaniment and two young lieutenants unfurled makeshift colors. The two hastily sewn flags were made of cotton rather than silk and moved only slightly in the humid air. The reds, whites, and blues of the ensigns were vivid and the American Eagles at their centers were compelling. It was all inspiring and glorious. Campaigning seemed a lot more fun than spending dawn to dusk behind a plow.

Pop, pop, pop! 15 British muskets lashed out and everything changed.

Chapter Nineteen

Archibald Grimes wheezed his death rattle at four that afternoon. He was lucid his last hours and Daniel Parke stayed by his side. He held his hand and spoke gently to him. They talked of many matters ranging from the trivial to the profound; of joys, regrets, missed opportunities and loose ends to be wrapped up in the very, very near future.

The word love was never spoken yet it was plain on both men's faces. Parke did not conceal his friend's condition from him and supplied no false cheer. His friend knew and accepted what must shortly be. Parke's own wound smelled badly. The surgeon had been sent for, but Parke knew from the growing finger of green that expanded from his shoulder that the gangrene might be too far advanced to be stopped. He really did not care much. He was an object of obloquy and guessed the authorities or the mob would come for him soon. His will provided plenty of funds for his family and his children would be raised by his sister and her husband. They were good and worthy individuals, unlike himself.

It saddened him the way he would be remembered. He considered shooting himself directly, but he did not want his children to live with that legacy. It would also convince people that all of the calumnies associated with his name were true.

He left the house and decided to take a short stroll on the grounds. The British did not bother him and did not even seem remotely curious. He gathered from the steady stream of pack horses that his plantation was being used as a supply center and would shortly be overrun with thousands of redcoats. The Pennywhistle fellow seemed a decent man. He would speak to him about the tobacco crop and ask that soldiers be enjoined from damaging the fields. They certainly were not the destructive hordes of Old Testament locusts that they had been made out.

He begged God, not for his life, but for forgiveness. He had transgressed God's law grievously with Archie, but even the two criminals next to Jesus had been forgiven because they sought redemption with open, honest hearts. He hoped Jesus was listening, but a few minutes later his mind drifted back to Archie. He would see him again on the other side and soon.

*****

Pop, pop, pop. Eight men fell as a second disciplined volley crashed into Beems' long column.

"Form line! Form line! By companies! Don't run! Don't run!" Packard shouted orders at the top of his lungs but his words were lost in the general din of screaming men and rattling musketry. He tried to find a drummer so his commands could be relayed in a way that would penetrate the noise but the only one he could spot was madly running in the opposite direction.

Beems' column devolved in chaos as men with little training struggled to form line; a maneuver that would enable them to direct a reasonable amount of lead toward their attackers at the edge of the woods. Yet even if they could have managed a volley, the line of enemy marines lying prone behind old logs would have presented poor targets.

"Time to go!" said Gates as he moved down the red-coated line." We've got 'em rattled. Head for the rally point." The operation was intended as a series of discharge and dash actions--wear down and run. Never tarry long in a single spot.

The Colonial Marines rose up silently and moved briskly back up a wooded trail familiar to slaves but not to whites. Having several marines who knew the area was a godsend as it enabled the British to use interior lines to stay hidden from any white pursuers.

There would be no immediate pursuit, however, because the column was in such disarray. The marines would have plenty of time to prepare another ambush at the rally point, two miles away. A messenger would convey the situation to Mr. Pennywhistle and he might well send forward further reinforcements. The black marines were acting as a magnet to white militia men and drawing them toward a reception at Mount Prosperity that they would never forget.

One marine glanced back toward the milling mob where the column had been. "And you thought we could only pick cotton," he said derisively.

*****

Tracy felt the large goose egg on the back of his neck. The nasty bitch could really hit. He staggered to his feet. His head swam and he cursed himself for being an idiot. He was usually so cynical about women and the one time he had let chivalry overcome common prudence he paid a painful price. He had been right about her, but had been infected by his brother's selective blindness. Country girl, indeed! She could teach Talleyrand a thing or two about guile. With a little polish and training, she would be a court intriguer of the first magnitude.

He checked his watch. He had been out for ninety minutes. The sun rode low on the horizon, but if he left immediately and really put the spurs to his swift mare, she could deliver him to Mount Prosperity before dark. He intended to have a few very crisp words with Miss Sammie Jo, but what she really needed was a smart horsewhipping. The lump would furnish his brother proof of her duplicity, but he feared he was too completely under her spell to listen to reason.

He shook his head in disgust and spat on the ground. His brother was in love. What a pity. It sometimes hit the reasonable ones like that. A creature had skipped into his life who was the absolute opposite of everything he believed in and needed for his happiness.

Sammie Jo was something like the Gorgons of ancient myth. The Gorgons turned men into stone by their sheer ugliness. Sammie Jo's loveliness turned men's reason to stone. No, that was not quite the right comparison. She was like one of the Fallen in the Bible: beautiful angel outside, dark inside.

He slowly got into the saddle. His head hurt but he could manage. Some part of his brother probably knew her for just what she was, but he had apparently exiled it to a faraway part of his consciousness. Perhaps one more example of her perfidy would finally allow that portion of his conscience to take control and make some reasonable decisions.

*****

Pennywhistle finished the final placement of his swivels as a colonial marine delivered a message he had expected for some time. He read the communication with satisfaction but realized he had only about three hours until the advance forces of the Americans appeared in front of his works. He dispatched ten men to return with the marine and reinforce Gate's efforts.

Everything was ready. The two leagers of wine a mile and a half distant from the front gate had been opened and the wolfsbane mixed in. Thirsty soldiers would only have five minutes of life after their first draught. Pennywhistle had qualms about employing poison yet anyone fool enough to trust Greeks bearing gifts deserved his fate.

The conventional swivels were fixed behind the hedges but the Chambers Swivels were all bolted to the bases of small carts each pulled by a single horse. The carts would serve as mobile artillery that could be rushed to any threatened spot.

The six mines had been placed on either side of the approach road. Anyone not on the road would be subject to random death. In truth, their explosions would not have much destructive power but their primary value was inducing shock and disorientation. The Americans would have no way of knowing just how many he possessed.

He had placed Gabriel in charge of keeping the horses ready for their big moment. He assured Pennywhistle that he could manage something that seemed an oxymoron: a controlled stampede.

Dale inspected the tiger pits making sure they were perfectly concealed and that the punji sticks at their bottoms were sharpened to razor sharp points. To the untutored eye, the approach to the main gate was a flat, featureless expanse of grass.

Once the pits were revealed, attacking troops would have to go around them by advancing along narrow corridors that could be swept by concentrated fire. Narrow corridors meant columns and limited firepower. The British would be in line and the firepower of the line always trumped the column.

The men were in the trenches talking quietly and eating. They could stand to at a moment's notice.

He had the two front windows flanking the entrance to the main house stove in and swivels placed in the lintels. They would be weapons in a last stand that he fervently hoped to avoid. Each passing hour brought Ross's Army closer. The stage was set, the props were ready, and the actors all knew their parts. All that was needed was an audience. He would give them a performance that would literally blow them away.

Sammie Jo rode hard for Mount Prosperity, both eager and worried. Eager to see Pennywhistle but worried about the reception she would receive. She knew a life with him would open up undreamed-of vistas. Observing Gabriel's transformation from slave to warrior had taught her that almost anything was possible. She had always evinced sympathy for blacks because she knew what it was to endure discrimination because of something you could not change. Her height, background, and gender had always made her feel a second-class citizen. Pennywhistle made her feel like royalty.

*****

Pop, pop, pop. The clattering of musketry had continued on and off for fifteen miles as Gates and his reinforced marine reconnaissance party tormented Beems' column. Beems' men were in a proper fury because every time they had stopped to volley at their tormentors, the colonial marines had simply vanished into the woods like wraiths only to emerge minutes later in an entirely different spot and began the process anew.

Gates' job was done. Mount Prosperity lay only two miles away. He formed his men up and quick marched them back toward the entrenchments. The Americans were disorganized and off balance, eager to lash out at anything and likely to fight with more stupidity than strategy. It was time to turn them over to Mr. Pennywhistle and let him finish what they had begun.

*****

Manton's men were only ten miles from Mount Prosperity. At the usual marching speed, they would reach it sometime just after dark. It could not come too soon. His men were exhausted and hungry. "Just a few miles more," became his constant refrain. His men believed him, but he was not sure how long that would continue.

*****

Sammie Jo came to the final bend in the road. Mount Prosperity lay less than a mile-and-a-half ahead. Pennywhistle would be very, very surprised. He would probably not be pleased. She could spin a very tall tale about his brother and he would probably suspect very little of it was true. She debated exactly how she should put it. The trouble was if she gamed the truth on that matter, he might take a very cynical attitude when she told him the truth about her feelings for him.

She was about to proceed that last mile when she heard a low muddle of noises, indistinct voices probably a quarter-league away. She cocked her head toward the source and pricked her ears. It grew louder each passing minute. A very large group of people was coming down the main road.

She decided to investigate. If it was what she feared, Pennywhistle would definitely appreciate a warning. She didn't like the idea of people threatening her man, Americans or not. Well, he was not her man yet, but she would make him so if she had to defy every power in Heaven to do it. She had her rifle and she might just teach a few of these rat bastards a lesson.

*****

Dale heard the same noises Sammie Jo did. A good poacher needed keen ears. He was experienced enough to be able to calculate composition and distance even though he could see nothing. It was not unexpected. He would have been more worried if he had heard less. That kind of talking meant that even if the force was reasonably large, it had little in the way of discipline. It had to be militia that were little better than an armed mob. He would investigate more closely then warn the captain.

*****

Gabriel made his final inspection of the horses and decided they would do just fine even if they had likely never heard gunfire. Mr. Pennywhistle was very pleased with him, said he had done an exceptional job managing beasts that he had never understood. He was a fine man to work for and treated men with respect. He wondered what had happened to Pennywhistle's servant. He gathered that he had died somewhere along the way and Pennywhistle had simply been too busy to find a replacement. The twelve-year-old Rufus could never be anything but a temporary substitute.

He had no training for it, but he wanted the job. He could learn what he had to know. Mr. Pennywhistle had called him brave. Even now he puffed with pride when he thought of his words after Bladensburg. It was the prettiest compliment he had ever received. He had no idea what Britain was like, but they certainly could not have many blacks about. He would speak to the captain about it when things settled down.

*****

Peter Spottswood's company was down to forty men from ninety because of heat and straggling. He had not seen

Pennywhistle since before Bladensburg and wondered how he was faring. He greatly looked forward to joining him again in a few hours. He hoped that disgusting Sammie Jo creature was finally gone. She was a viperous witch who appeared to have cast some inexplicable spell over his friend. She was a beauty, but nothing compared to Carlotta.

He could never understand Pennywhistle's fixation with the idea that a man was allowed only one chance for long-term happiness with a woman. He believed any number of women would be a perfectly suitable mate. He was a long way from being ready to settle down, but when he was, he had no problem believing he would find a fitting partner in short order. Until then, he would be quite content with a string of delightfully meaningless liaisons with a variety of lovely ladies. He was a Royal Marine after all: it was almost expected.

Pennywhistle had been alone for too long and Spottswood wondered if Sammie Jo was merely the wrong woman in exactly the right place at exactly the right time. Sheer convenience often compensated for a variety of glaring defects.

*****

Beems halted his unruly column when scouts had reported the main enemy installation lay just a few miles ahead. Word quickly got around and soon shouts of "no quarter, no quarter" rippled the formation.

Packard rode over to confer with Beems. He asked Beems to consider things carefully before acting, but the colonel would not hear of it. He cautioned Beems that he had less a militia battalion than an oversized armed mob. 1200 had reported present for duty, but there was a big difference between present and competent.

He respectfully asked Beems about his plan, but the colonel dismissively silenced him, saying he would make his dispositions when the enemy came in sight. He strongly implied he had some secret plan, but Packard doubted it. He wondered if he thought Jesus would miraculously invest him with gifted military insight at the last possible moment. Packard had his faith, but had never considered the Man from Nazareth as a military chieftain.

From what Packard could puzzle out, Beems plan was more about fire than firepower. The unarmed portion of his men had traded pitchforks for torches soaked in pitch and would be utterly worthless if confronted by a determined armed force. He guessed he was simply going to set fire to the whole estate and shoot any fugitives who fled the conflagration. Beems knew little about tactics, possibly less about actual combat. The only fight he had been in was with his congregants over what constituted proper attire for ladies on Sunday. He was of a decidedly Puritanical cast.

Beems had a personal grudge against Parke. Packard had grown tired of his intemperate rants. Wasn't judgment best left to God? Maybe Parke was a pervert although that was mostly wild rumor and lots of wild rumors had flown about in the wake of the British invasion. But the militia was supposed to defend the Republic, not be a morality posse out of the Middle Ages. It was supposed to be about attacking a British military post. Packard wondered if the reason Beems was so zealous was because he feared the same unnatural impulses were present in himself.

Packard persuaded Beems to leave the completely untrained behind. 600 militia who had training marched in a sloppy imitation of a column. They could deploy into a line if necessary, but it would take a lot of time. Of the 600, probably 20 had actually fired their muskets in anger. Many of the rest had never actually fired their pieces with a live round against a human target.

"Hey! Hey! Everybody! Wine! Wine!" Two groups of thirsty men immediately broke ranks and raced over to the scouts who had just discovered two giant barrels of wine. It had been a long, hot march and the men felt they deserved a reward. No one stopped to think that open wine barrels had no business being where they were.

Twenty men eagerly plunged their cupped hands into the open leagers and began madly hurling wine into their wide open mouths. They paused for a few seconds to savor a delicious taste. It was very, very sweet and reminded some of almonds.

A minute later, smiles gave way to faces beset with shock and then fear. Men coughed long and hard and then clutched frantically at their throats. They fell to the ground and rolled about crazily, moaning and then wheezing.

Beems came galloping up. "No! No! Stay away from the wine! We need no Dutch Courage to fight our battles."

"Poison! Poison!" Screamed one fat man in a beat-up coat who had been about to drink. He threw the wine in his palms to the ground in disgust and continued to shout his warning.

Men broke ranks to watch in horror as five minutes changed twenty of their neighbors into corpses.

"Bastards! Whoresons! Renegades! Monsters!" Were just a few of the things Beems' men called the British. The entire column was badly shaken but bristling with a huge appetite for revenge.

Beems was shocked but rallied his wits and determined to exploit the disaster. He called upon his preacher's cunning as he bellowed from his horse, "This will not stand, men! It will not stand! We are not facing men but outlaws who fight as cowardly dogs! These rabid dogs must be put down! Now! Follow me and let us avenge these deaths with fire and blood!"

The men cheered, huzzahed, and then began a spontaneous chant. "Death to the British. Death to the British! Death to the British." It took ten minutes, but Beems got the men back into ranks and resumed his march. The men continued their dirge-like chant as they marched and every face in the column now wore a scowl, a frown, or a look of fierce determination.

It was an hour after sundown when Beems stopped the column a mile from the front gates of Mount Prosperity. It was clearly time for some inspired, religious oratory.

"Men, there is a very bad man in the house over yonder. He killed many of your friends through his stupidity. He is a coward and a traitor. The British occupy his plantation, but I have every reason to believe he invited them in. He is also a traitor to God and a prisoner to dark and unnatural desires, absolutely monstrous uncleanness!" Angry murmurs rippled through the crowd. "It is up to us to mete out the justice he deserves and to smite the British invaders with the full force of American wrath!"

Loud cries of "hear, hear!" and "No mercy! No quarter!" echoed through the crowd. Beems smiled malevolently. Being a preacher had advantages. He was employing the same instruments he used Sundays in his pulpit. Fear and its handmaidens, anger and hatred, were fine tools to stoke bloodlust in a crowd, cause them to detach themselves from the reason that might counsel caution. Hate was a particularly splendid motivator, especially when it could all be focused on one opponent who could be transformed into Satan incarnate.

"Many of you have never seen battle before and are naturally worried about your conduct. Fear not, I feel God's hand upon our work this night and I can assure you, you will all do your duty and very much more. We are like the children of Israel meeting the Canaanites. I have read many books about battle and I will guide you to a victory you will boast about to your grandchildren. I will meet with the company commanders momentarily and explain my dispositions. I only ask you to follow their orders.

"The British think we are weak! The British think we are feckless. The British think we are just farmers!" Angry choruses of boos raced through the crowd. "Tonight we will show them just how mistaken they are." Cheer after cheer continued for a full minute. He wanted them worked into a proper frenzy.

"Our attack will be swift and savage. We will be avenging angels. We ask no quarter and will give none. When we are done Mount Prosperity will be a black crater of burned-out iniquity. We will tar and feather Daniel Parke then hang him from the highest oak tree. Victory or death! Who's with me?" The crowd went wild. Man after man shouted, "I am!" at the top of his lungs.

The chanting resumed. "Death to the British! Death to the British!"

*****

Dale watched the scene through his glass and smiled wryly. It was just as he suspected: a mob of damn fools. Only a rabble would chant like a horde of angry monks. They were silly men, little men who were all mouth and trousers. His marines would give them an education on the "joys" of battle.

*****

"Horseshit!" muttered Sammie Jo. She knew nonsense when she heard it. She loaded the *Widowmaker*. It was time to let it speak for her. The American commander sounded like a preacher and she hated preachers.

Chapter Twenty

Dale raced back to the main house. He found Pennywhistle hunched over a large ledger spread out on delicately ornate Louis XIV writing table. The captain put down the quill, shifted slightly in his chair, and favored Dale with a quick smile of relief at the interruption.

Pennywhistle detested paper work, but one of the joys of command was an unending supply of it. War was far more about foolscap than fighting. Ross needed an exact accounting of all the supplies laid in and Pennywhistle was determined he should have it.

Dale tersely explained the situation. Pennywhistle merely nodded at intervals. When Dale concluded he quietly said, "So death to the British is it? I think those fellows need to be taught a lesson. Have the men stand to their posts, Sarn't," he said in a calm voice at odds with his increasing pulse rate. "I shall be along directly."

"Very good, sir," said Dale who touched his hat in quick salute and vanished. Pennywhistle considered his advantages. A fight in the dark was a very stupid thing for amateurs to attempt. Night battles were very difficult to control and it was quite as easy to shoot a friend as it was to kill a foe. He would have his men tie white strips of cotton around their arms. It was an elementary precaution, but he did not believe the enemy would think of it.

Rufus appeared at his side trumpet at the ready. "Can I help, Captain?"

"Certainly, Rufus. Your music is always welcome." He found the boy's earnestness infectious.

He heard the bugle sound in the distance. He picked up his Ferguson and walked out into the yard. He unfurled his glass and panned it along the trenches even though he knew exactly what he would see. Every man was at his post with his weapon loaded and bayonet fixed. The marines had practiced the drill a dozen times and so doing it before actual combat was no different. He felt a surge of pride at his own men and confidence that the new Colonial Marines would one day be as good citizens as they were soldiers.

Gabriel came running up to him, carrying a musket. "Cap'n, cap'n. I'm a fixin' to fight and I want to do it at your side. Y'all ain't got no servant and that ain't fitten for a right proper gent like yourself."

Pennywhistle blinked and wondered why he had not thought of something so obvious. Gabriel was a good man, intelligent as well as brave. "I'd be honored to have you as my batman, Gabriel. We can discuss arrangements later assuming we both survive this fight. You may stay with me for the first few volleys but then I am depending on you to manage the horses. Your expert knowledge of their behavior may well prove decisive today."

Gabriel nodded with pleasure that his specialized knowledge would play a part in smiting those who kept his people in bondage. He and Pennywhistle began walking briskly toward the trenches.

The two had not gotten far, when an unexpected sight came running up to them, badly out of breath. It was Parke, looking ashen but determined.

Pennywhistle stopped in puzzlement. "What are you doing here, sir? You should stay indoors. Things are about to get very hot."

Parke spoke with great emotion. "It's me they want, more than anything, which makes it my fight. I don't have long to live, I think, and I'd rather go out defending my hearth and home than cowering in a cellar. Better a bullet than the gangrene. People have called me a pervert."

Pennywhistle's expression remained tactful, appropriately neutral. "It's quite all right. I am sure you have heard. Well damn it, even perverts can fight! I am willing to bet Colonel Beems is in charge. He will not be delicate."

He quickly explained Beems' character and outlook. Pennywhistle said nothing but listened intently. First-rate intelligence on the mind of an opponent was a godsend. Beems was exactly the opponent he wished for: hot-headed, impulsive, and a military neophyte. He was also full of delusions of military grandeur which give him the unwarranted confidence to take foolish risks.

"Thank you Mr. Parke. Far be it from me to deny a dying man his last request, particularly when he wants to assist me. Find yourself a position, sir, and add your musket to our numbers. I wish you the best of luck."

Pennywhistle walked very deliberately to the hedgerow. His unhurried steps were those of a man with all the time in the world and bespoke a confidence that the outcome of the fight ahead was never in doubt. Gabriel mimicked his almost theatrical steps because he understood the message they sent to the men. Rufus walked behind, minus his outrageously large turban. Pennywhistle had thought it far too tempting a target for angry men who had no love for freed slaves.

Scouts were unnecessary. The mindless chanting made the present location of the enemy clear. The explosions of the mines would signal Beems' advance. Beems would come straight at him. No diversions, no feints, just direct action launched from very close range. Beems struck him as the sort of chap who favored a battering ram over a ballista, a bludgeon rather than a rapier.

*****

Beems ordered everyone with muskets to place lighted candles in the muzzles of their weapons. The column blazed with light, brilliantly silhouetted against the cloudy sky. It was a dramatic gesture and pleased both him and the men, but it made them excellent targets. The men continued to chant, "Death to the British."

Sammie Jo tracked Beems. She had heard something about a fire and brimstone preacher named Beems and from his earlier loud blathering she gathered he was the man in her gunsights. She was in total darkness, but the column's many torches and candles illuminated the preacher's tall, emaciated frame perfectly.

She had him, but at the last second another officer spoiled her shot by stepping in front of him. No matter, one officer would serve as well as another. She fired from a prone position, rifle balanced on a log. The shot caught him square in the temple, and a small squirt of red-grey mist issued from his head.

Sammie Jo smiled. It was at least two hundred and twenty five yards. She and the *Widowmaker* made a great team. She reloaded quickly and moved stealthily thirty yards to the right.

It took Beams a few moments to realize what had happened. Who would fire on them? His scouts had detected no light infantry in the woods. A second later, another officer clutched his chest and pitched forward. Beems halted his column and began to bark orders. His men were excited but confused. He ordered Captain Hale's company to scour the woods to the right. The men moved forward and gradually spread themselves out, but they were a poor imitation of light infantry.

She had time for one more shot. She looked for Beems but he was in the midst of a crowd and she had no clear shot. She looked for another officer but it was hard to tell in the flickering light who was who since many of the militia had nothing directly discernible as uniforms. She waited until the line of scouts was a hundred yards out.

She centered her sights on a man's chest because he wore large, cheap brass epaulettes and squeezed the trigger. The shot penetrated the heart and knocked him backwards to the great surprise of his men. They walked over to the corpse and milled about in confusion. It had just begun to occur to them that real battle was not the game they had practiced at musters, but something quick and lethal.

Militia discipline was poor. Without orders, Captain Bork's company broke ranks and angrily joined Hale's company in the hunt for his killer. They found nothing. If this continued, the column would dissolve.

Boom! Boom! Boom! All six of the mines detonated within a few seconds of each other. Ten men were blasted off their feet and two no longer had legs when they hit to the ground. Bork's men had spread themselves out on either side of the road searching for the sniper but had instead discovered weapons outside the rules of war.

Beems raced over and looked at the writhing wounded and the five corpses. "Monstrous! Monstrous!" he shouted. "The cowardly actions of the unrighteous and the ungodly." Men gathered round him in shock but nodded agreement. "Is there no end to the diabolical perfidy of the British?" Cries of *terrible, horrid,* and *awful* raced through the crowd.

"Take heart men," thundered Beems. "We shall not be stopped! Back in the ranks, everyone! We shall advance like the Israelites at Jericho and sweep all before us. But we must keep our column tight and never leave the main road."

Sammie Jo congratulated herself briefly, but knew it was time to go. She raced to the rear and jumped on her horse. She was committed. She had killed her own people. She could never go back, even if they never figured out who the shooter was. She had done it not out of political principle, but because of love. Yes, damn it, she loved him. And she would fight for him.

*****

Manton halted his company. A mile in front, Spottswood did the same. It was fully dark now. There would be one last fifteen minute halt and then they would push onto Mount Prosperity for the night. Spottswood told his men to take heart. They had only five more miles to go. Discipline was holding.

*****

Tracy had pushed his mare so hard that she was ready to drop but his determination paid off. He caught sight of Sammie Jo galloping madly a few hundred yards ahead. Her silhouette was distinctive. He had his own rifle with him and he was positive she had not seen him. He was sick to death of her "cornpone cutie" imposture and should do the world and his brother a favor by ending this murderous bitch. He calculated her path and knew it would take her directly in front of him. He could definitely manage it.

Angry though he was, he could not do it. He had never cold-bloodedly shot a woman even though he had killed plenty of men in battle. There was no reason to let anger turn him into a barbarian. Besides, his brother would never forgive him. He had the infection of love and cold reason could make few inroads against it. Better to follow her. It took no great imagination to guess where she was headed.

*****

Beems' column marched slowly up the Charles Road. The candles turned it into a winding ribbon of light. Beems could see the main gate to Mount Prosperity just ahead. The clouds parted dramatically exposing the newly risen moon. He thought it some kind of omen.

He decided it was time for one final speech, one final push toward battle frenzy. He halted the column, faced it directly, and began a thunderous speech. "Your actions of the next few minutes will make your reputations for a lifetime. God and your country are watching. Do not disappoint them!" As the minutes passed slowly, his oratory and passions became more heated. His voice rose and he windmilled madly at the sky with his hands.

Pennywhistle and his men had heard the mine explosions and knew the opening round of the fight lay only a few minutes in the future. Beems' words came through loud and clear in the warm night air. They were as Pennywhistle expected: utter rubbish, monstrously provocative drivel. Beems' harangue was heavily flavored with religious imagery that seemed straight out Cromwell's puritanical England. What a windbag!

Pennywhistle was suspicious when men of the cloth took up arms. They were generally the most bloodthirsty of all, cloaking gory deeds in religious respectability. This Beems fellow would have been right at home with some of the murderous priests he had encountered in Spain. Goya was right, when reason slept, monsters awoke.

His men waited patiently. He walked over and checked each swivel gun. The pair would fire directly into the faces of oncoming attackers. Each piece was loaded with short rounds of canister, one round containing 44 three-ounce balls. Five of the Chambers volley guns converted to improvised horse artillery were positioned on the left flank and five on the right. They each contained 120 small balls that have a tremendous physical and psychological impact when delivered from an unexpected direction. He would need the militia close--under one hundred yards. It was kind of Beems to provide illumination.

He saw someone on horseback gallop out of the night onto the main road. His men saw the mounted figure but held their fire. The Americans saw it too and shots rang out. Stupid waste of ammunition, the range was too great. The horse raced directly toward his position. Dale raised his Baker.

"No wait," he said in astonishment. He could not have been more surprised if it had been Medea riding Pegasus. He recognized the silhouette of Sammie Jo, but how was that possible? "Let her pass," he said quietly.

He saw another figure bound out of the night, perhaps two hundred yards astern of Sammie Jo. Someone was following her. He would deal with it personally. He raised the Ferguson and waited. It was very difficult to hit a fast moving single target at night unless the range was very close.

*****

Beems finished his speech and his column began to move. The column dared not change into line to increase firepower because Beems feared more mines. The British were dishonorable tricksters and he feared they might have other horrors planned.

The column retained most of its integrity and shuffled slowly forward trusting to the shock value of sheer numbers. It resembled a large flowing puddle rather than a disciplined force marching crisply. The alignment of the files was poor and the men frequently bumped into one another. Drummers beat the cadence, but no one seemed to pay attention.

Pennywhistle ordered two of the Chambers carts forward. Time to soften up the poor fools.

*****

Sammie Jo raced past the hedgerows, oblivious to Pennywhistle's hidden men. Her pursuer approached. Pennywhistle centered his sights on the rider's chest then recognized the huge hat. He slowly lowered his weapon. Things were truly out of joint this evening. He motioned for his men to hold their fire although he did not recall his makeshift horse artillery.

Pennywhistle unfurled his night glass and quickly surveyed the column. He angrily snapped it shut. He had five minutes before they would be in range. "Take over," he said tersely to Dale. Dale merely nodded.

He ran back to the long avenue behind the gate. Sammie Jo leaped from her horse and ran toward him. His brother slammed his horse to a halt and started to dismount.

She hit him like a battering ram and leaped into his arms. He was seldom at a loss for words but he was now. "I could not leave you, Sugar Plum. I just couldn't." She kissed him wildly and he had to push her back.

"What is the matter with you, you idiot! I sent you to safety. We are about to come under fire. Do you think you can make sport taunting the Grim Reaper?" He spoke in anger, but it was laced with obvious concern. A part of him was glad to see her.

His brother's voice boomed out behind her. "I told you, Tom. She is pure willfulness and nothing but trouble. She knocked me on the head and slipped the leash. I suppose I should be grateful she didn't kill me," he said with heavy sarcasm.

Pennywhistle spat his reply. "Blast! I don't have time for this. John. Do me a favor, keep her out of the way. We can sort this mess out later."

"No!" shrieked Sammie Jo. "God damn it! I ain't gonna let anybody harm you. The *Widowmaker* here ain't ready to be put to bed just yet. Already killed me three men this evenin', aim to kill me a few more. The die is cast. I am throwin' in with you. Don't argue, ain't nothin' you kin say gonna change my mind. My place is here with you."

Pennywhistle stared at her in astonishment. Her eyes glowed with the fire of battle and an absolute certainty of purpose. He had thought Amazons mythical beings. It was insane to permit her anywhere near the firing line, but yet the cold logic of it made perfect sense. She would do what she liked anyway. Might as well put her rifle to work, turn a liability into an asset. At least he could keep an eye on her.

"Very well, Hawkeye," he said resignedly, "I hope your luck is in."

Tracy clearly disapproved. "Foolish, Tom, but I can see your mind is made up. My parole forbids me to fight as a soldier, but honor surely allows for defending kin."

"I'm grateful for the offer, but don't bother about me." He said to Tracy, "I may be distracted in the fight. Sammie Jo could use your help. Keep her safe."

Tracy glowered. "I will honor your wishes, even though it is against my best judgment."

"Don't need no protecting from...him," Sammie Jo snarled. Both men ignored her.

Pennywhistle turned on his heel and broke into a run. He had already wasted too much time on a purely ancillary matter. He heard them following closely behind.

He crouched down behind the hedgerow and again unfurled his glass. Good, two hundred yards out, he had time.

Beems' column continued chanting, "Death to the British, Death to the British," but Pennywhistle's men found it more amusing than threatening. It was the behavior of amateurs using mindless slogans to give their hearts a ferocity they did not really feel.

The two Chamber's carts halted only fifty yards from the right flank of the column. The carts would have been easy to capture if the Americans had had the wit to order an immediate charge. They seemed mesmerized by these two odd looking intrusions and oblivious to the danger.

The two marine privates leapt from the backs of their horses in full view of the 600 men and vaulted inside the carts. In perfect synchronization, they swung the two weapons toward the mass of aspiring soldiers. They touched slow matches to the vent holes and 240 pieces of hot lead slammed into the column like the discharge from Vulcan's forge.

Gaps opened in the formation as men fell shrieking to the ground. The column ground to a halt and confusion reigned. Beems galloped over and looked at the bloody harvest. "No! No!" he cried as he put his hands to the side of his head seemingly intent on squeezing out the confusion besetting his brain.

The two marines mounted up like lightning, jerked the reins to their beasts, and yelled, "ha'ah." The carts sped back to the safety of the entrenchments touched by nothing worse than rapidly fading shouts and curses.

Pennywhistle ordered the second pair of Chamber's carts onto the field to follow up the initial success. They unlimbered 100 yards behind where the first pair had opened fire. Another 240 rounds peppered the column. The shrieks grew in numbers and volume.

Pennywhistle's stomach lurched a second later when he saw a scarlet form about to perform a completely stupid act of "Death or Glory."

"Charge and give 'em hell!" Chivers face was locked in the madness of battle.

Blast that bloody idiot! When you were badly outnumbered you stayed put, used any cover you could find and delayed a counter attack until the enemy were broken reeds.

Apparently inspired by the horse artillery's success, Chivers jumped up and vaulted over the hedge. He howled an indignant challenge worthy of Milton's Lucifer, waved his sword like an angry Hun, and singlehandedly charged toward the front of the column, headed straight for Beems. A fine gesture in a melee, but a damned fool one in Pennywhistle's carefully choreographed battle.

Chivers obviously hoped his men would follow, but they were as sensible as he was not and declined to do so. He was attracting the wrong kind of attention as numerous Americans pointed their swords and bayonets in his direction. They were angry and under no discipline after the Chamber's gun attack. Chivers would serve as a target for a bewildered enemy who wanted to focus their fury on something that was not going to speed away.

The callow subaltern was trying to play the hero headquarters types had told him he should be; leading from the front and exposing himself boldly. The trick for that sort of leadership was in the timing and that only came from experience. You had to choose the precise moment when the enemy stood on a knife's edge between order and disarray. Chivers was conflating élan with excellence. He was novice trying to prove himself; compensating for ineptitude with foolhardiness.

Bang! Chivers' pistol fired and felled a charging American fifteen feet away. It was the luck of a novice since the weapon was normally only good at point blank range. He had no time to reload so he threw the pistol away and made a sweeping gesture with his sword that was unmistakable as a challenge.

Clang, clang, clang. Sparks flew as he struggled manfully against a barrage of blades.

Two officers and two sergeants had dashed ahead of their charging company and trained their attention on Chivers like a pack of predators scenting a wounded animal. His beginner's luck held and the attacks against him were pressed home with a singular lack of energy and skill. The American's failure to coordinate their efforts enabled him to deal with each blade in succession, but he yielded ground after each parry. He was fighting hard but clumsily, his strokes that of an officer far better acquainted with fashionable debutantes than fencing masters. He would fail any second with fatal results.

"Bollocks!" muttered Pennywhistle. He could handle four men but a company was beyond his skill. Much as he wanted to intervene, such an action would probably change nothing and result in his own death. He snarled in frustration and then saw something that made him smile. He was not the only one who had noticed Chivers' plight.

Peebles galloped onto the field with a Chamber's Cart. He halted the cart at right angles to the on-rushing Americans, leapt from the saddle, and jumped inside. He trained the weapon on the leading edge of the company and applied a glowing linstock to the touch hole. One hundred twenty pieces of lead smashed into the mass of Americans like a swarm of carnivorous locusts.

In an instant, 30 men lay unmoving upon the ground, their arms and legs splayed in odd positions of startling indignity. The same number writhed about violently shrieking, moaning, and cursing while clutching their stomachs, pissing their trousers, and voiding their bowels. The 20 men left unscathed halted abruptly and milled about in shock. They would play no further role in the battle.

Peebles waved to Pennywhistle. The momentum of the charge had been broken. The odds were now four against two. The Americans didn't stand a chance.

Pennywhistle jumped the hedge and broke into a run, his brain seeing the upcoming fight in its entirety well before the first blow was struck. Victory had to first exist in the mind before it was conjured into reality. The fight ahead was like a piece of music; a linear succession of violent notes fused together to form one seamless melody of battle. It was performed in 4/4 time with slash and thrust standing in for pitch; parry and riposte for rhythm.

Against multiple attackers, standing still for even an instant meant surrendering the initiative and certain death. Your only hope for victory lay in quick, continuous motions: slash-n-dash. Your movements became a ballet of battle with arms and hands exquisitely coordinated with precise leg and footwork. A superior sense of timing was imperative as your body flowed sinuously from one foe to the next while the enemy stood rooted to small patches of ground.

Chivers' luck finally ran out. He slipped on a mud slick and fell with his sword arm splayed out to his right. His chest was completely exposed and an American sergeant cocked his arm and prepared to deliver the death thrust through Chivers' heart.

Pennywhistle's swift cutlass was visible only as a blur as it sliced through the back of the sergeant's neck like a ripsaw cutting reeds. The man collapsed like a burst balloon.

Without missing a beat, Pennywhistle kept his blade moving as he pivoted on his right heel and aligned his elbow with a lieutenant's Adam's apple. He sliced sideways as the lieutenant turned toward him and severed the man's trachea. The lieutenant tried to cry out but all that issued forth was a terrible wheezing sound. He slowly toppled clutching his throat.

A second sergeant took a wild swipe at the top of Pennywhistle's head, the fear in his eyes supplying the reason for the crudity of his stroke. Pennywhistle easily ducked under it and corkscrewed his body upward as he rammed his blade through the underside of the sergeant's jaw. Its tip emerged from the top of his skull in the twinkling of an eye as the man's own eyes rolled upward without understanding.

The last lieutenant faced Pennywhistle directly, the saber he gripped with white knuckles shaking visibly. He held it vertically in front of his face thinking only of defense. He had a bad case of acne and probably wasn't more than eighteen. Pennywhistle felt sorry he would never see nineteen. The man plunged to the ground seconds before the marine's blade touched his chest.

Pennywhistle lowered his weapon in surprise and saw a prostrate Chivers smiling up at him. Chivers had slashed the man's legs while he had been staring at Pennywhistle.

Pennywhistle grabbed Chivers arm and yanked him violently to his feet.

"I say old man, that was deuced exciting and you were smashing! Bravo and thank you!" He grinned broadly and extended his hand.

Whapp! Pennywhistle slapped him hard in the face. "God's death! You could have gotten us both killed. Thank heaven your men remembered what I told them. When I tell you to hold and wait for my orders you bloody well do so! You ever pull a stunt like that again I will see you cashiered, but not before I give you a damned good horsewhipping." He shoved his face close to Chivers' and his voice came out an icy whisper. "Is that clear, mister?"

"Uh...uh...yes, yes Mr. Pennywhistle. Never again, Captain, never again." Chivers sounded like a schoolboy whose backside had just been tanned with a hickory rod.

"Now get back to the trenches and resume command of the men you deserted. They will obey the rank but you will have to work your arse off to gain their respect! I can't replace you so I will just have to make do with you. For God's sake keep your head down, your mouth shut, and your legs inside the earthworks. Inspire the men by staying alive."

Chivers flashed a chagrined salute, pivoted on his heel with the speed of a weathervane in a tornado, and ran back to the entrenchments like a spooked deer.

Why couldn't his family have found a living for him in the church, thought an exasperated Pennywhistle? *He'd only have to concern himself with keeping his surplice clean and his collection plates full.*

Pennywhistle raced back to the hedge and again vaulted over it. He hoped Chivers was chastened by his close call, but he'd have to keep an eye on him. He assumed his former position but it was hard to sit still because his blood was hot and racing. He breathed deeply to calm himself, his better judgment instructing him on the virtues of patience. It was better to sit tight and let the tiger pits work their magic.

Sammie Jo dashed up and crouched down next to him. If there was anyone who needed a lecture on patience it was she. He turned to her, "Wait for my command. Not a second before." She nodded fiercely. By God, she was a cool one. There was not even an ounce of sweat on her dangerously lovely face. She might be an outlier in peacetime, but she appeared to have been specially bred for what was about to come.

His men made one last check of their flints, made sure the edges were flat and sharp to guard against misfires. They opened their cartridge boxes and made sure all cartridges were fully dry. They tightened their sword bayonets on the end of their Bakers one last time.

He noticed Sammie Jo pull out a tomahawk. Where the blazes had she gotten that? Then he remembered American riflemen often carried them in lieu of a bayonet. She probably was as skilled with it as she was with a rifle.

Tracy calmly loaded his weapon. He thought about his parole and concluded family was more important. He would not fire on his countrymen save if one threatened his brother, and he reluctantly conceded, Sammie Jo. Then he would not miss.

AAAARRRRR! AIYEEEE! AHHHH ! FUUUUCCCK! All manner of incoherent screams and curses turned the air blue as the front of the column disappeared into the first tiger pit. Beems narrowly missed being pushed in himself. The column dissolved. As fleeing men raced headlong in all directions some fell into the other two tiger pits. Screams and shouts erupted like a hideous chorus of Satan's songbirds.

To Pennywhistle's surprise, Beems kept his head. He galloped toward the rear but instead of fleeing stopped and began shouting, "To me! To me! Form on me! Don't let the lobsters win!"

Pennywhistle despised the crass summoning of raw emotion and the manipulative oratory of hellfire preachers but he had to admit those abilities were serving Beems well tonight. Against all expectations the terrified militia men stopped, listened, and heeded his words. Instead of fleeing the field, they began to form up for another attack.

Pennywhistle had to concede Beems was persistent. He was going to have to implement his full plan of defense after all. He passed the word along the line to be ready for volley fire and sent messages to Gabriel and the horse artillery men to stand by.

The column took a quarter-hour to re-form and Pennywhistle's men used the time to check and then recheck all items of equipment. There was no such thing as too much preparation in wartime.

The column finally began to lumber forward with the gracelessness of an intoxicated elephant.

Someone in the column thought he saw a flash of movement in the hedgerows. He abruptly stopped marching, panicked, and loosed off a round. It was infectious and thirty other men, the entire front rank of the column, ground to a halt and fired a second later. Men in the rear stumbled into the front rank, unaware of any order to stop.

Beems raced in front of them. "Stop it, stop it, you fools! Don't fire unless I give the order."

Good, thought Pennywhistle. The first volley was the most decisive and the Americans had just squandered it. One hundred yards, not long now. The column resumed its march, 75 paces to the minute.

Sammie Jo found an officer and locked her 'V' sights onto his chest. Dale targeted a company officer marching to the side of the column and fixed his Baker on him.

Pennywhistle would take Beems. Three quick volleys should do it. Hit the head of the column, then pour in enfilade fire, and trust to the bayonet. The horse artillery would attack after the first volley and Gabriel would stampede the horses after the third.

The privates manning the two swivels were ready and eagerly looked toward Pennywhistle. He shook his head--not yet, just a little closer.

Tracy admired his brother's cool judgment. It saddened him that his countrymen had to die for such a foolish, pointless exercise but battle was very unforgiving about poor choices. He just hoped the column could be stampeded before many died.

Beems felt triumph. He was almost there and in his imagination he could see Parke hanging from the large oak tree near his front porch. It was sad but not unexpected that he had taken casualties but nothing important was achieved without sacrifice. After a fiery denunciation amidst flaming torches, hanging Parke after smiting the British would have just the right dramatic effect. It would cement his developing reputation as the big man in the county. He knew a great future lay ahead, perhaps even the supreme position in Annapolis. Yes, Governor Beems sounded just right.

Fifty yards, close enough, thought Pennywhistle. "Play *Garryowen*." He whispered to Rufus who immediately blew the first notes. Pennywhistle's cutlass rose in the air and flashed down. "Fire!" he bellowed. 120 Colonial Marine muskets crashed out, fired by three separate groups of 40, each at a different angle to the column.

Beems' column was in the position of a man who had stuck his head into a hat and fire hit it from three sides. The marines automatically began to reload in quick time as soon as they had fired. The hedgerows winked bright spots of red as the Bakers of the Special Reconnaissance Force cut loose a fraction of a second later. Sammie Jo blew a ragged round hole in a captain's chest and he crashed to the ground.

The two short rounds of canister, 88 balls, slammed the column's front at waist level: a giant fist of lead crumpling it like a human fist smashing cardboard. The five remaining batteries of Chambers raced onto the field and deployed without interference, this time on the left side of the column. Half a minute later, they poured over six hundred shots into the column from thirty yards range. The ground turned a sickening crimson and the grass slicked with blood.

Strangely, Pennywhistle had missed his man. Beems had ducked, as if warned by some supernatural instinct, and Pennywhistle's shot hit the sergeant next to him. Gabriel had aimed at the same sergeant. The man dropped like a boulder, two fatal rounds his chest. After Gabriel fired he dashed to the rear, toward the corral of horses.

The column had stopped and become a shouting mob, too frightened to run. The swivel gunners reloaded. They had only one round of canister left apiece, but they would make it count. They had a perfect target; a large compact body of men almost frozen in place.

"Fire!" yelled Pennywhistle. A narrow whip of flame shot out from the hedgerows. Sammie Jo fired a second later and her man went down, shot through the heart. The swivels fired and a storm of lead tore through the air.

What was left of the column resembled a field of corn that had been beaten down by a hailstorm. Beems remained miraculously untouched. The men in the rear started to back away. A few soiled themselves.

One more volley! Thought Pennywhistle. It was time for boldness; enfilade, really close. He waved his sword, jumped up, and yelled "follow me and form line." He would have been taking a huge risk in front of experienced regulars, but it was trifling with these frightened, sad excuses for soldiers.

He formed 120 men quickly into line at a ninety degree angle to the column. It took less than half a minute. The range was thirty yards. "Fire!" Twenty Americans fell. Again, Beems remained unscathed, although frightened out of his wits.

He waved his sword at Gabriel. He bellowed through a speaking trumpet. "Now!" Gabriel opened the gate of the small corral holding 60 horses and began running among them, swatting as many rumps as he could manage with the flat of a cavalry saber. It was a dangerous job and a less experienced man could have easily been trampled. Gabriel, however, moved with the grace and sinuosity of an experienced dancer.

The horses did as their natures demanded and panicked, seeking the quickest avenue of escape. A stampede ensued and the horses headed straight at the tattered column. Pennywhistle ordered his men to lie down knowing that even when frightened, a horse avoided stepping on a prone man.

Horses would however be merciless to a standing man. They barreled through the column like a whirlwind toppling the pillars of a ruined temple. Men not trampled gave way to abject fear and fled the field as fast as they could go, heedless of anything but their personal survival.

" Damn, damn! Damn!" shouted Beems as he threw his hat to the ground in disgust. "White men beaten by nigrahs! Impossible! Impossible!" Beems' men were shocked. The Reverend had never been heard to utter anything resembling a curse word. His profanity told them better than any single event that their cause was lost.

Sammie Jo drew her tomahawk and ran madly forward. She was lost in the hot blood of the moment and looked determined to obliterate anything blocking her path.

"Charge!" yelled Pennywhistle. His men ran forward with fixed bayonets and time seemed to slow to a crawl. The battle's conclusion happened as it usually did when amateurs faced cold steel. The last fragments of column simply vanished like grease dissolved by lye soap. Not a single bayonet touched flesh because the Americans were running well before a single marine could press an attack home.

The marines wanted to chase, but he reined them in quickly. The column had been thoroughly broken and those men would not be fighting anytime soon. His job was to defend the plantation not achieve an annihilating victory. The most dangerous thing was to let a triumphant charge run wild. British cavalry often did so after sweeping the enemy before them and got savaged by counterattacks from fresh riders. It was far wiser to regroup and husband strength.

Restraining Sammie Jo was another matter entirely.

Chapter Twenty One

Berserkers were highly useful in battle as the Vikings had demonstrated but they were also like arrows, once fired they were impossible to control.

Sammie Jo was a force of nature answering only to her primal instincts. She raced past the redcoats waving her tomahawk wildly and howling a feral battle cry that sounded like a cross between a wounded lion and a shrieking panther. It set some nearby dogs baying. She was a fast runner and reached a hapless American who had lagged behind. She brained him from astern and he dropped to the ground a second later amidst a shower of gore.

Rather than sating her appetites, the tomahawking stimulated them. She saw groups of candles moving slowly through the trees as bewildered militia fled the open fields and sought the imagined safety of thick woods. She plunged headlong into the dark forest and raced madly down the first trail she could find.

Silly bitch just signed her death warrant, thought an angry Tracy. He should let the giantess fry in her own grease but he had given his word to his brother. He rose and raced after her, muttering curses and wondering why a sensible man had such abysmal taste in women. Other women his brother had known had died as if by some hidden curse so why couldn't this one just have followed the pattern.

Pennywhistle saw Tracy run after her and wanted to join him but a presentiment of danger caused him to restrain his foolishness. He was in command and his first duty was to hold Mount Prosperity until relieved. He believed he had repulsed the main effort but with a man like Beems you could never be sure. Amateurs sometimes acted in the most unexpected ways.

He would keep his men close to the plantation until he was certain no further threats materialized. As an added precaution he would send three patrols out north of the main tobacco fields. There were no roads in that direction according to the maps and an attack from that direction was unlikely but he wanted to be sure.

Sammie Jo had vanished by the time Tracy reached the forest's edge. Two trails presented themselves and with so many footprints blurred together, he could not tell which she had taken. He saw trees on fire a hundred yards ahead on the second trail because some scared militia men had never withdrawn their candles from their muskets and had dropped them as they ran.

The flames were spreading fast and the heat was already starting to build. He heard a sinister pop-popping up ahead and winced. Rounds were cooking off in the cartridge boxes of men too badly wounded to continue. The girl would have followed those noises and the fires.

He walked briskly, rather than ran, down the second trail. It was not just caution over navigating an unfamiliar path. He had to dodge scores of terrified squirrels, foxes, rabbits, and other small beasts dashing madly to find haven from the approaching flames. When he had advanced a quarter-mile or so, he felt a sharp pain in his calf and a tremendous blow across his shoulders. Packed dirt suddenly rushed up to meet him.

The ground knocked the breath from his lungs and he saw stars briefly, but he retained consciousness. He heard some rustling noises. He slowly turned himself over, feeling fire in his calf, and found himself staring up into four stupid faces. They had the muddy eyes of bewildered men angrily casting about for someone to blame for a recent beating. As his vision cleared, he realized three of them were pointing decrepit fowling pieces at his head, while a fourth brandished a bloody hunting sword that likely accounted for the pain in his calf.

"Who the hell is this bastard?" said the swordsman whose arrogant posture proclaimed him their leader. "That's an American uniform but from the direction he come, he suren't wudden fightin' with us. I didn't see no regulars tonight and Colonel Beems would have told us if any were about."

"Think he has something to do with that big girl that ran past yelling like a damned banshee?" slurred a second with the face of a ferret and possessing a similar intellect.

"Don't know 'bout that, maybe he be one of them dicked in the nob cowards who got their arses tanned by the lobsterbacks! Cost us Washington City!" volunteered a snaggle-toothed third who then spat a jet of tobacco juice.

"Yeah look at his uniform. It's all dirty, likely he seen some fightin' but he wouldn't be here lessen he run away! He sure run a fur piece in a short time, must have been real scared," slurred ferret-face.

"No, I bet it's dirty from him playing possum when the redcoats attacked!" said snaggle-tooth.

"Yeah, a damn white-livered swell!" said a huge man at least five inches above six feet but so wide that he was known as "blubber boy."

"Boys, I think Mister Fancy Pants here needs a little homegrown justice from our boots!" said the swordsman.

"Damn right," chorused the other three.

The smell of rum from their breaths was suffocating Tracy and he half expected the heat from the flames to ignite the air. They had probably fortified themselves with plenty of liquid courage before the just concluded battle and had likely added to it to relieve the sting of defeat. They were jumping to conclusions like fleas on a hot stove and likely were not very amenable to reason.

Normally he would not have wasted any time with these louts and would have taught them some manners with his fists. He was reckoned the toughest boxer in the Marine Corps, a considerable distinction, and would have had them down for the count within minutes. But the shooting pains in his calf burned like jabs from Satan's trident and he was certain he could not stand. The heat was increasing and the fire was close now.

A cheap boot crashed into his stomach. He wheezed and instinctively curled himself into a ball. He steeled his will and determination. He would survive this! Damn, these were his own countrymen, the people he had risked his life for!

A second boot was poised to stomp his face when a brown blur flashed through the blazing air snarling a cry that defied description. The fierce, reclusive wolverine was angered because one of the men had stepped on her den where she had been trying to protect her young from the fire.

The animal's eight razor-sharp front claws slammed into Blubber Boy's left leg like needles thrown at a pincushion. The beast clamped her vice-like jaws firmly onto the calf muscles. Her grip made a pit bull's seem weak and she exerted hundreds of pounds of pressure while wearing a look that suggested she would not let go until Judgment Day. She whipped her 60 heavily muscled pounds angrily from side to side and shredded the man's leg as efficiently as a blast of canister.

Blubber Boy crashed to the ground and rolled in agony but he could not shake the beast. Tracy saw things clearly from his ground's-eye view. God! He had the perfect opening if only he could stand. He couldn't use his fists, but he still had one good leg. He lashed out with his boot and connected solidly with snaggle-tooth's shin. The man howled in pain, hopped on one foot, and clutched at his injured leg.

The furious swordsman started to thrust toward the prostrate Tracy. "No you don't, pea brain," sneered a twangy, feminine voice from behind. A knife tip slid slowly out from the front of the man's throat, as if his Adam's apple had suddenly birthed a silver snake. He gurgled in surprise and clawed desperately at his throat. He stood transfixed for a few seconds. When the knife was retracted, he collapsed like a paper mache sack loaded with grapeshot.

Tracy blinked in surprise as great as if he had just seen an avenging angel. Perhaps he had, but this one sported muscled limbs rather than heavenly wings. Sammie Jo stood over the corpse like a wildcat contemplating a kill. The flames served to highlight her blazing eyes, high cheekbones, and the determined set of her jaw. She was angry Mother Nature in human form.

The ferret-faced man quivered in shock and terror then froze. Who, or more appropriately, what was this creature?

His uncertainty was emblazoned upon his face and it froze him as well as his associates.

Sammie Jo was on him in three quick strides. She was a soaring inferno of feminine fury, less a woman than an elemental force of nature; five-eleven-and-a-half inches of determined energy that weighed in at one hundred and sixty pounds. Ferret-face was five-one, bony, and a hundred pounds soaking wet.

She clamped her left hand on the scruff of his neck and jerked him to face level. She looked him contemptuously in the eye and the terrified man wet himself. She contemplated him for a few seconds, as a cat would a mouse, then savagely thrust her knife upwards into his groin and corkscrewed it viciously.

The man screamed hideously, twisted violently, and blood flew everywhere. She looked upon him with contempt and cruelty. Her eyes made it clear she merely had a detached curiosity about how few seconds he would last before he expired. He ceased jerking after a minute and Sammie Jo dropped him like a girl bored with her rag doll.

Tracy's horror overpowered his pain. My God, this creature was one of Lucifer's handmaidens! And his brother had thought of her as a mere woman!

Snaggle-tooth lay on the ground, mewling, moaning, and clutching at his shin. She covered the yard to him quickly, a like a cat lured by a fish wagon. She wanted no loose ends. She wondered why she was defending the life of a man who despised her but Pennywhistle valued him and that was all that mattered.

Snaggle-tooth stopped groaning and looked up at her. The solemn expression on her blood-spackled face made plain what she intended. He offered up no pleas for mercy and resigned himself to what was about to happen. It was the only brave thing he had ever done.

She respected a man who chose to die with dignity but it in no way cultivated her mercy. She raised her right foot high in the air and slammed it down hard on the man's windpipe. She crushed it completely but the man did not die immediately. He began to buck, gasp, and wheeze. Death would take a few minutes.

She heard shouting men coming down the trail, evidently determined to help their mates. There was no time to lose.

She dashed over to the astonished Tracy and remembered how he had relentlessly bad-mouthed her. She looked down at him mockingly. "So, looks like you can't get it up." She saw him wince. "The leg, I mean."

His face turned red with anger. His mind acknowledged he needed help, but his tongue was still a free agent capable of independent action. "Why you cornpone cur..."

"Shut up! Ain't got time for that." She glanced at his leg. "Can you stand?"

He bit his tongue. He was an honest man where survival was concerned. "No, I can't. But if you can help me to my feet and lend my arm a shoulder, maybe we can hobble out of this mess."

The shouts on the trail were getting louder and closer. She made some calculations and decided what he proposed wouldn't work. Walking slowly together would only ensure both of them were captured. They needed speed. She looked at Tracy carefully, One hundred seventy pounds give or take. She was strong but not strong enough to manage what she had in mind for more than a hundred and a half yards. She guessed the distance to safety was a quarter mile.

She felt despair closing round her until she remembered an incident she had seen on the Marlboro road two months before. She had watched in awe as an ordinary woman had lifted an upturned wagon many times her weight to rescue her child who was being crushed beneath. She had tapped into some cosmic emergency power that made the impossible possible.

Trouble was that exceedingly rare power was capricious in the extreme so it could not be turned on with the pull of a mental switch or wished into activation through prayer. Its influence was of extremely short duration. She guessed the power flowed from a deep and abiding love for someone in imminent danger of extinction. She usually scoffed at love and certainly felt quite the opposite for the man who lay before her. She sometimes wondered if she were a freak incapable of that emotion.

No, blast it! The stuff her father had said about her unloving nature was a damn load of horse dung. She focused her mind's eye on an image of Pennywhistle's face. She concentrated on the danger he was in. She felt a deep anger that anyone dared menace him but a second later a far different emotion cascaded over her and begged her to take a leap of faith. She cast aside her fears and the emotional armor plating protecting her heart fell away. She did not care in the slightest if the entire world noticed her complete vulnerability. That vulnerability enabled her to reach deep inside her heart for the first time, find her love for the Englishman, and embrace its incredible strength.

She saw stars, shuddered for an instant, and the color drained from her face. An instant later a sunburst of understanding exploded in her brain. Waves of power rocketed through her veins and a feeling of certitude such as she had never known settled upon her face. She could lick a regiment of giants single-handed! Her shoulder wound abruptly stopped hurting and her skin glowed with unearthly health. Damnation! She could do this! But she had only three or four minutes before the power vanished like a carriage turning into a pumpkin. Could she cover four hundred and forty yards with one hundred seventy pounds of deadweight?

"Come on, old man, time to go." She grabbed Tracy's hand and yanked him to his feet as easily as if he were a wooden marionette. Instead of girdling his arm around her neck and shoulders, she simply hoisted him over her left shoulder in the manner of a large sack of potatoes. She immediately began to plod forward but that changed to a steady walk thirty seconds later as she adjusted to her burden. She wasn't the least out of breath but she knew the power could vanish at any second.

"What the hell are you doing?" bellowed a bewildered Tracy. His brain actually knew exactly what was happening but it was just too fantastic to credit.

"Saving your life! A girl rescuing the big bad marine! Imagine that!" She laughed scornfully then abruptly ceased talking. She could not spare an ounce of lung power for the ordeal ahead. She moved to a brisk walk then a slow jog. She felt giddy and god-like from the raw power coursing through her. It was as if she had ingested a hogshead of sugar and drunk a leager of coffee. She thanked the lord for making her a country girl instead of one of those citified, pasty-faced creatures in *Sense and Sensibility*. Still, everything had a price. When the power departed she would likely be limp as a dishrag and as useless as teats on a bull.

The shouts were growing closer. She heard the sound of angry hornets zipping past her. They would have her range in a few seconds. It was time to throw caution to the winds and push this quirky energy right to the edge.

She transitioned into a fast jog and was astonished at the vigor of her legs and lungs. Strength seemed to be building not diminishing. Tracy felt as light as a small sack of grain. A voice in her head kept calmly repeating, "You can do this." The voice increased in intensity and tempo. She began to run.

"Faster, faster, faster, ain't no boy can beat you!" This time it was her father's voice. What the hell? Her body responded instinctively before her mind recovered from the shock. Her long muscled legs moved even more swiftly; machine-like pistons mimicking a Boulton and Watt Engine. Her arms were as windmills in a gale and her lungs were as bellows hooked to an inexhaustible supply of oxygen.

Every sense organ responded eagerly as her consciousness heightened. The details of the forest speeding by were recorded in exquisite detail. She heard the gun shots, felt the heat, and noted the flames but the only thing that mattered was the trail ahead. No power on earth could stop or hurt her. She felt it in her bones.

She was running with long loping strides, pouring in every ounce of energy from her body and soul. She had always been known as a fast runner but her previous speeds were snail-like compared to now. The path curved from time to time and she had to duck low-hanging branches. The world was flying by and Tracy felt light as a feather. This couldn't last.

The shouts behind were growing fainter now save for the heavy breathing and footfalls of one man moving steadily closer. Her heighted hearing detected a distinctive cadence in the running; the left foot striking the ground more strongly than the right. She had heard it before because she had raced against this southpaw. It was Adam Fairchild who boasted of being the fastest man in Maryland. She had beaten him at 15 in an informal matchup but the result had been thrown out because she was a girl.

He had grown into a religious prig who did not drink, smoke, and likely would never make love. Just the sort of unsmiling fanatic to throw his lot in with Beems. The men behind him clearly hoped their best runner could do what they could not. He nursed a grudge against her and was probably bent on fatal vengeance. She could take him in a fight but if she stopped his friends would catch up and pile on. She tried for a burst of speed but it was as if she had hit a wall and nothing happened. The power had reached its limit and a slight tremor in her arms suggested it was about to fail. Sweat poured down her forehead and began stinging her eyes.

"Low branches." Tracy yelled. He had said nothing until now. Yes, the low-hanging branches were an annoyance but why mention them? "Weapons!" he bellowed.

Of course! She grasped his meaning in a flash and wondered how she could have been so blind. She saw three ahead. Two were unsuitable, but one branch was perfect. It was thick oak yet supple enough to have plenty of whiplash. It was breast high for her but face high for Fairchild.

"Hold on tight!" She shouted over her shoulder. She extended her long arms and hit the branch with every ounce force in her being, propelling it violently away from her. She held it for only an instant but when she let go it snapped back ferociously and caught Fairchild square between the eyes. It crushed his skull and he lived but a few seconds.

She could see the trailhead now. Pennywhistle was waving frantically and a squad of marines stood poised to deliver a volley. She was almost home, just a few more yards. She felt a thud on her back but experienced no pain. Tracy groaned in agony from the bullet.

Her legs suddenly buckled as the power vanished. She collapsed on her knees then lazily toppled like a drunken sailor after one too many grogs. She lay inert, feeling as if she had been trampled by a herd of elephants. Everything was moving in slow motion and her vision grew fuzzy around the edges.

"Fire!" She heard Pennywhistle's voice clearly and felt a large rush of air above her head. She heard a chorus of groans behind her followed by a chorus of cheers in front of her. She also heard loud and labored breathing a foot away and slowly turned her head toward the unconscious Tracy. Blood oozed slowly but steadily from his back.

Pennywhistle, Dale, and O' Laughlin dashed forward to help the fallen pair.

Pennywhistle could see Sammie Jo was moving but Tracy was not. He knelt gently down next to him and remembered what he could from medical school. He checked the carotid artery and examined the back and chest. Tracy's pulse was thready and the bullet that had penetrated beneath the left scapula had not exited. The wound was bad and the bullet would have to come out. There was no surgeon handy and although he knew anatomy he had never had surgical training.

Sammie Jo slowly got to her knees and a few seconds later clawed her way to her feet. She felt slightly dizzy and shook her head to clear away the cobwebs inside. She could see Pennywhistle's distress and it pained her as did the idea that her entire run might have been in vain. She slowly walked over to Pennywhistle. "I done my best for him."

Pennywhistle looked up, his expression a mixture of relief and disapproval. "You have my thanks," he said tersely, "we can discuss things later."

Pennywhistle took a small bottle of smelling salts from his haversack and waved them slowly under Tracy's nose. He came round with a start. He moved slightly then grimaced in pain. "I kept my promise, Tom, but it looks like no good deed goes unpunished. How bad is it?"

"I don't think you are going to be doing any dueling in the next few days," said Pennywhistle as cheerfully as possible.

"That bad, huh?" said Tracy. "I knew my luck would run out sometime."

"Don't move, John, we'll get you back to the house." He stripped off his sash and coat. He bandaged the leg wound with his sash and used his dirk to cut small crude pads from the lining of his coat. He packed the shoulder wound with them and told Sammie Jo to keep pressure on them. Dale asked how he and O'Laughlin could help.

The three of them fashioned the remainder of Pennywhistle's coat into a crude stretcher suspended between two weapons. Dale and the O'Laughlin slowly bore Tracy along, while Sammie Jo walked to the side and kept her palm pressed against the wound. It took them fifteen minutes to reach the house. They got Tracy into the main parlor and laid him on the couch. He was breathing heavily and drifting in and out of consciousness.

Chapter Twenty Two

Beems rallied a few of his men but most were headed home to their farms just as fast as their legs would carry them. He had lost the battle but he was far from beaten. Nigrahs whipping white men? No! God would not allow it!

He had thought he would not need March and so had kept those 1000 men as a reserve. Now they would come in very handy for a plan he should have used in the first place. He would have to do some fast talking to March to convince him the stinging defeat at the plantation was merely a tactical reverse but evangelical preachers specialized in deception and this would be little different from what he did every Sunday.

*****

Pennywhistle wished he had finished his medical education. He looked at Tracy's wound repeatedly and considered a radical option. He might be able to extract the ball, but his technique would be so crude that shock would probably kill the already weakened Tracy. He could only make his brother comfortable and hope that the army and a competent surgeon arrived in time. His brother mercifully lapsed into unconsciousness after manfully fighting the pain.

*****

March argued with Beems for ten minutes but in the end the preacher's fanaticism gave his tongue a zeal and a power that overwhelmed March's rationality. March agreed to let Beems use his men for a new assault. The 1000 men of Beems' new command marched in darkness on a seldom-used path but it would take them where he wanted: just north of the largest tobacco field. He estimated it would take an hour to get into position. He should have done this the first time around, but he had been arrogant and God had punished him for it. He had repented and now God was showing him another way. It was the Old Testament solution: fire.

*****

Spottswood's men were nearly asleep on their feet, but they staggered on. The plantation was only two miles ahead. "Come on, Come on, my hearties. You can do it, I know you. Compared to you, the Spartans of old were weak! A tot of rum to the first man to touch the door of the mansion house. We are marines and have to set an example for the army!" A few weak laughs rose from the column.

It was pure bad luck that the marine reconnoitering groups missed Beems' men. They naturally scouted the main roads and the cow path Beems had chosen was unfamiliar even to most local slaves. At one point the forces were only a quarter mile apart but it seemed much greater in the deep wood.

Chivers and Peebles led the main force of 75 men. Chivers was chastened by Pennywhistle's earlier dressing down and was trying to redeem himself by exercising extreme caution. He was in command but repeatedly deferred to Peebles' more worldly judgment. He was learning that rank did not confer wisdom but experience did. He was urging the men along when he saw a flash of blue in a tree. Sniper: zeroed in on Mr. Peebles.

He had no time to shout a warning, but time enough to act. He ran a few steps and jumped headlong, shoving Mr. Peebles out of the way. The bullet meant for Peebles took him between the shoulder blades and he crashed to the ground wheezing heavily. Several marines saw the powder flash, targeted the sniper, and fired. The corpse tumbled from the tree.

Peebles raced over and knelt down to Chivers. His face was graying fast and bloody froth spewed from his lips. "Why?" Peebles asked in astonishment.

"I owed you a debt," he whispered. "You saved my life. A gentleman always repays a debt to another....gentleman. You are a gentleman you know; a real one that can only come from the heart and soul. I was a fool not to have understood that when I met you. I'm only one by pedigree, you see. I wish I could have got..." He stopped talking and light left his eyes.

Peebles eyes misted over and he gently closed Chivers'. "Nothing became him in this life like the leaving of it," he said quietly to no one in particular. Glancing up he saw flashes of blue ahead in the woods. His face turned angry. "Let's get those bastards!" He shouted to the marines.

They responded eagerly.

*****

"I don't know what to do with you Sammie Jo," said Pennywhistle angrily, hands on his hips and pure exasperation in his face. "You are a perpetual headache to me, a nuisance of large and lethal proportions. You have caused me to endanger my cause, my reputation, and worst of all, my men. You are like the Lorelei of old. You bewitch men with your country siren song and cause them to abandon their reason. You move men about like a grandmaster in chess, all the while pretending you are only capable of a game of draughts. I thank whatever God rules in heaven, that I have not entirely taken leave of my wits."

His venom retreated and he sighed in frustration. "God's blood, Hawkeye! Why can't you just be like ordinary folk?"

She looked him straight in the eye with unexpected kindness and vulnerability. "Ain't no way to dress it up, I got to speak plain. I got a volley for you, direct from the heart." She paused for just a second and spoke slowly and deliberately. "I love you, Sugar Plum. It don't make no sense to me, but I know it's true. First time in my life I ever put anyone ahead of myself. Never thought it would happen. Y'all make me want to be the best woman I can be."

She walked a few steps to him and put her hands gently on his shoulders. She felt him shudder slightly. "You are more stubborn than a just woke up jackass hooked to a hay wagon! Climb down off your cross Tom Pennywhistle and admit it to yourself. You love me too. I can see it in your eyes. Don't hide from it, don't fight it."

Of all the brazen arrogance! The rustic hussy's hubris knew no bounds. How dare she presume to know his heart! A wave of anger flooded him. "Sammie Jo, I have never heard a more fantastic or outrageous statement. I..."

He froze in mid-sentence, two things were badly wrong. First, she was right! Damn and blast, she was right. The second was far more dangerous. He didn't see it, but smelled it. Fire and close. They were going to burn him out.

"Get inside the house, Sammie Jo. Now!" Thank God, she didn't argue for a change, but raced directly toward the heavy front doors. Dale ran up a few seconds later. "Spotted 'em just a minute ago. Hundreds of them. One minute nothing, then suddenly a blaze of torches. They set fire to the north field. They're headed this way."

"Assemble the men and get them inside the mansion immediately. The rest of our men will hear the gunfire and head this way on the double. We'll make our stand here. Get the swivels ready. One more hour and we will be all right."

As if to laugh at his confidence, a bullet sang by his head. There was no time to lose.

*****

Spottswood checked his map and conferred with the two scouts who had reported in. They claimed to have heard gunfire. He looked into the sky and saw large plumes of smoke framed against the bright moon. They were a mile and a half out and the columns of smoke would act as homing beacons. He assembled the company, explained the situation frankly. Pennywhistle was in danger. That was all they needed to hear. They formed into column and broke into the Moore quick step. They passed exhaustion in the first seconds and continued on sheer spirit alone. They would not be late.

Pennywhistle's men took positions on the first and second floors and waited. Rufus trilled out *The Roast Beef of Old England*. It heartened the men and shouted defiance at the enemy. The Americans were cautious and only moved forward in short rushes when the smoke formed an effective cloak for their movements. They advanced no closer than fifty yards and lay flat on their bellies. They merely took pot shots. They were not eager to die. It was hard to see much through the smoke, but they mostly looked to be poorly armed. Pennywhistle waited to return fire until the range was almost point blank. Distance shooting was futile in the smoky murk.

Shots hit the window frames from time to time, but no one was hurt. The desultory shooting continued for half an hour, but decided nothing. Redcoats fired back now and then, mainly to keep the American heads down. The exchange was fine with Pennywhistle, he was glad to stall for time.

It was most certainly not fine with Beems. He wanted a decisive result. His men were generally poor shots and smoke and the enemy's concealment made hits almost impossible. It was stalemate, the one thing his developing reputation could not afford.

It hit Beems that the smoke was all to the good. He had 20 of his men relight their torches and had the rest open a covering fire. The 20 raced forward in groups of five and tossed their flaming packages at various portions of the front porch. The dry tinder of the wooden porch flared into life.

The choking smoke rose in great clouds and drifted inside the house. Pennywhistle coughed heavily and tried to clear his head .The mansion's rear exit was still clear, but would not be for long. Making a run for it was logical but it would also be fatal given the disparity of numbers. His brother could not be moved and he had to make his stand here.

Pennywhistle could see barely a yard in front of him. He coughed again and his eyes watered. He had Dale bring the men down from the second floor. If the enemy was sensible they would simply wait them out and shoot them as they exited the building. But from what he knew of Beems, he was not sensible. He had no patience and wanted glory. He would assault the house.

The marines formed in the front hall and waited with the bayonet. Parke came up with a loaded musket. It was his home he said, and he would defend it with his dying breath. Sammie Jo grabbed her loaded rifle and took her place next to his side. She reached out and squeezed his hand. Pennywhistle acknowledged her fierce expression with a quick nod and knew she was willing to trade her life for his.

His brother hobbled over, barely able to stand. He looked a deathly grey, but he had his rifle and wore a determined expression. "If I am going to die," he said defiantly, "It will be standing up and facing the enemy." Pennywhistle's eyebrows arched slightly in surprise. "They mean to hurt you," Tracy added, "and that makes them my enemy as well."

Pennywhistle and his men were expendable. His job was to protect the supplies laid in and nothing else mattered. He determined to sell his own and his men's lives dearly. It was a bloody shame, though, about Sammie Jo, his brother, and Rufus.

Rufus bravely played *Heart of Oak*. Appropriate.

He had his men stand five feet back from the doors, wanted to give them a clear field of fire. He and Dale stood by the two swivels. The first militia group rushed forward a minute later. The militia men had not heard the term "forlorn hope" but they were it. Forlorn hopes usually died. He and Dale jerked the lanyards on the swivels at the same time. The canister blasted the lot into bloody fragments of muscle. There was no time to reload and slaughter the group immediately behind.

A burst of white light caused everyone to blink and an ear splitting crack rattled the windows. A gigantic bolt of lightning had struck the roof. A wind sprang up and dissipated the swirling smoke. A second later, a wave of rain slammed into the side of the house. It was another outbreak of the freakish weather spawned by the awful heat, but this time it did not save the Americans, but the British.

It all happened very fast. The rifles of Pennywhistle's men fired as soon as the second group of ten Americans came through the door. The noise sounded tremendously loud in the confined entrance hall and the volley killed all but two. One left alive was Beems. To his small credit, he at least was first through the door.

Beems had his pistol out, saw Parke, and fired angrily at him. The shot hit Parke in the neck and death was almost instantaneous. But Parke had leveled his gun at Beems and the final spark of life caused Parke's finger to spasm on the trigger. His shot caught Beems in the stomach and he dropped to the floor squealing like a gutted pig. The wound was exceedingly painful, but not immediately fatal.

More Americans rushed through the door amidst a giant hissing sound as the driving rain swiftly snuffed out the flames on both the house and fields. The fighting was brutal and hand-to-hand. This time British bayonets savaged American flesh. Time slowed once more for Pennywhistle.

He saw Gabriel nimbly gore an intruder with his bayonet, saw his brother gut a man with his sword, saw Dale expertly sidestep a sword thrust and riposte accurately with his bayonet. He vaguely remembered hours later, that his flashing cutlass had amputated one man's arm and skewered another through the eye.

Sammie Jo spotted a rat-faced man about to bayonet the barely breathing Tracy. She could not stop him in time but her tomahawk could. With a blood curdling yell she hurled it expertly and it embedded itself deeply in the man's right temple. The man made no sound and collapsed like a spent bellows in front of Tracy. Tracy turned his head toward the tomahawk's source. He smiled wanly and waved weakly in acknowledgment.

Her predatory instincts aroused, Sammie Jo raced over and wrenched the tomahawk free from the rat-faced man. She sought a new target for its bloody blade and quickly found one in the prostrate Parson Beems. She smiled like Lucifer's daughter at the thought of sending him to that lake of fire his ilk preached constantly about. The abject terror in his face likely matched that of the dying children to whom he had administered last rites. He was the kind of preacher who warned everyone, regardless of age, about the dangers of passing away "unsaved."

She raised the tomahawk high above her head and slammed the blade down with every ounce of muscle she could summon. He reminded her of all the preachers in her life and that hatred increased the force of the blow exponentially. The expert stroke split the Beems' face as neatly as if she were bisecting a rotten tomato. Bits of red flew in every direction and what remained of each half wore a bewildered look; astonished that God had not intervened.

Beems' extinction and all of the violence blurred together in a strange, mad tapestry of death as things always did during the heat of battle. Pennywhistle was exceptionally alert when it happened, yet it always took an effort to recall precisely what he had done in the days after.

It ended as swiftly as it had begun. It was the faint music that did it. The sound was unmistakable; bagpipes. *Garryowen;* his favorite! His men heard them at exactly the same moment as the Americans did. Both sides knew exactly what it meant. The Americans broke and ran.

The rest of Pennywhistle's marines came dashing up after a two-mile run that had started when they heard gunfire. He ordered them to join in the pursuit.

But a last shot from the fleeing Americans did horrid damage. It hit Rufus, still playing, square in the chest. He hit the floor clutching his beloved trumpet. Pennywhistle dropped his gun, raced over, and bent down. He cradled the boy in his arms and hoped against hope for some sign of life. There was none. A great talent had been silenced and would never bring joy to a larger world. His eyes moistened.

Spottswood's men moved forward confidently in loose skirmish order, followed by the rest of the Marine Brigade. The sheets of rain soaked the redcoats to the skin and made musket fire all but impossible, but it did nothing to dampen their spirits or determination. The Americans were already running, so all the British had to do was encourage their flight with leveled bayonets. They saw them off the field amidst much cheering.

The cloudburst stopped as suddenly as it started. The sopping wet redcoats continued their steady advance.

The 4th moved up behind the Marines in support. Manton's light company took point. His men scattered the last remaining fugitives.

CHAPTER TWENTY THREE

Pennywhistle and his men plopped down where they stood, utterly silent. He and they were exhausted from days of wild exertion and stress, unrelieved by very much sleep. The fight just ended had stolen their remaining reserves of strength. A strong wind blew through the smashed front windows and made the candles flicker violently. They gave a peculiar elfin light to the grave, haggard faces. The cloudburst had dropped the temperature drastically and chased away the humidity. For the first time in days, the climate turned civil and the gusts of wind brought blessed relief to everyone.

Nobody spoke for some minutes. Then one man laughed slightly and another joined him. A third chimed in. The ripple soon changed into a low, rolling chorus. The laughter had nothing to do with mirth but everything to do with relief and the expulsion to stress. Despite the Grim Reaper's best efforts, they had confounded him one more time. They rejoiced in the infinite joy and glory of simply being able to draw breath while those lying motionless nearby could not. Pennywhistle told everyone to rest.

His brother lay slumped against the wall. His pallid face showed he was fading fast. The last effort had been too much for him.

Pennywhistle rose with great effort, walked over to him and knelt down. "Don't go. It's too soon. Stay with me, I will get you back to health. There is so much we can learn from each other."

Tracy looked resignedly into his eyes and sighed. "My hourglass is down to its last few grains and nothing can prevent its emptying." His grey face took on a thoughtful cast. "Brother, you are so civil in your every address, so upright in your conduct, so steadfast in cleaving to your duty that it is easy to misread you as an overzealous prig. I despised you at our first meeting and consider myself lucky that in our short time together I was permitted the honor of discovering the good man beneath your heavily starched collar. My parting wishes are that you cease demanding perfection of yourself and realize that you alone cannot solve every problem. Show the same concern for yourself that you now confine to others."

He shuddered as if hit by Boreas's breath. "I grow cold and can hardly breathe. I cannot feel anything below the waist. I wish I had some suitably heroic final observation to make, but none presents itself." He coughed then tried to smile. "You're good with fancy words so you'll just have to invent a gallant epitaph. I think most inspirational parting words are inventions of playwrights and poets anyway." He wheezed a short laugh.

He coughed violently for a few seconds then continued in a whisper. "I have a confession to make. I am not the man of honor you think. When I was on board Gordon's ship I had a chance to see some of his papers. I found out about the upcoming attack on Baltimore and I passed that information along. I know it was wrong but my guilt over helping you got the better of my honor."

Pennywhistle spoke gently. "Don't trouble yourself, your patriotism remains intact. You fought like a Titan at Bladensburg and put your life on the line for your country a hundred times in those two hours. You were only on *Seahorse* because of me. You fell from grace one time marking you as merely human. Only the man from Nazareth achieved perfection. Besides, given the ineptitude of your government, that information may well be permanently lost among the underlings in the corridors of power. Empires rise and fall and governments come and go, but the bureaucratic cast of mind is unchanging and eternal."

Tracy wheezed a short laugh. "Yes, bureaucrats are like cockroaches. For every one you stomp, there are five more waiting in the dark. I have something for you."

With great effort, he reached into his pocket, extracted a document and handed it to Pennywhistle. Pennywhistle's eyebrows arched in surprise as he read the time honored words: *I, John Thomas Tracy being of sound mind and body...* "Not sure if it's legal, Tom. Wrote it out yesterday. Couldn't shake a presentiment that my race with Father Time was almost over. No attorney was handy but Captain Gordon and his First Officer witnessed it as a favor to you. The word of honorable men should count for something."

"Why me?" said Pennywhistle, touched yet puzzled.

"I didn't have any living family till I met you. You gave me something priceless that I had always coveted: a past, and an honorable one to boot. The knowledge that my father was a good man removed a gigantic weight I'd carried since childhood. That knowledge means more to someone hatched on the wrong side of the blanket than a person of legitimate birth can ever know. I like to think our father would be proud of me for saving the President."

"Be in no doubt of that," said Pennywhistle gently.

Tracy smiled wanly. "Not much in the will except a small house in Norfolk, a couple of hundred dollars in silver, and five hundred shares in a gold mine near Charlotte. Mines been a worthless money pit for years, but just when I don't need money, it looks like those paper certificates have suddenly become valuable. I got a letter last week from the chief prospector. The assay office confirmed he'd found three twelve-pound nuggets of almost pure gold and he is certain they are splinters from a very rich vein."

He coughed hard and then wheezed weakly. Bloody froth bubbled out. "The mine's like Sammie Jo: have faith and the grit to plough through tons of mud and dirt and someday you'll find your gold. I was wrong about her just like I was wrong about you. All that's gold does not glitter. Some women will cry for you, some will lie for you, and some will turn a blind eye for you, but not many will die for you. You can't spare that girl, she fights!"

He clasped Pennywhistle's hand tightly. "One last favor. Like the Crusaders of old, allow my heart to make the journey my body cannot. Bury it in the family sepulcher in England and help me to connect with a legacy for the ages. I have not been a Pennywhistle in life but perhaps I can be one in death."

Pennywhistle's eyes moistened. "Zeus's thunderbolts could not prevent me from carrying out your wish. You shall lie with our family in Saint Cuthbert's Church. The gallant sprits there will glory in your enlistment to their eternal ranks. When my time comes, I shall rest beside you."

He sighed deeply. "Bless you, Tom, God bless you!" His watery eyes glowed for a brief second as if viewing an awesome prospect. He spoke with joy. "Ah...I see them now.

Yes! Yes! Thank you all!" He smiled and a wave of serenity stole over his face as if he had just perceived distant trumpets sounding. A portal had been opened that no living man could see and voices were speaking that only Tracy could hear. "Yes, yes, follow the light, follow the light, time to go." He whispered calmly, as if answering a benevolent guide. His whisper faded out gradually as he passed into the world to come. "Beautiful, beautiful, beautif..." He stopped quietly in mid-sentence and his eyes stared straight ahead, unseeing.

Pennywhistle gently shut them. After all the horrible battlefield endings he had witnessed, it was a relief his brother had been granted a good passing. Death had come as a forgiving friend and not a frightening foe. Nevertheless, tears began to stream down his face. Two brothers lost. He was alone again. It was too much.

His hands and arms started to shiver. His shoulders began to shake and he felt as if he were naked in the Arctic. God, it was embarrassing.

Sammie Jo came over and sat down next to him. She was bleeding slightly. She had popped several stitches on her wound. She wrapped her left arm around his right shoulder like a warm blanket on a winter night. She squeezed gently and a wave of heat engulfed him. The shaking stopped abruptly. "I'm here, Sugar Plum," she said quietly.

Her touch seemed strange, alien. If he didn't know better, he would say he felt compassion from her. Had she grown a real woman's heart or was he so deluded by grief that he was simply imagining what he wanted to feel?

"I thank my lucky stars you made it, Hawkeye." He spoke absentmindedly, his careless tongue seemly independent of his disciplined mind. "I couldn't stand to lose a brother and you as well." Why had he said that? Of course! He was exhausted and it was sheer fatigue talking. And yet, there was a spark in his heart that he could not deny.

Manton and Spottswood walked in a second later. Water cascaded from their sodden uniforms and they looked like refugees from a capsized boat. They recoiled instinctively at the carnage, but quickly sized up what had happened. They noted with sadness Pennywhistle's grief-stricken face. Sammie Jo's arm clasped Pennywhistle's shoulder tightly, very protective.

Spottswood whispered briefly to Manton whose eyebrows arched in surprise. They exchanged dubious looks.

Spottswood bent down and tapped Pennywhistle on the shoulder. Sammie Jo shot a fierce glance at him and said, "Don't you bother him none, he's been through a lot. That's his brother."

A brother? Spottswood glanced at the corpse. The resemblance stunned him. He looked at Sammie Jo with evident distaste and wondered why this vile creature was still alive. "Don't be an impudent trollop. Tom and I go back a long way." He spoke gently, knew exactly what Pennywhistle would want to know. "We beat them, Tom. They run. Egad, they give way everywhere. You did it!"

Pennywhistle came back to himself. "Thank God for that. I thought you'd never get here."

Manton sat down next to them. "I am so sorry about your brother, Tom," he said with sympathy. Then his face brightened. "General Ross will be here directly. I have an idea what he is going to say. I think you will be pleased. You're going home!"

Pennywhistle's physical and spiritual exhaustion caused him to misinterpret the well-intended news. Home? How?

Why? Had he done something wrong? Was he being cashiered? Likely not, to judge by Manton's hearty grin.

General Ross walked in, followed by a pack of agitated aides. Ross managed to look elegant, despite his wet clothes. All of the weary men in the hall instantly jumped up and came to attention. Pennywhistle was the last to rise and did so slowly, but Ross did not seem to care. He favored Pennywhistle with a courtly smile.

"I am most pleased to see you Mr. Pennywhistle, most pleased." Ross quickly surveyed the corpses, but refused to look downcast. "A very close run thing, sir, but it looks like you've won a handsome little victory. I am most impressed with your conduct, as is Admiral Cockburn. He suggested since it was your report which made possible this campaign, it is you who should carry word of our victory at Washington back to the Prince Regent. I concur fully and I will prepare the final dispatches tomorrow. If everything goes well, and I think we have passed the final hurdle, you will sail for England within the week."

"Thank you, sir, I am greatly honored," he said, with as much formality as his fatigue enabled him to muster. It was indeed a great honor. Bearers of dispatches proclaiming great victories were generally promoted and knighted. *Major Sir Thomas Pennywhistle, Knight of the Most Honorable Order of the Bath.* It sounded a bit grand. But Sammie Jo would love it. Why did he think of her?

General Ross spoke kindly, "Forgive me, Captain Pennywhistle, for being so impetuous. I have startled you. You have been through a horrendous ordeal. I should have waited and allowed you to recoup your energies. You need food and rest. Please sir, refresh yourself and call upon me at your leisure."

"No, General, I am flattered by the honor you have bestowed upon me and gratified you have undoubtedly put aside more weighty matters to come here and acquaint me with your decision. Before you depart sir, permit me the singular honor of introducing you to Miss Samantha Matthews."

He hesitated for a fraction of a second as a flood of conflicting thoughts shot through his weary brain. She was feral, dangerous, and violence was her preferred solution to most problems. His friends strongly disapproved. She was also manner-less, blunt, and lacked education. Her tempestuous soul could never be tamed and probably could never be trusted.

Yet she had twice acted decisively to save his brother's life. She had given Pennywhistle the chance to say a heartfelt goodbye and ease Tracy's passing. Her conduct had moved his brother to retract his initial negative judgment and in the end argue that real character undergirded her coarse exterior. Perhaps his friends and others of their kind might change their opinion as well if they could move beyond class prejudice and focus on the rough virtue that only needed tutoring.

She loved him without reservation. The strength, depth, and power of her passion awed him. It was as plain as day in her face, voice, and body language. Most importantly, she loved him not as he could be, should be, or might be, but simply as he was. She cared nothing about his defects of character or his past misdeeds. She wanted him as a man, not a source of means: his fortune, estate, and reputation were of no consequence.

Unlike the painted maids of Bath, she would love him just as much if he were a beggar or a brigand. She also challenged him and dared him to explore uncharted horizons. Life with her would never be bland, insipid, or predictable. The lovemaking would be magnificent and often.

She showed great courage and possessed a quick natural intelligence. She deserved better than the lowly niche to which she had been condemned by an accident of birth. She was a work in progress and the final result might be quite striking if someone took an interest in sculpting her essential humanity into civilized form.

He could retire comfortably and creditably into private life if he chose. He could cast nightmares and tremors into the well of forgetfulness and live as a contented prisoner of his upbringing and station. His knighthood would give him minor celebrity and doubtless attract influential well-wishers. His saved prize money, The First Folio, and the inheritance from his half-brother would enable him to purchase a very respectable estate; a home by far the most convincing lure to attract a well-bred, well-pedigreed wife with a comely dowry. No one would think less of him after 12 years of battle; genteel retirement with a manor, a wife, and several squalling brats would be logical and expected.

But the man who could live a safe, dull existence as an easy-going country squire had died years before, yet another victim of a very long war.

He had always been an independent thinker and had never cared very much what polite society thought. Sammie Jo obviously did not either. He was being furnished a chance to shatter the illiberal shackles of caste and unreason and be a true servant of the Enlightenment he valued so highly. He could liberate Sammie Jo as well as himself. They were both outsiders of a kind, irrevocably altered by war and moved far beyond the traditional barriers of convention and class.

They had seen and done things pampered, peace-loving civilians spoke of only in the lowest whispers. It made them a well matched, if unexpected, pair. War had taught him that the best laid plans vanished in the first five minutes of fighting and that battle had an agenda of its own beyond any human agency. Love was like that too. He could forge whatever destiny he chose with Sammie Jo, if he possessed the courage and wisdom to trust his heart as she had hers. *For once, just roll the dice,* his heart demanded.

"She is my fiancée." He spoke with a quiet certitude that he did not quite feel. Sammie Jo looked at him with a mixture of shock and satisfaction, her expression a cross between that of a lottery winner and a just-fed tigress. She clasped his right hand in hers, and whispered in his ear, "You are my sugar plum now and forever!"

Ross favored her with a courtly bow and spoke the right gallant words. Sammie Jo responded with a dazzling smile, a graceful curtsy, and a simple, "enchanted, General." Ross smiled broadly back, apparently bewitched by her unaffected New World sincerity. He saluted Pennywhistle crisply. "We shall speak later, Captain. Once again, my felicitations on your victory."

Spottswood and Manton stared at Sammie Jo, Pennywhistle, and then each other in stunned disbelief, their eyes shouting, "Is Pennywhistle mad?"

Pennywhistle saluted Ross and the general departed. Sammie Jo swiveled her tall frame to come face to face with the much shorter forms of Spottswood and Manton. Spottswood's prim mouth, disapproving eyes, and knitted eyebrows made clear his contempt for her, while Manton merely looked astonished that such an odd creature could bewitch his friend.

"Don't care a jot what you think of me, this here's my man and I aim to take care of him. Now why don't you two gents make yourself useful someplace else." Sammie Jo's imperious blue eyes glowed with sparks of fire and her voice pulsed with menace.

Spottswood and Manton stood frozen in shock at the sheer gall of a backwoods hussy claiming to be their friend's Rock of Gibraltar. Why, he hardly knew the woman!

"I mean it. You'uns clear off, or so help me God, I will make you both sing soprano." She whipped out a knife and pointed it directly at their private parts. "I ain't afixin to tell you again." The look on her face was that of a mother bear protecting a wounded cub.

Spottswood and Manton wisely retreated, both realizing the emotional residue of battle caused many to behave in an outrageous manner. Now was not the time to warn their friend about the grave mistake he was making. They would however remonstrate with him strongly in the days to come.

Dale approved, although his poker face betrayed no opinion. As a worldly NCO of long service, he had observed enough unhappy officers to know that many oh-so-proper arranged marriages actually resulted in long-term misery for the two principals concealed behind a façade of expensive fashions, emotionless faces, and twittering conversations. Observing real passion between a married couple of the better classes was as rare as spotting a hummingbird in your garden.

The almost palpable lust this couple had for each other gave their marriage a more than fair chance of success. Dale's military experience had taught him that personality and passion were far better predictors of a man's long-term prospects than pedigree and manners. The same went for women and marriage.

His officer and the unusual American might be opposites in terms of class and upbringing but they shared a quality that was as extraordinary as a rose blooming after a hard frost: indomitable strength of will. It was if as each believed the very fabric of existence could be bent simply by demanding it with the proper resolve.

They were at their best when circumstances were at their worst and possessed a grace under pressure that gave them the power to act while others froze in indecision. They would be far from the ideal neighbors if you believed in an exquisite attention to class and propriety, but exactly the sort of people you would wish in your life if things started to go wrong.

Gabriel was astounded by what he saw yet it was no more fantastic than a former slave reclaiming his manhood and becoming a red-coated warrior. He prayed the new couple would prosper. The Good Lord helped worthy folk and these two certainly were that, although their martial spirits might not adapt easily to peace.

Pennywhistle had risked his life to free him from slavery. He had never asked anything in return save that Gabriel live his life with dignity. Gabriel believed the Englishman was destined for great things and wanted to be part of that journey.

Pennywhistle had accepted Gabriel's offer to serve as a replacement batman even though he understood the Colonial Marine had only a vague idea of what was expected of a gentleman's gentleman. Gabriel did know that the subservience of a slave was no part of the deal. In a country where no black men were held in bondage, he would be treated not just as a servant but as Pennywhistle's trusted confidant.

Pennywhistle was willing to give a man a chance to learn and blaze a distinctive trail that was his alone. His choice of Miss Samantha showed he truly believed that no man's destiny was charted in stone.

He would be just as out of place as Miss Samantha in a strange new land but he felt they could help each other adjust to greatly changed circumstances. He would also be a living link to the home she had left behind.

Pennywhistle wanted to explain his choice to his friends, but he was just too damned tired for words. He understood they had legitimate reservations but a deep part of him counseled that it was wiser to wager the future on what could be rather than what was. Sammie Jo might be a back country rustic, but that need be no permanent state of affairs. She was a fast study and was just beginning to grasp how far her gifts could take her.

He did not delude himself about the purity of her heart. It contained a great deal of darkness; fully as much as his own. The killer within might be disciplined and cloaked but it could never be entirely expunged. Still, she had killed out of love for him and thus rendered herself a woman without a country.

She would always be an opportunist who shrewdly balanced the key moment against the main chance to reap maximum advantage. There was no reason to expect married life would change her manipulative ways. She would just act with greater sophistication as her education increased.

Like a sorceress, she projected a beguiling glamour. She deceived men lusting after her into thinking she was just an unsophisticated country girl who did not quite grasp her effect on men. She maneuvered them into performing her will by tacitly promising much and delivering little.

Any trace of artifice was gone now and her eyes glowed with a heartfelt, pleading honesty. She touched his hand gently and spoke a simple incantation of enormous power: "I love you."

"I love you too," his lips replied instinctively.

She could learn the social graces but she would always have a primal edginess about her. No one would ever mistake her for a traditional chatelaine. But given a little guidance--his godmother Lady Leith would be perfect--he had no doubt that she would someday be as much a doyen of the drawing room as she had been a Diana of the woods.

Navigating her hidden depths would be an extraordinary voyage of discovery. Whether with knowledge or love, he was a seeker, a perennial explorer, someone for whom the unknown perpetually beckoned. He had only a limited idea of what he might find spending a life with her, but the journey promised unending excitement and great reward.

She smiled at him with simple, guileless joy. Her welcoming mouth and unexpectedly kind eyes suggesting she possessed a sentimental side that could be unshackled under the right circumstances.

The smile faded a moment later as she considered his unspoken reservations and pondered his mixed motives. Something flickered briefly in his emerald eyes that she doubted any man had ever seen: fear. Like so many Englishmen, he had a terror of raw emotion leaving him vulnerable. His protective shields were gone and the door to his heart was wide open. She had but to step through.

She knew the almost magical power of simple touch. Laying on of hands was no mere figure of speech but a powerful method of healing. She put her left arm gently around his shoulder and softly pressed her right hand on his. She silently stroked his hand for several minutes, her kind touch a far stronger restorative than mere words.

His eyes grew relaxed and dreamy as he felt the world of blood and carnage fading away. Unambiguous peace descended upon him as his usual rationality and skepticism retreated into the background. A second later he experienced that most evanescent of all emotions: joy. Far different from pleasure, joy was a creature of the soul rather than the body.

It had cost him twelve years of struggle, suffering, and death to reach this place and he had no wish to leave anytime soon. It felt a homecoming of a kind; to a strange, unexplored, exotic country that yet seemed exactly where he belonged. Sammie Jo, strong, beautiful, transcendent, was the mistress of this land, as if she had always been there and always would be. He had no idea if he could make a permanent home in this extraordinary kingdom, but it was surely worth a try.

His right index finger twitched several times. Sammie Jo softly covered it with her palm and the movements ceased. She wanted to hold him close forever and make sure those tremors never returned.

She placed his head in her lap and cradled it lovingly. She stroked his hair and cooed soothing words to him, as if comforting a child woken by night terrors. "It'll be alright Sugar Plum, it'll be alright."

He exhaled a deep sigh. His eyelids fluttered for a split second then closed softly. Dreams took him gently and no nightmares troubled his long sleep.

THE END

JOHN DANIELSKI

Tom Pennywhistle will return in
"'Attaché Extraordinaire"

AUTHOR'S NOTES

"The greatest disaster in American military history." A number of historians have described Bladensburg thus, yet it remains unknown to most Americans and exact accounts of the battle are confused and contradictory. There are disagreements among reputable historians with regard to the numbers involved, the amount of artillery on the American side, and even the time it took to fight the battle. Most accounts say it took two hours but several historians argue it took closer to four.

People naturally like to remember events which bring glory to their national heritage and forget those that did not, so it is not surprising that Bladensburg has remained in the shadowlands of America's historical consciousness. While I have taken a few liberties with the details of the battle in the interest of drama, the general description of it in *Capital's Punishment* is accurate.

At Bladensburg, as with the whole Washington Campaign, the British did everything right and the Americans did everything wrong. The British had unity of command, excellent small unit cohesion, singleness of purpose, plenty of combat experience, and a tradition of victory.

Capital's Punishment

The Americans had far too many people making unhelpful command suggestions, many units which had never even marched in anything larger than a company formation and numerous militia officers who owed their positions to election by their neighbors. The vast majority of the American army faced battle for the first time at Bladensburg and the American command had no real plan for victory save to stand on the defensive and hope for the best.

The British accomplished much with little while the American accomplished little with much. That a small, fast-moving army could occupy and burn an enemy capital and get away scot free despite much greater numbers of their opponents says a great deal about a well-trained, well-led, professional army matched against amateurs in arms.

Congreve rockets contributed much to the American discomfiture at Bladensburg but they were quirky, unpredictable weapons chiefly useful in generating terror. The real Congreves had no one like Pennywhistle to fit them with guidance fins and their flight paths were erratic. Wellington at Waterloo had no faith in them and at one point suggested that The Royal Artillery Rocket Troop discard their rockets and fight as artillerists manning traditional field pieces.

The one bright spot at Bladensburg from the American point of view was the conduct of Commodore Joshua Barney's sailors and marines manning a battery of artillery. They fought well and skillfully. A low point in American history nevertheless brought honor to the reputations of the United States Navy and the Marine Corps.

Barney's men only ceased firing when they ran out of ammunition due to the cowardly conduct of civilians in charge of the reserve ammunition. Barney was captured and paroled and many of his men compelled to surrender. Some of his men escaped and went on to render useful service against the British at Baltimore.

Their heroic conduct was remarked upon by nearly all of the British who wrote accounts of the battle. That the British spared the Marine Barracks in Washington on account of the gallantry of US Marines is true, according to legend, but much less certain when looking at the facts.

The portrayals of General Ross, Admiral Cockburn, Commodore Gordon, Commodore Barney, and General Winder are as close to real life as I could make them.

Cockburn is much maligned in American history and is chiefly remembered as a piratical, Snideley Whiplash cartoon villain who had the gall and bad taste to burn the White House. In truth, he was a skilled commander possessed of gifted strategic insight who likely would be remembered as a great hero if he had fought on the American side. It was he who later escorted Napoleon into exile on St. Helena and the Emperor found to his surprise that Cockburn was impervious to intimidation.

Cockburn did not care for Americans and made war ruthlessly but he was no monster and had a civilized, chivalric side to him. He actually did offer to provide a safe escort for Dolley Madison and did relent on burning the patent office when a number of well-manicured ladies begged for his help. He did employ the old custom of beating the parley in an effort to come to some kind of terms with Americans. He and Ross made the final decision to burn Washington only after they were fired upon by Americans barricaded in the Capitol building.

I have found no references to beating the parley and the volley from the Capitol building in recent works on the Washington Campaign and base my information on a 1987 biography of Cockburn by Dennis Pack: *The Man Who Burned the White House*. Pack took the trouble to consult the many volumes of Cockburn's personal correspondence which were purchased by the Library of Congress in 1909. That correspondence has been sadly ignored in more current books.

While the battle at Mount Prosperity never happened, the Chambers Volley Guns were real and appear to have seen action on several American warships.

Pennywhistle's breech-loading Ferguson Rifle was also real. It was years ahead of its time. Few examples exist today and any that might come on the market would fetch a price well into six figures.

Pennywhistle himself is a fictional character but he is loosely based on Royal Marine Captain Thomas Inch. John Tracy is loosely based on United States Marine Corps Captain Samuel Miller who was wounded at Bladensburg.

The Colonial Marines were an experiment that had a short but honorable history. They were disbanded at the end of the Napoleonic Wars but the British kept their word to them. The black marines not only retained their freedom but were given land in what is now Venezuela for their service. Their descendants live there to this day.

The racial attitudes expressed in this book may offend some modern sensibilities. They are far from my personal beliefs, but are accurate for the time: Pennywhistle's view of blacks represents an Enlightenment European attitude, while Tracy's reflects a viewpoint common to American men of means. Beems' outlook is closest to that of an average American. The use of the word Negro was common as was its nasty derivative. I resisted using any variants of the *N word* but felt sacrificing accuracy in the interest of avoiding unpleasantness would be a mistake.

The conspiracy to assassinate President James Madison is a creation of my imagination but a real and serious secession movement existed in New England. New England had suffered harsh economic consequences from the British blockade and considered a separate peace with Britain. The Hartford Convention actually occurred but moderate voices prevailed and talk of secession ceased.

Homosexuals were closeted at this time and any conduct in that vein was against the law, yet there was some measure of tolerance. Prosecutions for "uncleanness," the euphemism for almost any gay behavior, were few and far between. The Napoleonic Period was a boisterous, irreligious age as well as an unsentimental one. Outright persecution of gays only came in with the grim religiosity of Victorian Era.

London contained districts where it was relatively easy to arrange almost any kind of gay assignation. Molly Houses were somewhat like modern gay bars and were generally let alone by the authorities. You could rent a room by the hour with no questions asked. They were easily located by paying a savvy street urchin a small amount of coin to guide you there.

The description of what happened at the White House is accurate in a general way although I made educated guesses as to the décor and the food served. There were actually two large 12-foot-high mirrors in what is now The East Room and a large portrait of President Adams did hang above a marble fireplace but descriptions of the White House interior before the 1817 rebuild are barren of decoration detail.

The War of 1812 was a misbegotten war that brought no glory to any of the participants. It was not a second war of Independence as some older historians have maintained and can only be fully understood as a sideshow of the much greater Napoleonic Wars. It was fueled by the British impressment of American sailors, British attempts to use their blockade of Napoleon to close the Continent to American shipping, and American land hunger for Canada.

The Americans declared war by the slimmest of margins. It was a foolish, quixotic decision considering they faced a world class power and possessed only a small navy and an inexperienced army. The British had dispatched a message to Washington announcing the ending of the impressment of seamen, but the message only reached Washington two weeks after the start of hostilities.

The war had little effect on Britain in the long run but it did give the Americans a national anthem and a national hero in the form of Andrew Jackson. Oddly enough, the greatest battle, New Orleans, was fought three weeks after the peace treaty had been signed because word of it had not yet crossed the Atlantic.

For further reading on the War of 1812, the best single volume is history is Donald Hickey's *The War of 1812: A Forgotten Conflict.*

If you seek a detailed, scholarly treatment on the causes of the war, I would recommend Gordon S. Wood's new book, *Empire of Liberty: A History of the Early Republic 1789-1815.* Sadly, his account of the Washington Campaign is short, bland, and jejune. He repeats a number of old canards and includes no new insights or information.

For an amusing, acerbic, and insightful view of the American war effort in the conflict I recommend John R. Elting's *Amateurs to Arms! A Military History of the War of 1812.*

The best account of the Washington Campaign is Steve Vogel's *Through the Perilous Fight: Six Weeks that Saved a Nation*.

For those who enjoy documentaries, I recommend the PBS series, "The War of 1812." Most of the episodes are available free on Youtube.

CAPITAL'S PUNISHMENT

Next in the Pennywhistle saga:
"Attaché Extraordinaire"

The Congress of Vienna is sorting out the final results of the Napoleonic Wars and redrawing the map of Europe. Every country, empire, kingdom, and principality on The Continent has sent its top diplomats to argue its case and shape the destiny of Europe for the next century. Many crowned heads-of state lead their respective delegations and the concentration of Emperors, Czars, and Kings is something never before seen in Europe. An unofficial army of spies, high ranking military officers, minor royals, and prostitutes follow the negotiators and swell Vienna's population by 100,000.

Newly promoted Royal Marine Major Thomas Pennywhistle is seconded to the British Delegation of Lord Castlereagh as the Assistant Naval Attache but his embassy title is merely a cover for his real missions. One is official; recover a cache of documents highly damaging to the British Royal Family that could undermine the British bargaining position at the Congress. The other is very, very personal: find the man who murdered his brother.

Both covert missions plunge him into a world of palaces and profligacy where duplicity is the order of the day and a guileful soul always trumps a stout heart. The grand ballrooms, opulent drawing rooms, and sumptuous salons form a different kind of battlefield where information becomes ammunition and words become weapons. Fusillades are delivered with polished tongues, soft voices, and refined manners. Motives are mixed, intentions veiled, and every day reveals a new round of plots and counter plots. Little is as it seems and the elaborate masks of diplomacy often make evil appear attractive.

A shadowy presence known only as "The White Tiger" seems to anticipate Pennywhistle's every move, leading him to suspect that the British diplomatic cipher has been compromised by a mole. The trails of his investigations begin to intertwine and point to perfidy at the highest levels, perhaps even Czar Alexander himself. When the woman he loves is kidnapped, the stakes become even higher.

As Pennywhistle wades deeper into the swirling intrigue, he finds his brother was a far different, far more complex man than the shallow sibling from whom he had been long estranged. His investigation becomes a journey of enlightenment as he discovers his brother's true face and one of redemption as he seeks to honor his memory by solving his murder.

About the Author

John M. Danielski

John Danielski believes you learn best by doing and actually carried out many of the ordinary tasks Tom Pennywhistle performs in *The King's Scarlet*. He worked his way through university as a living history interpreter at historic Fort Snelling, the birthplace of Minnesota. For four summers, he played a US soldier of 1827; he wore the uniform, performed the drills, demonstrated the volley fire with other interpreters, and even ate the food. A heavy blue wool tailcoat and black shako look smart and snappy, but are pure torture to wear on a boiling summer day.

He has a practical, rather than theoretical, perspective on the weapons of the time. He has fired either replicas or originals of all of the weapons mentioned in his works with live rounds, six- and twelve-pound cannon included. The effect of a 12-pound cannonball on an old Chevy four door must be seen to be believed.

He has a number of marginally useful University degrees, including a magna cum laude degree in history from the

University of Minnesota. He is a Phi Beta Kappa and holds a black belt in Tae-Kwon-do. He has taught history at both the secondary and university levels and also worked as a newspaper editor.

His literary mentors were C. S. Forester, Bruce Catton, and Shelby Foote.

He lives quietly in the Twin Cities suburbs with his faithful companion: Sparkle, the wonder cat.

IF YOU ENJOYED THIS BOOK
Please write a review.
This is important to the author and helps to get the
word out to others
Visit

PENMORE PRESS
www.penmorepress.com

All Penmore Press books are available directly
through our website, amazon.com, Barnes and Noble and
Nook, Sony Reader, Apple iTunes, Kobo books and via
leading bookshops across the United States, Canada, the
UK, Australia and Europe.

More Books by John Danielski and others below.

King's Scarlet

BY

John Danielski

Chivalry comes naturally to Royal Marine captain Thomas Pennywhistle, but in the savage Peninsular War, it's a luxury he can ill afford. Trapped behind enemy lines with vital dispatches for Lord Wellington, Pennywhistle violates orders when he saves a beautiful stranger, setting off a sequence of events that jeopardize his mission. The French launch a massive manhunt to capture him. His Spanish allies prove less than reliable. The woman he rescued has an agenda of her own that might help him along, if it doesn't get them all killed.

A time will come when, outmaneuvered, captured, and stripped of everything, he must stand alone before his enemies. But Pennywhistle is a hard man to kill and too bloody obstinate to concede defeat.

PENMORE PRESS
www.penmorepress.com

BLUE WATER SCARLET TIDE

BY

JOHN DANIELSKI

It's the summer of 1814, and Captain Thomas Pennywhistle of the Royal Marines is fighting in a New World war that should never have started, a war where the old rules of engagement do not apply. Here, runaway slaves are your best source of intelligence, treachery is commonplace, and rough justice is the best one can hope to meet—or mete out. The Americans are fiercely determined to defend their new nation and the Great Experiment of the Republic; British Admiral George Cockburn is resolved to exact revenge for the burning of York, and so the war drags on. Thanks to Pennywhistle's ingenuity, observant mind, and military discipline, a British strike force penetrates the critically strategic region of the Chesapeake Bay. But this fight isn't just being waged by soldiers, and the collateral damage to innocents tears at Pennywhistle's heart.

As his past catches up with him, Pennywhistle must decide what is worth fighting for, and what is worth refusing to kill for —especially when he meets his opposite number on the wrong side of a pistol.

PENMORE PRESS
www.penmorepress.com

The Lockwoods

of Clonakilty

by

Mark Bois

Lieutenant James Lockwood of the Inniskilling Regiment has returned to family, home and hearth after being wounded, almost fatally, at the Battle of Waterloo, where his regiment was decisive in securing Wellington's victory and bringing the Napoleonic Wars to an end. But home is not the refuge and haven he hoped to find. Irish uprisings polarize the citizens, and violence against English landholders – including James' father and brother – is bringing down wrath and retribution from England. More than one member of the household sympathizes with the desire for Irish independence, and Cassie, the Lockwood's spirited daughter, plays an active part in the rebellion.

Estranged from his English family for the "crime" of marrying a Irish Catholic woman, James Lockwood must take difficult and desperate steps to preserve his family. If his injuries don't kill him, or his addiction to laudanum, he just might live long enough to confront his nemesis. For Captain Charles Barr, maddened by syphilis and no longer restrained by the bounds of honor, sets out to utterly destroy the Lockwood family, from James' patriarchal father to the youngest child, and nothing but death with stop him – his own, or James Lockwood's.

PENMORE PRESS
www.penmorepress.com

Fortune's Whelp
by
Benerson Little

Privateer, Swordsman, and Rake:

Set in the 17th century during the heyday of privateering and the decline of buccaneering, *Fortune's Whelp* is a brash, swords-out sea-going adventure. Scotsman Edward MacNaughton, a former privateer captain, twice accused and acquitted of piracy and currently seeking a commission, is ensnared in the intrigue associated with the attempt to assassinate King William III in 1696. Who plots to kill the king, who will rise in rebellion—and which of three women in his life, the dangerous smuggler, the wealthy widow with a dark past, or the former lover seeking independence—might kill to further political ends? Variously wooing and defying Fortune, Captain MacNaughton approaches life in the same way he wields a sword or commands a fighting ship: with the heart of a lion and the craft of a fox.

PENMORE PRESS
www.penmorepress.com

WINDMILL POINT

BY

JIM STEMPEL

Gripping historical fiction vividly brings to life two desperate weeks during the spring of 1864, when the resolution of the American Civil War was balanced on a razor's edge.

At the time, both North and South had legitimate reasons to conclude they were very near victory. Ulysses S. Grant firmly believed that Lee's Army of Northern Virginia was only one great assault away from implosion; Lee knew that the political will in the North to prosecute the war was on the verge of collapse.

Jim Stempel masterfully sets the stage for one of the most horrific battles of the Civil War, contrasting the conversations of decision-making generals with chilling accounts of how ordinary soldiers of both armies fared in the mud, the thunder, and the bloody fighting on the battlefield.

"We must destroy this army of Grant's before he gets to the James River. If he gets there it will become a siege, and then it will be a mere question of time." – General Lee.

PENMORE PRESS
www.penmorepress.com

Penmore Press

Challenging, Intriguing, Adventurous, Historical and Imaginative

www.penmorepress.com

www.ingramcontent.com/pod-product-compliance
Lightning Source LLC
Chambersburg PA
CBHW050607170726
48283CB00001B/143